Hanging by the Moment

H.B. PATTSKYN

Published by
Dreamspinner Press
5032 Capital Circle SW
Ste 2, PMB# 279
Tallahassee, FL 32305-7886
USA
http://www.dreamspinnerpress.com/

Hanging by the Moment

Cover Art by L.C. Chase
http://www.lcchase.com

ISBN: 978-1-62798-127-9
Digital ISBN: 978-1-62798-128-6

Printed in the United States of America
First Edition
September 2013

I am as always amazed by and grateful for the love and support I get from my incredible husband and his family. Love you, Mom!

I've made a lot of new friends along my journey from fanfiction writer to published author, people who have helped me grow and learn, who have beta read or acted as "cheerleader" when I doubted myself. I'm especially grateful to Shira Anthony for helping me get through the doubting phases of this one. I might have thrown in the towel on it if she hadn't kept telling me how much she loved Pasha and Daniel.

Although she passed away long before my first book came out—and I have no idea what she would think of what I write—I'd like to acknowledge and thank my grandmother, Helen Garzia Braund. Like Pasha's family, my grandmother's parents were Russian immigrants, and a lot of the conversations Pasha and his father have about his sexuality mirror conversations my grandmother and I had over mine. She was very much a product of her era and upbringing, but she was generous, accepting, and the single greatest influence on me, not only as a writer, but as a human being. No matter what I did, she believed in me and supported me and hardly a day goes by that I don't think of her and miss her with all my heart.

A note about the Russian translations:

I made the decision to translate the Russian words in *Hanging by the Moment* phonetically rather than letter by letter. Although I caught a little flack from one of my translation sources, the decision is based on two things: One, there are thirty-three letters in the Russian alphabet; two of them are always silent, many of the others don't have an English equivalent (Pasha and Daniel actually have a conversation about that on their first date). Two, the words are all in dialogue. I thought it was more important for readers to "hear" what was being said than it was to try to translate each letter according to its nearest English equivalent.

CHAPTER ONE

"MAKE sure you wipe down ketchup and mustard bottles," Pasha Batalov's father called over his shoulder as the pair trudged into the back door of the little diner. "Sharon said they looked like shit when we closed up Wednesday night." Even after twenty years in the United States, Ivan still sounded like he'd just stepped off the plane from St. Petersburg.

Pasha bit his tongue on his initial sour response, that if Sharon had thought the ketchup and mustard bottles needed wiping down, she should have done it herself. It was just as dead at the end of her shift as it was at the beginning of his.

"You hear me?" Ivan snapped when Pasha didn't answer right away.

"*Da*. Yes, I heard you."

"Then say something so I know you listening!"

Pasha kept mute. Five thirty in the morning was too early to start arguing about stupid shit. He hung his coat up on the peg next to the back door and headed into the dining room, where he turned up the heat and started a pot of coffee. The little diner had twelve booths and three small tables that sat a grand total of sixty customers, sixty-six if people wanted to get cozy. Another five seats were available at the counter for anyone who wanted to look into the kitchen through the window separating it from the dining room. The walls were painted an uninspired shade of beige to match the scuffed brown floor and dull upholstery, and framed posters of Greek temples and vases hung on the walls. On Wednesday, Sharon had decked the halls for Christmas with twinkling lights, velvet bows, and red-and-green garland. Everyone else said it looked pretty, but Pasha thought the whole thing was overdone and gaudy.

"Put on news," Ivan yelled from the kitchen.

Pasha groaned but didn't argue. When the old man said "news" he didn't mean MPR—Michigan Public Radio—or even some middle-of-the-road station that might give an even view of the world around them. No, he meant WJR, the local home of Rush Limbaugh. Limbaugh wouldn't be on until later in the day, but Pasha wasn't too keen on listening to the morning guy, either. Choices, however, were a luxury that was in short supply in Pasha's life.

He tuned the radio to WJR and took stock of what needed to be done to get the place ready for breakfast service, not that customers were likely to start pouring in when they opened. Starting with his least favorite job, Pasha got the ketchup and mustard bottles out of the pie case behind the counter. Sharon was right, they did look like shit, although those probably weren't her exact words. In the twelve years he'd known her, Pasha had never heard Sharon swear or raise her voice. After combining the half-empty plastic squeeze bottles, he took the empties back to the dish room for his cousin Samara to wash when she came in at nine, and grabbed as many clean bottles as he could find on the shelves.

While he was in the back, he headed to the prep area to grab a few lemons out of the walk-in cooler. A quick glance at the shelves assured him they had enough milk to get through breakfast and probably lunch as well. Just the same, he added "milk" to the grocery list hanging on the cooler door. *For all the good it does.* Dad would wait until they were completely out of something before sending someone across the street to the grocery store to buy more.

When he got back to the dining room, Pasha set the lemons aside, filled up the mustard and ketchup bottles he'd found in the dish room, wiped them all down, and started setting the bottles out at every other booth.

"How come you don't put ketchup and mustard on all tables?" Ivan hollered.

"Because these are all the clean bottles we have."

"So wash goddamned dirty bottles! I don't pay you to do half-ass job, I pay you to *work*! It's going to be busy day, Pasha. I want every table set up."

Pasha couldn't remember the last time they'd had a truly busy weekday breakfast, but he didn't argue. The only days he made any real money waiting tables were Saturday and Sunday—and lately, even the weekends weren't so hot. What had been seventy- and eighty-dollar days were now fifty-dollar days, and it *wasn't* because customers weren't tipping. Half the buildings around the diner stood empty with "for sale" or "for rent" signs in the windows.

"I'll run a load of dishes as soon as I get everything else done," he promised his father. He would have anyway, just to stave off boredom.

Thirty minutes later—with all of his sidework done, and the dish machine loaded and running—Pasha turned on the neon "open" sign. "*Crap*," he swore under his breath when he saw a big silver and black delivery truck sitting in their lot, taking up most of the meager parking space. If Dad saw it, he'd have a conniption. The old man *hated* truckers who parked in their lot, even when they didn't have any customers. Without bothering to get his coat, Pasha darted out the front door and across the lot to get rid of the guy before Dad noticed him.

As he approached, the driver rolled down his window and offered up an amiable "Hey."

Pasha stopped dead in his tracks. It wasn't just the guy's unexpectedly friendly attitude that made him stop short, it was that the man was *gorgeous*. He had caramel-colored skin, warm chocolate-brown eyes, and thick jet-black hair that hung in a loose braid draped over one shoulder. And his smile.... God, what a smile. Heat rushed to Pasha's cheeks as he realized he was gawking. He cleared his throat. "You ah, you're blocking our lot. We just opened up."

"Sorry about that. My GPS died and I'm trying to get someone on the phone to help me figure out where I am, but nobody's picking up in the office. Which I s'pose isn't your problem." The driver's smile turned apologetic. "I'll get out of your lot." He leaned back into the cab.

That *should* have been the end of it, but instead of heading back inside, Pasha stepped closer to the truck and asked, "Where are you trying to get to?"

"Jay's Party Store. Any chance it's around here somewhere?"

"Sorry, never heard of it," Pasha told him. "What street is it on?"

"Wattles."

"Jeez, you really *are* lost."

The driver let out a rueful little laugh. "Story of my life. I don't suppose you could help me get un-lost?"

Pasha grinned; un-lost, that was a new one. "Wattles is Seventeen Mile Road. This is Main Street." He pointed to the road in front of the diner. "Twelve Mile is the next light up." He pointed north, but it didn't seem to help, the trucker still looked confused. A gust of wind cut through Pasha's thin white uniform shirt, making him shiver. He crossed his arms over his chest and asked, "Where exactly are you trying to get to?"

"You wanna hop in out of the cold?" the truck driver offered.

Pasha hesitated—but seriously, what was the guy going to do, drive off with him as a hostage? *I could think of worse fates.* "Yeah, thanks."

Instead of motioning him around to the passenger's side, the trucker opened up the driver's side door and slid over, making room for Pasha behind the massive steering wheel. "I'm the one who should be saying thank you. It's been one of those days from the get-go."

Pasha returned his smile. "Same here." His dad had been in a foul mood long before they got to the restaurant that morning. Yesterday hadn't been any picnic either. Holidays never were, but after everything that happened last year, family gatherings were more tense than ever. Pasha didn't want to even think about what Christmas was going to be like. "I can't believe this weather. It's not even December yet, and I swear it's going to snow today."

"They're saying up to six inches," the trucker told him.

He groaned.

"Not a fan of snow?" He looked like he was trying not to laugh at Pasha's sour expression.

"Not a fan of *shoveling* snow."

"No arguments there. I'm Daniel, by the way." The guy pulled off one of his heavy gloves and held out his hand.

Daniel's grip was strong but not overpowering, and his hand was big and warm and thick with calluses. Heat crept into Pasha's cheeks again as he realized it was his turn to introduce himself. "I'm Pasha."

"Interesting name."

"Yeah, I get that a lot." "Interesting" was one of the nicest things people had to say about his name. "It's sort of short for Pavel, which is Russian for Paul. I tried going by that for a while, but…." But he was babbling. He pulled his hand into his lap. "Sorry. You're probably more interested in getting back on the road."

"Only because I have to get this stuff delivered by seven or my boss is going to have my ass. And *not* in a fun way." Daniel's brows shot up and his lips curled into a mischievous grin.

Pasha blinked—then gave himself a good mental shake. There was no way Daniel meant that the way it had sounded. Statistically speaking only one, maybe two, out of every ten people were gay, which meant that no matter where he went, the odds would always be against him meeting another gay man. Except at a gay bar. *And if I ever ran into this guy there, he wouldn't give me the time of day.* It was like his friend Ty said: the beautiful ones stuck together.

And Pasha wasn't beautiful.

He wasn't Quasimodo or anything, but he wasn't tall or fit and he'd never been thin. A thirty-eight-inch waist might not make him *obese*, but add to it very average looks and short ash-brown hair that was starting to thin, and you came up with the kind of guy other men simply were not clamoring to meet. Pasha cleared his throat. "The ah, the easiest way to get to Wattles from here is to head north on Main. Take a left out of the lot," he clarified. Then added, "Main turns into Livernois when you hit Fourteen Mile Road. What cross street are you looking for?"

"Dequinder." It came out sounding more like a question than a statement.

"When you get to Wattles, make a right. Dequinder's only a few miles down. It'll be the next main road you come to after John R. You'll be there in no time," he promised.

"Thanks, you're a real lifesaver."

"Anytime," Pasha told him. The warmth of Daniel's smile made his stomach turn summersaults.

Daniel's grin turned mischievous again. "Guess I'll have to remember that the next time I get lost out this way. Or maybe I should get lost on purpose, just to have an excuse to come see you again." He waggled his brows and just for a second, Pasha forgot how to breathe. Daniel *was* flirting with him, he had to be! But why on earth would a guy who looked like that flirt with *him*? Daniel could walk into any club and have his pick of the guys lined up along the bar.

Daniel cleared his throat. "Well, I guess I should let you get back to work. Thanks again for helping me get back on track here."

Did he really sound as disappointed as Pasha thought he did? *Or am I just hearing what I want to?* He supposed there was only one way to find out. "Do you want to come in for a cup of coffee or something before you hit the road?" What was the worst that could happen anyway? He'd get a polite brush off and never see Daniel again?

"Wish I could, Sugar, but I'm behind schedule as it is."

"Yeah. Right. Sorry." *Polite brush off it is.* He turned to open up the door, but the sound of Daniel's voice stopped him.

"You here all morning?"

Pasha nodded, dumbfounded. "All morning, every morning."

"What, no time off for good behavior?"

"Who says I behave?" he quipped back without thinking. *Shit, where did* that *come from?* Pasha had never quite figured out how to flirt. Sometimes he managed to say something funny but most of the time he fell flat on his face. "I ah, it's a family business. There's no such thing as time off when you're the owner's son." *Face, meet pavement.*

But Daniel smiled. "I guess I know where to find you, then."

This couldn't be happening. Guys who looked like Daniel never came on to him. "I um, I really have to go back to work."

"Yeah, me too. See you 'round?" he asked.

No longer trusting his voice, Pasha nodded. He climbed back down out of the cab as gracelessly as he'd clambered in. It was hard to tell what was really making his stomach flutter so madly, the fear that Daniel was only trying to be polite, or the possibility that he might *actually* come back. Shivering, he stepped away from the truck and watched as Daniel maneuvered the big rig out of the lot. Before turning onto Main, Daniel leaned out of the cab and waved good-bye one last time.

Please…, Pasha started to pray. But it was stupid. God didn't answer prayers like that. If he did, Pasha would still be together with Michael. He headed back into the restaurant, where Dad was cooking off more bacon than they could possibly need on a weekday.

"What were you doing outside?" the old man wanted to know.

Pasha settled on the easiest answer he could think of. "Giving directions to a guy who was lost."

"We're not Yellow Pages, Pasha, we're *business*! Next time some *paskudnyak* gets lost, you tell him to go buy map from gas station across street!" He waved angrily toward the corner gas station. "I pay you to *work*!"

"Everything's set up," he contended. "There's nothing left to do except wait for customers to show up."

"There's *always* something to do. You can mop floors, wipe down counters. You can clean goddamned windows! Maybe when you own business, then you understand you don't got no time to waste on people who do nothing for you, nothing but take up your time and energy. That's all people are good for, Pasha. Only people you can count on is *family*."

Pasha didn't respond. They'd had this argument before, back when Pasha was still trying to have a social life, real friends outside the bar and Facebook. Back when he was still with his ex, not that Dad knew Michael was his boyfriend. The old man would have lost it if he'd ever caught on that they were more than just friends. As it was, Dad thought they spent too much time together. Friends, the old man argued, would only hold Pasha back. Sometimes he wondered what had made his father so cynical and bitter. Dad had been that way for as long as Pasha could remember.

Before Pasha could come up with any kind of reply, something that wouldn't totally piss the old man off, he spotted Nate Archer's big blue Bronco coming around the corner. He'd never been happier to see the retired Marine as he was just then. Nate and his dad could sit around for hours bitching about everything they thought was wrong with the country. It was exactly the distraction Dad needed today; Pasha too. "Nate's here," he pointed out, in case his father hadn't seen the Bronco.

Ivan nodded. Rather than head back into the kitchen—Nate never ordered breakfast anyway—the old man poured two cups of coffee. He set one on the counter and the other on the ledge in front of the pie case. When he reached for a creamer, Pasha stopped him.

"Dad, you're supposed to be using skim milk. Remember your last checkup? Your cholesterol was through the roof."

Ivan waved him off. "What do those damned doctors know, huh? There's nothing wrong with my heart. It's this damned place that's killing me."

"Come on, you need to take better care of yourself."

"Who are you to tell me what to do? Did you wipe my shitty ass when I was baby? Or did I wipe yours?"

Pasha's jaw tightened, but he stopped trying to argue. One of these days, the old man was going to keel over from a goddamned heart attack, and with any luck, it *wouldn't* kill him. Pasha stalked into the kitchen to finish cooking the bacon his dad had left on the grill.

A moment later the cowbell over the door clattered and Nate walked in. "God damn! It's as cold as a witch's tit out there!" he announced, his voice booming through the empty restaurant. "You hear the news this morning? They're saying six inches of snow by noon!"

"No, that much?" replied Ivan. He took a seat at the counter.

"You better believe it. My goddamned knees are killing me! Arthritis always acts up before a big storm." Nate shrugged out of his coat and sat down next to Ivan. "Those idiots in Washington keep crying 'global warming' then turn around and say 'snowpocalypse.'"

"What do they know, huh?" Ivan agreed. "All I know is with price of gas going up, it's gonna cost *fortune* to keep this place going all winter."

"Maybe you oughta take a vacation."

In the kitchen Pasha rolled his eyes; Dad *never* took time off.

Chapter Two

NATE was on his second cup of coffee when Pasha spotted Belinda Freeman's beige Kia Sorento pulling into the lot.

Since Nate and the old man were still sitting at the counter complaining about the world's problems, Pasha grabbed a couple of eggs from the fridge for Belinda's omelet. Like most of their regulars, she was predictable, breakfast was always an egg white omelet with tomatoes, spinach, and mushrooms. Pasha had just gotten the eggs separated when Ivan joined him in the kitchen. "I'll finish," he said. "You go take care of customers."

What customers? Pasha thought, but there was no point in saying it aloud. He swapped out the white cook's apron for his black waiter's apron and went up front to pour two cups of coffee, one for Belinda and one for himself. He set hers on the counter and reached into the pie case to get a creamer for his. Then he changed his mind and grabbed the quart of skim milk instead. He didn't have his dad's heart problems—yet—but back in high school, he'd worn size thirty-two jeans. At only five foot six, even that had been considered a little chunky, but these days, he was wearing size thirty-eight pants and he hated it. It made him wonder about that trucker from earlier. God, what was he, some kind of chubby chaser? Not that there was anything wrong with that. Pasha just didn't want to fall into the category of chubby, even if, when he looked in the mirror, he knew it was true.

The cowbell clattered and Belinda came in, bringing with her a gust of icy wind, a flurry of snowflakes, and a bright smile. "Good morning, gentlemen."

Ivan returned her greeting in Russian. "*Dobryeah ootra.*"

"Hi, Belinda," said Pasha.

"What brings you out in this cold?" asked Nate.

"Work doesn't stop just because of a little snow." Belinda unwound the long blue-and-bronze knitted scarf from around her neck, slipped off her coat, and took her usual seat at the counter. "Do you have raisin bread this morning?"

"*Nyet*," said Ivan. "Not 'til bread man gets here, and who knows when that's gonna be." He gestured toward the window and the snowstorm outside.

Like all of their regular customers, Belinda accepted the situation without complaint. "Did everyone have a nice Thanksgiving?"

"Bonnie cooked so damned much turkey, we'll be eating it 'til Christmas!" Nate told her. "I swear, sometimes that woman forgets it's just us two these days."

"Your kids not come home?" Ivan asked.

"Marie's still in Spain with her boyfriend," Nate explained, his expression souring. "You know, the Canadian." Nate had yet to call his daughter's beau by name. "But we got to video chat with Nathan. Couldn't talk long, but it was good to see him."

"How's he doing?" Pasha asked. Nate's son had enlisted in the Marines straight out of high school and was currently stationed somewhere in the Middle East. Pasha had had a mad crush on him since the first time they met, not that it would ever go anywhere. Nathan's politics were a lot like his father's.

In answer to Pasha's question, Nate shrugged. "There's a lot he can't talk about. It goes with the territory, but you know Bonnie worries." He stood up and put his coat back on.

"You leaving already?" said Ivan.

"I'm supposed to be at the mall already. Bonnie sent me out of the house this morning with a Christmas list as long as my goddamned arm." He dropped two bucks on the counter: a dollar sixty-three for his coffee, the rest for Pasha's tip. He might have been upset about a thirty-cent tip if Nate weren't so easy to wait on. Or if it had ever been any different.

Ivan brought Belinda's breakfast to her, then went to refill his coffee cup. Pasha didn't say a word when he dumped two creamers in it.

Instead of going back into the kitchen, Ivan leaned on the counter. "What about you, you have good Thanksgiving?" he asked Belinda.

"I drove out to Portage to visit my gran."

The old man shot Pasha a dark, sidelong look. "See. It's like I keep saying, Pasha. Holidays for *family*. Not for staying out all night at *bar*."

"I wasn't out 'all night.' I was only gone for a couple of hours."

Belinda gave Pasha a soft, sympathetic smile. "Any word from your mom?"

Ivan answered for him. "Vera's still in Chicago. She's visiting Lena, helping out with boys."

Belinda's smile hardly faltered. "That's awful nice of her."

"*Da*," Ivan agreed. "She's good woman."

Sometimes Pasha wondered if the old man actually thought he was fooling anyone. *Or maybe he's told the same lie so many times, he's starting to believe it himself.*

"So how's the rest of the family?" Belinda asked.

Pasha shrugged. "Nadia and the kids are doing pretty good, I guess." Nadia was his younger sister. She had four children and a *paskudnyak*, a good-for-nothing, for a husband. Yesterday had been a little rough on… well, on everybody, honestly, but Nadia's five-year-old son had been hit the hardest. RJ was just old enough to realize that something was wrong, that the Christmas tree wasn't up in the living room on Thanksgiving like always. He'd asked if it was because *Babushka*, Grandma, wasn't there, and wanted to know when she was coming home.

No one would give him a straight answer. Nadia tried to shush him while Dad lied and said she was visiting Lena. Peter, Pasha's older brother, didn't say anything; he just walked out of the room, leaving his wife standing there looking uncomfortable. Nadia's husband remained oblivious, hunched over his DS, just like always. When Pasha suggested maybe they could call Mom to say hi, Dad went ballistic. That was when he headed to the bar, where he hooked up with a stranger and got his brains screwed out in a by-the-hour motel. It wasn't the first time.

Belinda's voice cut through his unhappy thoughts: "Has Ryan had any luck finding a job?"

Pasha shrugged. "It's a tough market." *Even tougher when you spend your days playing computer games.*

Ivan made a rude noise. "It's not so tough. Peter got promotion at work. He's managing supervisor now." He beamed with genuine pride.

Pasha didn't get it. Dad had been furious when Peter moved to the other side of the state last year to take that job. *Then again, Peter was always the one who walked on water.*

"Tell him I said congratulations," said Belinda. She slid her empty plate across the counter. "I'd better get going. I have to be in West Bloomfield in half an hour."

"Have a good one." Pasha didn't bother writing up a check for her. He just took her money, punched the amount she owed into the register, and handed back her change.

Belinda put a five-dollar bill on the counter. "Chin up, kiddo. It really does get better."

"Thanks. Take it easy out there. The roads look pretty bad."

"I will. See you later, Ivan." She waved to the old man as she headed out the door.

Pasha set her plate into the bus tub. As he was wiping down the counter, the door opened again. He looked up, hoping—but it wasn't his gorgeous truck driver, it was some couple he'd never seen before. "Have a seat wherever you like," he told them with a practiced, professional smile. He filled two plastic tumblers with ice water, grabbed a couple of breakfast menus, then followed his customers to one of the tables by the window. Outside, the snow was coming down harder than ever.

BY THE time Samara came in at nine, there was a thick blanket of white covering the sidewalk and lots of gray slush on the road. The storm didn't show signs of letting up anytime soon, either.

"How bad is it out there?" Pasha asked his cousin.

She scowled as if that was the dumbest question anyone had ever asked. Maybe it was. He was just trying to make conversation.

Thin and gangly, with a long, narrow face, Pasha's cousin wasn't what anybody would call a pretty woman. Neither was her sister Lena, but Lena had managed to land herself a husband. When Samara turned thirty, Pasha's aunt gave up on her ever getting married and talked Ivan into giving her a job. Being the good Russian daughter that she was, Samara took the only position he had available without complaint.

She stomped the snow off her boots at the door and clomped over to the coatrack just outside the restrooms. "Salt trucks haven't been out yet," she told Pasha over her shoulder. "It took over an hour to get here." Normally it was only a twenty-minute drive from her parents' Bloomfield Hills home to the restaurant. After hanging up her coat and swapping out her snow boots for a grungy old pair of tennis shoes, she trudged into the dish room.

AT TEN thirty, Pasha only had twelve bucks in his pocket—and five of that had come from Belinda—so when his lunch-shift partner called to say she'd be late, he told her not to worry about it. *Of course she should have been here a half an hour ago*, he thought as he hung up the phone. But Amy was always running late. Ivan let it slide because she'd been with them for seven and a half months, which was longer than anyone else except Samara, who was family, and Sharon, who might as well be. All restaurants had a high turnover rate, but Pasha suspected theirs was higher than normal.

The only customers he had when Amy finally showed up at eleven thirty were Art, Jimmy, and Rueben, a trio of older gentlemen who came in every day. The three were at their usual table at the back of the dining room. Jimmy made a big show of looking at his watch. "You're late," he told Amy gravely—but the grin on his face made it obvious he was teasing.

Ivan, who was at the counter reading the paper, turned around and scoffed. "So what else is new? She's gonna be late for her own funeral." Amy ducked her head apologetically, but Ivan waved it off. "Maybe for Christmas, I buy you alarm clock." His tone was gruff, but like Jimmy, he was grinning, teasing her.

"I don't think a new clock will help," said Jimmy.

"I swear it was the snow," Amy pleaded, shedding her coat. Underneath it, her uniform—a white blouse and black pants—was a disheveled mess. "It took me almost half an hour to dig my stupid car out."

"Yeah, but what time did you *start* digging?" wondered Rueben.

"I plead the fifth," Amy responded with a grin.

Pasha just chuckled and took Amy's coat so he could hang it up on the coatrack by the restrooms.

"We'll take some decaf when you get a second," Rueben said to no one in particular.

"You got it," Pasha answered with a smile. What Rueben actually meant was that *he* would take some decaf. Jimmy and Art never touched the stuff.

Amy leaned back against the counter next to Pasha as he got the pot started. By then she'd pulled her curly red hair into a haphazard ponytail, straightened her blouse, smoothed her slacks, and tied a black apron around her thick waist. The final touches were dark-red lipstick and a pair of big silver earrings in the shape of Buddha heads. She turned to Pasha. "How was your holiday?"

"Good, I guess. Everyone was there." *Almost.* "We celebrated Nadia's birthday. She was born on the twenty-sixth," he explained.

"That must be fun." Her tone was ripe with sarcasm.

"Yeah. One year, Mom had put candles in the pumpkin pie." At the time, Pasha thought it was funny. Now he wondered whether that was his mother's odd sense of humor or the illness. He shoved his hands into his pockets. "What about you? You do the big family thing?"

"I avoid big family things."

"Lucky you."

"Luck has nothing to do with it."

AT ONE thirty, Pasha had twenty-seven dollars in his pocket and there was still no sign of Daniel. *Which means he wasn't really interested.* He tried not to feel too disappointed. Why should a guy who looked like Daniel be interested in him, anyway? Or maybe he'd read the whole thing wrong and Daniel wasn't flirting with him at all. Maybe he was just trying to be nice. After all, what were the chances of meeting Prince Charming in the parking lot?

"Pasha!" Ivan hollered from the kitchen.

"*Da*? What is it?"

"Come cook. I have to go to store."

Pasha nodded and traded in his black waiter's apron for a white cook's apron without complaint. Dad usually left between one and two, either to go home and take a nap or to go to the store, or both. Sometimes Pasha wondered what it would be like to work in a restaurant where they didn't run out of wheat bread and orange juice halfway through breakfast, or where the owner ran the business instead of running himself ragged. But what choice did Dad have?

For one thing, he could sell the fucking place, Pasha thought irritably. But he knew it would never happen. Dad would work himself into an early grave before he admitted it was time to throw in the towel.

As soon as Ivan was out the door, Amy changed the radio station to Doug FM. Their tagline, "we play everything," was pretty accurate. Adele might be followed by ZZ Top, who might be followed by Sara McLachlan, Lady Gaga, or Taylor Swift. Since the holiday season had officially begun, they were just as likely to play Burl Ives or Bing Crosby. Pasha could do without the latter two. Thankfully, Katy Perry was playing instead.

"Turn it up," Pasha called to Amy. She was happy to oblige.

Samara poked her head out of the dish room and scowled. "Ivan doesn't like that station."

"Well, Ivan isn't here, is he?" Amy quipped back.

Samara turned her glare on Pasha. He ignored her. He liked Katy Perry's "Firework" and hummed happily along to the upbeat lyrics as he scraped off the grill. He was so engrossed in the music that he barely heard the clatter of the bell over the front door.

"Hi," he heard Amy say. "Go ahead and have a seat wherever you like."

"Thanks."

Pasha's head jerked up. He *knew* that voice—but it *couldn't* be.

Only it was.

Daniel.

And he looked even better than Pasha remembered.

CHAPTER THREE

PASHA'S heart hammered so loud in his chest he was sure the whole world could hear it, and when Daniel flashed that smile of his, he thought he was going to die on the spot. And suddenly, he wanted to because they weren't sitting in the cab of Daniel's truck anymore, they were inside the restaurant where everyone could see them. If Samara came out front and noticed the way Daniel was looking at him, if she figured it out… *oh God.* How was he going to get out of this?

He watched Amy pour Daniel a glass of water and hand over a menu. "Anything else to drink?" she asked in her usual cheerful tone.

"Water's good for now," Daniel answered. He had set a tattered paperback on the counter and shed his coat. The tight black T-shirt underneath it showed off an incredible physique: a trim waist, broad shoulders, and the kind of strong arms Pasha had always wanted to have holding him. *Only guys like that do* not *go for guys like me, not even at 2:00 a.m. when the bartender announces last call.* Pasha had been snubbed enough times to know better than even *trying* for guys who looked like that anymore.

But when Daniel smiled at him, it was like he was looking at the only thing in the room worth noticing. A warm, fluttery feeling spread through Pasha's chest and he smiled back, but fear kept him rooted to the spot even though all he wanted to do was go over and say hi.

What if Amy noticed the way Daniel was looking at him and started asking questions? Pasha liked her, but it wasn't like they were friends. She didn't know he was gay, and he wasn't ready to tell her. He wasn't ready to tell anyone.

"Do you need a few minutes?" Amy asked Daniel.

Mischief twinkled in his eyes. "I dunno. What's good here?"

Pasha wished he could sink into the floor and disappear, but Amy just shrugged, seemingly oblivious to the way Daniel kept staring over her shoulder into the kitchen. "Some things are better than others," she said. "It depends on what you're in the mood for." Pasha couldn't see her face, but he imagined Amy flashing a mischievous little grin of her own. She flirted with practically every guy who came in. After all, she was a woman—she could get away with it.

Daniel's smile got broader and his brows shot up. "Oh, I know what I want all right. I'm just not sure yet whether or not it's available."

And for a second, Pasha couldn't breathe. Amy turned around to look at him, and he knew by her stunned expression that she'd figured it out. What he didn't know was what she was thinking. Her brows were drawn together and her mouth tugged downward into a frown—then suddenly, as if realizing what she was doing, Amy schooled her features into a mask of neutrality and turned back to her customer. "Why don't I let you have a couple of minutes to figure it out?" Without waiting for his answer, she hustled into the kitchen.

"Amy—" Pasha began.

She cut him off. "I'm stepping out for a ciggy. Hold down the fort." It wasn't a request.

Pasha just wished he could figure out what she was thinking. Amy was an art student and by all accounts she seemed pretty liberal. She should be okay with it—but what if she wasn't? What if some ex-boyfriend had dumped her for a guy and now she hated gay men or…? *Just breathe.*

"I'm taking your coat," Amy added as she grabbed it off the hook. "See you in ten."

"Yeah. Sure." How the hell could he have been so *stupid*? Pasha had let himself get so carried away this morning that he hadn't stopped to think about what would happen if Daniel came back, and now…. He swallowed past the lump in his throat and glanced toward the dining room. Daniel's expression was as difficult to read as Amy's. He shot

Pasha a questioning look—and Pasha picked up a cleaning rag and started scrubbing the counter next to the grill.

All I have to do is walk over there and say "hi" and maybe... maybe Daniel would ask him out. Maybe he'd ask Daniel out. Maybe they'd totally hit it off and... and he couldn't. Because if he went over and started talking to Daniel, Samara would overhear every word. She was probably in the dish room now, listening in, trying to figure out what she'd missed and why Amy had stormed out like that. If Samara thought for one second he was gay, she would run straight to Ivan.

No.

Samara would run to her mother, and *she* would run to Ivan. It would be one more thing for Pasha's Aunt Anya to hold over Dad's head.

He glanced back up to see Daniel studying him over the top of his menu. He offered Pasha a smile, and Pasha turned back to the task of scouring an already clean counter. This was *exactly* why his ex had dumped him. Michael hated coming into the restaurant and being treated like just another one of Pasha's friends. He had every right to hate it, but he didn't understand. Just because they weren't living in Russia didn't mean Pasha's whole family didn't still act like it.

Finally, Amy came in from her smoke break. When she saw Pasha standing in the kitchen scrubbing the counter, she stared at him like he'd sprouted a second head. Her brows furrowed and she started to say something, but then she changed her mind and walked into the dining room to ask Daniel if he was ready to order.

"How about a burger and fries?" he answered. "Medium rare on that burger, if you can do it."

Pasha didn't look up. He didn't need to. He could tell by Daniel's voice that he wasn't smiling anymore. *He must think I'm the world's biggest ass hat for jerking him around like this.*

"Are you all set with water or did you want something else to drink?" he heard Amy ask.

"I'll take an orange juice, biggest one you've got."

"Sorry, we ran out. I've got cranberry," she offered.

"Sounds good. Let me have a small Greek salad too, with whatever low-fat dressing you guys have."

"Sure thing." She turned to the kitchen. "You catch all that back there?"

"Yeah," Pasha answered without looking up. He took a hamburger patty from the freezer and then remembered it was supposed to be medium rare, so he set it on his freshly scrubbed counter, gave his hands a quick rinse, and donned a pair of ugly blue gloves. Out of the corner of his eye, he watched Amy drop off the juice. Then she slipped around the corner, out of view. Which left him no choice but to face Daniel. "You ah, you want everything on your salad?" he asked in the most professional tone he could muster.

The look on Daniel's face made knives twist deep in Pasha's gut. He could see Daniel was hurt. Confused. But all he did was flash Pasha a rueful little smile and answer, "Life's short, right? Might as well give me the works."

"Yeah, I… um… sure. Everything on that burger too?"

"Why not?" Daniel gave him another little smile then picked up his novel and opened it to somewhere in the middle.

Pasha tossed a handful of iceberg lettuce onto a plate—iceberg lettuce was the only kind Dad ever bought—and added a teaspoon of feta, one onion slice, half a tomato slice, two beet slices, and one dinky little pepperoncini. It was the saddest salad he'd ever seen. Even if he didn't already feel like shit for the way he was treating Daniel, he couldn't serve him something so pathetic. He added more of everything, and since Amy hadn't reappeared, he grabbed a couple of soufflé cups of low-fat dressing out of the cooler and took the salad out to his customer.

Daniel put his book down but didn't make eye contact. "Thanks."

"Anytime." Which was exactly what he'd said to Daniel this morning. He was pretty sure Daniel realized it too, at least if the tight smile on his face was any indication. Pasha glanced toward the dish room; Samara was nowhere in sight. He kept his voice low anyway, just to be safe. "Look, I didn't mean to give you the wrong impression this morning. I'm sorry."

"I guess I got my signals crossed. No harm done?" It sounded more like a plea than a question.

"No harm done. But you didn't get anything crossed," he admitted. He couldn't let Daniel walk out of here thinking he'd made that kind of mistake. "I just… it's a little hard for me. This place. My life. For a minute I think I forgot how impossible things were the last time I…." Warmth crept into his cheeks. The last thing he should bring up was his ex. "My life is really complicated right now."

"Everybody's life is complicated, Sugar. It's what you do with the complications that counts."

"I wish it was that easy."

"It's as easy—or as hard—as you make it."

Pasha didn't know what to say to that, so all he did was shrug. "I'd better get back to work. Let me know if there's anything else you want."

"There's lots of things I want. But I guess… what's that line? You can't always get what you want?"

Pasha smiled. "But if you try sometimes, you might find you get what you need."

Daniel chuckled. "I wonder if Mick knew what he was talking about or if that was just wishful thinking."

"Me too."

FIFTEEN minutes later, Daniel paid his bill, left a fat tip, and put his coat back on. He gave Pasha one last lingering look.

Pasha turned away.

CHAPTER FOUR

"WHAT are you, some kind of friggin' *idiot*?" Amy hissed.

"Shhhh!" Pasha looked frantically toward the dish room, but there was no sign of his cousin.

"Don't you shush me!" But at least she lowered her voice. "That guy was totally hot and he *totally* was checking you out!"

"I'm not—"

"Bull hockey!" she spat, before he could get the lie out of his mouth. "Damn it, Pasha, if I had a guy that hot checking me out, I would *not* be standing back here flipping gyro meat while he got away!" The gyro meat was for a customer who had come in while Daniel was eating. Pasha was just glad it wasn't one of their regulars. It was bad enough Amy was causing a scene in front of a stranger.

"You already have a boyfriend, remember?" he snapped.

She settled her hands on her hips. "Do *you*?"

"No."

"So I repeat: what kind of friggin' idiot are you?"

"The kind who's trying to do his job."

She grabbed the spatula out of his hand. "I can make a fucking gyro. Now go after that guy!"

"I can't."

"Why the hell not? He wasn't *just* butt-fucking gorgeous, Pasha, he seemed really nice. From where I'm standing, this is a no brainer."

"I know." He was sure he sounded as glum as he felt. All he wanted was to race out the back door and try to catch Daniel before he left and ask—*beg*—for another chance. But guys who looked like Daniel didn't give second chances. They didn't have to. If some idiot blew them off, there was always someone else waiting in the wings. "He's probably already gone."

"Pasha—"

"Amy, *please*. You know my family. My dad. My fucking cousin. Even if I wanted to, I couldn't go after that guy."

"You *do* want to."

"It doesn't matter."

"You're an adult, you can do what you want. Hell, you don't even *like* working here. Your old man would be doing you a favor if he fired you."

"It's not that simple." Six months ago, Dad had put Pasha's name on the business license and the bank account. Technically, he didn't just work there: he was a partner, an owner. But he didn't want to tell Amy that. He didn't want to tell anyone because he didn't want anyone treating him differently. "I feel miserable enough as it is, okay? I just blew the best opportunity I've had in… in *ever*."

"And whose fault is that?" She tossed the spatula on the counter; it landed with a loud clatter.

Samara poked her head around the corner.

"Don't say a word," Pasha warned her. "Not today. Not now." He pulled the gyro meat off the grill and assembled the sandwich in angry silence. It wasn't Amy he was pissed at, it was himself.

After he set the plate in the window, Pasha got a piece of apple pie from the case behind the counter, put a huge wedge of sharp cheddar cheese on top—the good stuff he brought in for himself, not the shit his dad served—and popped the pie into the microwave to heat up. While it was going, he poured himself a cup of coffee, dumped in a packet of cocoa mix, and topped the whole thing off with a mountain of whipped cream. *Screw the diet.* What difference did it make whether he dropped a few pounds or ended up with a potbelly like his dad? As long as he was stuck working for the old man, he'd never be able to have a boyfriend.

Pasha took his plate and cup to the counter and sat down to read the Food section of the newspaper.

Amy joined him. "You okay?"

"Do I *look* okay?"

"No." She leaned in closer. "You know I'm totally cool with… you know," she said in quiet tone, eyeing the doorway between the dining room and dish room. "I just wish you would have told me."

"Why?"

She frowned, looking surprised. "Because we're friends. You've known me for what? Like seven months now? You have to know I wouldn't care."

"Amy, friends hang out outside of work. We've never so much as gone out for coffee together."

"Fair enough. I'm going out tonight. You wanna come?"

It was Pasha's turn to frown. "What, you find out I'm"—he glanced toward the dish room, but there was no sign of Samara—"gay and suddenly you want to play Will and Grace?"

"Excuse me?" She pulled away from him. "I'm trying to be *nice*. If you don't want to be my friend, just say so."

"I'm sorry. It's just… yesterday was pretty shitty for me. This whole year's been bad."

Her expression softened. "Maybe you need a little Grace in your life." Amy grabbed a clean fork from the silverware roll in front of her and helped herself to a bite of his food. "Cheese and pie is weird."

"So get your fork out of my pie," Pasha quipped back with a grin.

Amy raised her brows. "Maybe I *like* sticking my fork in your pie."

"Dream on." He took another bite of pie.

She laughed. "So what do you say about tonight?"

"I don't know. I really don't want to impose or anything."

"I'm just going over to a friend's house for beer and movies. No way you can impose on that. I'll even come back and pick you up so you can leave the car for your dad."

Pasha ate the last bite of his pie. He'd started carpooling with his father into work a few months earlier when his Escort died. Even before that, the old man was constantly badgering him into driving in together. He said he only wanted to save Pasha gas money, but sometimes Pasha suspected his father had ulterior motives. Pasha usually got off work between four and six—or whenever Dad came back to cook for the dinner shift—but because they'd driven in together, Pasha had to come back to the restaurant at the end of the night to pick Dad up. It made him think his father was sabotaging what little social life he had left by making it almost impossible for him to go out after work.

"Just beer and movies?" he asked Amy. "It won't be a big deal if you bring me along?"

"Just beer and movies," she promised. "We don't even have to stay late if you don't want to."

AFTER a quick shower and a much-needed shave, Pasha wrapped himself up in his bathrobe, careful to avoid looking at his image in the steamed up mirror on the back of the bathroom door. He'd started feeling guilty about that pie and whipped cream less than an hour after he ate it.

When he got to his room, he stopped dead in his tracks. Amy was pawing through his closet, making disparaging noises at nearly everything she saw.

"Are you *sure* you're gay?" she asked over her shoulder.

Pasha blinked, momentarily taken aback. Then he shook his head. "No, this is all a sneaky plot to get you alone in my room with me practically naked."

She snickered. "Guess it worked."

"You were supposed to wait downstairs."

"I got bored." But then she flashed a mischievous grin. "Besides, I wanted to see what else was hiding in the closet around here."

He rolled his eyes. "Find anything interesting?"

"Yeah. A gay man with no fashion sense."

"There's nothing wrong with my fashion sense."

"Pasha, I hate to break this to you, but you have *the* most boring wardrobe I've ever seen."

"Compared to you, *everyone* has a boring wardrobe."

Amy had come back to the restaurant to pick him up wearing a purple velvet mini dress and hot pink go-go boots. "Here, try this." She thrust a burgundy long sleeved Henley at him. "And please tell me you own a pair of jeans that don't make your ass look all saggy, the way your work pants do."

Pasha balked.

"It's not like I was staring, I'm just saying your work pants don't do jack shit for your tush."

"Why don't you let me worry about my own 'tush'?"

"No offense, but if this afternoon was any example of you taking care of yourself, you need some help."

He grabbed the Henley from her. "I freaked out, okay? Can we please not talk about it anymore?"

Amy's expression softened. "Okay." But then she turned back toward his closet. "This, however, is completely unacceptable. You and me are going shopping, mister, and real damned soon."

PASHA took another swig of his beer, some artisan brand he'd never heard of, and glanced toward the window. Snow was still coming down fast and furious outside the spacious downtown Detroit loft, but inside it was like sitting at an island resort, complete with bright tropical colors, huge plants, and bamboo furniture. *The only thing missing is a cabana boy.*

The loft's owners, a middle-aged couple named Ben and Teddy, had welcomed Pasha in, warmly proclaiming "the more the merrier!" before handing him a beer and telling him to make himself at home. But Pasha had never felt *less* at home in his life.

Watching the pair now, snuggled up together in an oversized chair with Ben sitting in Teddy's lap and Teddy's arms wrapped casually around his lover's waist, didn't help Pasha feel any more comfortable. It wasn't their fault. They weren't doing anything wrong, and even if they had been, it was their home and they could do whatever they wanted. Pasha took another big swig of his beer. Seeing how happy Ben and Teddy seemed together made him miss Michael more than ever.

Another couple, Cliff and Marla, were on the sofa. She was stretched out with her feet in his lap and he was rubbing them, making her smile. Amy and Leon were curled up together on the floor. Thank God the last couple in the room wasn't really a couple. According to Amy, both Mark and Brett were single—and gay. They were both cute, too. Mark had shoulder-length honey-brown hair and a neatly trimmed goatee; Brett was clean-shaven with delicate features, huge brown eyes, and short, bleach-blond hair. Both were on the tall lanky side, although Brett more so. He looked like he could have been a dancer; maybe he was. Neither had said much to Pasha when Amy introduced them. Actually, *no one* had said much to him after the introductions were made.

Pasha took another sip of his beer. As he lowered the bottle, he noticed Brett had turned toward him. He flashed a shy smile and Brett smiled back. Then he turned back toward the big flat screen TV on the other side of the room. Pasha did the same. The movie had been going for about half an hour, but Pasha still had no idea what it was about. The plot, such as it was, seemed split between some old space station's decaying orbit and subsequent crash to earth and a bunch of squatters doing heroin in an Australian slum. One of the heroin addicts was played by some guy who'd been a big name musician back in the eighties. According to Ben, the guy had hanged himself.

"Hey," said a soft voice.

Startled, Pasha looked down to see that Brett had scooted over to the foot of his chair and was looking up at him.

"Hey," Pasha whispered back, not wanting to disturb the others, who were clearly enjoying the film a whole lot more than he was.

"You look bored."

He shrugged. He went to take another sip of his beer only to discover the bottle was empty.

"Here." Brett passed up his glass. It looked like cola but smelled like rum. Pasha hesitated. "Go ahead," Brett told him with a grin. "Honest, I don't have cooties."

He snickered and took a sip. It was a rum and Coke all right. Or rather, it was a glass of rum with barely enough Coke to give it a little color.

Brett's glossy lips curled upward in a grin. "Come on into the kitchen and I'll make you one. Or you can take that one and keep me company while I make another one for myself."

Pasha rose to his feet and offered Brett a hand up. Once up off the floor, Brett kept hold of his hand and grinned as he tugged Pasha toward the kitchen.

Brett closed the door behind them and leaned up against the counter. "Jesus Christ, I was bored out of my mind! What a fucking snooze fest!"

Relief flooded Pasha. "I thought I was the only one who didn't get it."

Brett shook his head. "Teddy and Ben have the *worst* taste in movies—but the best taste in booze!" he said gleefully. Brett helped himself to a glass out of the cupboard nearest the sink and filled it with ice before pouring in a generous helping of dark rum and a splash of Coke. While he was adding the cola, Pasha picked up the rum bottle. Cruz Single Barrel. He'd never heard of it, but then again, his knowledge of liquor wasn't very extensive.

Brett leaned back against the counter again and studied him a moment. "Amy says you're Russian."

He frowned. When had Amy told Brett that? *And why?* But he answered anyway. "Yeah. I am."

"Cool. I don't know what all I am. I mean, you know, there's the usual, English, Dutch, German, and whatever." He sipped his drink. "But who knows, right?"

"I guess."

"Do you speak Russian?"

Pasha nodded. He felt like a monkey on display at the zoo. *Look kids, over here we have a Russian….*

"The only Russian word I know is Stolichnaya," Brett told him.

Pasha nearly rolled his eyes at what he assumed was an attempt to be clever. "Your accent is terrible."

"Oh yeah? You say it."

"*Stoleechnaya*." He put the stress on the correct syllable and pronounced each of the letters the way they were meant to be pronounced.

"Wow, whoever said Russian wasn't a sexy language never heard it spoken by someone as cute as you."

Heat crept into his cheeks.

"You're even cuter when you blush," said Brett, and before Pasha knew what was happening, Brett's mouth was on his. The kiss was hot and demanding, and there was only one option: surrender. Pasha closed his eyes and let Brett push him back against the wall. Brett ground into his crotch so hard it hurt, but that only made Pasha kiss him harder.

It was only when Pasha felt Brett's hand pushing between them, reaching for his zipper, that he broke the kiss. "I don't think…," Pasha began. Even dazed and breathless, he didn't want to think about what Amy would say if she walked in on them like this. But God, he didn't want to stop. "Is there somewhere else we can go?"

"How about the bathroom?"

Pasha nodded. "You have anything?" he asked, because the last thing he'd thought to bring with him was a rubber.

Brett smirked. "Nice thing about bathrooms. There's always a medicine cabinet, and I happen know that's where Ben and Teddy keep at least one box of condoms."

PASHA had to bite his lip to keep from crying out. He was bent over the cold porcelain sink with his jeans and boxers sagging around his ankles, and a long, thick cock buried balls-deep in his ass. "Oh Christ, right there," he grunted as Brett hit his prostate. "Harder. Fuck me harder. As hard as you can." He ignored the pain, the sharp edge of the counter digging into his stomach, and the burning in his ass.

"That good?" Brett asked as he slammed into him again. He was holding onto Pasha's hips so tight, Pasha was sure he was going to have bruises in the morning.

"More," Pasha urged. "*Please*. Make it hurt!"

Brett dug his fingers in harder and picked up his pace so that all Pasha could hear over the pounding of his heart was the relentless slap-slap-slap of flesh against flesh. "So good," he moaned. Everything ached. "Feels so fucking good."

"You too. Tight. Hot," he murmured in between fast, hard thrusts. "Fuck, I'm getting close." He reached around for Pasha's cock, but Pasha shook his head.

"Don't." Tears stung in his eyes, but he wanted it to go on all night. Being on the edge of climax was the best part of getting fucked.

"Whatever you want." Brett slipped his hand into Pasha's hair and grabbed a fistful of the short strands. He pulled Pasha's head into an uncomfortable angle. "Good?"

"Good," Pasha confirmed. He lost himself to the haze of pleasure and the agony of being so ruthlessly fucked he couldn't see straight. Brett pulled his hair and pushed Pasha harder against the counter. Nearly every brutal thrust sent Brett's cock slamming against his prostate. It hurt. It *should* hurt. Pasha bit his lip again to keep from screaming as he came way too soon, splashing cum against the cabinet door.

A second later, Brett grunted, his strokes becoming erratic. "Sweet Jesus," he gasped, then went slack against Pasha's body.

"Yeah," Pasha agreed.

They lay slumped together for several long moments catching their breath. Brett was a dead weight on top of him, but Pasha didn't utter a word of protest. He waited patiently and completely still until Brett was ready to get off of him, even when it became difficult to breathe. When Brett finally stood up, Pasha straightened too. Without a word, he pulled up his drawers and then his jeans. At his request, Brett hadn't taken his pants down, he'd simply undone his fly and fucked Pasha fully clothed. All he had to do now was remove the rubber, tuck, and zip.

They cleaned up in silence, carefully wiping away all the evidence of the tryst. Then Brett announced he had to take a leak, so Pasha left the bathroom first. He padded quietly back to the living room and resumed his seat, doing his best not to look like a man who'd just been fucked senseless. He ignored the angry look Amy shot him and the weird vibe coming from Mark. It wasn't like he'd gone off and slept with the guy's boyfriend or something. Amy said they were both single; that meant Brett was fair game. And anyway, Brett had started it, hadn't he?

When the movie ended, Amy decided it was getting late and they should leave.

"You're such a party poop," Brett whined at her.

"Some of us don't get to sleep in 'til noon on Saturday," she shot back.

Brett heaved a melodramatic sigh and turned to Pasha. "Can I see your phone?"

Pasha handed it over and watched, mouth agape, as Brett punched a phone number into his contact list.

"There." He handed it back to him with a cocky grin. "Now you don't have any excuse not to call me."

Pasha was about to offer up his number in exchange, but Amy tugged at his arm, sending a very clear message: they were leaving. *Now.* He offered a wan, apologetic smile to Brett and trudged after her.

Amy didn't say a word the entire way back to Pasha's house, and every time he tried to strike up conversation, her responses were terse and cold.

"I don't know what you're so upset about," he said finally, when she pulled up to the curb in front of his house. "We cleaned up—"

"That is more information than I needed, thank you."

"So what's the big deal?"

"The big deal is that I took you there to meet *Mark*, not to go screw Brett in the goddamned bathroom!"

Pasha blinked. "Mark? But he didn't say two words to me."

"Neither did Brett!"

She had a point. It hadn't taken very many words to get him into the bathroom with his jeans down around his ankles, a total stranger fucking him so hard his poor ass protested every bump in the road. Working tomorrow was going to be sheer agony, but it was what he wanted, what he always asked for. "What difference does it make that I hit it off with Brett instead of Mark?"

"Mark's a nice guy. Brett's a whore. I love him to death, but he'll fuck anything that moves."

"Thanks a lot."

"I didn't mean it that way," she insisted, but he was pretty sure that was *exactly* the way she'd meant it. Amy went on, "I just thought you and Mark should get to know each other. You've got a lot in common and he's such a good person. Brett's only interested in one thing."

"Maybe that's the only thing I'm interested in."

"I don't believe that."

Pasha didn't believe it either, but what else was there? Celibacy? "I'll see you in the morning," he told Amy as he got out of the car.

"Yeah. Good night," she answered, her tone still cold.

Pasha let himself in the front door. The house was cold and dark. Empty. Instead of going upstairs for a shower, he headed straight for the fridge and to the pint of Ben & Jerry's Cheesecake Brownie ice cream he'd stashed in the back of the freezer. He sat down on the floor in front of the heat vent to eat it.

After shoveling half the container into his mouth, Pasha pulled out his cell phone and almost called Brett. Maybe he wasn't as bad as Amy said. Maybe he'd like to go out for drinks sometime. But then he changed his mind and texted Michael instead. It was only the second message he'd sent since they broke up last year, and he didn't expect a reply. After all, if Michael couldn't be bothered to answer back when Pasha texted him with "happy birthday" back in July, why would he bother to answer now? But it was worth a shot.

I was thinking about u today. Just wondering how u been. Give me a call sometime, I'll buy u a cup of coffee. God, he sounded pathetic, but that didn't stop him from hitting Send. They'd dated for almost eight months, the longest Pasha had been with anybody. Why didn't that count for something? Why had it been so easy for Michael to not only dump him, but never want to speak to him again?

Pasha snorted. *Because after he dumped me, he hooked up with another guy.* A *gorgeous* guy. Pasha would never forget the night Ty dragged him to the Rainbow Room and there was Michael, his arms around a handsome blond. *I'd forget me too, if I had a guy like that hanging on my arm.* They'd exchanged awkward hellos and then Pasha left, preferring to pay forty bucks to get a taxi and go home rather than stick around and watch Michael and his new boyfriend make out.

He finished his ice cream and went upstairs to take a shower and wash off the stench of stale sex and latex. He was sure there'd been a time when sex was more than getting screwed on his hands and knees in a cheap, by-the-hour motel room or over the bathroom sink in somebody's apartment. Closing his eyes, Pasha tried to remember what it felt like to be touched by somebody who loved him, somebody who wanted him—*him*, not just a warm hole that needed filling.

"I know my life is messed up and maybe it's my fault, but all I want is somebody who'll love me. Somebody I can love back. Why is that so hard?" He blinked the water out of his eyes and stared up at the steam-filled bathroom ceiling. "Is it because they're right?" Was being gay really a sin? "But if it's wrong, why do I feel this way? If you wanted me to like women, all you had to do was flip a switch inside my head or something, right?" If God made everyone, everything, why would he make some people gay and then say being gay was wrong? It didn't make any sense.

CHAPTER FIVE

AFTER several hours of tossing and turning, Pasha finally gave up on sleep and got out of bed. He couldn't get his mind off Daniel. More than anything, he wished he could go back in time somehow and fix things. If he could change the past, he would run out the back door, catch Daniel in the lot, and beg him for another chance. Or better yet, he wouldn't act like an ass in the first place. He would quietly tell Daniel that he was in the closet and ask him if they could meet somewhere later. Dinner. Drinks. Whatever Daniel wanted would be fine with him.

But there was no going back and the chances of ever seeing Daniel again were slim to none. Even if he did, what would he say? Sorry I was such a jerk, you wanna try again? I promise not to be a total ass hat this time? Yeah, right.

Miserable to the core, Pasha started rooting through the kitchen cupboards as quietly as he could. There was nothing he could do about having screwed up with Daniel, but he could at least try to make it up to Amy for being such a jerk in front of her friends. Not that he would mind hooking up with Brett again, but maybe next time they should do it somewhere *other* than someone else's bathroom. *And maybe Amy really is wrong about Brett. Maybe he hasn't found the right guy yet.* It was worth a shot—wasn't it?

By the time five o'clock rolled around, the kitchen was toasty warm and smelled of vanilla and brown sugar, and Pasha was humming along with Kylie Minogue on the radio.

"What the hell are you doing?" His father's voice rose above Kylie's.

Pasha scrambled to turn down the radio. "Sorry. Did I wake you up?"

"No." But he was still scowling. He stalked over to the radio and turned it off. "It's five o'clock in morning. What are you doing up? And what is that?" He scowled down at the nine-by-thirteen-inch pan Pasha had just pulled out of the oven.

"Blondies."

"What the fuck is blondie?"

"They're kind of like brownies," Pasha explained. The ones he'd made had walnuts, pecans, and swirls with homemade caramel. Pasha had even sacrificed some of his Ghirardelli white chocolate chips because white chocolate was Amy's favorite. He owed her big time, and he knew it.

Dad, however, didn't look impressed. "Last thing we need in this house is more *shit*."

The words stung. Pasha told himself all his father really meant was "junk food," but that didn't make his actual words hurt any less. "I didn't make them for you. I made them for Amy." He'd planned on cutting a few pieces for his father, but if Dad was going to act like that, why bother?

"Why you cooking for her?" Ivan wanted to know.

"What difference does it make to you why I do anything?" He turned and refilled his coffee cup, then poured a cup for his dad, too.

"I'm not blind man, Pasha. I see what's going on."

Fuck. Pasha wiped his hands off on the dish towel. How had Dad figured it out? Unless Samara—

"Amy very pretty girl."

"What?"

"Amy. She pretty. Young. Smart. Never on time, but…." He shrugged. "She nice girl. But she has *drook*, Pasha."

Pasha frowned. "I know she has a boyfriend." Everyone did. "What are…? Wait. You think me—*and Amy*? Dad, honest, we're just friends."

Ivan gave him a long measured look. "Okay. So maybe you're 'just friends.'" He didn't sound like he believed it. "I know you're good boy, Pasha. I know you don't mean to do wrong things. But maybe Amy's *drook*—what's his name? Leon? Maybe this Leon no like her having…." He hesitated, as if searching for the right word. Failing to find it in English, he said in Russian, "*Bleezkiy drook*." A male friend, someone close, but not romantic. "Maybe he thinks you trying to steal her, huh? Why cause trouble between them? Let Amy be. It's no good to go sniffing around skirt of another man's woman."

"Jesus Christ, Dad, do you realize what you just *said*?"

Ivan bristled. "So now I'm stupid old man? I know how world works, Pasha. I know Amy's boyfriend not gonna like you baking her fucking cake. Don't go making trouble."

"Amy doesn't need Leon's permission to have friends."

"Not girl friends maybe, but you're *man*, Pasha. Men and women aren't friends like that. Only reason man hangs out with woman is because he wants her in his bed."

"Seriously, Dad? That's what you think of me?"

"Don't be stupid. I know you're good boy, I'm telling you what Amy's boyfriend gonna think."

"You've never even met him!"

"You think I let your mother run around with other men?"

Pasha's jaw tightened. "I really wouldn't know. Excuse me. I need to take my shower."

Ivan grabbed his arm as he tried to pass—Pasha yanked it back.

"You listen to me," the old man seethed. "You leave those at home. Or how about you give them to Nadia when she comes in for breakfast?" he suggested, brightening some. "Kids—"

"*Nyet*. I made this for Amy and she's who I'm giving it to. I don't know why you're making such a big deal out of nothing—"

"If it's nothing, how come you don't want to give this to your sister for kids?"

"Because I didn't make it for them!" Why did everything always have to be such a battle between him and his dad?

"You think you know everything, don't you? Well you don't know *nothing*!"

Pasha took a deep breath and counted to ten and then back down again. It only helped a little. No matter what they were fighting about, it always ended the same way, with his father accusing him of thinking he knew everything and/or Dad telling him how much he *didn't* know. "Dad, I don't think I know everything. I just know that Amy's boyfriend isn't going to care that I baked her a pan of blondies. If it makes you happy, I'll make some brownies for Nadia and the kids tonight." Because he loved his nieces and nephew but they weren't getting Ghirardelli chocolate. Nestlé was good enough.

Ivan waved him off. "Do whatever the fuck you want. It's not like I can stop none of you nohow. You kids don't appreciate nothing I do for you."

"Dad, I *do* appreciate you—"

"Go take your shower. We're gonna be late."

AMY came running in the front door at ten minutes after seven. Ivan didn't look up when she apologized for being late, he just kept scooting the bacon around on the grill. She shot Pasha a questioning look, and he stepped around to the coffee station, motioning her to follow him.

"What's going on?" Amy whispered once they were out of Ivan's line of sight.

"Me and Dad got into it at home this morning. It was probably my fault for losing my temper."

"Not *everything* is your fault, Pasha."

He just shrugged. His and the old man's argument wasn't anything she needed to worry about. "I'm sorry about yesterday. I know I totally crossed a line and that I was a real jerk."

Amy tugged off her coat. "No arguments there."

"I hope this makes up for it." He reached up and got the plastic container of blondies down off the shelf where he'd stashed them when he came in.

Amy cocked her head to one side. "Bribery, huh?" she asked as she opened the container.

"I figured it couldn't hurt."

"Hmm. We'll see." But as soon as she tried a bite, she smiled. "What was I mad at you for, again? I seem to have forgotten all about it."

He chuckled. "I promise to behave the next time you take me out. Assuming there is a next time," he added hopefully.

"Please. If you think I give up on my friends that easily, you really don't know me very well. Besides, I believe I owe you a shopping trip."

"Yeah."

"Don't sound so excited," she teased.

He rolled his eyes, then glanced around the corner and into the kitchen. Dad was attacking the job of slicing vegetables with such ferocity someone might think the tomatoes had personally offended him. Pasha turned back to Amy. "I don't suppose there's any chance you're wrong about Brett? Maybe he just needs to find the right guy?" he suggested.

"I've known Brett since the sixth grade. All he wants is Mr. Right Now."

Pasha sighed. That's what he'd been afraid of. "What about Mark? Any hope of him still wanting to hook up or something?"

"Sorry, sweetie. Not after last night." Amy poured herself a cup of coffee. "But there are lots of great guys out there. You don't have to settle for the Bretts of the world. I mean, look, I really do love him, but I worry about him too. If all you're looking for is a little fun—"

"No. You were right before. I want more than that. I just don't know how to make it work. You know what Dad's like." When the Supreme Court made its ruling against DOMA earlier in the year, the old man nearly lost it. Ivan said he couldn't believe they'd come out in favor of "those damned gays." "Maybe I should just stick with fun," Pasha said sullenly. "It's all I seem to be any good at, anyway."

"Don't settle for less than what you want. You deserve to be happy. Everybody does."

He peered into the kitchen again, but this time he didn't see Dad at all. Ivan had probably gone to get something out of one of the coolers. "My last relationship ended… it was a mess, Amy, and it was all my fault. Michael *really* loved me. And I loved him. I thought he was the guy I was going to spend the rest of my life with."

"So what happened?"

"He wanted us to move in together. I said no. He broke it off and started seeing someone else."

"Why did you say no?"

"I couldn't move in with some guy and expect my family to think we were 'just friends' for the rest of our lives. Even if we got a place with two bedrooms, what would I say in five or six years when Dad or my aunt Anya wanted to know why I still wasn't married? As it is, I get shit from Anya about being almost twenty-five and not having a girlfriend."

"Don't you think you're going to have to come out eventually?"

"No. Maybe. I don't know. But last year, when Michael asked me to move in with him, it was just lousy timing. Peter had just announced he was quitting the restaurant to take that job in Grand Rapids and Dad took it really hard." Peter had only been working at the diner part-time, mostly just to keep the books balanced, but Dad had still been clinging to the belief that when he retired, Peter and Pasha would take over the business together. It was never going to happen, but Dad refused to see it until Peter moved to the other side of the state. "And then all the shit with my mom… it just… everything came to a head all at once. There was no way I could move out. It would have killed my dad to lose me, too."

Amy gave him a long, thoughtful look. "Okay. You can tell me this is none of my business if you want to, but what's the real scoop with your mom? I mean, I kinda figured she wasn't *really* visiting relatives in Chicago for a whole year. Did her and your dad split up or something?"

"I wish it was something that easy. My mom has Alzheimer's disease."

"Oh God. Pasha, I'm sorry." She laid her hand on his arm. "How old is she?"

"A little older than Dad. The doctor called it 'early-onset Alzheimer's.'" Pasha set his hand on top of hers and let their fingers intertwine. "She was diagnosed about six years ago, but last year it got to the point where she couldn't be left alone anymore."

"Is she really in Chicago?"

"Yeah. My cousin Lena's a nurse. She found a place for Mom near her and visits a couple times a week. I think Peter's been out once or twice."

"What about you and your dad?"

"You're kidding, right? Sometimes I think he sent her so far away just so he'd have an excuse not to visit." *Or maybe so he doesn't have to think about her anymore.*

"I'm sure that's not true."

"You weren't there on Thanksgiving when he threw a fit because I wanted to call her, let the kids say hi. I thought maybe she'd enjoy hearing from us, but Dad put his foot down, said it was wrong to put the kids through that. I think the truth was that *he* didn't want to go through it." What kind of coward hid behind his grandchildren? If Dad didn't want to talk to Mom, he could just have said so. "By the time I was finally able to get away to call on my own, Mom was already asleep, so I went to the bar." *And got screwed by a total stranger in a cheap motel.* But he wasn't going to tell Amy that.

"Next time call me, okay? You've got my number, right?"

"I… yeah, I have it. Thanks."

"Anytime." Amy hesitated but then said, "Look, Pasha, I'm the last person who should be telling anyone what to do when it comes to family, but here goes. You need to start thinking about yourself and what *you* want out of life, not what your father needs or wants. Ivan's a big boy. He can take care of himself. He can run his own life—or he can ruin it. But he has no right to ruin yours too. Stop letting him walk all over you."

"It's not that easy."

"Yes. It is. But the longer you stick around here, the harder it's going to be to leave. I know the economy kind of sucks right now, but there are other jobs out there. You're a good cook, Pasha. Or if you don't want to cook, you can go back to school—"

"It's too late for that."

"You're only twenty-four. You can still go to school get some other kind of job—"

"My name's on the business, Amy. I'm stuck."

"Damn."

"Yeah."

Amy tightened her grip on his hand. "That doesn't mean you can't have a life outside of this stupid place."

Why did Pasha suddenly hear Mick Jagger's voice singing, "You can't always get what you want, but if you try sometimes, you might find you get what you need"?

"UNCLE PASHA!" RJ cried as he ran at Pasha and flung his arms around Pasha's waist. It was the same every Saturday, but it never got old.

"RJ!" Nadia scolded the youngster. "Your boots! You're tracking snow all over the restaurant. People are going to think you were raised in a barn!"

"It's okay," Pasha assured her. He hauled RJ up into his arms and carried him back over to the mat by the door so he could stomp off his boots. There were less than half a dozen customers in the dining room, but that wasn't unusual for nine o'clock on Saturday morning. *Only five years ago, we would have been slammed.* Five years before that, they'd needed three people on the floor on Saturday and four on Sunday.

Once the kids had gotten the snow off their boots to their mother's satisfaction, Pasha helped RJ and his four-year-old sister, Clara, out of their snowsuits.

"You two look just like abominable snowmen," he teased as he brushed the snowflakes out of Clara's long hair. She giggled and Nadia shook her head. She had her arms full with her two-year-old, Bailey, and the baby, Abbey, who was still little enough to ride in a carrier. As soon as Pasha had RJ and Clara divested of their bulky snowsuits, he took the carrier from his sister so she could get her own coat off.

"*Spaseeba*," said Nadia, stretching out her arm. She was about Pasha's height, but thin as a rail with long dark hair that framed a face Pasha had always thought would be pretty if she weren't always frowning. "I can't believe those *paskudnyakee* at the clinic think she's *under*weight," Nadia grumbled. "Just let one of *them* haul her around for an hour."

Pasha shot her a concerned look, but Nadia waved it aside. "You know what those idiot doctors are like, always thinking they know what's best. They don't know shit." Nadia headed for her usual table near the coffee station. "Seriously, you'd think by now they'd realize I have *some* clue about how to take care of my own goddamned kids." She stood Bailey up in the booth and tugged off the youngster's coat. "Do you mind getting them settled? I need to talk to Dad."

"Sure." He set the carrier down on the table and took Bailey from his sister. Pasha could guess what Nadia wanted: her mortgage was due in a couple of days, and more likely than not, she didn't have enough money to cover it. It was the same almost every month.

"I got Bailey's big-girl chair," Clara announced. She was standing next to Pasha holding a brown plastic booster seat, grinning with pride over her accomplishment. RJ was right behind her with a highchair for Abbey.

"Is Bailey big enough for a big-girl chair?" Pasha questioned.

"Mommy put her in one at Cheesies's last night," said Clara.

Pasha forced a smile. She meant Chuck E. Cheese's. If his sister could afford to take the kids out for pizza, why the hell was she in the kitchen asking their father for money? *Because she can*, he answered his own question.

"I'm gonna build a snow fort when we get home," RJ announced proudly.

"You are, huh?" said Pasha as he tried to settle his squirming two-year-old niece into the booster seat. "That sounds like an awful big job. Think you're up to it?"

RJ grinned. "Daddy's gonna help."

"*Moladyets*." "Good for you" was the best answer Pasha could come up with. RJ's father didn't get up off the sofa for snow forts or much of anything else, and Pasha knew it. He suspected RJ knew it too.

"I think we need another high chair," he told his nephew. There was no way Clara was going to sit still in a booster seat.

Obediently, RJ trotted over to where they kept the high chairs and brought one back. Pasha got Bailey settled easily and was about to offer the kids some milk when Nadia returned.

A deep frown creased her forehead. "Bailey can sit in a booster—"

"We tried," Pasha told his sister.

She heaved an exasperated sigh and picked the two-year-old up out of the high chair and put her into the booster seat, where Bailey proceeded to wriggle, fuss, and slap her hands against the table, much to the obvious ire of the other diners in the restaurant. Ignoring both her daughter's antics and the glares from other customers, Nadia got herself a cup of coffee and sat down at the table.

Pasha glanced up to see Amy giving him a sympathetic look. He smiled back. While he'd been wrangling with his niece, three tables had walked in, and she'd picked them up without complaint. *Then again, she probably appreciates the chance to make a few extra bucks.* Pasha turned to RJ and Clara. "Sharon got us some new coloring books last week," he said. "You wanna color with me for a minute?"

RJ's face lit up. "Yeah! Is it Transformers?" he asked hopefully.

Pasha did his best to hide his snicker. "No, it's Frosty."

"That's for babies!" RJ protested.

"I like Frosty!" Clara informed her brother. "And *I'm* not a baby!"

"*I* go to school," RJ countered.

Nadia gave them each a sharp look. "If you two start fighting, *nobody's* coloring," she warned.

They settled down quickly, but anyone who looked could see that RJ was pouting. Pasha got the coloring books and was about to sit down and color with them, hoping to prove to his nephew that there was nothing wrong with Frosty the Snowman, when the front door opened up again. It was Belinda. She waved at Pasha to stay where he was and helped herself to a cup of coffee before coming over to say hello. "Looks like you guys are having a party over here."

"We're coloring," Clara told her.

Belinda nodded sagely. "So I see. Looks like fun."

"You want to color with us?" asked RJ.

Nadia frowned at him. "Mrs. Freeman is a grown-up. Grown-ups don't color."

"Uncle Pasha colors with us," RJ protested.

"That's different," said Nadia.

Belinda smiled down at the youngsters. "I'm not very good at coloring, anyway. I tend to go outside the lines."

Pasha snickered. He didn't know Belinda well, but he had little trouble believing that. She had been a regular for four years, ever since the day her car broke down a few blocks away and she had to wait at the restaurant for AAA. It had been one of those damp, yucky days where the cold seeps right through to the bone. Ivan told Belinda her lunch was on the house and he sent her home with a piece of fresh apple pie. It wasn't the first time Pasha had seen his father be nice to a customer, despite what the old man sometimes said about people. Dad's moods were just mercurial. *And I seem to be the one who always catches the brunt of his temper.*

"Are you having your usual this morning?" Pasha asked Belinda.

"Yeah, but no rush. My brother-in-law's meeting me for breakfast."

Pasha nodded and went to see if Amy needed a hand with anything. Her customers all had drinks and she was taking the last table's order now, but the tickets for the first two tables were still hanging in the window. When Pasha looked into the kitchen to see what Dad was doing, he saw that the only thing the old man had plated were three giant Mickey-Mouse-head pancakes and a big bowl of fresh fruit. Ivan topped the fruit with whipped cream and proceeded to carry everything out to Nadia's table.

"Dad!" Nadia admonished when she saw. "There's no way they can eat all that!"

"So?" said Ivan.

"So it's a waste," she countered.

"It's mine to waste if I want. Now what about you, you want eggs? Or maybe I make you pancakes?"

“I’m fine with coffee.”

“You’re too skinny. Pasha!” he hollered across the dining room. “Make your sister some eggs, huh? Make her some potatoes too. Make it nice plate. I’m gonna sit.”

Before going into the kitchen, Pasha stuck his head into the dish room and asked Randy, the high school kid who washed dishes for them on the weekends, if he could come out and bus tables. Then he asked Amy which of her orders needed to go out first. He wished today was the exception rather than the rule, but it wasn’t. Saturday mornings were always this chaotic. It made Pasha wish his sister would just stay home. *But why would anyone pass up a free meal?*

WHEN Amy came in from her post-lunch smoke break, Pasha asked if she was okay with him going outside for a little fresh air.

“I’ll hold down the fort,” she promised with a smile. Pasha returned it, got his coat, and headed out the back door. An icy blast of wind hit him square in the face as soon as he stepped outside, but up above the sky had gone from nasty dark storm clouds to clear, vivid blue. Pasha let himself into his dad’s car to get out of the cold and slumped against the passenger seat, hoping beyond hope that the bright sun shining down was some kind of good omen and that what he was about to try would actually work. He fished his cell phone out of his coat pocket, connected to the Internet, and did a Google search for Jay’s Party Store in Troy, Michigan.

Nothing.

Okay, how about J’s Party Store? He typed in the new search.

Still nothing. There was nothing for Jae’s Party Store or Jai’s Party store, either.

Pasha sagged in defeat. His only hope of ever seeing Daniel again had hinged on being able to talk to someone at Jay’s Party Store and pray they could remember, and would tell him, the name of the company that had delivered something (Pasha didn’t even know what) Friday morning at 7:00 a.m. If he could get the name of the company Daniel worked for…. Pasha sighed. Even if he was able to get ahold of Daniel’s company, *his* Daniel might be one of eight Daniels who worked there. And God, wouldn't he sound so sane and rational if he called up and asked to talk to the really gorgeous Daniel with the long black hair and beautiful smile. Even if there was only one Daniel, calling him at work might get him into trouble with his boss. Besides, what would he say if he actually got Daniel on the phone? *"Hi, I'm the ass hat who asked you to come back to see him, then freaked out and blew you off? You wanna do it again sometime?"*

Right. No way Daniel was sitting around waiting for a phone call from him. Maybe he should just call Brett. Brett might only be after one thing, but it was one thing he was awfully good at—but damn it, there had to be more to life than a series of one-night stands. Pasha pocketed his phone. One night, two nights, it didn't matter. He was sick of it. *Only what's the alternative?* Spending the rest of his life single and celibate? God, that was too fucking depressing to think about. *All I want is to meet one nice guy.* Why was that so hard?

A shadow passed across Pasha's face, causing him to look up. Someone was standing right outside the car. Pasha blinked, not believing he was really seeing… *Daniel?*

Chapter Six

DANIEL leaned over, resting his head against the top of the door, and Pasha cranked down the window. His heart hammered so hard he was afraid the whole world would hear it.

"Hey," Daniel greeted him with a smile that made Pasha's whole body feel warm and weak.

"Hi." It sounded more like a frog croaking than an actual word. Pasha cleared his throat and tried again. "Hi." He wasn't sure it sounded any better the second time around.

Instead of the thick, dirt-smudged Carhartt jacket and faded jeans he'd had on yesterday, Daniel wore a leather coat and snugly fitting black jeans. His hair hung loose and wavy around his shoulders. "Am I interrupting something?" he asked, still smiling that gorgeous smile of his.

"I… no," Pasha croaked out. He cleared his throat again. "I was just checking my messages," he lied. "It's quieter out here."

"Colder too."

At the moment, Pasha didn't feel the cold. "You here for lunch?"

"Nope. I was hoping to see you."

"Me?"

"I ah, I kinda wanted to apologize for yesterday," Daniel explained.

"Why? I was the jerk."

"You weren't a jerk, Pasha. It never occurred to me that you might be in the closet. It should have. I'm sorry I came charging in like some kind of bull in a China shop. That's what my sister calls it," he added with a rueful little smile. "I hope I didn't cause you any problems."

"No, it's fine. It would have been bad if my cousin had figured it out—"

"Please tell me your cousin wasn't the gal who waited on me."

"No, that was Amy. She's cool. My cousin is the dishwasher. The one with the attitude problem," he clarified. Samara had come stomping out of the dish room a couple of times while Daniel was eating his lunch yesterday.

"Ah. Well." He didn't seem to know quite what else to say.

"Don't worry, nobody likes her," Pasha assured him.

"I ah… I'm just glad I didn't make things rough for you around here. And I um, was kind of hoping you might be interested in going out for coffee or something, sometime?"

Oh God. "I'd *love* to." He glanced at the back door; there was still no sign of anyone coming to find him. "But there's something I need you to understand. I mean…." He took a breath and tried to start over. "When I say my life is complicated, I just… the last guy I dated knew I was in the closet when we started going out." He hoped he wasn't assuming too much. Coffee wasn't exactly a major commitment. *But every relationship has to start somewhere.* And his and Michael's had started over coffee. "Michael broke it off with me because… I guess it was a lot of stuff, but it all revolved around me not being able to come out. Nothing's changed since then. Nothing's ever going to change, either."

"If I said 'never say never,' you'd probably take it the wrong way, so I won't say it. Truth is, it's your life. No one has the right to tell you how to live it, least of all some guy you just met."

"I just don't want to go through that again. If it's going to bother you down the road, I'd rather not start something that's only going to end up…." *With me heartbroken.* "Like it did before."

"Pasha, who you tell, what you tell them, isn't my business. It isn't anybody's. I can respect the fact that you've gotta be careful, and

I'm willing to just follow your lead. But I guess maybe I should warn you that I'm *not* in the closet and if ah… I mean, I don't want to assume too much here, but…. Look, why don't we just start with coffee and see where it goes, okay? You might decide after one date that you never want to see me again."

"I doubt that." Warmth rose in his cheeks, but Daniel's smile made him glad he'd said it.

"What time do you get out of here?" Daniel asked.

"Around four." Which wasn't strictly true, he got out of there when his dad felt like coming back and letting him go home. *But Amy's right. I have the right to a life outside this place.* "Maybe we could meet up around five thirty?"

"Just tell me where, and I'll be there."

"There's a coffee shop called the Bean and Leaf a few blocks down from here. South," he clarified. "It's right next door to a restaurant called Diablo's, which is pretty hard to miss."

"I'll see you there." Daniel straightened.

"Daniel." Pasha called him back, berating himself mentally for not being able to simply accept the fact that the universe had decided to give him a break for once. But he had to know. "Why?"

Daniel leaned back in and shot him an inquisitive look. "Why what?"

"Why are you asking me out?"

He seemed puzzled. "Because I can't think of another way to get to know you—unless you *like* the creepy stalker types." He winked. "If that's the case, we can skip the coffee, and I'll just go back to peering in your bedroom window while you're asleep."

"That's only sexy in movies."

"I s'pose that means I'll have to delete those pictures of you off my phone, huh?"

Pasha laughed. "Let me guess, you've been covertly stalking me for weeks and only just yesterday decided to make your move by pretending to be lost?"

"Guilty as charged."

Pasha shook his head. More than anything, he wished he didn't have to go back to work, that he could just hang out with Daniel now. "You sure you don't want to come in for lunch?"

"Nah, I'm good." Daniel stepped back so Pasha could get out of the car.

"I ah… I guess I'll see you in a few hours," he said.

"Wild horses couldn't keep me away. Neither could another broken GPS," Daniel added with another wink.

Pasha grinned back at him. Maybe meeting just one nice man wasn't too much to ask for, after all. *Now I just have to not blow it on the first date.* Which meant *getting* to their first date.

"WHAT the hell were you doing outside?" the old man demanded when Pasha stepped into the kitchen.

"Just taking a break." He hung up his coat and walked over to the slicer, where Dad was working on a huge brisket of corned beef, probably for tonight's dinner special.

"You take your breaks *inside*, like everybody else."

"If smokers can go outside for a cigarette, I can go outside for a little fresh air." Pasha tried to keep his tone neutral, but it wasn't easy with his dad scowling at him. The conversation was already off to a bad start. *And it's going to go downhill from here.* "Look, I need to leave on time today."

"What do you mean, 'on time'?"

"I mean that I need to leave at four."

Ivan's scowl deepened. "How come you gotta leave so early?"

"I have to be somewhere by five thirty," Pasha answered, rather than point out that the other daytime servers got to leave before three.

"So I gotta change *my* plans because *you* gotta be somewhere?" Ivan demanded.

Pasha bit his tongue. He couldn't begin to count the number of times he'd rearranged his plans to accommodate the old man. "This is important, okay?"

"Fine. You wanna go at four, you fucking go at four. But I want you to remember something, Pasha. Someday *you* gonna be boss. This gonna be your place and you won't be able to spend all your time chasing around, goofing off. You're gonna have to grow up."

Pasha swallowed back the angry words that welled up in his throat and walked out of the kitchen. He knew he was asking a lot when he asked his father to give up part of his afternoon. The break Dad took between lunch and dinner was the only time off the old man got. *But it's his choice to be here open to close.* Which was only partially true. They couldn't afford to pay another cook. *But we could close at four like half the other Coneys in town.* Hell, they could probably close for one full day and save money in the long run. Lots of small restaurants were closed on Sunday or Monday. But Dad was afraid to do anything that might upset their regulars, even if it meant putting himself in an early grave to stay open seven days a week.

Amy caught Pasha's eye, then headed around the corner toward the coffee station. Pasha followed.

"Okay, what the hell was that all about?" she asked.

"I told him—"

"Yeah, I got the part about you wanting to leave at four today, what I'm asking is what's going on."

Heat enflamed Pasha's cheeks. The whole restaurant had probably heard the old man yelling at him. Thankfully, the only customers were regulars. Belinda and her brother-in-law were looking at something on her laptop, and Art and Jimmy sat at their usual table doing a decent job of pretending they hadn't heard. Sam McMiller, who only came in on the weekends or at dinnertime, was sitting in a corner booth reading his paper, looking like he really *hadn't* heard—maybe his hearing aid was turned off.

And Amy was still waiting for an explanation.

"Daniel was here," Pasha told her.

"Who?"

"The delivery truck guy."

"When? Where? How did I miss him and what the hell happened?"

Pasha couldn't help but laugh. "He came by while I was outside. We're going out tonight. It's just coffee," he added quickly. "But who knows, right?"

"Just take it slow," she advised, "no screwing in any bathrooms." The lightness of her tone took the sting out of the admonishment. "Now, let's talk about what you should wear...."

IT WAS almost six when Pasha finally pulled into the crowded parking lot behind the Bean and Leaf Café. The old man had gotten back at three thirty. He'd come in, fixed himself a sandwich, and sat down to eat it at the counter. He didn't get back up again until exactly four o'clock on the dot. Pasha didn't care. He'd kept his mouth shut and kept working until Dad came into the kitchen to take over. Pasha had made good time getting home, where he'd showered and shaved quickly, then gotten dressed in the outfit Amy suggested. Everything was going perfectly until he ended up stuck in a huge backup on I-75. And of course he didn't have any way of contacting Daniel to let him know he was running late because they hadn't exchanged numbers.

Please, please, please still be here, Pasha prayed as he circled the lot behind the Bean and Leaf for a third time, desperately searching for a parking spot. The diner might be dead, but the rest of Royal Oak appeared to be jam-packed with people out Christmas shopping.

At last, Pasha spotted a little white car pulling out of a space near the back of the lot. *Wouldn't it be just my luck that that's him, leaving?* Since he couldn't see the driver, all he could do was hope Daniel was still inside the café, and that he wasn't the type of guy to get pissed when someone was late. Pasha pulled into the vacant spot, fed the meter, and jogged across the slush-covered cement.

By the time he reached the café, his heart was pounding both from nerves and his sprint across the parking lot. Through the big garland-decked windows, Pasha had a clear view of the half-dozen tables closest to the door; Daniel wasn't seated at any of them. Steeling himself against disappointment, Pasha opened the door and stepped inside. The aroma of roasting coffee hit him at once; so did the cacophony of noise. Nearly every seat was occupied, and everyone seemed to be talking. Couples held hands and friends laughed while a few solitary souls were hunched over laptops with headphones on.

Pasha scraped the slush off his shoes and began winding his way through the long, narrow room. Daniel was nowhere to be seen, but by then, it was almost six thirty. He couldn't really blame Daniel for leaving. How many chances did one guy get, anyway? He was just debating whether or not he wanted to wait in line at the counter and drown his sorrows in a latte and maybe something from the pastry case when someone stood up near the front of the café.

Daniel.

And damn, he looked good. He was wearing a black turtleneck tucked into his jeans, with a narrow belt around his slender waist—but the best part was the way he looked at Pasha, as if he was truly the only person in the room *worth* looking at.

There *had* to be a catch. Guys like Daniel didn't settle for ordinary.

But there he is. Butterflies danced in Pasha's stomach as he closed the distance between them. "Sorry I'm so late," he said in lieu of hello. He wanted to explain about the accident, but was afraid it would only sound like a lame excuse.

Daniel just shrugged. "No worries. I had good company." He nodded down at the tattered paperback sitting next to a paper cup with a couple of teabags floating in it.

Pasha wasn't sure how to respond to his comment, so he simply offered up a weak smile and shucked out of his coat—and became acutely aware of Daniel's gaze sweeping over him, seeming to take in every detail. Heat rushed to Pasha's cheeks. Not even Michael had looked at him the way Daniel was now.

"You look good," Daniel said.

"Thanks. I ah, I had some help. I mean, I got a little fashion advice from a friend."

"The clothes are nice, but I was talking about the man wearing them, Sugar."

Breathe. Just breathe. Think of something to say... anything.... "You too. I mean... you look really great," he stammered.

Daniel's expression warmed. "Glad you think so. Can I buy you a coffee or something?"

"Yeah, thanks. I really am sorry," he repeated.

"For what?"

"Being so late."

"I said no worries. Stuff happens."

How could anybody be so easygoing?

"So. Coffee, tea, latte?" Daniel questioned.

It felt strange having someone ask him what *he* wanted for a change. "Latte, I guess. With skim milk. I'm trying to shed a few pounds."

"I don't see why. From where I'm standing, you look perfect."

More heat crept into Pasha's cheeks but that didn't stop him from admitting the truth. "I had a thirty-two-inch waist in high school."

"And?"

"And it's not thirty-two inches anymore."

"You don't have the metabolism of a sixteen-year-old anymore either. Or the acne," he pointed out with a wry grin.

"I never had acne."

"Just for the record, I hate you."

Pasha blinked—then realized Daniel was teasing him. He smiled and took a closer look at Daniel's face, where he saw a few tiny pockmarks, all that remained of Daniel's teenaged acne. "I'll still trade you," he said, eyeing Daniel's waist.

"You wouldn't say that if you saw a picture of me at sixteen. And at the risk of sounding like a broken record, there is nothing wrong with the size of your waist. I'll get you that latte with skim milk if that's what you really want, but if you prefer something else...." He left it open-ended.

Pasha gave in. “Two percent milk. And maybe extra foam and maybe a shot of cheesecake flavoring?”

Daniel’s grin was nothing short of triumphant. “You got it. You want anything else while I’m up there? I saw some red velvet cake in the case.”

“No, I’m good.”

“No arguments there.”

Oh God. Please let this be real.

As Daniel turned and walked toward the counter, Pasha found himself admiring the view. Daniel’s ass was firm, round… perfect. *And you’re leering*, Pasha chided himself. He sat down and picked up Daniel’s paperback. *The Catch Trap*, by Marion Zimmer Bradley. The front cover showed a pair of circus performers in old-fashioned looking costumes. He flipped the book over and read the back cover—then blinked and read it again, just to make sure he’d read it correctly. He had.

The story was set in the nineteen forties and fifties and revolved around a pair of male trapeze artists.

Gay male trapeze artists.

Lovers.

By the time Daniel got back with his latte, Pasha was on page fifteen. “Sorry,” he said, putting the book back down.

“About what? It’s a novel, not top-secret documents.” He set Pasha’s drink on the table next to him and resumed his seat. “So what did you think?” He nodded at the paperback.

That guys don’t read romance novels. Except he’d been sitting there reading it, himself. “Um. It’s interesting, I guess.”

Daniel laughed. “Go ahead and say it, men don’t read romance books.”

“No… I just… I’ve never read one, so I have nothing to compare it to.” Pasha popped the lid off his latte and sipped down a mouthful of sweet creamy foam.

“I think somebody’s glad I talked him out of skim milk,” Daniel teased.

"I still want to drop six inches." *Crap.* He hadn't intended to say aloud how badly he'd let himself go.

"You're worked up over *six* inches?"

"Yes. Six big, fat, ugly inches." If he was going to say it aloud, he might as well own it.

Daniel just shook his head. "Pasha, you look great exactly the way you are."

"Says the man with, what, a thirty-inch waist?" he hazarded.

"Twenty-nine," he corrected gently.

"Uh-huh."

"It's just a number, Sugar."

"Guys who look like you can afford to say things like that."

Daniel let out a frustrated-sounding sigh and changed the subject. "MZB, Marion Zimmer Bradley," he clarified, nodding to the paperback, "is a real pioneer in LGBT fiction. Most of her work is in science fiction and fantasy. I think *Catch Trap* is the only contemporary—or sort of contemporary—book she wrote."

"It ah…, I guess I don't know a whole lot about gay literature." The truth was he didn't know much about any literature.

"If you're interested, you can borrow it. Bradley's a great place to start. But I should warn you, *Catch Trap* is kind of a bittersweet pill."

"What do you mean?"

"Two gay men in the forties and fifties…." He left it open-ended for Pasha to fill in the blanks on his own.

Pasha nodded. "Yeah." It sounded like something he could relate to. "Let me know when you finish it."

Daniel pushed the book back over to him. "I've finished it five or six times already."

"Why are you reading it again? It's not like the ending is going to change." He ducked his head apologetically; just then he'd sounded *exactly* like his father.

But Daniel was still smiling. "Good books are like old friends. Sometimes you have to check back in on them, see how they're doing, even if you know nothing's really changed."

He had no idea what to say to that.

Daniel offered up a sheepish grin. “My mom teaches literature. I guess it’s her fault I’m kind of a book nerd.”

“You’re way too good looking to be any kind of nerd,” Pasha blurted out. Embarrassment heated his cheeks.

Daniel either didn’t notice or didn’t mind—or he was simply too polite to comment. “Trust me, I am. I read every single one of Bradley’s Darkover books when I was a kid, borrowed ’em from my mom.” It was his turn to blush. “Well, I sorta started out helping myself to her bookshelf when I was ten or eleven. Ma wasn’t too happy at first. She wasn’t sure they were all age appropriate. After I came out she understood why I liked Bradley’s writing so much.”

Pasha shot him a questioning look.

“She writes LGBT characters without painting them as villains or creeps or stereotypes,” he explained.

“Oh.” Not sure what else to say or do, Pasha bought himself a little time by taking a sip of his drink. “I didn’t do real well in LA—Language Arts—back in high school.” Truth was, he hadn’t done real well in anything.

“Mind if I ask how long ago high school was?”

Pasha found it easier to stare at the framed photograph over Daniel’s left shoulder than to look at his date. “I graduated seven years ago.” Most guys his age didn’t talk about high school anymore, but he’d only gone to community college for a couple of semesters, and only part time.

“That’d make you… twenty-four, twenty-five?” Daniel guessed.

“I’ll be twenty-five in February.” He took another sip of his latte. “You?”

“Coming up on the big three-oh next week. I hope that doesn’t make me too over-the-hill for you.”

He was kidding, right? “No way. When, next week?”

“Tuesday.”

“Happy early birthday.”

The warmth of Daniel’s smile sent that swarm of butterflies flapping around in Pasha’s stomach again. “It’s starting to look that way, anyway." Color tinted Daniel's cheeks and he cleared his throat. "So when in February do I get to tell you happy birthday?"

"The seventeenth." *Please let that mean he wants to stick around that long.* Pasha hadn't been on very many first dates, but so far this was the worst. He could only hope Daniel didn't think so too. He gulped down some more of his latte, wishing it was spiked with something a lot harder than cheesecake-flavored syrup. "I ah… I guess… it must've sucked when you were a kid, having a December birthday. I mean, you know with it being so close to Christmas and all." *God, I hope that didn't sound as dumb to him as it did to me.* "My sister's birthday is the day after Thanksgiving. She always hated having her party be a part of Thanksgiving dinner. Christmas must have been even worse."

"Nah, my folks never did the combined birthday/Christmas thing. But maybe they had a little extra incentive since there's two of us."

"Two of you?"

"I'm one of a pair, identical twins."

Somewhere out there, there was another Daniel? "Is your brother…?"

He chuckled. "Straight as an arrow, but other than that we're almost exactly alike." Daniel faltered a little, his gaze settling on the contents of cup. "Or we used to be. I guess it's been a long time since we could fool anybody into thinking I was him and he was me."

"You didn't seriously do that, did you?"

"Yeah, once or twice," he admitted sheepishly.

"Did he have a hard time with it when you came out?" Pasha wondered if that was why Daniel seemed to pull into himself a little a second ago.

Daniel drained the last of his tea and shook his head. "Davis took it better than anybody."

He was pretty sure that wasn't the whole story, but he didn't press the issue. "How old were you when you came out?" he asked instead.

"Sixteen. I told Davis first, then my folks, and then my sister."

"What happened? I mean… how'd they all take it?" Pasha was sure that if he'd come out at sixteen, Dad would have kicked him out of the house. *He probably still would.*

"Pops told me he didn't care who I loved just as long as they treated me right—and as long as I treated them right too. Ma took it a little harder. She was kind of quiet for a few days," Daniel explained. "Eventually we talked. Turned out she was mostly just worried, afraid I'd end up getting picked on or something." He smiled. "I grew up in a pretty small town and I, ah… I took my first boyfriend to the homecoming dance, if that gives you an idea of how *not* in the closet I was, even back then."

"Shit. That took balls."

He snickered. "Maybe. Ma would tell you I'm just a troublemaker."

Pasha couldn't help but laugh a little, too. He could see Daniel as the class clown. It didn't take long for him to sober, though. "I'll never be able to tell my family." And he envied that Daniel could.

"Sometimes family surprises you, Pasha. I'm not telling you what to do," he added quickly. "I'm just saying that you can't always predict what someone's going to say or do. I knew my parents would be okay with me liking guys. They're both pretty open-minded. I was pretty sure my sister would be all right with it too. But I was *convinced* Davis was gonna lose it—that's why I told him first. Only it turned out I'd worked myself into a real dither over nothing. All he did was laugh and tell me it was about time I figured out I liked guys. *He'd* known since we were twelve. I don't know how. I didn't know myself until I met Jared."

"I think I always knew something was wrong with me. I mean, not *wrong*, just… different. But when I was a kid, I was so mixed up. I remember watching *Buffy* with my older brother. He had a thing for Willow." He rolled his eyes. Peter had had posters of Alyson Hannigan, the actress who played Willow, all over his bedroom when he was a teenager.

Daniel smiled. "Let me guess, you like Angel better?"

"Yeah." Even back then, he'd had a thing for big strong guys.

"Me too."

Pasha sipped his latte. Maybe they should have met at Pronto!, the bar down the street. At least there he could have gotten himself a drink. If Daniel *still* liked big strong guys… *that's not me.* "I ah, I wanted to be like my brother Peter, but no matter how hard I tried, I just couldn't look at girls that way."

"Being different's hard."

Pasha shrugged again. He didn't want to say out loud how many times he'd gone to bed praying that God would fix him. He wasn't sure what was worse, not knowing what was "wrong" or finally having the courage to acknowledge that he was gay. "When I was fifteen, my brother caught me looking at men's swimsuits in a sportswear catalogue. The ah… the models were pretty hot and I was… you know."

"Jerking off?"

"God no! I was just hard. But it was pretty obvious why."

"What did your brother say?"

"He broke my nose."

The smile that had begun tugging at the corners of Daniel's mouth vanished. "He *hit* you?"

Pasha shrugged. "What he said hurt more than having him punch me. It wasn't like we were close or anything, but I just…." He could still see the pained expression on Peter's face. "I hadn't… I mean, I didn't pick up the catalogue to look at the models. It was just one of those things that came in the mail and I was flipping through it because I was bored. When Peter called me a faggot, I just sat there. I wanted to say I wasn't, but I couldn't deny it anymore."

Daniel muttered something incomprehensible under his breath and reached over like he was going to take Pasha's hand—then drew his hand back before actually touching him. "Sorry."

Pasha shook his head. He wished Daniel *had* touched him.

"How old was your brother?" Daniel wondered.

He shrugged again, not seeing how it mattered. "Twenty."

"What did your parents say?"

Pasha scoffed. "You think I told them?"

"You had to say *something* to explain a broken nose."

"Peter told Dad I got into a fight at school."

"Your father believed that?" Daniel clearly didn't seem to think he should have.

"Dad believes everything Peter tells him. Besides, I got hassled over my name all the time, so even though I'd never been in a fistfight before, it sounded plausible enough." Didn't it? It must have—Dad bought it. "Spending a few weeks grounded was better than what Dad would've done to me if we'd told him the truth. Anyway, it was a long time ago. It doesn't matter anymore." Daniel didn't look like he believed that any more than Pasha did. He drained the last of his latte and set the cup next to Daniel's, wondering if two empty cups signaled the end of what had definitely turned into a miserable date. "Maybe we should call it a night."

"I put my foot in it, didn't I?"

"Huh? No. No, you're great company. I'm the one… I ah, I think my mom would say I'm a wet blanket tonight. I swear, I never talk about stuff like this. You know, family."

Daniel offered up an apologetic smile. "I didn't mean to pry."

"You didn't. I just started babbling." Maybe he really should stick with anonymous hookups, after all. Dating was too complicated.

"I don't suppose I could talk you into hanging out a little more? I noticed a couple of restaurants across the street. We could grab a bite to eat if you're interested."

Pasha was too stunned to give Daniel anything but the truth. "I'd like that. If you really want to." If Daniel was just trying to be nice, he'd rather go home and eat ice cream.

"I'd like to spend some more time with you, Pasha. It um… it's been a while since I've been out on a date. This is nice."

He nodded. Today was obviously his day for second chances and he was not going to blow this one. "What are you in the mood for?"

Daniel's smile turned mischievous, although his tone remained neutral. "This is your neck of the woods, Sugar. What do you recommend?"

Heat crept into his cheeks again, but Pasha ignored it. "If you like Asian, Little Tree is the best place around. I've never been to Diablo's but I've heard it's good, or there's Andiamo's if you want Italian. Or we could go to Beirut Palace. They serve a really good fattoush." He realized he was talking too fast and forced himself to take a breath. "I'm up for whatever you want."

Daniel's brows shot up in a way that made Pasha squirm, but all Daniel said was, "How about Asian?"

"Asian's good. But I should probably go put some more money in my meter before we head over."

"Me too. I parked up front. You?"

"In back."

"I'm not sure, but I think there's a really dirty joke in there somewhere," said Daniel, his grin growing more mischievous than ever.

Pasha snickered. "I think so too. How about we leave it where it is and meet up at the restaurant?"

Chapter Seven

WARMTH spread through Pasha's chest when he walked into Little Tree and saw Daniel watching the door. Waiting.

For me.

Daniel was seated at a table on the far wall, and he was looking at Pasha the way he had when he came into the diner yesterday, the way he had when he spotted Pasha in the café, like Pasha really was the only person in the room worth noticing.

God, I could get used to this.

Daniel got to his feet as Pasha approached the table. "Long time no see," he teased.

"Yeah." He didn't know what else to say, but it didn't seem to matter. Daniel reached out and gave his arm a light, friendly squeeze and suddenly all Pasha wanted to do was lean up and find out if Daniel's lips were as soft as they looked. He broke eye contact before he gave into temptation, and Daniel's hand fell away from his arm. At times like this, Pasha envied straight couples. Or gay couples who were brave enough to be out of the closet.

When the waitress came over, he ordered a cup of black tea. Daniel already had a cup of green tea in front of him.

"So what do you recommend here?" Daniel asked, after she'd gone again.

"I guess it depends on what you like."

Daniel's gaze fell squarely on him. "I can think of at least one thing I like, but I'm pretty sure it's not on the menu."

For a second Pasha couldn't breathe. Gorgeous men did *not* come on to guys like him! "Tell me again why you're here," he pleaded.

Daniel shook his head, but he didn't quit smiling. "I'm here because I met this really cute guy the other morning and instead of telling me to get the hell out of his parking lot, he offered to help get me to where I needed to be. Of course it doesn't hurt his case any that he's got the prettiest pair of hazel eyes I've ever seen. One of the sweetest smiles, too," he added, his own smile deepening.

"He's also got a thirty-eight-inch waist and thinning hair."

"Sugar, if all I wanted was something pretty to hang on my arm, I'd go out and buy a bracelet." He sounded irritated. "Not that I don't like the way you look. I do, I like it a lot. But that's just the icing on the cake. Life is too short to get hung up on superficial stuff. Besides, in thirty or forty years, neither of us is going to look so hot." Color tinted Daniel's cheeks. "Sorry. I have a tendency to jump the gun a little."

"I don't mind." He ignored the nagging voice at the back of his head that reminded him how Michael had wanted thirty or forty years, too. They hadn't broken up because they fell out of love. *But if you love someone, how can you go from asking them to move in to never speaking to them again?*

"Why don't we just work on getting through dinner," Daniel suggested.

"Yeah, good idea."

THE next hour was spent eating, laughing, and trading stories about growing up, school, work, and family. And even though Pasha was way more interested in hearing about Daniel's life than he was in talking about his own, he found himself saying more than he'd planned about himself. He talked about his brother and sister and nieces and nephew, and he learned that Daniel was from the Upper Peninsula, from "a speck on the map" called Hannahville.

"It's not too far from Escanaba," he offered. That didn't help much, but instead of asking where Escanaba was, Pasha decided to look it up online later. "What about you?" said Daniel. "You live in Michigan all your life?"

Pasha shook his head. "I was born in St. Petersburg, Russia," he added. "Not Florida."

"Whoa. You don't sound like it. I mean… sorry. I just meant you don't have any kind of accent."

He shrugged. "I came here when I was five. I've spent most of my life speaking English."

"Do you still speak Russian?"

"*Da. Svabodna.*"

"I'm impressed."

Pasha laughed. "By two words?"

"It's better than I could do." He set down his chopsticks and regarded Pasha thoughtfully for a moment. "What was the hardest part of moving here?"

"You know, you're one of the few people who have ever asked me that. Most people just assume it was learning English, but really it was learning the alphabet. It's really different."

"How so?"

Pasha flagged over their waitress and asked if he could borrow a pen and something to write on, then he turned back to Daniel. "What's your dad's name?"

"John. Why?"

"I suppose we're on *tee*—on informal terms," Pasha explained. "But if we were in Russia, I might still be calling you *Daniel Johnovich.*" As he spoke, he wrote out Daniel's name in Cyrillic cursive—although "Johnovich" was far from a traditional patronymic name.

"Okay, I recognize about half the letters," said Daniel, "but why's there an *H* in the middle of my name?"

"That's an *n*," Pasha told him.

Daniel shot him an incredulous look. "So why do both Daniel and Johnovich start with *D*?"

"Because there isn't a *j* in Russian."

"Right. Note to self: do not try to learn Russian to impress boyfriend," Daniel muttered. Then he blushed. "Sorry. I'm honestly not trying to get ahead of myself here, promise."

"I don't mind," Pasha repeated what he'd said earlier

"You sure?"

"It's kind of pointless going out with someone if you don't at least hope there's the possibility for something, right?" He held his breath waiting for the answer.

Daniel's smile made his heart surge. "Yeah. Absolutely right."

And it was all Pasha could do not to reach across the table and take hold of his hand.

They continued talking while they finished their dinner, and Pasha learned that both Daniel and his twin brother had played football and hockey all through high school. Daniel had even played a little football in college. No surprise there, given Daniel's build. What did surprise Pasha was that Daniel had been involved in drama in high school, and had even landed the leading role in *The King and I* his senior year, which meant he could sing, too.

"I couldn't carry a tune if it had handles," Pasha admitted.

"I'm not sure I'm really all that good. It's a small town. There weren't that many guys in my class clamoring for the role."

"I'll bet you're better than you think."

Daniel looked almost embarrassed as he shook his head. "What about you? You do sports or anything?"

"I wanted to try out for baseball in eighth grade, but…." He shrugged. Mom kept forgetting to make the appointment for his physical. At the time, he thought she did it on purpose so he couldn't play, but looking back, he realized it was probably the Alzheimer's. They didn't know she had it then, of course. Sometimes he wondered how they could have missed it. *Except everybody forgets stuff.* "I wouldn't have had time for baseball, anyway."

"Why not?"

"Daniel, I started helping out at the restaurant as soon as I was tall enough to stand in front of the sink and scrub pots. We all did. By the time I was sixteen, I was cooking four nights a week and waiting tables on the weekends."

"That doesn't seem right."

He shrugged again. It was just the way things were. "When Peter cut his hours at the restaurant so he could go to college full time, I picked up his shifts. I don't think anybody even noticed that I almost flunked out of high school because of it."

"I hope you'll forgive me if I say I don't think much of your brother, Sugar."

"Yeah. It's okay. I don't think much of him either most days. So, um, you haven't told me where you live now," he said, mostly to change the subject.

"Ypsilanti."

"You drove all the way back here in this weather?" *Just to see me?* Ypsilanti was almost an hour away.

Daniel flashed another one of those knee-weakening smiles. "Some things are worth a little extra effort." His tone made Pasha feel warm. Wanted. It was a really nice feeling. Then his smile morphed into a silly, lopsided grin. "'Sides, where I grew up you're almost always forty minutes away from wherever you wanna be, and this weather is *nothin'* compared to what we get in the UP."

Pasha smiled back at him. "What brought you down here in the first place?"

"School. I wanted to get away from home, or at least small-town life, so I got myself accepted to U of M."

"You went to U of M and you drive a delivery truck?" Embarrassment heated Pasha's cheeks. "I'm sorry, I didn't mean it like that."

"It's okay. Truth is, I wasn't as ready to be on my own as I thought."

"What happened?"

"I dropped out. It's a long story."

Pasha took the hint and didn't ask Daniel why he left school. "How come you didn't move back home?" he asked instead, hoping it was a less tender subject.

"I did for a while, but you know what they say, you can never go home again."

"I wouldn't know. I never left."

"That's nothing to be ashamed of, Pasha. Heck, my sister Joyce moved back home a few years ago when her and Robert split—her ex-husband," he explained. "She still hasn't moved back out again."

"But at least she moved out for a while."

"Only when she got married." Daniel nudged his foot under the table, coaxing another smile out of Pasha. "It's still pretty early. You feel like walking up to the movie theater and seeing what's playing?"

Pasha glanced down at his watch. It was only a little after eight. The movie theater was only about a block away—unless Daniel meant the Main Art Theater, which was two blocks up. Either way, it would be a short walk.

"If you'd rather just call it a night—"

Pasha shook his head. "I'd love to go to a movie with you, it's just…. God this is embarrassing. I have to pick my dad up from work at eleven. My car died a few months ago and I haven't gotten around to buying a new one yet."

"Why is that embarrassing?"

"I'm almost twenty-five years old, I still live at home, I work for my dad, I'm borrowing his car to come see you tonight, and I guess while I'm laying it all out there, I might as well tell you that I dropped out of community college after two semesters."

"You did catch the part where I told you I dropped out of U of M, right?"

Pasha nodded. He had. But at least Daniel had gotten *into* U of M. That was more than he could have managed. "I just wish I'd done more with my life."

"You're only twenty-four, Sugar. You've got plenty of time to do something else if you want. Thing is though, it's your life. If you're not happy with it, the only person who can change things is you."

"I wish it was that easy."

"It's as easy—or as hard—as you make it," Daniel reminded him.

"Yeah. I know. It's just… I feel like my whole future is tied up in a restaurant that's probably going to go under in a year. When that happens, I won't have anything." God, he was doing it again. "I'm sorry."

"For what?"

"I'm usually not like this."

"Pasha, I'm enjoying your company. If I wasn't, I wouldn't have asked you if you wanted to stay out a little longer. If you don't have time for a movie, we can walk back across the street for more coffee and maybe some dessert."

The last thing his waistline needed was dessert. Pasha glanced at his watch again. "If we catch a movie starting in the next half an hour or so, I should be okay." And if he was few minutes late, what was the old man really going to do? Fire him? "What did you want to see?"

"Why don't we just take a walk and see what's playing, then go from there?"

"Why are you so easygoing?"

"Because life is too short to sweat the little stuff, babe. There's plenty of big things out there to worry about."

"I HAD a really nice time tonight," Pasha said, as they headed back down Main Street toward the coffee shop after the movie. Their timing at the theater had been perfect. There were only a couple of shows they both wanted to see, and one of them was scheduled to start ten minutes after they got there. That left enough time to buy tickets and hit the concession stand without being rushed, but without having to sit through a bunch of commercials before the previews, either. Since Daniel had picked up the tab for dinner, Pasha paid for the movie. Neither wanted popcorn, but Daniel accepted Pasha's offer of something to drink. *And* he talked Pasha out of getting a diet soda. They both got plain bottled water instead, which was something Pasha probably needed to drink more of anyway if he wanted to lose a few pounds.

It was ten forty-five when the movie let out and the streets were almost empty. A fresh blanket of snow had fallen, making the world look pristine and everything feel somehow quieter. Blue-white lights twinkled around the trunks of every tree lining Main Street and colored lights decked most of the shop windows they passed. Pasha smiled as he realized he was starting to feel just a little more optimistic about the holidays.

His smile faltered, however, as seconds ticked by turning slowly into minutes, and Daniel still didn't respond to what he'd said about having had a good time.

"I ah, I'm sorry I have to take off like this," Pasha said as they approached the street corner. On the other side, they'd part company. "I wish I could stay out longer."

The light changed color and they crossed the street. But Daniel still wasn't talking.

"If you want to do this again sometime, you know where to find me," Pasha told him. By then he was racking his brain, trying to figure out what he'd done wrong. The evening had started off a little rough, but dinner had been amazing and nothing weird had happened at the movie.

"I had a really good time too," Daniel finally said, his voice so soft, Pasha almost missed it. "I just…." He hesitated, looking like he wasn't quite sure what to say. Then he shook his head. "Can I walk you to your car?"

"Sure." His heart skipped a beat. Maybe Daniel was just trying to figure out how to get a good-night kiss. God, all he had to do was ask. It was late and there was hardly anyone around. What were the chances of anyone noticing? Pasha led the way to where he'd parked.

Barely a dozen snow-covered cars were still parked in the lot behind the strip of shops that included the Bean and Leaf, and the lot was dark except for a few pools of light created by streetlamps.

When they reached the El Dorado, Pasha turned and looked up at Daniel expectantly—hopefully. But Daniel shoved his hands into his coat pockets.

"I ah—" Pasha began, but he stopped talking when Daniel leaned in close.

"If you weren't so worried about someone seeing us, I'd kiss you good-night," he whispered, his voice little more than a rumble in Pasha's ear.

"You could. I wouldn't mind."

"What if someone saw?"

Pasha shut his eyes and let his whole world become the warm woodsy scent of Daniel's cologne, the soft sound of his voice. The nervous flutter of his own heart. "Right now I don't care."

"Tell me how you like to be kissed."

"Slow. Soft. Gentle." It was the opposite of everything he'd been asking for, for the last year, but it was everything he really wanted. "I want you to kiss me. I wanted to hold your hand in the café and I wanted to kiss you in the restaurant—"

"Shhhhh," Daniel's breath was warm on his skin. He grazed his lips against Pasha's cheek with the bare ghost of a kiss, then he pulled back. "I should let you go."

"No. I…." He cleared his throat. "I just meant…. Yeah. I've gotta get my dad."

Daniel took his wallet out of his pocket and handed Pasha a business card. It read *Taps Micro Brewery* in large letters. Under that was the name *Daniel Englewood* and a phone number. "That's my cell number. It's easier on everybody if my customers call me directly when they need something. You saw the other morning how reliable the office is." He shot Pasha a wink. "'Course, all things considered, I'm glad I couldn't get through."

"Me too. I um…." He didn't have anything as classy as a business card to give Daniel.

"Why don't you shoot me a text when you get home? That way I'll know you made it okay, and I'll have your number, too." For a second, he looked like he wanted to say something more, but then just shook his head again. "Drive safe, okay?"

Pasha nodded. "You too."

THE happy, hopeful feeling in Pasha's chest died away as soon as he pulled into the restaurant parking lot and saw the old man scowling out the front window. It was barely eleven thirty. The diner had closed at eleven and Dad *should* still be cleaning up.

Before he went in, Pasha tucked Daniel's paperback into his coat pocket, where his dad wouldn't see it. Predictably, Ivan was waiting for him at the back door, looking angrier than ever. "You have good night?" he snapped.

"Yes. How was dinner?"

Dad ignored the question. "Where did you go?"

He wanted to tell his father that it was none of his business, but he knew if he didn't offer the old man something, he'd never let it drop. "I met a friend for coffee. Then we went for sushi."

"What friend?"

He didn't answer. "Do you need help cleaning up, or are you ready to go home?" he asked instead.

"So now you're keeping secrets from me?"

"Dad, I'm tired. We have to be back here early tomorrow. Can we please not fight?"

"Who's fighting? I just wanna know where my son went tonight. Is that crime in this country?"

"Why are you making such a big deal out of this?"

"Why are *you*?"

Pasha let out a long sigh. "Fine. I had dinner with a guy named Daniel Englewood. Happy?" His tone was probably snider than it needed to be, but maybe if his dad had been *half* this nosey about what Mom did in her spare time, they wouldn't be in such shit now. Dad hadn't found out about all the bills she forgot to pay until several of their vendors refused to make any more deliveries to the restaurant. A couple of them refused to do business with Dad again, even after he settled up his debts. But that wasn't the worst of it. When Dad took the bookkeeping away from Mom and gave it to Peter to handle, Mom stayed home more and began spending her days ordering stuff off eBay and those cable shopping channels. She bought clothes she would never wear, jewelry and kitchen gadgets she didn't need. She even bought exercise equipment, a stationary bike, a Thighmaster, and a Pilates ball.

When Ivan finally figured out what was going on and confronted her, she said buying things made her happy, and wasn't it her money as much as Dad's? She'd put as much work into the restaurant as he had.

By then, their savings account was almost empty and half their retirement account was gone.

PASHA waited until he was safely in his room with the door shut to text Daniel with, *Home safe. Had a really great nite.* He stopped short of saying how much he wanted to see Daniel again. Needy wasn't particularly sexy.

He shed his clothes and put on a pair of sweats, a thick sweatshirt, and warm wool socks. Too giddy to sleep, Pasha curled up under the blankets and carefully opened Daniel's tattered paperback up to the last page he'd read back at the coffee shop. He'd never read a gay romance before—or any romance for that matter—but it was interesting, especially with all the stuff about trapeze artists and circus life. Only it was hard to concentrate on the words when he kept glancing at his cell phone, trying to calculate how long it would take Daniel to get home, wondering if he'd text back tonight or just go to bed. Maybe it was silly to wait up; after all, it was just a first date. Daniel would probably text him in the morning. *Or the next time he wants to go out.*

God, did he *really* have a shot with a guy like Daniel? Daniel wasn't only gorgeous, he was nice, down to earth, levelheaded, and he seemed *so* sincere. It was hard to believe he didn't already have a boyfriend. The nagging voice in the back of Pasha's head warned him that there had to be something wrong, some kind of catch—but before he could give into doubt, his phone chirped, alerting him to a new text message.

It was from Daniel. *Just got in. I had a great time, 2. Is it OK 2 call u at this number?*

Pasha's heart beat harder as his fingers flew over the keys. *Anytime u want.*

What time do you get off 2morrow? Daniel wanted to know.

Pasha smirked. *Depends, that an offer?* He hit Send before he lost his nerve, and then held his breath, waiting.

He was just starting to think he might have gone too far, when Daniel texted back, *Guess I set myself up for that 1. :) What time do u get off WORK 2morrow?*

Pasha snickered and texted back to tell Daniel that during the week, he usually got out between four and six, but Daniel could call him anytime after three. *Afternoons are usually pretty dead,* he explained. Then he asked Daniel when he got off work.

Daniel texted back, *Depends on the day. Usually 4 or 5.*

Which would have been perfect, if Pasha didn't always have to drop whatever he was doing in the evening and run back up to the restaurant to get his dad when the restaurant closed at eleven. Of course, if he had his own car…. He opened his web browser and surfed over to Craigslist to check out used cars. His budget was pretty limited, but there were a few in his price range that *seemed* decent. At least they were newer models—under ten years old, anyway—and didn't have much more than a hundred thousand miles on them. After a few minutes of looking, and feeling increasingly out of his depth, he shot Daniel another text. *I don't suppose u know anything about cars?*

A little, Daniel texted back. *Y?*

He explained what he was doing. There was only a brief pause before Daniel replied: *Let me ask around at work. Somebody's always selling something.*

Pasha smiled. He typed in, *OK.*

Another moment later, Daniel sent: *Talk 2 u soon. G'nite.*

Goodnite, Pasha typed back. He set his phone on his nightstand and put the book inside the drawer before turning off the light and snuggling down into the down comforter. He closed his eyes, but he still couldn't sleep. All he could think about was Daniel and that kiss that hadn't happened, the kiss he wanted so badly he could almost feel it. Almost *taste* it.

Pasha slid his hand slowly down his stomach, keeping his touch light, lingering a long moment at the waistband of his sweatpants, drawing it out even though his cock was throbbing, desperate to be touched. He skimmed his fingertips over it through the cloth and bit his lip to keep from making any noise. Finally, he slipped his hand underneath the waistband of his sweats to touch the skin underneath. He shuddered but forced himself to go slow. Closing his eyes, he pictured Daniel's face. That smile. God, and those eyes. He moaned as he took hold of himself, wondering what Daniel's mouth felt like, what his cock looked like. How it tasted.

He bit back a moan as his hips started to buck, almost of their own accord. He pictured Daniel's hand around his cock and whispered Daniel's name into the darkness. Bringing his knees up, he teased at his entrance with one finger. "Soft," he whispered. He reached for the bottle of lube in his nightstand drawer and somehow managed to get it open, to get some on his hand. Tonight, he wasn't going to shove his finger in dry like he usually did. "Slow," he murmured as he breached the tight ring of muscle with his slicked up finger. "Gentle. So gentle. So slow." He writhed as he fucked himself, wanting it to last all night, wanting it to be real. Pasha rolled onto his side and turned his head, muffling uncontrollable moans in his pillow as his hips pumped harder. "Oh Christ!" He exploded into his sweatpants. "Daniel… Daniel…." *Daniel.* Aftershocks rocked him for several long moments as he lay there in a stupor with sparks dancing in front of his eyes. He couldn't remember the last time he'd come so hard just from masturbating.

Finally, Pasha shimmied out of his soiled sweats and pushed them out of the bed.

CHAPTER EIGHT

PASHA'S mother had once told him that morning was wiser than evening, that a good night's sleep put things into perspective, and that the light of a new day let you see things differently. Dad didn't seem to subscribe to the same theory. The old man was snappish and surly the whole morning, and the fact that their first customer didn't arrive until almost nine o'clock probably didn't help. Pasha was just glad it was someone who would overlook his father's foul mood.

Belinda stomped the snow off her boots and waved to Ivan as she headed over to her usual spot at the counter.

Pasha already had her coffee poured—but he handed it to Jill, who worked with him on Sunday mornings. "Why don't you go ahead and take her?" he offered.

"You sure?" Jill asked.

Since Pasha had come in first, the first table should be his, but he didn't mind letting Jill take Belinda's order because Jill would inevitably go home before him. That didn't make her happy. In most restaurants, the server who came in first left first, but unlike his coworkers, Pasha was paid a flat salary. He doubted Dad actually saved much money by letting everyone else go home and making him stay, but it was the way the old man wanted to do business.

All he's really doing is guaranteeing we won't ever keep anyone worth keeping.

The diner was Jill's second job. During the week she taught yoga at some studio in Ferndale. Not being dependent on her tips the way a couple of the other servers were, she could quit anytime she wanted, and Pasha knew it.

"I'll get the next table," he told her. He'd just started tearing down the coffee station anyway, pulling the cups and boxes of cocoa mix and tea off the shelves and the bags of coffee out of the drawer so he could wipe everything down. The job did need to be done, but mostly, Pasha had wanted to find a chore that put him out of his father's sight for a while.

Looking at the stained coffee cups, he decided tonight would be a good time to bleach them. Sunday was the only day he closed, so it was the only day he could get extra sidework done, things like bleaching the coffee cups or emptying and washing salt and pepper shakers. He tried to get Sharon to do it during the week, but she never seemed to find the time. Dad said Sharon had enough work to do, and what difference did it make whether or not the salt and pepper shakers got washed? Pasha sighed. It probably didn't make a difference, it just made him feel better when things were done right. When he was a little kid, before Mom got sick, they never slacked off on anything. Every Sunday, the salt and pepper shakers and sugar containers were emptied and washed, and on Monday morning, he, Peter, and Nadia came in to help the waitresses fill them back up again. Then Mom drove them to school and came back to run the register and take carryout orders. Daniel might think it wasn't fair—and maybe it wasn't—but Pasha would do anything to have those days back. *Back then, Dad used to smile all the time.*

When the next table came in ten minutes later—some couple who looked like they were on their way to church—Pasha told Jill to go ahead and pick them up too, because he was working on the coffee station. Then he made the tactical error of heading toward the dish room to get some fresh bleach water.

"Pasha!" Ivan snapped, as soon as he rounded the corner.

He looked up at his father, doing his best to keep his expression bland. "Yeah?"

"How come you giving away tables, huh? You no wanna work today?"

"I'm in the middle of something—"

"I don't pay you to fuck around, I pay you to work!"

Pasha noticed the church couple giving both him and his father dirty looks and forced a smile. "Yes, Dad." He was sure he sounded as insincere as he felt, but getting into an argument in front of customers wouldn't help anybody.

Pasha walked into the dish room, dumped the dirty water, and refilled his bucket. When he came back out to the dining room, he found Jill working on the coffee station, putting everything back together again. She shot him a sympathetic look.

"Thanks," Pasha told her.

"No sweat."

Belinda came around to corner toward the coffee station carrying her cup, and Pasha picked up the pot. "Sorry—"

"I'm fine on coffee," she told him. "Come on over here and sit down with me a minute." She motioned him to one of the booths on the far wall, out of his father's line of sight.

Pasha joined her. "What's up?"

"I know it's none of my business, but I understand what you're going through. Both of you."

Her tone was full of warm sincerity, but there was no way she could understand; no one could. Pasha forced a tight-lipped smile and started to get up. "I should get back to work—"

Belinda laid a hand gently on his arm. "Pasha, my grandfather has dementia."

"I…." But he didn't know what to say. Belinda had never mentioned it before.

"I just wanted you to know that if you ever needed someone to talk to, you can always call me." She slid over one of her business cards. "Believe me, I know how hard this can be."

"Thanks. It's been a pretty rough year," he admitted.

"I'll bet. It tore my gran up when we finally had to find a nursing home for Grandpa. Gran was… angry. She felt betrayed. By him, by God. By the doctors, not that it was anyone's fault. But her and Grandpa were supposed to spend the rest of their lives together. They were going to take a cruise around the world." She laughed. "I doubt they would have gotten any farther than Mackinac Island, but that wasn't the point. It was something to dream about." Then her tone sobered. "Your mom was a lot younger than my grandfather when he got sick. Your parents were supposed to have so much more time together."

"I know it's not fair and I know he's angry, but it was his decision to send her away."

"He didn't have a choice. I was here the day the fire department had to go to your house, remember?"

"Yeah." He remembered. That was the day Mom put one of her mother's antique bowls in the microwave to heat something up. Either she didn't remember that the gold accents on it were real or that you can't put metal into a microwave. One of the neighbors saw the flames and called 911. The fireman who talked to Dad said they found Mom hiding in the bedroom closet like a scared kid. She knew the fire was her fault, but she didn't seem to understand how it had started.

"Lately it just feels like I can't do anything right," Pasha told Belinda. "It's like he's taking everything out on me. None of this is my fault." It wasn't anyone's.

"I know it doesn't seem fair. But try to put yourself in your dad's shoes for a minute. What would you do if someone you loved didn't recognize you anymore?"

Pasha didn't have to put himself in Dad's shoes to imagine that. The last time he'd talked to her, Mom only remembered one son, Peter, and she thought Pasha was him. However…. "I don't know," he had to admit, because while he knew what he *wouldn't* have done—he would never have shipped Mom off to Chicago—he couldn't say what he *would* do if he'd been in Dad's shoes after the fire last year. What if he'd moved in with Michael and somewhere down the road, Michael got sick?

"It would be really hard to see my… to see the person I'd planned to spend the rest of my life with like that," he said.

"So try not to judge your dad too harshly, okay? Cut him a little slack, even if he doesn't seem to be cutting you any."

"I'll try."

BY ONE o'clock, Jill had been cut from the floor. Randy was on his way out the door ten minutes later, leaving Pasha to wait on customers and wash dishes all by himself. By the time he walked out the back door with his dad at four fifteen, all he could think about was going home and taking a long, hot bath. All of his regular sidework was done, plus the coffee cups were soaking in bleach water, and he'd swept, mopped, and helped his dad close down the kitchen for the night.

"We're gonna stop by Nadia's on the way home," Ivan told him as they got to the car.

"Dad, I'm exhausted. Just drop me off at home, okay?"

"You don't wanna see your sister?"

"No. I mean yes, of course I do. Just not tonight. I'm tired."

"Maybe you should've thought about that before you went fucking around last night."

Pasha leaned back and closed his eyes. It was going to be a long night.

NADIA lived in northeast Detroit, near Six Mile and Telegraph. It wasn't a safe neighborhood—not that the Hamtramck neighborhood where Pasha and his father lived was great, but at least there weren't any boarded-up houses on their street. When Pasha helped his nephew learn how to ride a two wheeler last summer, he'd seen so many burned-out, boarded-up abandoned homes in her neighborhood it made him sick. *But when you've got a husband who won't work....* He knew why she'd married him, he just didn't know why she stayed with him.

Before Pasha could knock, the door flew open and RJ threw his arms around Pasha's waist. "Mama said you were coming over! I was waiting!"

Pasha laughed and hauled his nephew into his arms.

"Let your uncle and *Dadushka* in," Nadia scolded. "Sorry, Dad," she said, planting a kiss on the old man's cheek, when he and Pasha finally cleared the threshold.

"Daddy, look who's here!" RJ hollered into the living room, where Ryan was hunched over his laptop. He flashed a friendly smile and went back to his game.

By then, Clara had come downstairs to see what was going on. She gave Ivan a hug, then tugged on Pasha's coat and held up her hands. He scooped her up in his other arm. "Someday you guys are going to be too big for me to pick you both up at once," he warned with a grin.

"Nuh-uh!" Clara shook her head, sending chestnut-brown curls flying everywhere.

Nadia heaved a sigh and shook her head at their antics. "Come on, Dad, there's coffee in the kitchen. Pasha?"

"Yeah, I'll be in in a sec." *What would happen if I came out?* He wasn't sure how Nadia felt about homosexuality; they'd never talked about it. They'd never talked about much, really, even though there was only a year separating them.

He remembered the two gay kids from high school—or at least the two who were out—Rich Addison and Jeff Olinski. Pasha had been too afraid to try being friendly with either of them, not that he thought he had much in common with them, anyway. Or maybe that was what he'd told himself to make it easier to avoid Rich and Jeff, because they caught a lot of flak from some of the students over being gay. Other kids didn't care, of course. *But neither of them tried to bring a date to prom.*

God, Daniel had guts to have done that, especially in a small town way up north. Pasha could never have been that brave in high school. He wasn't sure he could be that brave now. Was going after what he wanted—a home with a man who loved him, maybe even kids of his own someday—really worth the risk of losing everything he already had? *What if Nadia said I could never see these guys again?* A sharp, cold ache lanced through his heart, and he buried his face against RJ's shoulder.

"Love you, Uncle Pasha," RJ whispered.

"I love you too. Both of you," Pasha added, kissing Clara's forehead.

He was about to set the kids down so he could join Dad and Nadia in the kitchen, but then he changed his mind. "How's that snow fort coming along?" he asked RJ. His nephew's expression said it all. There was no snow fort. Pasha wasn't surprised. "Why don't you two get your coats and come help me make a snowman outside?" he suggested. RJ's eyes lit up and Clara grinned. Pasha grinned too.

Please, God, I don't want.... He didn't want to lose the things that mattered most in his life.

IT WASN'T until Pasha got back into the car and picked his phone up off the passenger seat that he realized he'd missed a call. He got so few phone calls that he hadn't bothered to take it into his sister's house.

The name on the caller ID was *D. Englewood.* A wide grin spread across Pasha's face—quickly, he schooled his features. Dad didn't seem to have noticed the smile. *Thank you, God.* It was horrible, Pasha knew, but just then he didn't want to talk to his father about anything, least of all Daniel.

The message Daniel left on his voice mail was short and sweet. Daniel was just calling to say hi and hoped to hear from Pasha soon. It made Pasha feel… light. Giddy. *Like I did when I first met Michael.*

They'd met at OCC—Oakland Community College. Even though Pasha lived in Wayne County, OCC's Royal Oak campus was right down the street from the restaurant, so he could take classes between shifts or right after work. Besides, OCC had a better culinary program than Wayne County Community College—although all of the actual cooking classes were held at the Farmington Hills campus, which wasn't so close. It didn't matter; Dad had berated Pasha for going to school for cooking. *You've been working in kitchen since you were sixteen,* Dad yelled. *Why waste your money?* In a way, Dad was right, he could cook, but Pasha thought there was something to be said for learning how to make more than gyros and fried egg sandwiches.

Dad had begrudgingly supported Peter's going to school because Peter was taking up accounting, and the old man figured he could use the knowledge to manage the restaurant's books better than Mom had. That, and Peter hadn't actually given Dad a choice. He simply went and did what he wanted without consideration for Dad or Pasha or anyone else.

Nadia didn't go to college. She got married a month after she graduated high school. Seven months later, RJ was born. Dad liked to tell everyone he was preemie, but RJ had weighed almost eleven pounds at birth. De-Nile, it seemed, wasn't just a river in Egypt.

At last, the old man pulled onto their street.

"You're gonna have to shovel driveway," Ivan told him as they neared the house.

Dad was right. Before they could pull into the driveway, it would have to be cleared. *One more reason we should have come straight home.* It was petty, but Pasha thought Dad was trying to punish him for yesterday by keeping him out when he knew all Pasha wanted was to come home and go to sleep. *And if he'd dropped me off at home, I could have gotten the driveway when it was still light out.* At least one of their neighbors had hit the sidewalk with a snow blower, so all Pasha had to do was shovel the drive enough for Dad to pull into the garage.

By the time he got up to his bedroom, Pasha was ready to drop. He flopped back on his bed and stared up at the water stains on his ceiling, thinking about everything Amy had said to him yesterday—everything Daniel had said too. If he was ever going to have the kind of life he wanted, he was going to have to make some awful big changes. Scary changes. But what if it wasn't worth it? What if *Daniel* wasn't worth it? What if the whole thing blew up in his face?

But God, Daniel seemed so… perfect. Only no one was perfect. *And I guess there's only one way to figure out what his flaws really are.*

Pasha fished his phone out of his pocket and hit Call Back.

Daniel picked up in two rings. "Hey, Sugar. I was starting to think you were avoiding me or something." He was obviously making a joke of how long it had taken Pasha to get back to him, but Pasha thought he heard some underlying uncertainty too.

Is it possible he's as scared as I am? Pasha was sure he had way more to lose than Daniel. Daniel was already out and his family accepted him. "Sorry about that. I just got home," he said into his phone.

"I thought the restaurant closed early on Sunday."

"What, jealous?" Pasha couldn't help but tease.

"Should I be?"

Pasha rolled over onto his stomach, propping himself up on his elbows. "You're kidding, right? A guy like you could have anybody he wanted. Or have you *not* noticed how good-looking you are?"

Ivan hollered at him from the hallway, "You gonna take shower?"

"No, go ahead. I'll get one in the morning." Then, into his cell, he said, "Sorry."

"No worries. And just for the record, having good looks isn't a guarantee of anything." There was a sharp edge to his tone. "It doesn't mean the guy you're interested in is gonna be interested in you."

In two short sentences, Daniel had managed to make Pasha feel more chastised than Dad could with an hour of yelling. "I'm sorry."

"I just don't know why you're so hung up on looks."

"It's hard not to be. You're gorgeous, Daniel. But you're right, that isn't the part that matters." Pasha felt like he was treading into murky water. He couldn't see what lay ahead, and the river bottom under his feet was slippery and uneven. "I like the way you look at me, like you're seeing something… something other people don't seem to see." *Something worthwhile.* "I like the way you make me feel about myself."

"I think you're selling yourself short, babe."

"Maybe. And anyway, you don't have any reason to be jealous. Dad dragged me over to my sister's house tonight after work. Although," he added, intentionally slowly, because he desperately needed to lighten the mood, "her neighbor *did* manage to come up with *another* excuse to 'drop over' while I was there." It never seemed to fail that the twenty-something divorcée from across the street dropped in to visit Nadia *every* time Pasha visited.

"So I *should* be jealous," said Daniel, though the smile in his voice was audible. "Like I said, being good-looking isn't any guarantee of anything. Not that I'm half as good-looking as you're making me out to be."

"Yes, you are, but maybe this is the right time to tell you that the neighbor is a woman."

"Lots of guys like women, Sugar."

"I'm not one of them." Pasha hesitated. "Are you?"

"Would it be some kind of deal breaker if I said yes?"

Which pretty much answered the question. Pasha still took a couple of seconds to mull it over. He'd only dated a couple of guys before Michael, and neither of them for very long, but he was pretty sure neither was bi. Michael *definitely* wasn't into girls; bisexuality was a major deal breaker for him. He'd ranted to Pasha on more than one occasion about how bisexuals were either only doing it to be trendy—apparently some people thought being bi was cool—or because they couldn't make up their minds whether they were gay or straight. Pasha had never thought it was that simple, but he hadn't contradicted Michael, either.

Maybe this was the catch, the reason Daniel didn't already have a boyfriend.

"No, it's not a deal breaker," Pasha finally told him.

"You sure?"

"I don't think I want you ogling women in front of me, but I don't want you ogling guys in front of me either." He tried to sound like he was teasing but really, deep down, he was nervous as hell.

"Pasha, being bi doesn't mean going out with a woman one night and a man the next." He only sounded a little defensive. But then he heaved a sigh and his tone softened. "When I'm with someone, that's who I'm with. I appreciate someone who looks good, but you won't catch me 'ogling' anybody but you. I just hope you don't mind if I do that every chance I get."

Heat rushed to Pasha's cheeks—farther south, too. "No, I don't mind."

"Good. Because you have one *very* ogle-able butt."

CHAPTER NINE

"SO?" AMY leaned across the counter. Monday was one of her days off, but she'd dropped by the diner after class to talk to Pasha. Her timing couldn't have been better. The old man had left fifteen minutes ago and the place was dead. Sean, who waited tables on Monday and Tuesday mornings, as well as on Saturday nights, was sitting in a booth over by the windows playing Angry Birds on his cell phone.

Amy spoke in a hushed tone. "How'd your date go?"

Pasha smiled. "It was a little rough at first but by the end of the night, it was really, really good." He recounted dinner and the movie and told her about last night, too. "We talked for over an hour." He'd discovered that Daniel was almost one hundred percent Native American, mostly Potawatomi—he'd had to look them up because he'd never heard of that tribe before—some Cherokee, and, if Daniel's great-great-grandmother's stories about an illicit affair with a fur trapper were to be believed, maybe a little Portuguese. Pasha didn't get the impression that the rest of Daniel's family was entirely convinced. He'd also learned that Daniel's sister taught elementary school art and Potawatomi culture and that his brother was an engineer working on a wind and solar energy farm in Arkansas. And of course Pasha felt obliged to tell Daniel more about *his* family.

But Christ, we sound like a bunch of paskudnyakee *compared to Daniel's family.*

"So when are two getting together again?" Amy asked. They were both being careful to avoid pronouns. Sean was engrossed in his game, but Samara kept coming out of the dish room, bringing up one and two plates at a time, glaring at Pasha and Amy each time she passed by.

Pasha leaned over and rested his chin on his arms. "I have no idea. Maybe I'm crazy to think this'll work out. I told you why the last person I dated broke up with me. Nothing's changed since then. Hell, if anything, my life is even more messed up now than it was a year ago."

"Do you *like* this new person?"

"Yeah. A lot." More than he wanted to admit.

"Well, then it seems to me that you're just going to have to figure out some way to make it work."

God, when Amy said it, it sounded so sensible. He turned his head so he was looking up at her. "That's easier said than done. I'm here seven days a week, remember?"

"I know." She laid her hand on his arm and gave a little squeeze. "But you deserve to be happy, Pasha. And you deserve some time off. No one should have to work seven days a week."

"Dad puts in more hours than I do."

"That's his choice."

He opened his mouth but then shut it again. She was right. Dad had options. He might not be able to afford another cook, but they could close up early or close on Mondays, like other small restaurants did. "You know nothing around here is ever going to change."

"He won't have a choice if you put your foot down and *tell* him you're taking one day off a week." She lowered her voice further. "You're half owner; that makes you his partner. Start *acting* like it. You have a voice in how this place runs."

Before Pasha could tell her that pigs would fly before Dad agreed to give him time off, his cell phone chirped, alerting him to an incoming text message.

"I'll bet I can guess who *that's* from," said Amy, as he pulled his phone from his pocket to check the number.

Pasha rolled his eyes—but she was right. It was from Daniel. He couldn't help the smile that spread across his face as a happy, giddy feeling filled up his chest. It was the kind of feeling he could get used to.

"Somebody has it bad," Amy teased.

"I do not! I just…." Heat flushed his cheeks. "I don't know what it is."

"I do." She grinned. "You're falling in love."

Pasha shook his head. He knew he *could* fall in love with Daniel, but no way it was actually happening, not after just one date. "It's too soon for stuff like that."

"Says who? I fell for Leon on our first date."

"Me and… we haven't even kissed yet."

"*Good.*"

"How is that good?" Pasha wanted to know.

"Anticipation is a *huge* aphrodisiac."

Sean looked up from his phone. "Dude, when did you get a girlfriend?" He called everybody "dude."

"We just started going out," said Pasha. "It's no big deal."

"It is if you're falling in love with her," said Sean.

"I'm not falling in love with anyone," Pasha snapped. He knew he was angrier about Sean's assumption than he had the right to be. Everyone assumed he was straight. *And it's because I let them.*

Oblivious to Pasha's mood, Sean got up and ambled over. "So is she hot?"

Amy gave an exasperated sigh. "Is that *all* you think about?"

He looked dumbfounded. "What else is there?" Sean was twenty-three and a student at Wayne State University; he'd been at the diner for two months. "I mean I guess it matters whether or not she's good in the sack, but if she's fugly—"

"Oh, grow up!" Amy punched his arm hard enough to leave a red mark.

Sean grinned. "That's the way it's gonna be, huh?" He went straight for her ribs, making her squeal and shriek in protest.

Samara stomped out of the dish room, an angry scowl plastered across her face. "Stop horsing around!" she said, snapping as if she were rebuking ill-behaved children. "It doesn't look good."

Amy and Sean froze.

"To who?" Amy wanted to know. "We're the only people in here. Besides, *you're* not in charge. Pasha is."

Oh God. The last thing he needed was Amy making waves between him and his cousin. Amy seemed to have her own ideas.

"You're Ivan's *niece*," she went on. "Pasha's his son. Who do you *really* think carries more weight around here?" She shot Pasha an expectant look.

There was no getting out of it now. He had to say something. Doing his best to sound professional, Pasha turned to his cousin. "If you're done with the dishes, we could use some potatoes peeled for tonight."

Samara's jaw clenched and for a second Pasha was sure she was going to say something—but then she turned on her heel and stalked back into the dish room.

"See," Amy said. "That wasn't so hard."

"Yeah." But Pasha knew he'd have hell to pay later.

"I'm going out for a smoke," said Sean. "If anybody comes in—"

"I'll get them started," Pasha promised.

"Thanks, dude." He grabbed his coat and went out through the front door, no doubt to avoid the dish room and Samara.

Pasha's phone chirped again.

"Someone must really want to talk to you," said Amy.

"It's just a text."

"Uh-huh. Let's see." Before Pasha could stop her, Amy picked his phone up off the counter and started reading the text. Her brows shot up. "Somebody's in the neighborhood and wants to know if they can drop in to see you." Her grin was mischievous.

"No—"

"Yes," Amy countered.

"Amy!" He made a grab for his phone, but she swiveled in her seat and started typing. "Would… love… to see you," she spoke aloud as she typed.

Irrational, blind panic made Pasha's stomach churn when he saw her hit the Send button. "Are you out of your mind?" he hissed.

She handed him back his phone. "You said yourself you don't know how often you're going to get to see each other. You have to learn to take advantage of the little opportunities life throws you."

"What about Sean? What about *Samara*? Do you *want* me to get caught?"

Amy gave him an exasperated look but kept her voice low. "Men have male friends, Pasha. I'm pretty sure as long as you two don't start making out in the middle of the dining room, no one will think anything of it, even your nosy-ass cousin."

He tried to get a grip on himself. "Yeah, okay. I guess you're right."

"Of course I am. Now how about some Greek fries? I'm starving. Oh and I want *your* tzatziki sauce, not that stuff your dad makes."

TEN minutes later, Pasha saw a familiar big black-and-silver truck pulling around the corner. He wiped his hands off on a towel and tried to look casual, standing by the counter with Amy while she ate her fries, but as the seconds ticked by, his chest felt tighter and tighter. At least Samara was in the back, peeling potatoes like he'd asked. There was no reason for her to come up front anytime soon, and she couldn't see the dining room from where she was either.

Sean had been back from his smoke break for a while. As soon as the front door opened, he poured a glass of water. "Have a seat wherever you want," he said to Daniel, clearly oblivious to the way Pasha's heart was about to pound right out of his chest.

Daniel hesitated, as if trying to assess the situation, but Amy jumped in. "He's not a real customer," she told Sean, "he just came up to see me. Hope you don't mind sitting at the counter." That last was directed at Daniel.

He returned her smile like they were old friends. "Counter's fine." He shucked out of his coat and sat down next to her.

"Greek fry?" Amy offered, nudging the huge platter of feta covered fries over toward him.

"What exactly is a Greek fry?" Daniel wanted to know.

Pasha snickered at the perplexed look on Daniel's face. "Basically, they're french fries with garlic, oregano, thyme, feta, and tzatziki sauce," he explained.

Daniel scooted the plate back over to Amy. "I'll pass, thanks. What kind of soup you guys have today?"

"Chicken lemon rice," said Pasha. "I made it this morning."

Amy wrinkled her nose, but Daniel looked pleased. "Works for me."

Before Sean could move, Pasha ladled up a bowl of soup.

"You know, if you dudes don't actually need me," Sean grumbled, "I can go home."

"Think of it as an easy tip," Amy quipped back. "Is there still orange juice left from breakfast?"

"Yeah, why?" asked Sean.

"I'll take a tall one, thanks," said Daniel.

Pasha poured the juice. He was standing closer to the pie case, anyway.

Sean just shook his head, got himself a bowl of soup, and went back over to the same booth he'd been at when Amy came in earlier. Pasha came around to the other side of the counter and, after a few second's debate, sat down next to Daniel. Sean didn't seem to be paying attention; he had his phone out again and was either playing a game or surfing the Web. Pasha relaxed. "How's the soup?" he asked.

Daniel's smile sent a jolt of heat through Pasha's whole body. "The soup is amazing," he said, but it was the cook he was looking at.

Pasha smiled back at him. "What time you off work?"

"I'm done now. You?"

He shrugged. "Whenever my dad comes back."

"How do you make plans for after work if you never know when you're… getting off?" he asked, brows raised.

Amy smacked his arm.

"Problem?" he asked her.

"You are awful," she said. "I approve."

Daniel chuckled and Pasha shot her a dark look. Too much goofing off might bring Samara back up front. But Amy ignored him and ate the last of her fries. In answer to Daniel's question, Pasha explained that his social life was a little complicated at the moment.

"I'm gonna hear that word a lot from you, aren't I?" Daniel asked.

"Probably. Sorry."

"No worries," Daniel assured him, but his expression told a different story, like maybe it *was* something to worry about.

Pasha nibbled his lower lip. "It won't be so bad once I have my own car again," he promised.

Daniel waved it off. "My sister waited tables through college, Sugar, I know how it goes. I'll see you when I see you." That only made him feel worse—but before Pasha could come up with anything to say, the back door opened. It wasn't the old man, it was Sharon, and she was carrying a huge cardboard box.

"I need some help, please!" she hollered into the restaurant.

Pasha and Sean both got up to go give her a hand. There were three more boxes of groceries in the trunk of her car and two bags from the market across the street in her back seat. This wasn't anything unusual; Sharon did most the restaurant's shopping. A lot of it came from Gordon's Food Supply or Sam's Club, but some came from the grocery store across the street. Ivan said it was better to buy in smaller quantities, purchasing only what he thought they needed at that very moment, rather than to buy in bulk from wholesale vendors like they used to. He was half right; the weekly bills were smaller, but in the long run, it cost a lot more to buy from the grocery store than it did to buy wholesale. *And you don't need a degree in Culinary Management to know that*, Pasha thought irritably as he hauled the last heavy box in and set it on the counter. While Sean and Samara put away the groceries, he paid Sharon out of the till. He knew sometimes Dad gave her extra, but that was between them. He paid her exactly the amount on the receipt, then tucked it under the drawer. Sharon didn't look happy but didn't say anything about it. She just took her coat and purse and put them in the office.

And Pasha saw that Daniel's soup bowl was empty. "Can I get you anything else?" he asked.

Daniel's eyes sparkled. "Lots of things. But I ah, I was kinda hoping maybe we could grab dinner or something after your shift."

"I wish I knew when that was going to be. I'm sorry."

"It's okay. Like I said, I'll just see you when I see you."

"Can I call you later?" Pasha really didn't mean for it to come out sounding so much like a plea, but it did.

Daniel smiled. "I should be home in an hour, hour and a half, tops."

"It won't always be like this, honest. I want to make time for… for whatever." *For you. Us. A relationship.*

"Pasha, I really do understand that restaurant work comes with unpredictable hours. I'm okay with it, just as long as I get to see you once in a while." He leaned in closer and lowered his voice so no one else could hear. "But I wouldn't mind it if the next time we go out, I get to hold your hand and kiss you good night."

Pasha felt light enough to float away. "I'd like that too."

IT WAS nearly eight thirty when Pasha finally pulled into his driveway. Dad hadn't gotten back to the restaurant until almost seven forty-five; that was the latest he'd ever been getting back from his break, and more than late enough to make Pasha worry. But when he asked the old man if everything was all right, Ivan waved off his question and told him to go home. Pasha was too exhausted to argue.

He headed inside and dialed Daniel's number before he was even out of his coat.

"Hey, Sugar," Daniel said by way of hello. "I was starting to give up on hearing from you tonight."

"Dad didn't get back 'til pretty late." He pulled his coat off and tossed it over the back of a chair.

"I hope you didn't mind me coming in to see you at work today."

"No, it was really good to see you. I'm just sorry I couldn't get out of there early enough for us to get together tonight." He toed off his shoes and headed up to his room. Every muscle ached and all he wanted to do was go to sleep, but in an hour he had to go back out into the cold to pick his dad up from the restaurant. "Any chance you're free some other night this week?" Maybe with a little notice, he could get out earlier.

"I'm afraid this week's pretty tied up."

Pasha bit back his disappointment. Sometimes he really hated his life. "I guess there's always next week."

"Count on it." Daniel's tone made him smile.

"So ah… any big plans for the holidays?" Pasha asked, mostly trying to make small talk, but suddenly afraid he was sounding nosy. *Or worse, presumptuous.*

But Daniel didn't seem to notice. "I'm heading home on the twenty-second."

"When are you coming back?"

"Not until the fourth."

"I'm jealous," Pasha told him. Mostly he was teasing, although it was hard not to be just a little jealous of anyone who got to take vacations from work. "I only get four days off a year."

"Man. There really is no rest for the wicked over there."

"It's just part of running a business." He leaned back and closed his eyes.

"Yeah, I guess. Most years I only take a couple days for Christmas, but this'll be the first time in a while both me and Davis could make it home at the same time, so we decided to burn through pretty much all our vacation time and stay as long as possible."

"*Moladyets*," Pasha said, even though his heart wasn't in it. It was selfish, and it wasn't like he would have been able to spend Christmas with Daniel anyway, but it might have been nice to see him the day after or something.

"*Mola*-what?" Daniel questioned.

"Sorry. It means 'good for you.'"

"Thanks. Ma's pretty excited to have us both home for once. I'm just a little bummed about being away for so long."

"Why?"

"I ah, I hope I don't sound like I'm getting too ahead of myself if I say I would have liked to spend a little time with you over the holidays. I figure Christmas is tied up with family stuff, but maybe I could have stolen you away for New Year's Eve."

Pasha was sure his heart was beating double time. Daniel was right about Christmas, but New Year's Eve was wide open. "You can call me at midnight if you want," he offered. Or maybe that was lame.

"Consider it a date."

"I'll hold you to that," Pasha warned.

"I expect you to."

The conversation drifted toward other things, and they talked until Pasha looked over at the clock on his nightstand and realized it was almost nine forty-five. "Crap. I have to go pick my dad up."

"Drive safe out there, okay? I don't know what it's doing by you, but over here we've got sleet coming down pretty hard."

Pasha got up and walked over to his bedroom window. "So far, it's just cloudy." But a lot of snow had melted during the day and the drive home had been less than pleasant. "Can I call you tomorrow?"

"You can call me anytime you want, Sugar. But I… look, I know I said I was tied up all week…," Daniel began tentatively.

"If you're busy tomorrow—"

"No. I mean, yeah," he sounded embarrassed. "Tomorrow night some friends are dragging me out for my birthday, but I was thinking that if you wanted to come, there's always room for one more. I'd really like to see you again, maybe finally get that kiss good-night."

More than anything, Pasha wanted to say yes. But the real answer was "It depends on when and where."

"The Spaghetti Bender in Ypsilanti, around six."

Pasha nibbled his lower lip. "If I can get out of work early enough, I might be able to make it for a little while, but I won't be able to stay late."

"That's okay. And don't sweat it if you can't come. I know it's pretty last minute."

"Believe me, I want to go, I'm just not sure what tomorrow's going to be like. Lately my dad's been…." He hesitated, searching for the right word. He couldn't find one. "Things are a little rough on both of us right now. Christmas was always… it was a big deal to my mom and without her here, things are a little weird."

"Can I ask what happened to her?"

"It's a long story." But he felt like he owed Daniel some kind of explanation. "I guess the easy version of it is that Mom has Alzheimer's and last year… last year Dad had to find somewhere for her. You know, a home. This'll be our first Christmas without her."

"Oh babe, I am so sorry." The sincerity in his tone made Pasha's chest tighten. It wasn't that Amy had been any less sincere, this was just… different.

Maybe Amy's right, maybe you are falling in love with him. He wanted to shove the idea aside, but he had to admit, he liked it. "Shit happens, right?" he replied, trying not to sound so bitter for a change. He really didn't know what he would do if he was in his dad's shoes. Maybe it was easier on the old man to have Mom so far away, so he didn't have to think about her too much, so he didn't have to watch her wasting away right in front of him or make up excuses not to go visit her. For all Pasha knew, Mom didn't know who Dad was anymore, either. "I really have to go. I'm sorry."

"Don't be. Just shoot me a text when you get back home so I know you made it okay."

"I will." Pasha disconnected the call and sagged against his bedroom wall for a few more seconds enjoying the warmth, the fluttering feeling in his stomach.

THE old man met him at the back door with a surly "You're late."

It was only ten thirty, so technically he *wasn't* late. The restaurant wasn't even closed yet. But most nights Pasha was there by nine thirty so Dad could let Kaja, the night dishwasher, go home. Kaja didn't mind staying later; Dad just minded paying him to. There was no point in arguing with the old man that keeping Kaja on for another hour and a half wouldn't break the bank, it would just keep Kaja from quitting. He was a hard worker and Pasha liked him, plus good dishwashers weren't easy to find. It wasn't a job most people wanted, even in a bad economy.

"Sorry I wasn't here sooner," he told his father. "The roads are starting to get bad again." Which might not be the real reason he was later than usual, but it was the truth. It looked like Dad had already sent both Kaja and Sharon home anyway, not that there were any customers to worry about. "Do you want me to start mopping the kitchen?"

"*Nyet*. You can mop in morning. Turn off Open sign."

Pasha blinked. He couldn't think of too many times Dad had closed up early.

"Weather this bad, no one gonna come in," the old man explained.

"Yeah. Sure." But when he went to hand his father the keys, Ivan shook his head.

"You drive. I'm tired."

"Dad, are you okay?"

"*Da*. Just old."

CHAPTER TEN

PASHA texted Daniel the next morning to say *Happy Birthday.*

Daniel's reply made him smile. *It is now.*

"Who you talking to at this hour?" Ivan wanted to know. They were driving in to work, with Dad behind the wheel and looking better than he had last night. Maybe he really had just been tired.

"A friend," Pasha answered his question.

The old man scowled, but didn't press the issue.

The roads were slick and dark and a thick layer of ice coated every tree branch and fence. Salt trucks were out—they probably had been all night—but traffic was moving slowly, which did nothing to improve the old man's mood. Pasha cringed every time they passed an accident. Most were fender benders, but when they got to the I-696 interchange, the state police directed everyone off the highway. Up ahead Pasha spied an accident involving a jackknifed semi and several wrecked cars, with two ambulances on the scene. Ivan cursed.

Pasha sent Daniel another text. *Roads look like hell. Take it easy, OK?*

Daniel answered just a few seconds later. *Always do, Sugar. But it's nice 2 know someone's worrying about me.*

ALL morning, Pasha was tempted to text Daniel, wanting to know for sure that he was all right out there, but the last thing he wanted was to be the one who caused Daniel to get into an accident by distracting him from the road. Finally, at ten thirty, he got a text and pulled his phone out of his pocket. When he saw Daniel's name on the caller ID, he breathed a little easier.

Just stopped 4 lunch, Daniel's text read. *Roads R awful. Must've passed a dozen accidents this morning. How's it going on ur end?*

Pasha's thumbs flew over the keyboard. *Slow. Made $12 so far.*

Daniel answered a few seconds later. *Ouch. Guess next time we go out, it's my treat :)*

Pasha sent back a smiley face of his own, then Daniel texted back that he had to go. He only had a few minutes to eat before getting back on the road; he was way behind schedule because of the weather. *TTYL*, he added. Talk to you later. Pasha beamed—then noticed his dad scowling at him.

"You got nothing better to do than fuck around on that thing?" the old man asked.

Pasha refrained from pointing out the obvious: there were only two customers in the place, Art and Jimmy, and they didn't need anything. "I'm going outside to take a break," he told his father.

Dad's scowl deepened. "What's wrong with you that you can't take break *inside*? What you doing out there?"

"Just getting a little fresh air." Before going out, he asked Sean to keep an eye on the floor. "I won't be long," he promised.

"No sweat, dude."

Pasha grabbed his coat and headed across the ice-slicked parking lot for the El Dorado. He didn't have to turn around to know his dad was watching him from the back door. Once he was inside the car, he pulled his phone back out of his pocket and dialed the number for the nursing home in Chicago. After exchanging brief pleasantries with the nurse who answered, he asked if he could talk to his mom.

"This isn't one of her better days," she warned him.

"Yeah, okay." Pasha knew that meant Mom wouldn't be speaking a whole lot of English. That was less problematic for him than it was for most of the staff of the nursing home; as far as he knew, only one woman there spoke any Russian at all. She wasn't a native speaker, but she'd taken enough of it in college to do all right. What Pasha was really afraid of was that Mom wouldn't know who he was. He did his best to brace himself for it. It wasn't her fault and it didn't mean she didn't love him. If it weren't for the damned disease.... He sighed. If it weren't for the Alzheimer's, *everything* would be different. Everything would be okay.

At last, the nurse came back and told him she had Mom there. A moment later, Pasha heard her voice. "*Da*?" She sounded so old.

"*Zdravstvoy, Mama*," he said and he held his breath.

"*Pyotr*?"

Pasha bit back his disappointment. Maybe she just thought he sounded like Peter over the phone. "*Nyet*, *Mama*, *eta* Pasha," he explained.

There was a moment's pause on the other end. "*Kto*?" *Who?* she asked.

"*Ya tvoy soin*, Pasha," he told her. *I'm your son.*

She continued on angrily in Russian. "My son named Pyotr! I don't know any Pasha. Who are you, why are you calling me?"

Pasha closed his eyes and fought back the sudden, overwhelming urge to cry. He didn't know why it was getting to him so badly this time. "I miss you, Mama," he told her, rather than pressing the issue.

She hesitated again. "Then how come you never visit?"

"I'll come soon." It was a lie and he felt guilty as hell, but by tomorrow, she wouldn't remember they'd spoken, so why tell her the truth when the truth would only hurt?

"How's school?" she asked.

Pasha wondered if she meant high school or college. Peter wasn't in school at all, of course, but sometimes she forgot that too. "It's going pretty good. How about you, how are you doing?"

"I can't complain, but I'd rather hear about your life." Which was her way of saying she was miserable. "Have you met any pretty girls?" Apparently she'd forgotten Peter was married.

Pasha hesitated, unsure of how he wanted to answer. But then said, "Yeah, I ah... I met someone last week. She's really nice."

"*Hmph*. I'd rather hear she's pretty. You're good-looking boy. Don't waste your time on ugly girls."

"She's not ugly, Mama," Pasha assured her. "She's beautiful." Well, it was only half a lie. Daniel was gorgeous. He just wasn't a girl.

"Is she Russian girl?"

He hesitated again. "No, Mama, she's Native American."

"*Indian*?" Mom sounded shocked. "Well. Just don't tell your father. You know what he can be like."

"Yeah," he agreed, smiling a little. If it weren't for the fact that she thought she was talking to his brother, it would be a pleasant conversation. "I haven't told Dad about her yet."

"You wait until it's serious before you do. Then he won't have any choice but to love her as much as you do."

That was never going to happen. But it didn't matter. "I love you, Mom."

"I love you too, Pasha."

Pasha's heart lodged in his throat. "Mama?"

"*Da*? Yes, what is it, *moy kotyonok*?" she asked mostly in English. The only Russian words were *moy kotyonok*, "my kitten." It was what she used to call him when he was a little kid. She never called Peter that, he was her "little fish."

Pasha brushed the moisture off his cheeks. "I… it's nothing. I just miss you a lot."

"I miss you too."

Movement caught his eye. Dad had opened up the back door and was motioning him to come inside. "I have to go, Mama," he told her, wishing desperately that his dad would just give him a few more minutes of peace. "But I'll call you again soon, I promise. And I'll try to come visit." God only knew how he'd manage it, but right then, all he wanted to do was drive straight to Chicago and wrap his arms around her. It wouldn't matter that if by the he got there, she didn't know who he was anymore. She knew now.

"I know you're working hard for your father. You be good boy for him, okay?"

"I will. I love you, Mom," he said one last time before hanging up.

BUSINESS picked up some at noon, and by the time Ivan left at two fifteen, Pasha had twenty-five bucks in his pocket. Considering how bad the weather was and how slow things had been last week, he was grateful for that much, but he doubted Sean had made more than ten or fifteen dollars. Hopefully, the rest of the afternoon would be better for him.

As soon as the old man was gone, Sean pulled a thick Web design textbook out of the backpack he'd stowed under the counter. "You cool with me doing some homework?"

"Go for it." The restaurant was empty again, and they'd cleaned everything they could think of cleaning before lunch. All Pasha was going to do was sit down and read the paper. Why shouldn't Sean take a break too? But when Samara rounded the corner carrying an armload of dishes, she scowled. "You're not allowed—"

Pasha cut her off. "I told him it was okay."

"Ivan—" she began.

"Isn't here," Pasha finished for her. "And as far as I know, he didn't put you in charge."

If looks could kill, Pasha was sure he would have dropped dead on the spot. As it was, his cousin was probably going to run straight to the old man like some kind of schoolyard snitch. *Or call her mother.* It wouldn't be the first time Samara had told Anya what was going on at the restaurant when Ivan wasn't around. Then Anya went to Ivan and Ivan came down on Pasha.

Samara huffed back into the dish room and didn't come back out again until Kaja got there at ten to four. By then, Sharon had replaced Sean on the floor—and Pasha's phone remained silent in his pocket. Finally, at five thirty, he gave into temptation and shot Daniel a quick text. *Just checking in*, he sent. *Text or call when u get a chance.* Hopefully that didn't sound too needy.

Twenty agonizingly long minutes later, Daniel texted back: *Just got off work. Heading home.*

It wasn't exactly an invitation, but…. "I'm going to step outside and make a call," Pasha told Sharon. The only customer she had was

Sam, and he already had his food. Sharon still didn't look happy about Pasha going outside. He didn't care. On his way out the back door, he grabbed the bucket of rock salt and tossed a few handfuls onto the ice-coated asphalt. Some of the ice had melted in the afternoon sun, but now that it was getting dark again, everything was starting to freeze back over. Pasha finished salting the lot, then leaned against the cold bricks of the building and dialed Daniel's number.

He picked up in two rings. "Hey, Sugar." His voice was full of warmth. "How's it going?"

"Don't ask. I…." He bit his lower lip. "I talked to my mom today."

There was a brief pause on the other end. "Everything okay?"

"Yeah. She knew who I was. I… sorry."

"For what?" Daniel asked, sounding startled by the question.

"Telling this guy I barely know how bad my life sucks some days."

"Last time I checked, the only way to get to know someone was to talk to 'em. That means the bad stuff, too. Besides, if your mom recognized you, isn't that a *good* thing?"

"Yeah. A very good thing," Pasha agreed. "The last couple of times we talked she didn't even remember that she had two sons."

"I'm glad today was different."

"Me too. Thanks."

"So, any chance you're calling to tell me you can make it tonight?" Daniel sounded hopeful.

"I wish I could, but I'm still at the restaurant. I have no idea when my dad's getting back."

"No worries."

Pasha spotted Belinda's Sorrento pulling into the lot. Jimmy's pickup was just behind her. "I'll probably have to cut this short," Pasha warned. "We're getting customers."

"Call me when you get home?"

"Won't you be out with your friends?"

"I should be able to drag myself away for a few minutes. You might even save me from having to sing, if Erika drags us out to karaoke."

"You don't like to sing?" he asked, surprised. After all, Daniel had landed the lead in *The King and I* in high school. That had to mean he had a great voice.

"I love to sing. I just don't like karaoke."

"How come?" Pasha wondered.

"Erika always wants me to do a duet with her."

"Should I be jealous?" He was only half teasing. Daniel did like women, after all.

But Daniel chuckled. "She has a girlfriend and no, Erika's isn't bi. Even if she were, there's this other person I'm really interested in right now, and he pretty much has my full attention."

"He's a lucky guy."

"We both are," Daniel countered.

His tone made Pasha smile. But his expression faltered when the back door opened and Sharon poked out her head. Her brow was creased and her lips were pursed. "Didn't you see Belinda and Jimmy come in?"

"Yeah," he told her. Then into the phone he said, "I've gotta go, but I'll call you later."

"I'll hold you to that, Sugar."

Pasha pocketed his phone and hurried into the restaurant. Jimmy was drinking hot tea and having a bowl of soup, probably waiting for Art and Rueben, and Belinda was sitting at the counter with a cup of coffee and the latest issue of *Victoria Magazine*. There were no tickets hanging in the window, no food that needed to be cooked. Sharon hadn't needed him. Biting back his anger, Pasha poured himself a cup of coffee and went into the dish room to talk to Kaja.

CHAPTER ELEVEN

IT WAS almost seven thirty when Pasha got home, and as usual, he was exhausted. He kicked the back door shut and set three cloth grocery sacks down on the kitchen counter. Two of the bags were from Aldi and carried the usual household supplies—milk, eggs, meat, coffee, yogurt, and cheese. The third bag was from his stop at Nutri-Foods, the health food store a couple of doors down from Bean and Leaf. Pasha had gone in hoping to find some kind of low-calorie sugar substitute that didn't taste like crap, but the guy behind the counter told him that there was no such thing as a magic bullet for weight loss. He'd said Pasha would have to do more than cut out sugar and coffee cream—although both were steps in the right direction—and had guided Pasha toward some things he promised would help. He ended up spending entirely more money than he'd intended, but hopefully the end result would be worth it.

Hopefully so will enduring Dad's ridicule. Every time anyone mentioned health food or herbal supplements to the old man, Ivan started going on about hippies, crystal worshippers, and snake oil salesmen. Pasha honestly didn't get the connection.

After putting everything away, he sat down at the table with a cup of Siberian ginseng tea and phoned Daniel.

It took him four rings to pick up. "Hey, Sugar!"

"Hey, yourself. Having fun?" In the background, he heard people laughing, loud music, and a woman telling Daniel they were up next.

"I don't know about *fun*. I'm about to get up and sing." He sounded miserable.

Pasha wondered if the woman, probably Erika, was giving Daniel a disgruntled look or if she'd swatted his arm the way Amy did. "Too bad I'm missing it. I'd love to hear you."

"I'd love for you to be here."

"*Daniel*!" the same woman he'd heard a second ago hollered in the background. "Tell the new boyfriend you'll call him back later! We have to get up there or we'll lose our turn!"

Pasha's heart skipped a beat. Daniel had told his friends he had a new boyfriend?

"Sorry, babe, duty calls," Daniel said. "Can I call you back later?"

"Sure."

"It might be late," he warned.

"I don't mind. Hey, *nee pooha nee pyera*."

"What?"

"It means 'break a leg.' Sort of. I'll explain later," he promised. "Have fun."

"Thanks, Sugar," he said, then he disconnected the call.

New boyfriend. Pasha was grinning from ear to ear as he made his dinner: half a grilled chicken breast and a salad of mixed field greens with tomato and cucumber slices. He mixed up a quick homemade dressing with half a tablespoon of extra virgin olive oil, fresh lemon juice, and fresh garlic, thyme, and oregano.

After dinner, Pasha changed into a pair of sweatpants and a T-shirt and then went downstairs to haul his mom's old exercise bike out of storage. He spent the next forty-five minutes pedaling to Lady Gaga and Kylie Minogue. When his time was up, he felt more tired and sweaty than after a busy Sunday morning, but it felt good. He had just enough time to grab a quick shower before heading back up to the restaurant to help his dad close.

When he got there, the old man was deep in conversation with Nate and Sam and hadn't gotten anything done. He didn't get up to help Pasha, either, and Nate and Sam didn't leave until eleven thirty, a half an hour after the restaurant was officially closed for the night.

Pasha swept and mopped around them, but it still took until after midnight for him and Dad to get out of there.

Ivan was just exiting the freeway onto Joseph Campau Road when Pasha's phone rang.

The old man scowled. "Who's calling you at this hour? Don't your friends know you gotta get up early in morning?"

Pasha ignored him and answered the call. Even before he saw the name on the caller ID, a surge of warmth began spreading through his chest. "Hi."

"Hey," Daniel responded.

"You finally get home?"

"Yeah. I hope I'm not calling too late."

"No, it's fine."

Ivan's scowl deepened. "Who is that?"

Pasha waved him off. "It's no one, Dad."

"No one, huh?" Daniel scoffed.

Ivan continued talking. "It's too late to be on phone. Tell 'no one' you gotta go to bed."

"I can decide for myself who I want to talk to and when I want to talk to them," Pasha snapped back. Then, into his cell, he said, "Can I call you back in five minutes?"

"I'll be here."

Dad continued to scowl the rest of the way home, and Pasha continued to ignore him. He was out of the car before the old man even had the engine turned off. Pasha headed straight up to his room without bothering to take off his shoes or coat and hit the Call Back button as soon as the door was closed behind him. "Sorry about that," he apologized when Daniel said "hello."

"No worries, Sugar. It sounds like it's one of those days over there."

"It's always one of those days." He tossed his coat into the corner and sat down on his bed to pull off his shoes. "How was karaoke?"

"Erika dragged me up for *two* duets."

Daniel's tone made him laugh. "What'd you sing?"

"'Need You Now' by Lady Antebellum, which admittedly was my choice, and 'I'll Cover You' from *Rent*. Erika picked that one for us." He didn't sound too happy about it, either.

Pasha knew the Lady Antebellum song, and even though he was completely unfamiliar with *Rent*, he could still take some pretty good guesses what 'I'll Cover You' might be about. "You're *sure* I shouldn't be jealous?" he teased.

Daniel's chuckle was a warm, welcome rumble. "Positive, Sugar. I—"

"Pasha!" the old man hollered. It sounded like he was standing right outside the bedroom door.

Pasha took a breath and let it out before asking Daniel if he could hold on for a second, then got up and opened the door. "Do you need something, Dad?" he asked, doing his best to keep his tone even.

"Who are you talking to?" He still wanted to know.

"Just a friend."

"*What* friend?"

"No one you know, okay? Now do you mind?"

"Yes, I mind! It's late. You should go to bed."

"Dad, I'm not a little kid. I'll see you in the morning." He closed his door and apologized to Daniel for the interruption.

"Don't sweat it, babe. I'm sure it just means he cares about you."

Pasha scoffed. "The only thing my father cares about is the damned restaurant."

"That can't be true."

"You don't know him. I think he pulls half the crap he does just to keep me under his thumb so I *can't* leave." Pasha knew how angry he sounded, how angry he *felt*. He'd given up everything he ever wanted and for what? Dad never even told him "thank you" at the end of his shift. He didn't say it to anyone. "I'm sorry," Pasha said into the phone.

"For what?"

"Sounding like some kind of ass hat. I know I should be grateful I even have a job right now. It's just that some days it's really hard." He closed his eyes and stretched out on the bed. A dull throb pounded at the base of his skull.

"If you want to talk, I'm happy to listen."

"I… it just feels like no matter what I do or how hard I try, it's never good enough. Peter was always the golden child. He fucking walked out, took a job on the other side of the state. I'm still here and all I get is crap."

"I'm sorry, Sugar."

Pasha took another deep breath and let it out again. "It's not your fault. It's not anybody's."

"I'm not real sure about that. But mostly I'm just sorry you're having to go through it. Family should be there to support each other."

"That's the funny part."

"What do you mean?"

"Dad's always saying how important family is, that family comes first, but I feel like I'm always coming in last. Shit. I really am sorry. I don't mean to dump on you."

"I invited you to, remember?"

"Yeah." He smiled again. "Thank you."

"Anytime, Sugar."

"Thanks." He rolled over onto his side and changed the subject. They didn't say good night until almost one thirty.

After hanging up, Pasha changed clothes, plugged his phone in to charge overnight, and climbed back into bed. But he couldn't sleep. He rolled over onto his side, hugging his pillow close to his chest. It was cool and smelled like cheap bargain-brand fabric softener. Closing his eyes, he tried to remember what the sheets used to smell like when he was a little kid, and how good it felt when his mom tucked him in at night. She used to kiss his forehead and tell him she loved him.

It had been a long time since he'd felt like that. A long time since he'd been happy at all.

Please, God, let this be real, let it work out between me and Daniel, he begged. And maybe it was a stupid prayer, given what the Russian Orthodox Church had to say about men like him, but how much could man know about God, anyway? "I love my dad, I really do," he whispered into the darkness. "I know sometimes I say I hate him—and maybe I hate him as much as I love him, and maybe that screws that whole honoring your parents thing, but he just pisses me off so much sometimes. Isn't there some way to make it all work out? All I want is somebody to love. Somebody who'll love me back. I want a life with someone, just one guy. I know I haven't exactly acted like it the last year and I'm not proud of that, honest, I just got caught up in the moment and… well, I'm sure you saw for yourself." If God was really out there somewhere, Pasha knew he was screwed. He didn't deserve any of the things he was asking for. "But if you just give me this one chance, I promise, I'll do better. I'll figure out how to do right by my dad and not screw it up with Daniel either."

PASHA ignored the disgruntled look on his father's face and sent Daniel another text message. He and Dad were on their way into work, so it wasn't like his texting was stopping him from doing anything important. All he was doing was sitting in the passenger seat.

"I'll never understand that thing," Dad grumbled.

"What, a cell phone? You have one."

"*Da*, but you don't see me doing that… *texting* all day long. It's like you can't go one minute not talking to somebody."

"I don't text all day long," Pasha retorted. Sometimes he exchanged a few quick texts or Tweets with his friend Ty or maybe spent a few minutes catching up with stuff on Facebook, but for the most part he hardly used his phone at all. *Which might be why the old man's giving me such a hard time now.* Dad had to realize there was someone new in his life and that someone wasn't just a friend.

His phone chirped again, alerting him to a new message from Daniel.

"Turn that damned thing off already!"

"I'll set it on vibrate," Pasha offered. His father didn't seem pleased by the compromise.

He and Daniel had been texting all morning. Daniel started it by sending a message to say hi, but somehow hi led to a flurry of texts back and forth, and Pasha was enjoying it too much to stop. Daniel seemed to be enjoying it too and since he wasn't on the road today, he had the time. He'd explained that although most days he really was just a delivery driver, once in a while he "got stuck" in the office doing paperwork and making sales calls. Pasha teased him that it sounded like a good way to spend the day after a night out partying, but Daniel responded by telling him all he'd had to drink the previous night was cranberry juice.

My partying days are long over, he added with a little smiley face. Then just a second later he texted, *Hope that doesn't make me seem 2 old.*

Pasha laughed and assured him it didn't. Truthfully, it made him feel better about Daniel not having a boyfriend already. He was still trying to figure out what was "wrong" with Daniel, why he didn't already have someone special in his life. If it wasn't the bi thing, maybe it was that he was in AA, and that was something Pasha could live with. He texted, *So what other bands do u like besides Lady Antebellum?*

Lots of stuff, Daniel answered. *Guess some of my faves are the Corrs, Proclaimers, Imogen Heap. Love Sheryl Crow. Stones of course*, he added with another smiley face.

Pasha made a mental note to look the Corrs, Proclaimers, and Imogen Heap up on YouTube later. He knew who Sheryl Crow was, and everybody knew the Rolling Stones, but as for the rest? He was clueless.

Daniel texted back asking what Pasha's favorite bands were. Pasha started to type out *Lady Gaga, Kylie Minogue, Pink,* and suddenly realized that all he had to do was add Abba to the list and he'd be making himself like a total queen. He erased the words he'd written and typed in *Lots of stuff* instead.

After several seconds of silence passed between them, Daniel pressed him for specifics. Reluctantly, Pasha admitted to how much he loved Lady Gaga. Next in line were Katy Perry, Pink, Kylie Minogue, and Adam Lambert. He sat back and waited for Daniel to ask why Abba wasn't on the list.

What Daniel texted instead left Pasha stunned. *I took Joyce to see Katy Perry in Grand Rapids a couple years ago. She put on a great show.*

He finally recovered enough to type out *Hate you.* But added a winking smiley face to take the sting out of the words. Then he added, *Your sister likes Katy Perry?*

Daniel answered with a smiley face of his own. *Yeah. Her taste is pretty eclectic, just like mine. Maybe if KP comes back to MI, we can go. Might have to invite my sister, tho.*

Pasha smiled. *OK by me.* Then he realized Dad had exited the highway and they'd be to work in just a few minutes. *Have 2 go soon. Almost at restaurant. TTYL?*

U bet. Have a good day, Sugar.

U2.

"MAYBE you should stay through dinner," Ivan suggested. It was five o'clock and he'd just gotten back to the restaurant. "It might be busy night, tonight."

There were only a few customers in the place, but Pasha knew what his dad was thinking; they'd been slammed at lunch and by the old man's logic that meant they'd be slammed for dinner too. The only thing was, it never worked out that way. There was a reason Dad only had one person on at night. "I'm sure Sharon can handle it."

Ivan frowned. "What, you got plans or something?" It sounded like more of an accusation than a question.

"I'm just tired."

"You think I'm not tired, Pasha? I'm *always* fucking tired. But when you're boss, you work long hours. You better get used to it. This place gonna be yours someday."

"Could we please not fight, Dad?"

"Who's fighting? I'm just telling you how it is."

Pasha took off his apron and headed for the back door. "I'll try to get back early tonight," he promised. "Night, Sharon!" he hollered—but he didn't wait for a reply. He just left.

"YOU home already?" Daniel asked, after they'd said their hellos.

"Yeah, Dad got back early." He only wished Dad had gotten back early on Monday instead. "What about you? You home or still stuck in the office?"

"Just got in a few minutes ago. You mind if I eat dinner while we talk? I just put it in the microwave."

"As long as you don't mind if I eat too." Pasha already had his meal started; the mushrooms, garlic, and shallots were sautéing in olive oil on low heat. He splashed in a tablespoon of wine and inhaled the pungent aroma wafting up from the pan. *Food Heaven.*

"What, you work in a restaurant and you come home hungry?" Daniel teased him.

"I have to be around that stuff all day. By the time I get out of there, I'm ready for something different." Besides, the food at work wouldn't help him get rid of those six fat, ugly inches. He just didn't want to say that aloud because Daniel still harbored the notion that Pasha looked good the way he was. Pasha was glad and he knew it annoyed Daniel when he got down on himself, but *he* wasn't happy with his body. *And there's only one way to change that.*

"So what's for dinner?" Daniel asked. "Leftover turkey?"

"No, we sent most of the leftovers home with my sister." *Thank God.* He liked turkey, but Dad always bought the biggest bird he could get his hands on. "I'm making a quick beef stroganoff." What he didn't say was that he was substituting the sour cream with nonfat Greek yogurt. He'd gotten the idea from a magazine and figured that every little bit helped, which was why instead of the big, fat egg noodles he usually cooked with, Pasha was serving the stroganoff over brown rice pasta from the health food store.

"You mean making, as in from scratch?" Daniel questioned him.

"Is there any other way to make it?"

"Maybe I shouldn't tell you what I'm having."

"Why? What's for dinner at your place?"

"Lean Cuisine lasagna."

Pasha made a face.

"I told you, Sugar, I can't cook to save my life."

"I guess I won't hold it against you. But I think I may have to show you what real lasagna tastes like." *Even if it isn't diet food.*

"Careful, I might take you up on that," Daniel warned. "You know what they say about the way to a man's heart."

"Then it's *definitely* a date," Pasha teased. Well, mostly.

Daniel was quiet for just long enough to make him start to wonder if he'd said something wrong, only he didn't know how to backpedal. "I'd like that," Daniel finally told him, all teasing gone from his voice.

Warmth bubbled up inside Pasha's chest. "Me too. Hang on a sec. I need to put you on speaker," he said, realizing belatedly that he probably should have sliced up the meat before calling. It really was a two-handed job.

"You've been on it on my end since we started talking. Sorry, I guess I should've told you."

"No big deal. So how was work?"

Daniel groaned. "Most days I love my job."

"Today wasn't one of those days, I take it?"

"Nope. I don't know what I'm gonna do when I'm stuck in the office full time."

"You in line for a promotion or something?"

There was another long pause on Daniel's end. "Or something. It's a long ways off."

"It doesn't sound like you want it at all."

"Yeah, well. Sometimes shit happens, right?"

Pasha slid the meat into the pan and washed his hands. "Is everything okay?" Most people got excited about promotions.

"Yeah, everything's fine." But Daniel didn't sound real convincing.

If they were together—really together—Pasha would have reached over, taken Daniel's hand. Held it. He would have done anything he could to put the smile back on Daniel's face. "You ah… you think there's any chance of us getting together tomorrow?"

"I'd love to, Sugar, but I have a doctor's appointment after work."

"Nothing serious I hope."

"Nah, it's just routine."

"Are you sure everything's all right?"

"I'm sure, babe. I'm just… everything's gonna be fine."

Reluctantly, Pasha let it drop. "So what about Friday? For getting together I mean. My treat," he threw in for good measure, so Daniel would know he wanted to pay for his fair share of dates.

"I've kind of already got plans for Friday."

"Saturday?" Pasha asked. "Maybe dinner and a movie, like last week?"

"Saturday isn't real good for me, either."

"Oh. Okay." Pasha tried to tell himself he was overreacting. Everybody had the right to have plans. He shouldn't feel hurt just because Daniel had a social life and he didn't. *Just because* his *social life is taking up both Friday* and *Saturday nights.*

"I *want* to see you again. I've just got a lot going on this week. I can cancel my Saturday—"

"You don't have to change anything for me."

"Pasha, I like you. But there's some stuff I need… I'm seeing somebody on Friday."

It was several long moments before Pasha trusted his voice enough to speak. "You don't owe me… I mean. Sure. Whatever." He tried to sound casual about it. Daniel didn't owe him anything. They'd only gone on one date. Hell, they hadn't even kissed. There was no expectation of anything. How could there be? *Just because we talk every day….*

"It's not a date. You are the only person I'm seeing right now, babe. But I…." He hesitated. "Aiden is someone I used to date." And he sounded guilty about it too. "We ah, we haven't talked in six years. I bumped into him the other day and he wanted to get together. It's… the way things got left between us—"

"You don't owe me any kind of explanation, Daniel. What you do on Friday night is your business, not mine."

"Pasha—"

"Look, I hate to cut this short but I've got a bunch of stuff to do tonight before I go pick up my dad." Which was at least partially true. He'd been spending so much time on the phone with Daniel that he hadn't had time to do his laundry—only that wasn't the real reason he was in a hurry to get off the phone.

"Please don't take me getting together with an old friend the wrong way."

"Don't you mean old boyfriend?"

Daniel heaved a sigh. "Yeah. I guess I do. I'll talk to you later, okay?"

"Sure."

CHAPTER TWELVE

"HE *SAID* it wasn't a date," Amy retorted the next morning at work, when Pasha told her about his and Daniel's conversation. They were standing over by the coffee station, both keeping a wary eye out for the old man. Ivan had been in a surly mood all morning.

"He also said this Aiden guy is his ex," Pasha hissed. All last night, he'd painted pictures in his head of how Daniel and Aiden's date would go. Aiden would say how sorry he was that they'd broken up. He'd ask Daniel if he was interested in rekindling the flame. Of course he was, after all, Aiden was gorgeous. He had to be. Besides, they had a history. What did Daniel have with Pasha? One date and a few phone calls?

"Pasha, they broke up for a reason. Even if you don't know the reason, what makes you think Daniel would want to go out with this guy again?"

"Because if Michael walked in that door today and asked me for a second chance, I'd give it to him, no questions asked," he admitted.

Amy gave him a long, measured look. The disapproval in her eyes nearly killed him. "I guess we're just different."

"What do you mean?"

"If I met a guy that I really liked, a guy who seemed to really like me, there would be *no way* my ex could come in and sweep me back off my feet."

"Even if it was Leon? If the two of you broke up or something? If he broke up with you?" he amended. "And then a year later, he realized he'd screwed up and wanted to get back together with you. You wouldn't do it?"

She crossed her arms over her chest. "If Leon broke up with me, there would be no way *in hell* I'd give him a second shot at breaking my heart."

"Michael was the first guy I ever loved."

"So?"

"So… isn't that worth a second chance?"

"It's your life, honey," Amy said, her tone full of heartbreaking disappointment. "You have to figure that out for yourself."

Pasha sighed. "It doesn't matter. Michael won't even return my texts."

"This isn't about Michael, Pasha. It's about *you*."

Guilt needled at him—but he was pissed, too. Amy was supposed to be on his side, not Daniel's. "You mind if I get something to eat?" He wasn't hungry, he just needed an excuse to get away.

"Sure, go for it. But remember what I said, okay?"

Pasha didn't answer her.

The old man looked up when he came into the kitchen. "I'm going to make a couple of poached eggs for breakfast," Pasha told him. Or maybe it was closer to lunch. It was almost eleven. "You want me to make you some, too?"

Ivan frowned. "Since when do you eat poached eggs?"

"I don't know." It wasn't like he'd *never* had poached eggs before; he just usually ate them over easy. "Do you want some or not?"

"I can make my own breakfast."

"Suit yourself, but remember what Dr. Mullins keeps saying about your heart, Dad. You need to be more careful what you eat."

Ivan scoffed. "Like you and that New Age crap?"

"It's not New Age crap." It was oatmeal, whole grain bread, raw honey, flax seed, dried goji berries, herbal tea, and açaí berry juice. Which he supposed probably looked a little like crap to his dad. "I'm just trying to make some healthy choices in my life."

"If you want to make healthy choices, stop going to bar and fucking drinking all night."

Pasha dropped it. He poured water into a shallow pan and set it on the stove to heat up then got some broccoli out of the cooler.

Dad's scowl deepened. "I thought you said you were having eggs."

"I am. I'm having some broccoli too. Do you want some?"

"*Nyet*."

Pasha cut up and carefully measured out a cup of broccoli and put it into a strainer so he could steam it over the boiling water after he'd dropped in his egg. When it was done, a little lemon juice would replace the salt he usually used. Maybe if he started now, he could avoid having to take all the drugs Dad had to take, just to keep his blood pressure under control.

The old man scowled. "I see what's going on here, Pasha."

Pasha blinked at him, confused. As far as he could tell, the only thing going on was him making himself something to eat.

"You're going to end up just like your sister, too goddamned skinny. It's not healthy what she's doing to herself."

Pasha opened his mouth to argue but then changed his mind; his dad was right about Nadia. Last Sunday at dinner all she'd done was scoot the food around her plate, picking at it now and then. Ryan finished off over half her meal. But it was nothing new. Nadia had been eating—or *not* eating—like that for as long as Pasha could remember.

"One of these days she's gonna make herself sick."

"I know, Dad." He dropped his eggs into the water and put the strainer of broccoli over it, then covered the pan. "But I'm not Nadia, okay? I really do need to lose a few pounds here."

"Who you trying to impress, huh?" He shot a glance out into the dining room where Amy was wiping down the shelves behind the counter.

"I'm not trying to impress anyone." *Liar.* But despite what Dad obviously thought, it wasn't Amy he wanted to impress. Pasha got his phone out; there were no messages, no missed calls. No nothing.

"Can't you put that thing away for one goddamned minute?" Ivan snapped. "Who's gonna call you anyway?"

"No one, I guess." He'd texted Daniel earlier, just to say hi, but so far Daniel hadn't gotten around to answering him.

"HONEY, if a guy tells you he's seeing someone else, he is *not* that into you," Ty said, when Pasha called him Friday night after work. He'd been down in the dumps all day and needed someone to talk to, someone who *wouldn't* take Daniel's side.

Pasha swallowed another spoonful of Ben and Jerry's Cheesecake Brownie ice cream. He was sitting on the kitchen floor with his back propped up against the heat vent. He hadn't heard from Daniel yesterday until almost ten o'clock at night—way later than anyone would have been stuck at a doctor's appointment. Worse, Daniel hadn't even called, he'd just sent a text to say "good night." He could have said good night live, on the phone. But only if he wanted to talk. Pasha had texted him back anyway, and texted again this morning, to say "good morning," but Daniel didn't get around to responding until noon. He didn't even apologize for taking so long to answer, he just sent a short *hi, got your text, will call u later*.

Only he didn't call. They sent a few short texts back and forth during the afternoon, but then Daniel said he was headed home and would talk to Pasha tomorrow. Pasha could fill in the blanks on his own: Daniel was headed home to get ready to go out. *With Aiden.* That was when Pasha bought a pint of Ben and Jerry's. *It's not like I've got anybody to impress, anyway.* Why should he starve himself into looking like Nadia for a guy who wasn't interested in him?

Or maybe Amy was right and he was overreacting.

Pasha ate another spoonful of ice cream. "Maybe they're just friends," he told Ty. But no matter how many times he said it, he didn't believe it. The pint of ice cream was almost half gone.

"Baby Doll, if they were 'just friends,' he wouldn't have made a point of telling you he used to date this guy."

"Maybe he's trying to keep everything on the level so I don't think he's going behind my back or something." Even to his own ears it sounded like he was making excuses for Daniel.

"I know you don't want to hear this, Pasha, but if this guy was really into you, the only plans he'd have for tonight would involve figuring out how many ways he could screw your pretty little brains out between now and sunrise. Telling you he's seeing some old boyfriend is like daring you to go out and get laid by somebody else. And it'll serve him right when you do it too."

"Who says I'm going to go out and to get laid?"

"Girl, who are you talking to? How many times have I seen you slinking off with some stud to that roach motel down the road from Menjo's?"

Another spoonful of cold, creamy goodness slid down his throat. Ty was right. Not just about him and picking up tricks at the bar, but about Daniel. Friday and Saturday nights were for going out and… and maybe not getting screwed, but they were for spending time with somebody you at least wanted to screw. *And instead of seeing me tonight, he's seeing his old boyfriend.*

Come Monday, Daniel would call him and say something like "I really like you, but me and Aiden have a history." How could Pasha argue with that? It was exactly what he'd told Amy he would say if Michael suddenly swept back into his life. *And if it was me and Michael going out tonight, it* wouldn't *be as just friends.* He'd be doing everything he could to get back together with his ex.

"Have you heard one word I've said?" Ty wanted to know.

"Sorry." Pasha set the empty ice cream container down next to him. "I guess I was daydreaming."

"Not a very happy daydream, from the sound of your voice."

"*Nyet*. No. Sorry." He tried not to speak Russian at his friends.

"What you need is to get out of that house. Go get yourself all dolled up and—"

"I can't. I have to be back to the restaurant at eleven."

"Intervention time," Ty told him. "You have two choices and two choices only. You can either drag your sorry ass up out of whatever pity-party food I hear you eating—which is *not* doing your girlish figure any favors, I might add—and get yourself dolled up so we can go out on the town, or I am coming over there and dragging you out of the house by the short and curlies. Now what's it gonna be?"

Pasha was suddenly very glad Ty didn't actually know where he lived, because he sounded serious. Then again, going out would get his mind off Daniel, but…. "I really do have to be back at the restaurant by eleven."

"Don't worry, Cinderella, I'll get you home before your coach turns back into a pumpkin. Or… that place is in Royal Oak, isn't it?"

"Yeah. Why?"

"How about you let your fairy godmother pick you up there? That way you can leave your car for the wicked queen, *and* you can get good and sloshed tonight." He sounded entirely too pleased with himself.

"I'm not sure that's such a good idea."

"Which part, you getting drunk or me picking you up?"

"I—"

"Oh, don't sweat it, honey. I don't have to come in to come and fetch you. I know I'm not the kind of girl you bring home to Daddy."

"Come on, you know that's not it," he protested, even though that was exactly what he was worried about. Ty wasn't just effeminate, he was black. *Talk about a double whammy.* The old man would have a fit.

Ty just laughed it off. "Honey, I'm not offended. I know I'm *way* too fabulous for some people. Now, what's the address?"

Pasha scraped the last drops of melted ice cream out of the bottom of the carton. Maybe going out wasn't such a bad idea. If anyone could cheer him up, it was Ty—wasn't that why Pasha had called him in the first place?

"MMMM, come to Mama!" Ty murmured over the top of his Long Island iced tea as another cute guy wandered past. Ty had declared it too early to even *consider* going to Menjo's and dragged Pasha to Pronto! in downtown Royal Oak instead. The idea was to grab a bite to eat before going dancing, but so far, all Ty wanted to do was ogle guys and drink—not necessarily in that order, either.

Pasha just stared at his phone. *God... dear God*, he amended, turning it into a formal prayer, *is it too selfish to wish Daniel's as miserable right now as I am?* Probably. He wished it anyway, because maybe if Daniel had a rotten time out with Aiden, he'd remember what a great time he and Pasha had had. Maybe he'd call. *I can't really be* this *pathetic, can I?* How could he have fallen so hard for a guy he barely knew? A guy he hadn't even *kissed.*

Ty elbowed him. "Earth to Pasha."

"Huh?"

They were seated at the bar because even though it was early, only eight thirty, the place was packed with attractive twenty, thirty, and forty-something-year-old men out for dinner or drinks and a good time—so much so that there weren't any tables available on the restaurant side of the restaurant/video bar. Pronto!'s website might not proclaim it as a gay hangout, but men outnumbered women by at least ten to one, and the ladies knew that didn't skew the odds in their favor—unless they happened to be looking for other ladies.

"Are you even paying attention?" Ty asked.

Pasha took a long pull off his bottle of Corona and shrugged.

"You are way too hung up on that loser."

"He's not a loser."

"He's losing you, isn't he?"

Pasha opened his mouth to argue, but no argument came out. "He said he wanted to call me on New Year's."

"And that means what exactly?"

"That he's going to miss me?" Pasha didn't actually mean for it to come out sounding like a question, but he questioned it, himself.

"Uh-huh. Sure he will. If he's half as hot as you say he is, he's already got his date for New Year's Eve all lined up. How do you know he's even going out of town for Christmas?" He signaled the bartender for another drink.

It looked to Pasha like the only one getting sloshed tonight was Ty. "I'm good," he said, when the bartender shot him a questioning look.

Ty paid for his drink and turned back to Pasha. "Honey, listen to your fairy godmother: this guy is full of nothing but hot air and empty promises. Anybody can talk a good talk, but if he don't walk the walk, he's not worth your time."

"But—"

"No buts. Except maybe *that* butt!" He pointed out another cute guy walking past. As if aware of the attention, the big beefy blond wagged his hips just a little harder as he walked away. Ty laughed. "You need to get yourself some new action," he said to Pasha. "Something to take your mind off this Daniel guy." He said Daniel's name as if it tasted like sour milk.

"I don't want action."

"*Everybody* wants action. Look, until a guy puts a ring on your finger, you are a free agent. If this man you just met doesn't want to be with you on Friday *or* Saturday night, you have every right to get out and meet someone who *does*. And the first thing you need to do is stop staring at *this* thing." He picked Pasha's phone up off the bar and put it in his pocket.

Pasha drained the last of his beer. Maybe Ty was right. He hadn't made any promises to Daniel. Daniel hadn't made any to him either. *And he's the one who wanted to be with someone else tonight.* When the bartender came back, Pasha ordered another beer and an order of the "smack and cheese," macaroni and cheese with chicken, mushrooms, and bacon.

THE first person Pasha saw when they got to Menjo's was the guy he'd been with on Thanksgiving. Fred? Frank? Something like that. He was leaning up against the bar, a bottle of beer held casually in one hand, surveying everyone who came in. When Pasha met his gaze, Fred… or Frank, smiled.

Ty leaned in and whispered in Pasha's ear, "Somebody's giving you the eye. Go forth and conquer, girlfriend!" He gave Pasha a nudge toward the bar.

Pasha started to dig his heels in—then changed his mind. Why shouldn't he go over and say hi? Fred or Frank… or maybe it was Ferris? Whatever his name was, he was right here, and if the look on his face was any indication, it wouldn't be too hard to talk him into a repeat of last Thursday night. *And why not? Ty's probably right. Daniel and Aiden are out there somewhere screwing like horny rabbits. Why should I sit around waiting for some guy who isn't interested in me?* Maybe tomorrow, he'd call Brett.

When Pasha was close enough to say hi, Fred or Frank or Ferris beat him to it. "I was hoping to see you again."

"Yeah, me too."

"So um, that guy you came in with…?"

"Just a friend," Pasha assured him.

He smiled. "Can I buy you a drink? Tequila, wasn't it?"

"Yeah. And thanks, I'd love a drink."

CHAPTER THIRTEEN

PASHA swiped his towel across the center of the steam-covered mirror and gazed at his naked reflection. He didn't like what he saw. Maybe it was guilt, maybe it was the hangover, or maybe it was just lack of sleep, because he hadn't gotten in until 2:00 a.m. last night.

"Pasha!" Ivan shouted up the stairs. "It's late!"

"I'll be down in a minute!" He swallowed a couple of açaí berry capsules with a full glass of water and tried to convince himself not to feel guilty about last night. A pint of ice cream, a plate of macaroni and cheese, a few beers, and four shots of tequila weren't the end of the world.

Missing Daniel's call, however, made him feel like shit. It had come in at ten, but Pasha didn't get it until Ty dropped him off at home and gave him his phone back. Hearing Daniel's voice and the message he left made Pasha feel more guilty—more angry at himself—than ever.

"Hey, Sugar. I just got home and figured I'd call and check in, see how things were going. Guess you're busy or something. Or just not answering your phone because you saw it was me." He let out a nervous-sounding laugh. "I'm sorry I've been kinda scarce the last coupla days. I've just been running my tail off at work, trying to set stuff up so everything doesn't fall apart while I'm on vacation. I'm not sure it's gonna help. The guy they've got taking over my route is a new hire—never even had a trucking job before. He just got his license last month. I've been training him all week, but it isn't going too good. Hopefully he'll get the hang of it before I leave. Otherwise you might just get stuck with me for Christmas after all. Ma'll be pissed, but I won't leave my customers with somebody who can't do the job. Not that you care about any of that, I'm sure, and this thing's probably gonna cut me off any second, so just… just give me a call when you get a chance, okay? I miss talking to you, Pasha. Maybe I needed a day or two for that to really sink in—and maybe I'd better shut up before I say anything too stupid. Talk to you later."

So far, Pasha hadn't even texted him back. He didn't know what to say.

"*Boistra*!" Dad hollered. It sounded like he was standing at the foot of the stairs.

"I'm hurrying!" Pasha hustled across the hall and shimmied into his uniform as fast as he could, then bounded down the stairs, taking them two at a time.

"You look like shit!" the old man snapped when Pasha finally got into the kitchen. "This is what you get for going out drinking all night! We should have left half hour ago!"

"I know, I'm sorry." Pasha had slept straight through his alarm, not waking up until the old man pounded on his bedroom door twenty minutes ago. "Just give me a second to get something to eat."

A deep crease appeared in Ivan's brow when Pasha slapped some organic almond butter between two pieces of whole grain bread. "What the hell kind of breakfast is that? Why don't you let me make you some eggs when we get into work?"

"This is fine."

"You're going to make yourself sick eating that shit. I know you're taking pills—"

"They're not pills." Which wasn't exactly true, but what Dad meant was diet pills and laxatives, the shit that really messed you up when you didn't use it right. "Look, I don't want to argue with you today, okay?"

"PLEASE just tell me you didn't do anything stupid last night," Amy said when Pasha explained why he looked like something even the cat wouldn't drag in.

They were standing by the coffee station. Pasha was on his third cup, but he still didn't feel any better. "I guess it depends on how you define 'stupid,'" he answered. He still hadn't texted Daniel back.

"*What* did you do?" Amy pressed him.

"I didn't sleep with anybody if that's what you're asking. I tried to, but—that came out wrong!" he said in answer to her angry glare. "I just meant that I ran into a guy I know and I let him buy me a drink."

"*And*?"

"What difference does it make what I did or didn't do?" he snapped. "I never promised Daniel anything. He didn't promise me anything either. *He* was the one out with some ex-boyfriend last night. *I* just went to the bar and had a drink."

"More than one, to look at you. And anyway, the fact that Daniel *told* you he was going out last night should have given you the clue that he cares about you. If he didn't, he would have gone out behind your back. Christ on a cracker, Pasha, how fucking stupid are you to not see how much this guy likes you?" She turned and started to walk away.

"Amy, wait! It's just… he's so good looking. And so smart and so nice."

"And you like him," she pointed out.

"And I *really* like him."

"So…?"

He sighed. "So last night I had a couple of shots of tequila with this other guy." Usually that put him in the right frame of mind to let some stranger pound his ass. "But I just… I wasn't interested. I made up some lame excuse and spent the rest of the night on the dance floor." Which he supposed at least counted for something; it was exercise. "I was ready to get out of there by eleven thirty, but Ty didn't want to leave yet so I was stuck until almost closing time."

"You could have called me, you know."

"I almost did, but I was afraid you'd think I was only there to get laid."

"You *were* only there to get laid. Look, I might have been a little pissed if you'd told me you were going to Menjo's last night, but if you'd called me to come and rescue you, I would have been there in a heartbeat, no questions asked."

"Thanks."

"What are friends for?"

Pasha didn't want to admit that it had been so long since he'd had any real friends he'd forgotten. "You ah… you maybe want to do something tonight? Dinner or a movie? My treat."

"You've got a date."

THE best part of Saturday morning was always seeing RJ and Clara. Pasha returned their eager hugs and helped them and their sisters get settled into the family's usual booth near the coffee station, while Nadia went into the kitchen to talk to Dad.

"Who wants to color?" Pasha asked the kids.

"Me!" Clara and RJ replied in unison.

Pasha laughed and got out the coloring books and crayons. He didn't get a chance to sit for long, however, because just as he was sitting down, Dad and Nadia came out to the dining room.

"I'm going to sit a while," said Ivan. "You go make breakfast." He waved Pasha off to the kitchen.

"But we just started!" RJ protested. "See, Uncle Pasha got us Transformers." He held the book up for his mother to see.

"He got me Ponies!" Clara added happily, holding up the My Little Pony coloring book.

Nadia made a sour face. "Uncle Pasha has to work. That's what you do when you're a grown-up."

Pasha let the dig go. "I'll come over and color later if I get a chance," he promised RJ and Clara.

Amy shot him a sympathetic look as he passed by her. He smiled back. It wasn't as if Dad and Nadia were doing anything new. They always acted like this.

Pasha had just gotten the kids' pancakes on the grill when Nadia joined him in the kitchen. "Hey, what's up?" Pasha asked her. "Can I make you something?"

"I'm good with coffee. What I want to know is what's up with *you*."

"What do you mean?"

"You and Amy," she said pointedly, not bothering to lower her voice.

"There *is* no me and Amy. We're just friends."

"That's not what Dad thinks."

"Well, he's wrong."

"He heard you asking her out this morning, Pasha. She has a boyfriend. Leave her alone."

Pasha flipped the pancakes and turned to face his sister. "You don't get to tell me who I can be friends with. Neither does Dad." He slammed three plates down onto the counter and sliced up a few strawberries and one banana between them.

Nadia gave him a disgruntled look and got more fruit out of the cooler for her kids. Pasha didn't bother arguing with her. If it came down to it, Dad would say what he always did: it was his money and he could waste it however he wanted to.

Nadia continued to regard Pasha as he worked in silence. "So that's it, then?" she finally said. "You're going to do whatever the hell you want no matter who it hurts?"

"Oh, please. That's just great coming from you."

She crossed her arms over her chest. "What's *that* supposed to mean?"

"Nadia, do you have any idea what's even going on around here?"

She frowned.

"We can barely pay our own bills, but every month you come in here with your hand out. Dad can't afford to support you. He can barely support himself."

"How dare you—"

"How dare I what? Tell you the truth?"

"So, what? You want for my kids to go hungry?" she snapped.

"No. But if you can't pay your mortgage, maybe you shouldn't go out for pizza—"

"Do you really think spending a few bucks on pizza is going to make a difference?"

“Pizza, cable, cell phones—”

“Oh, so now you want me to be cut off from the world?”

“No, I want that *paskudnyak* you married to get off his ass and get a job!”

Nadia’s face grew redder with each word that came out of his mouth, but Pasha didn’t stop.

“This place is going under, and I feel like I’m the only one who gives a crap. Peter ran off to the other side of the state and you—the only thing *you* care about is how much money you can get out of the old man before he works himself to death!”

Her palm connected with his cheek, stunning Pasha into silence.

“Pasha! Nadia!” Ivan hollered from the kitchen doorway. “What the hell’s going on in here?”

“Nothing.” Pasha took off his apron. “I’m going outside for some fresh air.” He didn’t give his dad a chance to respond. He just grabbed his coat and marched out the back door. His hands shook as he punched in Daniel’s number. Maybe Daniel was the last person he should be calling. Maybe he should call Belinda or try to talk to Amy, but just then, Daniel’s was the only voice he wanted to hear.

All he got was Daniel’s voicemail: “You’ve reached Daniel Englewood. I’m sorry I’m not able to take your call right now, but if you leave your name and number I’ll get back to you ASAP.”

Pasha slumped against the wall. “Hi, it’s me—”

A beep cut him off. *If that’s Ty….* Pasha switched over to the other line. “Hello?”

“Hey, Sugar.”

Oh God. Daniel. “Hey yourself.” He almost crumbled to the ground at the sound of the other man’s voice.

“You okay?” asked Daniel.

“No.”

“Wanna talk about it?”

“Maybe later. Right now it’s just really good to hear your voice.”

“Likewise. Did ah… you get my message?”

Pasha smiled. “Yeah.”

"I hope I didn't sound like too big of an idiot."

"You didn't sound like an idiot at all," Pasha assured him. "And I'm sorry. I know I acted like a real ass hat the other night. I just…just please tell me you're not dumping me for this Aiden guy."

"Pasha, I told you. Aiden is someone I *used* to go out with. It was a long time ago and I… I was a different person back then. What me and Aiden had, it was never very serious. I'm not that guy anymore."

Somehow, that only made Pasha feel worse. "I really like you, Daniel, and I'm really… I'm scared. I don't want to screw this up."

"I like you too—and I'm scared too." How could someone so good-looking be scared of anything? But there was no doubting that Daniel sounded it. Daniel went on, "Look, I was thinking, how about we get together tonight?"

"I thought you had plans?" Pasha hoped that came out sounding like the honest question it was.

"I can get out of it," said Daniel.

"I don't want you to cancel anything just for me. I mean that. Besides, I'm going out with Amy tonight."

Daniel hesitated for a second before speaking again. "Yeah, okay. If tonight's no good, how about tomorrow?"

"Tomorrow works."

"You want me to pick you up at the restaurant or…?" He left it open-ended.

"Here's good. How about one thirty?" The old man would have a fit when Pasha asked Jill to close for him, but he didn't care. Sunday used to be his day off, back when Peter still cooked part time.

"I'll see you then, Sugar," Daniel confirmed. Pasha was sure he could hear a smile in Daniel's voice.

"WHAT goes on in my restaurant is none of nobody's goddamned business!" the old man roared, his face beet red. Pasha was just glad that for once the old man had pulled him into the office before going off on a tirade. Hopefully the closed door and distance between them and the dining room were enough to keep the few customers they had from hearing. “Nadia’s *my* daughter!” He slapped his chest emphatically. “If I want to give her money, I give her money! She’s got four kids to raise—what do I got, huh? *You*? You’re man, Pasha. You can take care of yourself. Nadia don’t got nothing.”

“She has a husband—”

Ivan waved off his argument. “He’s *paskudnyak*! He don’t do nothing for his fucking family.”

“That’s not your problem—”

“So what, you want to see kids go without food, without warm coats for winter? Huh? Maybe you want them to get kicked out of their house! That’s what’s gonna happen if I don’t help. Nadia’s your sister. How come you don’t care what happens to her?”

“I do care! I’m just saying that you can’t afford to support them. What happens when you lose our house?”

“*Our* house?” he bellowed. “*I* pay goddamned mortgage every month! You don’t even pay fucking rent!”

“If you want me to pay rent, just say so!”

“I don’t want nothing from you. Go wait fucking tables. Let me worry about roof over your precious head!”

Anger and humiliation burned in Pasha’s cheeks as he stalked out of the office. His one consolation was that his sister and the kids were gone by then. With any luck Clara and RJ hadn’t heard any of it. He darted into the men’s room and splashed cold water on his face. When the door opened, he turned to apologize to the customer who had come in.

But it was Amy.

“The sign on the door says ‘men,’” he pointed out the obvious and turned off the tap.

Without a word, she wrapped her arms around him. Pasha didn’t realize until she did it that he was shaking. “I don’t know what that was about,” Amy said softly, “but I’m sorry.”

“It’s got nothing to do with you.” He held her tight. “God, I hate him!”

“I know.”

“I don’t hate him.”

"I know that, too." She straightened and smoothed her hands over his cheeks. "I'll hold down the fort for a few more minutes, while you get yourself together."

"Thanks."

THE old man didn't say another word to him all day, even to complain, and Pasha returned the favor. When Dad came back to work the dinner shift, Pasha told him Amy was picking him up and they were going out. She would drop him off at home, so Dad was on his own to close again. And since the old man was already pissed, Pasha figured it was as good a time as any to tell him he was going to ask Jill to close for him tomorrow.

"What's wrong with you?" Ivan wanted to know. "You no wanna work no more?"

"I just need some time off."

"You gonna be boss someday—"

"But I'm not the boss now."

Ivan glowered. "What you gotta do tomorrow that's so important it can't wait 'til after closing?"

Pasha hesitated—then told him the truth. "I have a date."

"With who?"

"It's none of your business, Dad."

IT WAS almost two thirty before Pasha was able to leave on Sunday. He'd worked through a slow morning trying not to stare at the clock. It wasn't easy. But he knew he couldn't ask to leave any earlier than one—which was when a party of ten walked in the front door, followed by two couples, and a family of five. Several more customers trickled in afterward. It was Murphy's Law, and any other time he would have been happy with the late rush. Today all he wanted was for the place to stay dead so he could get out of there. Pasha didn't dare ask to go until everyone had their food, and even then he'd been sure his dad would tell him he had to stay.

But Ivan just waved him off. "I can't stop you nohow," he said.

Pasha changed clothes in the office and hurried out the back door, right into a snow squall—and suddenly realized he had no idea what kind of car Daniel drove. They'd sent a couple of text messages back and forth over the past hour: Daniel texting to let Pasha know he was there, Pasha replying to apologize because he couldn't leave, Daniel answering to say "no worries." Pasha was about to text him again to ask exactly where in the lot Daniel was, when he noticed a green Mustang idling by the dumpster. As Pasha approached the car, Daniel leaned over and opened the door, and Pasha slid in. "Thanks."

"My pleasure." Daniel flashed a wan smile.

"Is everything okay?"

"Yeah." He didn't sound it, though. "Remember the other day when I said there was some stuff we needed to talk about?"

Daniel's expression made Pasha's heart seize up. "I thought that was just about you and Aiden."

"Aiden has nothing to do with it—well, not exactly anyway. I just… there's something you need to know before this goes any further. And I'm sorry I didn't tell you sooner, it's just… I *hate* this conversation."

"*What* conversation?"

"The one that starts out with me telling you I'm HIV positive."

CHAPTER FOURTEEN

THE world stopped spinning on its axis.

HIV.

HIV?

Pasha's brain couldn't quite process the word.

He knew what HIV *was*—who didn't—but what does it *mean*?

Prejudice.

Illness.

AIDS.

Death.

Sure, it wasn't the death sentence it had been thirty years ago. There were treatment options, even some glimmerings of hope for a cure, but… but it still meant….

AIDS.

It meant prejudice.

It meant getting sick.

Dying.

Maybe death wouldn't come today or tomorrow or even next year, but…. Pasha closed his eyes. It was like Alzheimer's. Eventually Daniel would die, and it wouldn't be pretty. "How long have you had it?" he heard himself asking.

"I found out six years ago. It's hard to say when I actually got it."

Six years. Daniel had been living—dying—with this thing for six years? And he hadn't bothered to say anything until… *until after I start to fall in love with him?* But how could Daniel know that? A dull ache began to throb at the base of Pasha's skull. "Could we just… would you just drive, please?"

"Sure. Where—?"

"I-75. South. To Joseph Campau." Home. It was the only place Pasha was sure he could successfully navigate to.

HIV.

AIDS.

Pasha fumbled with his seatbelt, but it seemed to take forever to get it to work right. Daniel was almost to the first streetlight before he finally got himself buckled in.

HIV.

How…?

But he was pretty sure he knew the answer. He doubted Daniel had ever done drugs—or at least nothing heavy, nothing that involved needles. He was just as sure that if it wasn't Daniel's fault, if he'd been exposed accidently somehow, he would have said so right off the bat. That only left stupidity. Sheer fucking stupidity. Anger roiled up inside him. Even as a small part of Pasha's conscience kicked at him, telling him he was being selfish, he couldn't help feeling cheated.

He *liked* Daniel.

At length, Pasha glanced over at the driver's seat. Daniel seemed to be trying very hard not to look at him, to just concentrate on driving. "It's why you dropped out of school, isn't it?" he asked.

"Yeah." The word was barely audible.

Pasha frowned. Six years ago, Daniel would have been twenty-four. "You were what, almost done with a master's degree?" That'd be about right for a twenty-four year old, wouldn't it?

"First-year law student."

"And you didn't know any better! *Fucking…!*" How could somebody so smart have been so stupid? "Dammit, Daniel." He turned away again as angry tears stung his eyes. HIV *wasn't* a death sentence, not like it used to be, but it changed *everything.*

Didn't it?

It had to.

It was HIV.

It was AIDS.

It was getting sick; it was pneumonia and skin cancer.

It was prejudice, fear.

"I know," said Daniel softly. "Believe me, I know. Whatever you're thinking, I've thought it myself a thousand times."

His tone broke Pasha's heart, but that didn't lessen his anger. "You have no *idea* what I'm fucking thinking." *He* didn't know what he was thinking, so how could anybody else?

"Maybe not," Daniel conceded. "But I know what everyone else thinks."

"Yeah." Pasha closed his eyes again and leaned against the window. Even the cold of the glass didn't ease his aching head—his aching everything. Daniel was the most beautiful guy he'd ever known. It wasn't just what was on the outside. He was so warm. So down to earth. So sexy. So sweet.

And someday he's going to die.

Pasha knew there were kids out there who treated HIV like it was nothing—some of them even claimed to want to get it. *Idiots.* He'd been going to the bar since he was seventeen and had known a few guys who were old enough to remember when HIV wasn't "nothing."

A lot of those guys weren't around anymore.

Was this how Dad felt when he heard the words "early-onset Alzheimer's disease?" If he'd known Mom would get sick, would he have married her? But you couldn't predict who would get Alzheimer's; it was just one of those genetic screwups. It wasn't anybody's fault. HIV was something you *got*. It was Daniel's fault he had it.

Pasha didn't look at him again, didn't speak to him, until Daniel told him they were coming up on Joseph Campau. "You need to make a left at the first street," said Pasha. His tone was hollow. Empty.

Daniel made the requested turn. "I know I should have told you sooner. I'm sorry." His tone was hollow and empty, too. "I didn't think… we only went on *one* date, Pasha. I didn't know if this was going anywhere. I figured if it did… if it did, I would tell you. And if not, no harm done."

No harm done? Was he fucking kidding? "We talked almost every day this week! For *hours*. I thought…." But he couldn't finish his sentence aloud. He'd started to fall for Daniel. He thought Daniel felt the same way. "I told you about my mother, Daniel, about my fucked-up family—about stuff I never tell *anybody*!"

"I know. I'm sorry. I *swear* I was going to tell you Monday. It's why I came to the restaurant to see you."

But I couldn't get out of work. God, if Daniel had told him then…. Pasha swiped his hand across his face. He *wasn't* crying, but everything ached. He'd never felt so betrayed. He'd opened up his whole life to Daniel, and Daniel hadn't bothered to tell him the single most important detail about his.

HIV.

"I'm sorry, Pasha," he repeated. "If you'd been able to come out on Tuesday night, I would have told you then."

His laugh was cold. "That would have made for a pretty shitty birthday."

"Only if you'd told me you never wanted to see me again." Daniel sounded like he was trying to smile, but when Pasha glanced over at him, he could see it wasn't working.

"Why didn't you just tell me over the phone?" he asked.

"I hoped telling you face-to-face would make a difference, that you'd see me and not some stupid virus or all the mistakes I made before we even met. I… it's been so long since I've gone out with anybody and this is why."

He heard what Daniel didn't say: he'd been rejected so many times it was easier not to risk getting hurt. The heartbreak in Daniel's tone made Pasha want to wrap his arms around Daniel and make all the hurt go away. But he didn't. He didn't even reach over to take his hand; he just looked away. "Turn left at the next street. My house is the last one on the end of the second block."

"Okay."

HIV.

AIDS.

It wasn't fair! Daniel was sweet. He was funny. He was sexy.

He's everything I want.

How could Pasha walk away from that?

Someday he's going to have AIDS and I'll fall apart. How was that fair to either of them? Didn't Daniel deserve someone who could take care of him? Someone he could lean on? Pasha wasn't that person. *I can barely take care of myself.*

Or maybe he was just making excuses.

Daniel pulled up to the curb. He didn't bother cutting the engine. "I ah, I guess this is it."

"I should give you back your book." He couldn't even look Daniel in the eye.

"Why don't you keep it? I already read it, remember?"

"Yeah. Thanks. I guess…." *I'll see you around.* Only he *wouldn't* see Daniel around. They didn't have the same friends or hang out in the same places. This was really good-bye, and it was so unfair!

No. Unfair is having your whole life messed up by one stupid mistake. It was meeting someone, liking them, and then having to figure out how to tell them you had HIV. It was wondering if everything that person felt about you would change the second they knew. *God, he must hate me. All I can do is whine about how complicated* my *life is.* No wonder Daniel was always saying that life was short—for him life *was* short.

"I should go." Pasha finally managed to get the words out.

"Pasha, I… I meant what I said before. About liking your company. If you maybe wanted to just… hang out? You know, just friends…?" His expression broke Pasha's heart all over again. It was like he was trying not to get his hopes up too high—trying not to give up hope altogether. "I promise I'll never push you for more than you're comfortable with."

Pasha swallowed hard. Suddenly he thought he knew why Michael had refused to ever speak to him again. "I can't," he told Daniel.

Daniel forced a tight-lipped smile. "I understand."

"No, you don't." He could never be "just friends" with Daniel; he wanted too much more.

But was he strong enough to face life with a man who had HIV?

Was he strong enough to walk away?

What happened when they decided to take the next step? Would he be able to be intimate with Daniel without totally freaking out and acting like some kind of ass hat?

Christ, for all I know, I've already been with someone who has it. It was a sobering thought.

Pasha spent several long moments just looking at Daniel, weighing everything in his head, all of the things he was afraid of—all of the things he hoped for—before he finally leaned in and pressed a soft kiss to Daniel's mouth. It took Daniel several seconds to react, to return the kiss, but when he did, Pasha closed his eyes. Daniel's lips were softer than he'd imagined and his kiss was so gentle. So sweet. Pasha reached over and cupped the back of Daniel's head. His hair was soft. Daniel's cologne was warm and woodsy, and for a second, Pasha was sure he heard the beating of Daniel's heart. Finally, Daniel wrapped one strong arm around Pasha's shoulders and Pasha smiled. He nipped at Daniel's lips until they parted, until Daniel let out a soft sigh. Instead of pushing past Daniel's lips, Pasha sucked on his lower lip for several seconds before beginning his exploration of Daniel's mouth, turning it into the kind of kiss he'd fantasized about all week. The real thing was a *lot* better than the fantasy.

When they pulled away from one another, Pasha found Daniel searching his face, looking very unsure of himself.

He pressed another, much softer kiss to Daniel's mouth. "Every time I see your number on the caller ID, I smile," he admitted. "For the past week I've been… you've been all I could think about. All I wanted tonight was to be able to kiss you."

"You can kiss me anytime you want."

"Daniel, I'm afraid that someday you're going to get sick and I'm going to fall apart. I'm afraid I'm not strong enough to handle all the complications that come along with this." Most of all, he was terrified he wouldn't be able to walk away after that kiss. "Please tell me you're taking care of yourself. Tell me you're seeing a doctor and taking some kind of medication. Tell me you're not going to get sick and die tomorrow."

"I'm not going to get sick and die tomorrow, I promise. I see my doctor regularly and I have a boss who knows what's going on. But guess you should know I'm not on any meds."

"Why the hell not? You said you've had it for six years! What are you waiting for? Please tell me you're not one of those people who thinks they can beat it with herbal tea and prayer."

Daniel smiled. "No. I do that stuff, believe me. I do everything I can to stay healthy and I pray all the time. I pray that my health holds out, that my numbers stay good. For the last week I've been praying like crazy that this really amazing guy I just met won't totally freak out on me, that he'll want to see me again even after I tell him I'm positive."

"I am freaked out." Pasha hated to admit it. He wanted to say that everything was fine, but he was still scared.

"I know. But the hardest part of all this isn't being rejected because I have HIV. I know that scares people. The hardest part is when someone says they're going to be around and then they start cancelling dates and ducking my calls."

"I won't duck your calls," he promised. "And I won't cancel dates. I just need to know you're okay."

"I've got a great doc. Me and her decided together that I don't need to start taking antiretrovirals yet."

"How come?"

"For one thing, the list of side effects is as long as my arm. Right now my CD4 count is close to eight hundred—that's a good number," he said when Pasha shot him a questioning, doubtful look. "And my viral load is next to nothing. As long as it stays that way, I'm okay."

"It can't be that easy."

"It's not easy. Pretty much every decision I've made for the last six years—every decision I'll make for the rest of my life—is affected by the fact I've got a bum immune system. I see my doc every six months to get my blood checked and every single time, I'm scared stiff that *this* will be the visit when we have to start talking about those antiretroviral drugs.

"But I'm even more scared that I'm gonna meet someone I really like and they're not going to be able to see past this stupid virus or all the dumb shit I did to land myself here. I'm afraid I'll… I don't need somebody who won't fall apart when things get tough, Pasha. I need somebody who won't judge me. Someone who isn't afraid to touch me. Someone who won't freak out the first time I get a cold."

Pasha reached out and took his hand; their fingers intertwined. "I can't promise I won't freak out the first time you get a cold," Pasha admitted. "But I'm not afraid to touch you." With his other hand, he stroked Daniel's cheek. Daniel leaned into his touch and feathered a soft kiss to Pasha's palm. Smiling, Pasha coaxed him into another kiss. This time it was Daniel nipping at his lower lip, trying to gain access to Pasha's mouth. Pasha gave it to him without hesitation. Daniel's tongue slid over his. It was soft and velvety, and his explorations were so slow, so gentle. So tender. It was just the way Pasha had told him he wanted to be kissed, and it left Pasha lightheaded and giddy.

By the time they separated, both men were out of breath, panting hard, foreheads pressed together. They both smiled. Pasha stroked Daniel's hair. He was still scared of what was going to happen somewhere down the road when Daniel got sick. *But that's a long way off.* He closed his eyes. Right here, right now, Daniel was everything he wanted, and he wasn't strong enough to walk away from that. He didn't want to be.

It was only when he opened his eyes again that he realized the El Dorado was sitting in the driveway, idling.

CHAPTER FIFTEEN

DANIEL followed his gaze. “Shit,” he breathed. “Pasha, I am so sorry. I swear, I *didn’t* see him drive up.”

“I know. It’s not your fault.” He looked at his watch. It was barely three twenty. Dad should still be at the restaurant closing up. God, what had the old man done, kicked everyone out and closed up early because he was pissed? Or had he broken every speed limit between Royal Oak and Hamtramck? Pasha looked back at his driveway, at the El Dorado. He felt… numb. Absolutely numb. He should be afraid, or maybe angry at himself for being stupid enough to sit in front of his own house, making out with a man in broad daylight. But he wasn’t mad; he didn’t feel anything. “I think I’m going to have to take a rain check on tonight.”

“Pasha—”

“You should go home.”

“I don’t feel right leaving you here like this. If things get ugly—”

“I’ll be fine. I *am* fine.” He took hold of both of Daniel’s hands again, twining their fingers together. “This was bound to happen sooner or later. Maybe not like this, but I couldn’t hide in the closet forever.” And maybe part of him *wanted* Dad to find out. Why else would he have been so careless?

“If he gets physical—”

Pasha snorted. “He’s fifty-six and has a bad heart. The worst thing he can do is kick me out. Fire me. If that happens… if that happens, I’ll call Amy and see if I can crash on her couch. Tomorrow

I'll start looking for a new job. I'll get my own apartment. Everything'll be fine."

Daniel didn't look convinced.

"I'm okay," Pasha repeated. If it really came down to it, he'd be better off if Dad disowned him and removed his name from the business. He leaned in and pressed a soft kiss to Daniel's mouth. What the hell, if the old man was watching, might as well give him a good show, right? He'd already seen them making out anyway, how much worse could another kiss make it? Besides, kissing Daniel was right at the very top of Pasha's list of favorite activities just then.

"Whatever happens, I want you to call me," said Daniel.

"I will. I promise." He kissed Daniel one last time before getting out of the car. As soon as he stood up, Dad gunned the El Dorado's engine and sped into the backyard so fast, Pasha was surprised he didn't slam into the garage door.

Pasha jogged across the street and up to the front porch. The snow was coming down harder than ever, but the pavement was warm enough that a lot of it had melted on contact, turning to slush. By the time Pasha got to the door, his shoes and socks were soaked clear through.

As he dug out his house keys, he tried to collect his thoughts and figure out what he was going to say.

Some people are gay. I'm one of them. Get over it.

Okay, probably not the best opening line, but what else could he say? Even if he could deny it, he didn't want to. He was sick of pretending to be something he wasn't—or at the very least, he was sick of letting everyone assume he was straight. *Only I'm not sure I'm ready for a rainbow flag T-shirt either.* Pasha heard Daniel pull away from the curb, but didn't turn around. He was afraid if he did, he would completely chicken out, run back to the car, and ask Daniel to just take him to Amy's. *But running away will just delay the inevitable.*

Pasha let himself into the house and set his wet shoes on the mat next to the door. He pulled off his socks and placed them over the heat vent to dry, then hung his coat in the front hall closet. He heard the kitchen faucet come on. Water splashed against the sink for a few seconds, then the pitch changed. Dad was filling the teakettle. Pasha made his way down the long narrow hallway—somehow, it seemed longer and narrower than ever before—but couldn't make himself cross the threshold into the kitchen, so he leaned against the doorframe instead. Dad didn't turn around. He didn't speak. He just got down a cup from the cupboard, took a packet of tea out of the caddy on the counter and dropped it into his cup.

Finally, he glanced over his shoulder. His expression was unbearably cold. Distant.

Bitter.

It made Pasha wish he'd let Daniel hang around because he realized suddenly he couldn't simply drive to Amy's when this was over; he didn't have a car of his own. The knots in his gut tightened. "I know we need to talk—"

The old man waved him to silence. "What you do… you're grown man, Pasha." Rage filled his voice. "But don't you *ever* shame me in my own home again!"

"I wasn't *in* your house."

"Don't you shame me in front of my neighbors!" His palm came down on the countertop so hard the dishes in the drainer clattered. He whirled around, facing Pasha. The anger drained from his face, leaving behind a look of utter defeat. "You do what the hell you want. I can't stop you nohow. I can't stop none of you kids. You… you just do what the hell you want," he repeated more quietly. The hurt in his voice tore at Pasha's heart, even if the next words out of his mouth enraged him. "But you do it somewhere else. I don't ever want to see that *pidoras* here again."

He swallowed back his anger. "You won't."

"I don't want to see that *pidoras* in my restaurant neither," he snapped, vacillating from hurt to anger and back again. "You hear me? You want to… to do what I saw when I pulled up, you go somewhere *else*."

Pasha bit his tongue on his initial response. *It was just a kiss.* If he'd been with a girl… but he hadn't been with a girl. He'd been with a man. "Fine," he agreed. They stared at each other until the kettle started whistling on the stove. Ivan made his tea. Pasha walked out of the kitchen and padded up the stairs toward his room. It was over. It had lasted less than ten minutes. *And it was mostly painless.*

It wasn't until he closed his bedroom door that his knees turned to jelly and he sank to the floor rather than fall flat on his ass. It had really been… well, okay, maybe it wasn't "painless," but other than a few short outbursts, Dad had barely raised his voice. Pasha drew in a ragged breath and pulled out his cell phone. His hands were shaking as he dialed Daniel's number.

Daniel picked up in two rings. Pasha barely let him get "hey" out before telling him that everything was fine. "It was a short conversation."

"How short?" Daniel wanted to know.

"He didn't kick me out or disown me, he just said he doesn't want to see it."

"That's it?"

"Pretty much." There was no way he was going to tell Daniel what the old man had called him. *Pidoras.* There weren't many Russian words for homosexuality, but of the options available, that was probably the worst. "But I'm guessing he's never going to want to hear about my wonderful new boyfriend," he managed to joke.

"New boyfriend, huh?" Daniel teased right back. "That mean I've been replaced already?"

"Not hardly."

"So when does your new boyfriend get to see you again?" Daniel wondered.

"When do you want to see me?"

"Would now be too soon?"

Pasha almost laughed. "How far did you get?"

"I'm parked two blocks away. I um… I just figured if things didn't go too good, you might need a ride or something."

"Thank you. What street are you on?"

"I'm at the corner of MacKay and… it looks like Pulaski," he pronounced it slowly.

"That's one block," Pasha informed him, "not two."

Daniel snorted. "So do you want me to drive up to the next block and *then* come get you?"

He rolled his eyes. "No. And I'll come to you."

"You sure? It's starting to come down pretty hard."

Pasha hauled himself back up to his feet. "Yeah, I'm sure. I'll be there in ten minutes."

He got a dry pair of socks from his dresser drawer and made his way cautiously back downstairs. Dad was in the living room. He didn't look up from his paper when Pasha walked past. He didn't say anything when Pasha told him he was going out either.

Right. What did I honestly expect? He didn't bother with good-bye; he just put on his boots and coat and headed out into the cold. A sharp wind cut through Pasha's jeans. He shivered and hurried down the sidewalk toward MacKay, snow crunching under his feet. The slush was starting to freeze over, and he slipped several times on the ice before reaching the corner. As soon as he did, he saw Daniel standing beside his car, waiting.

"Long time no see," Pasha teased when he got close enough to be heard.

Daniel smiled. "A little too long." He hesitated—then reached out and laid his hands lightly on Pasha's arms. "You sure you're okay?"

"I am now." He hadn't realized how close he was to tears until the moment Daniel touched him. He didn't even know why he wanted to cry. But it didn't matter now. Pasha stepped into the warm circle of Daniel's arms and closed his eyes. With his ear pressed up against Daniel's chest the way it was, Pasha could hear the soft thudding of his heart. He smiled.

"Much as I like this, you sure your neighbors aren't going to raise a fuss?" Daniel asked softly.

"I don't care." Life was too short. "Besides"—he looked up again and met Daniel's gaze—"who's going to recognize me in this?" The snow was coming down so hard, it could only be described as a blizzard.

"Let's get you out of the cold, anyway." With one arm still draped over Pasha's shoulder, he walked them around to the passenger side door and opened it up so Pasha could slide in. A few seconds later,

Daniel was sitting next to him. "I haven't seen this much snow since I visited home last." He grinned, shaking the snow out of his long hair.

"You look just like the abominable snowman," Pasha teased.

"I do, huh? You know, I've heard those guys sometimes sneak down to villages, abduct handsome guys from their bedrooms."

Pasha laughed. "In which case, I think I'm perfectly safe."

"I don't think so." He leaned in—then hesitated.

Pasha met the kiss halfway. It was soft, sweet. When they parted lips, Daniel was smiling, but it wasn't his usual, mischievous grin. It was soft and warm, and it made Pasha's stomach come alive with butterflies.

"You ah… you want to get something to eat?" Daniel asked.

"Sure. But there's not much open around here on Sunday, just a couple of bars and some pizza places."

"Either's fine, but no one says we have to stick around here."

"I was just thinking about the weather."

"I can handle a little snow. My friend Erika suggested this place called Pronto! in Royal Oak—"

"No." Just thinking about the place made Pasha feel queasy. "I mean… not tonight. I'm in the mood for somewhere quieter." Somewhere he could be sure he wouldn't run into anyone he knew.

"Yeah, okay. I just wanted to go somewhere I can hold your hand." He sounded disappointed, even though it looked like he was trying not to let it show.

Pasha reached over and took his hand, letting their fingers lace together. "You can hold my hand anywhere you want. I'm done hiding."

"Pasha, look, I love it that you want to come out, but I'm not real sure you're thinking clearly. You just had an emotional run-in with your dad. Maybe you'd better give yourself a little time to cool off before we go walking down Main Street hand in hand."

Reluctantly, he nodded, because he knew Daniel had a point. "If you really want to go to Pronto!, we can."

"I told you, all I want is to go somewhere I can hold your hand. If ah… if you're up for a drive, we can even go back to my place. The food's not very good, but I think you'll like the ambiance."

He hesitated. The thought of going to Daniel's apartment was *very* appealing, but snow was still falling hard.

Color tinted Daniel's cheeks. "I wasn't suggesting…. I'm not trying to rush you into anything, Sugar. I was just talking about lighting a fire and watching a movie. Heck, I don't even have anything… I mean… you know… I'm not assuming—"

Pasha laid his fingers over Daniel's lips. "You're not assuming anything I don't want, too. A movie sounds great. And if you want to stop somewhere and get a box of condoms, I'm not going to object to that, either."

"No. I mean, yes, of course I want to. You have no idea how much I want to. I just don't want us doing anything tonight you might wake up regretting, okay? There's a lot we still have to talk about. "

He swallowed hard. What they had to talk about was the one thing Pasha wanted to forget: Daniel's HIV. But he nodded anyway. "Yeah. Okay. And yes, I'd love to go back to your place. I'm just worried about the weather. You'll have to bring me back home again in a few hours."

"I don't mind. There's a great pizza place not too far from my apartment. I really wasn't kidding about being a lousy cook," he said with a grin.

Pasha looked down at his watch. It was almost five o'clock. If they left now, they'd get to Daniel's by six or six thirty, or maybe closer to seven, if they stopped for carryout. "We'd really have to leave your place by ten." Which would get Daniel back home at eleven. Pasha shook his head. That was too late for him to be out driving around, especially on a night like this. "Maybe I'd better take that rain check after all."

"There is one other option," Daniel suggested tentatively. "You could stay over. I mean on the sofa. Or you can have the bed and I'll take the sofa. I'm not asking you to sleep with me. I'm just thinking that if you stayed over, we'd have time to talk. If you want." He sounded so nervous. "Or we can make it a rain check for some time when Mother Nature isn't dumping so much snow on our heads."

Pasha gave his hand a tight squeeze. "I'd love to stay with you tonight, but I have to work in the morning. You'd still have to get me home."

"I have deliveries on this side of town pretty early tomorrow. I could drop you off at the restaurant if you wanted."

"Your boss wouldn't mind?"

"I'm not necessarily saying I would tell him, even though it's not the kind of thing he'd care about if it weren't for the insurance company. I have to drive back past my place on my way up here, anyway. I can pick you up after I check in. If I rearrange my first couple of deliveries, I can get you there by six, if that works."

"Six is good." The old man would have a fit—six was when they opened—but seriously, it wasn't like they got very many customers in that early. Pasha could get his morning sidework done in between waiting on the handful of people who walked in the door. "I just have to go home and get my uniform." *And let Dad know what's going on.* That was one conversation Pasha wasn't looking forward to.

"Will you let me drive you?"

"Yeah." He didn't want to walk through the snow again.

PASHA let himself in the front door and was surprised his father wasn't in the living room like usual, watching television. He was tempted to just go upstairs and pack an overnight bag without telling his dad what was going on. But he forced himself to head toward the kitchen anyway. Dad sat at the table, looking through a shoebox full of old photos.

He glanced up when Pasha came in—he looked older than ever. He didn't say anything; it didn't look like he knew what *to* say.

Several painful moments of silence stretched between them before Pasha finally found his voice. "I came home to pick up a few things."

"You're leaving?"

"Just to stay the night at a friend's house. He'll drop me off at work tomorrow morning."

"*He*?" The old man's eyes narrowed. "You mean that *pidoras*?"

"His name is Daniel, and you can't call him *pidoras*"—just saying the word made his stomach turn sour—"without calling *me* one too."

For a second Ivan looked like he was going to start yelling again, but then his shoulders slumped and he shook his head, looking defeated. That hurt Pasha more than if the old man had been angry.

"Dad—"

Ivan waved him to silence. "Don't say nothing. Don't…. I know you know right from wrong, Pasha! You're good boy. That's why I don't understand this." More than defeated, he sounded helpless.

"It's not about right and wrong, Dad. It's more complicated than that."

"It's not complicated! It's wrong! He's man. You're man. Men don't… men don't do what I saw you doing when I drove up!"

There was no point in arguing. Without another word, Pasha went up to his room and gathered up what he'd need for tonight. Tomorrow. After stuffing his clothes into an old backpack, he headed into the bathroom for his toothbrush and razor. When he came out he found his father waiting for him at the top of the steps.

"This… this *man*," said Dad, "did he put you up to this? Did he fill your head with some nonsense? Is that it? Is this *his* fault?"

"Daniel isn't my first boyfriend, Dad."

Ivan's face contorted. "*Boyfriend*? Men don't have boyfriends. What that makes you, huh? *Girl*?"

Pasha swallowed back his first response—anger—as well as his second. Getting mad wouldn't help and he'd be damned if he was going to apologize for being gay. "I'll see you in the morning. Daniel's dropping me off around six."

Chapter Sixteen

AS SOON as he slid into the passenger seat, Daniel asked what was wrong.

"Nothing." Realizing there were tears on his cheeks didn't help. Angrily, he wiped them away. He wasn't the kind of man to cry about every stupid little thing! Only when he felt Daniel's hand on his knee, he almost started up again.

"It's not nothing," Daniel said gently. "Did your dad say something?"

"Of course he said something! I'm sorry," he said. "I didn't mean to snap. It's just… could we please just go?"

"Whatever you need, babe." Daniel took his hand back so he could get the car in gear, but as soon as he pulled away from the curb, Pasha reached over and their fingers intertwined.

Pasha closed his eyes and tried very hard not to think about HIV.

AIDS.

Illness.

Prejudice.

Death.

He pulled Daniel's hand up to his lips and feathered a soft kiss over Daniel's knuckles.

"If there's anything you want to know, all you have to do is ask," said Daniel, his voice so soft, Pasha almost didn't hear it. "I won't hold back. I'm just not sure how much I should say right now."

"Me either." He gave Daniel's hand another kiss. He wasn't sure he wanted to know anything. It wasn't like the past could be changed. Besides, hadn't Daniel said he'd made mistakes? That could only mean he'd been careless. *And now he has this stupid life-changing disease.*

Suddenly Daniel pulled his hand away. Confused and a little hurt, Pasha shot him a questioning look.

"Don't," was all Daniel said in reply.

"Don't *what*?"

"Don't start looking at me and only seeing how many days you think I have left. I have years, Pasha. Decades. But all that time is meaningless if you start ticking off calendar days in your head, because the second you start doing that, you stop being able to enjoy this minute, right here, right now. I'm not a walking gravestone."

The image horrified him, but it was almost exactly what he'd been thinking. "Am I that transparent?"

Daniel shot over a rueful little smile, but when he spoke, the bitter edge was gone from his voice. "Only a little. You should have seen my sister when I first went back home. She couldn't look at me without breaking down. Pops neither."

"What about your mom?"

"If Ma ever lost her composure, I never saw it. She's always been the tough one. When I got sick, she came down to Ann Arbor and stayed with me for almost a month, got me through it. Kept me from doing anything permanently stupid, if you know what I mean."

"Yeah. I do. Can I ask… I mean, what happened? How'd you find out you had it?" It had a name, but Pasha wasn't ready to say it out loud, not yet.

"I ended up in the hospital with a pretty bad case of pneumonia. When it started, I thought it was just stress. I was coming up on midterms," he explained. "I'd pulled a bunch of all-nighters studying—and doing other things. I missed a few meals. I was living mostly on Red Bull and vending machine chow back then. Add in the occasional pizza or Ramen…." He shrugged. "But I just kept getting sicker and, well, the short version of it is that I ended up in the ER and after a couple of blood tests, they told me I had HIV and that my white cell count was down in the single digits."

"Shit."

His smile surprised Pasha. "That's what I said. Hearing that wasn't the hardest part, though. The hardest part was that.... I did a lot of dumb things, babe, stuff I'm not proud of. I had a lot of phone calls to make, a lot of people to tell that they might wanna get themselves tested. Five that I know of tested positive for HIV. Aiden was one of them. Friday was the first time… it was the first time he's spoken to me since he found out. That's why it was important for me to see him."

Pasha could hear the guilt in Daniel's voice, see it on his face. He reached over and took his hand again. "It takes two.... I mean, those other people could have told you that you had to wear a rubber. It's not just your fault. It's theirs too."

"That doesn't make me feel any less responsible. But thanks." He gave Pasha's hand a gentle squeeze and Pasha squeezed back. "When it was all over I quit school, went home for a while. I ah.... I'd lost pretty much everybody I thought of as a friend, anyway. Even people I'd never been involved with looked at me like I was some kind of leper. Or maybe Typhoid Mary."

"I can't believe people would be so unfair."

Daniel shrugged. "It wasn't having people say they were mad at me or even that they hated me that I minded. They were just being honest and I could respect that. What hurt was when someone said they'd always be there, that nothing had changed, but suddenly they wouldn't hug me anymore or even sit next to me on the sofa. They'd come over to visit and sit on the other side of the room looking nervous, staring at the clock. Staring at me like all they could see was how much time they thought I had left. To tell you the truth, I was more relieved when they finally went home than they were."

Pasha ducked his head apologetically.

"I'm sure most people don't even realize what they were doing," Daniel told him. "But eventually it got to the point where most of the friends I had left seemed to always be too busy to see me. Some of 'em even started dodging my calls. I took the hint and stopped calling. When I left, only a handful of people stayed in touch with me."

"So why come back?"

"Home wasn't much better. Every time I sneezed, Ma ran me to the doc's office to make sure I was okay. Pop and Joyce weren't any better. And believe me, in a small town, everybody knows your business, so it wasn't just them acting squirrely. Most folks were… nice. Only it was the kind of nice you'd be to somebody who only has a few weeks left to live. When one of the few friends I had left down here said he could get me in at the microbrewery where he worked, I jumped on it. I would've taken anything that got me away from Hannahville, but this has turned out to be a really good gig. They started me out in the warehouse, then when I got my CDL, they gave me a truck and route."

"Is that…. I mean…." Only he wasn't quite sure how to ask Daniel what he was wondering.

Daniel seemed to understand. "You mean am I going to be able to keep it up indefinitely? No. As it is there are days I come home so beat I barely have the energy to crawl into bed—although that just might mean I'm getting old," he teased, and Pasha managed to laugh too. Daniel went on, "There's an office job waiting for me when I can't handle making deliveries anymore. My boss had an uncle who died of complications due to AIDS."

Pasha swallowed hard.

"That was a long time ago, Sugar, before anybody had a handle on how to treat HIV. I promise you, I'm not gonna up and die on you."

"Yeah, okay." And he knew it was his turn to talk. The last year of his life seemed like the best place to start, only it wasn't something he was proud of. Pasha shifted in his seat. "I guess there's some stuff I should tell you, too."

"You don't have to tell me anything you don't want to."

"Thanks. But I feel like I do. I'm just afraid you're going to change your mind about… everything."

Daniel squeezed his hand. "Don't be. The fact that we're both here, now, that you didn't tell me to take a hike… I'm… you're not gonna run me off real easy."

Pasha nodded. He hoped that was true. "Last year was… it was really hard." Heat rushed to his cheeks. "Not as hard as your last year of school—"

"Pasha, you can't compare someone else's life with yours. We all get hurt over different stuff, and from what you've told me already, things 'round your place aren't any kind of picnic."

"No, I guess not. Last year, while everything was going on with Mom, my brother announced he was moving to the other side of the state to take a job in Grand Rapids. The only good thing in my life was my boyfriend, Michael. I really thought he was it, you know? The One. He was the only guy I ever really said 'I love you' to. He was the first guy who ever said it to me. Then a week later, it was all over and he said he never even wanted to speak to me again. I know this is going to sound stupid, but he even unfriended me on Facebook. We'd been together for almost a year and suddenly he was just *gone*. All I had left was this great gaping hole in my life, and I didn't know how to fill it."

"You mind if I ask why you two broke up?"

Pasha took a deep breath and let it out again. He was terrified of what Daniel was going to say when he heard that part of the story. "Michael wanted me to move in with him, but that would have meant coming out and I couldn't. Dad needed somebody. I was the only one left. I couldn't walk out on him the way my brother did. I still can't. If he kicks me out, fine, but I can't leave."

Daniel frowned. "Let me get this straight. This guy you've been with for a year tells you he loves you and wants the two of you to move in together and you tell him you can't 'cause your life's gone to shit, and he *dumps* you?"

"He said he couldn't live a lie anymore." Pasha didn't blame him.

"What lie?"

"The one where we pretended to be just friends when he came into the restaurant to see me. I told him I was in the closet before we started dating, but I guess he didn't believe me. Or maybe he thought I'd change." He shrugged. It didn't matter anymore.

Daniel shook his head. "For what it's worth, I think your ex is a damn fool, but I can't say I'm sorry you were single when we met."

Butterflies danced in Pasha's stomach. "Me either." He turned and watched the road go by for several long minutes, trying to figure out how to tell Daniel the rest of it. Snow fell in giant flakes. It was coming down slower than it had been earlier, but no one was going over fifty miles an hour on the highway—except for the occasional idiot in an SUV who sped past like he was king of the road.

"So what happened after you two split?" Daniel finally prompted gently.

"For a while, not much. I just went to work, came home. Ate ice cream." He smiled a little. Daniel smiled too. "I kept hoping Michael would change his mind, that he'd at least want to be friends. After about a month, I realized it was never going to happen, so I started going out again."

"Nothing wrong with that, Sugar."

"I ah…. I don't mean that I went out and had drinks with friends or even that I went on a few dates. I didn't go out on any dates. I just hooked up with whoever wanted to." *Please don't ask for too many details.* "I know it was stupid, but I just…. I was hurt. I wanted the hurt to go away. Sex felt good. Keeping it uncomplicated was… easier, I guess, than trying to have another relationship." He shot Daniel a hopeful look.

"Babe, I'm in no position to judge anyone," he repeated what he'd said earlier. "Just tell me you were careful."

"Always. Every time."

Daniel hesitated a moment before asking, "Can I ask when you got tested last?"

"Right after Michael dumped me. We… after we'd been together for a couple of months we ditched the condoms. We got tested first," he added quickly. "I'd never done it bareback before. I didn't think he cheated on me or anything. I just needed to be sure I was okay."

"I'm glad. If ah… if I asked you to get tested again, would you?"

"I guess so. Why?"

"Pasha, if you're really serious about taking things further, there's a lot for both of us to consider. It's not just your health. I can't afford to take chances, either. I'm not saying I don't believe you about being careful, I do. But another STI would really mess me up."

"Yeah, that makes sense." He nibbled his lower lip. He didn't want to say anymore, but he was afraid that if he didn't, he'd never be able to look at himself in the mirror again. "There's something else." Daniel deserved to know the whole truth.

"You don't have to tell me any more than you have already."

"Yes I do. Friday night I… I was really upset, so I let my friend Ty drag me out to Menjo's. It's this gay bar—"

"I know it."

"Ty said it would serve you right if I got laid. I didn't," he said quickly. "But I ran into this guy I knew. This guy I'd… you know. Been with." *Please don't ask me to be more specific.* "I let him buy me a drink." He watched Daniel's Adam's apple bob up and down. "That's *all* that happened, Daniel, I swear."

And maybe Daniel took his hand back because the road was slick and he wanted both hands on the wheel, and maybe he took it back because he didn't want to hold hands anymore. "I know we just met. If you want to see other guys—"

"I don't. I missed your call Friday because Ty got so pissed at me for staring at my phone that he took it away from me. I wouldn't have gone out in the first place if he hadn't dragged me."

Daniel gave a slow, thoughtful nod. "I really…. I don't want to come off like I'm trying to get ahead of myself or like I'm trying to push you into anything, and I *don't* want to scare you off. I just need to know if we're on the same page. If you're not ready to commit to something that's just me and you, it's okay. Maybe it's too soon to start talking about anything exclusive, anyway. I just… you need to know that I'm not comfortable taking the next step, getting intimate, until it's just you and me. If you're not ready to go there—"

"I am. I can do that. I don't want to go out with anybody else."

"Pasha—"

"I mean it. I… you're about all I could think about this week," he confessed.

Daniel's smile made him feel warm inside. "Me too," he said.

CHAPTER SEVENTEEN

"HERE we are, home sweet home," Daniel announced as he eased into the driveway of a big blue house on Washtenaw Road, Ypsilanti's main thoroughfare. Pasha smiled. He liked the sound of the word "home."

It looked like someone had shoveled the sidewalk and driveway at some point during the storm because there was less than an inch of snow covering the cement and gravel. More than five inches covered the grass. But at least the storm had stopped and salt trucks and plows were out, though the roads were still a mess. It made Pasha glad he was staying the night.

"How many people live here?" he asked as Daniel pulled into the backyard. Three cars sat parked under an aluminum carport. They looked like the kinds of cars college students drove: old, cheap, and dotted with rust spots.

"Seven, I think. Me and Becky are the only tenants who've been here awhile. She's got the other apartment on the main floor—doesn't look like she's home, though. She's a nurse up at U of M."

"Nurse Becky, huh?" Pasha teased.

Daniel just shook his head and pulled into an empty spot between a two-toned Ford Escort and an enormous old Cadillac. "You have enough room over there?"

Pasha surveyed the distance between his door and the Caddy. "Yeah, I'm good." When Daniel cut the engine, he got out and grabbed the pizza from the backseat.

At the initial suggestion of pizza, Pasha had been dubious, but figured beggars couldn't be choosers and in the middle of a snowstorm, he'd take whatever fast food was available. The pizza they'd come home with wasn't anything he would have expected: feta cheese, artichoke hearts, mushrooms, spinach, and fresh tomatoes. There was also a huge Caesar salad, an order of calamari, and, despite Pasha's objections, a pair of cannoli. Daniel said the filling was to die for.

Daniel grabbed the remainder of the bags and led the way up to the back door. "Watch out for the attack cat," he warned as he unlocked it.

Pasha stopped midstride. "The what?"

"Look up."

Pasha stepped over the threshold into a large, clean kitchen and gazed up in the direction Daniel had indicated. Sitting atop the fridge was the biggest, fluffiest yellow cat he'd ever seen in his life. It flicked its tail and glared down at him.

"What the hell is that?"

Daniel laughed. "*That* is my best friend."

The monstrous tabby jumped down from the refrigerator and landed on the tile floor with enough force to make the apples in the bowl on the countertop wobble. It stepped forward and Pasha stepped back.

"Um… Daniel?" he said, when his back was against the wall and the cat kept advancing on him.

Daniel was too busy laughing to be much help. The cat rose up on its hind legs and butted its face against Pasha's thigh, leaving behind a trail of long white and yellow hair. Pasha just hoped the loud rumble coming from its throat was really purring.

"See, I told you you'd get attacked." Daniel set the bags down on the counter and took the pizza box from Pasha's hands. "You're supposed to pet him, by the way," he advised. "But I should warn you, it's a catch twenty-two. He won't leave you alone until you do—but once he figures out you're willing to pay attention to him, he'll be all over you."

"Um… I ah… I've never been real good with animals."

"Allergies?" Daniel queried.

"No. I just… um, we never had any. Pets, I mean."

"Not even a goldfish?"

"My family owns a restaurant, remember? There was never any time for anything else. Besides, pets are… messy." Which was probably the nicest thing the old man ever had to say on the subject. Pasha wasn't sure he disagreed, either. Besides getting long hair all over his jeans, the cat had started to drool. He didn't even know cats did that; he thought it was just dogs who got all slobbery and gross.

Daniel finally came to the rescue and scooped the gigantic fur ball up into his arms, cradling it like a baby. The beast kept on purring, occasionally lifting its head to rub its face on Daniel's. Daniel seemed to genuinely enjoy its antics. "The only time I *didn't* have a pet was when I was at school." He brought the creature closer. "Pasha, I would like to introduce to you Alexander the Great. Alex, this is Pasha."

"Um… hi?" he said—but then took another step back when a giant paw came toward his face. His back hit the wall and the paw hit his nose. "I don't think he likes me."

"He's just trying to get your attention."

"Trust me, he's got it."

"Cats like their heads scratched."

Right. Pasha reached out and gave the beast's head a little pat. Its fur was softer and silkier than anything he'd ever touched. The cat captured his hand between both paws and it rubbed its nose eagerly against his fingers. He could feel its teeth, but its claws weren't out. Pasha was still dubious, however. "Is this good or bad?"

Daniel laughed. "He's marking you. Pretty much everything and everyone who comes into the house belongs to him, at least in his mind."

"Great." But when Daniel set the beast back on the floor, Pasha knelt down so he could continue petting its soft fur. He scratched behind its ears and under its chin. "What kind of cat is it? I mean, is it something special? I've never seen one this big before."

"He's a Maine Coon. My mom raises 'em," Daniel said over his shoulder. He was at the counter, getting down plates for their dinner.

"Are they always this big?"

"Alex is actually a little on the small side for a male. He only weighs sixteen pounds."

"*Only*?"

He chuckled. "Wait 'til you meet his dad. Caesar weighs in at twenty-four pounds."

Suddenly Alexander rose up on his hind legs and placed one giant paw on each of Pasha's shoulders. "Um, Daniel?" The cat rubbed his face against Pasha's nose, scraping his skin with sharp incisors—then he started licking Pasha's cheeks. His tongue felt like sandpaper. "Help?"

Laughing, Daniel intervened, scooping Alexander back up into his arms. "All right mister, Pasha is Daddy's boyfriend, not yours," he scolded gently. "You want a boyfriend, you go find your own." He set Alexander down on the counter and got a pouch of cat food out of one of the cupboards overhead. Alex purred louder, rubbing his head against Daniel's arm and shoulder. He pawed frantically at Daniel's hands as he opened the pouch and let out a plaintive meow when Daniel turned away so he couldn't get at it.

"Don't let him fool you," said Daniel, as he dumped the food into the fancy little bowl on the counter. Alexander went at it like he hadn't been fed in a week. "He's not starving, *or* unloved."

Pasha grinned and shucked out of his coat. Daniel had already taken his off and hung it on one of the hooks by the back door. Pasha followed suit. He took off his shoes and set them next to Daniel's too. Then he came back into the kitchen and leaned up against the counter next to Daniel. Pasha didn't realize he was smiling until Daniel looked over at him, until he smiled too, and a flurry of butterflies started swarming around in the pit of Pasha's stomach again. He leaned in and Daniel met his kiss halfway. If he could just forget about the great big ugly elephant in the room—HIV—everything would be just the way he'd imagined it the other night when they were talking on the phone.

When they drew apart, Daniel's expression was hard to read—but then he smiled again. "You want something to drink? I ah…. I'm afraid I wasn't expecting company. I don't have much to offer."

"Whatever you're having is fine with me."

"I was just going to make a pot of green tea," Daniel began tentatively.

"Green tea works."

"Do you want to eat in here at the table, or in the living room, in front of the TV?"

"I remember someone promising me a fire."

He chuckled. "Living room it is. If you want to go and make yourself comfortable, I'll start the tea and be in, in a sec."

Pasha nodded and started stacking up the carryout containers.

"Can you manage all that?" Daniel asked.

He scoffed. "Please. I'm a professional," he said and headed through the only available door into the darkened room beyond.

"There's a light switch on the wall to your right," Daniel called.

"Thanks." He hit it with his elbow, bringing up several pools of glowing yellow-orange warmth provided by track lighting overhead. At the same time, the nearly eight-foot-tall Christmas tree in front of the big bay window came to life with twinkling multicolored lights. There didn't seem to be a single branch left undecorated.

"I know it's a little early," Daniel said from the kitchen. "But I figured I wasn't going to be here to enjoy it for most of the holiday season, so I might as well put it up."

"Mom always put ours up the day before Thanksgiving, so it would be up when my nieces and nephew came over." Pasha set the boxes and plates down on the low coffee table in front of the sofa. "RJ—that's my nephew—wanted to know if it wasn't up this year because she wasn't there. Then he asked when she was coming home."

"If you want to turn it off…." Daniel offered.

Pasha turned and saw him standing in the doorway looking pensive. "Don't be silly, this is your house. Besides, it's beautiful."

Daniel crossed the distance between them and cupped Pasha's cheek. His touch was still tentative, like he couldn't quite believe Pasha wouldn't pull away. "I just want you to be comfortable here," Daniel said.

"I am."

While Daniel got the fire going, Pasha took a minute to look around at the rest of the room, wanting to get a better feel for the man who lived there. The living room walls were painted dark forest green—definitely not Pasha's first choice, but it suited Daniel. So did the dark hardwood floors, richly colored throw rugs, and huge, overstuffed pillows that were scattered everywhere. The furniture wasn't new, but it wasn't worn out either. Daniel's television sat in one corner of the room. It wasn't big or fancy, and Pasha wasn't even sure he had cable, but he doubted Daniel's TV got half as much use as the floor-to-ceiling bookshelves that dominated two of the four walls.

What held Pasha's attention the longest, however, was the collection of family photographs hanging over the mantelpiece. Some of the pictures looked so old, they had to be of Daniel's grandparents, maybe even his great-grandparents. Others looked more recent; some were professional photos, others candid shots; some were big, others small. The thing that struck Pasha the most was how happy everyone looked. The only photos Dad kept around their place were of Nadia's kids, and mostly those were just stuck to the refrigerator with magnets, the kind Ivan got from the bank or his insurance agent.

Daniel stood up and pointed out a picture of a young couple standing hand in hand, smiling. She wore a long, beaded dress; he had on a tuxedo, albeit a really hideous one. "That's my ma and pops on their wedding day," Daniel said. Daniel's mother had jet-black hair hanging down past her hips, and his father was a mountain of a man with broad shoulders and strong arms. His hair was about as long as Daniel's. "The next one over is my sister Joyce and her two kids, Josh and Roberta."

Pasha smiled. Daniel's nephew looked about RJ's age and was holding a giant Optimus Prime action figure. "My sister's boy loves Transformers." He felt a pang of loss… potential loss. If Nadia said he could never see RJ again, it would kill him. *Please let this be worth it.*

Daniel wrapped his arms around Pasha's waist and pulled him close. "This okay?" he asked softly.

"It's better than okay," Pasha assured him. He laid his hands on top of Daniel's arms and held them tight while the fire crackled in front of him. Daniel was warm, and his chest against Pasha's back felt so solid, so stable. Pasha closed his eyes and savored the moment. Having Daniel holding him like that felt better than Pasha ever could have imagined. Daniel was so strong, so… *alive*. How could he have HIV?

Except Pasha knew the answer: there were no outward signs of HIV. Anyone could have it.

And I've been with an awful lot of guys this past year. It really was a sobering thought.

Still holding on to Daniel tight, he opened his eyes again scanned the rest of the wall and eventually found what he was looking for: a photo of a pair of identical teenaged boys in red-and-white jerseys, their long hair done into braids, their faces riddled with acne. They had their arms around each other's shoulders, and they were both grinning ear to ear.

"I told you the acne was bad," Daniel said, apparently aware of what Pasha was looking at.

"You were still gorgeous."

"Can you even tell which is me and which is Davey?"

Pasha studied the photo a minute, then glanced over his shoulder at Daniel before looking at the picture again.

"Don't feel bad, no one—"

"You're the one on the left."

"You're just guessing."

Pasha shook his head. "I didn't have to guess. I know that's you."

"How?"

He shrugged. "I just do."

"The only person who never mixed us up was Ma," Daniel told him. "Especially back then." He pressed a soft, warm kiss to the back of Pasha's neck.

Smiling, Pasha tilted his head forward, hoping Daniel would continue. He thought he was going to melt into the floor when Daniel took him up on the silent offer. As the kisses became more fervid, Pasha felt a bulge growing between Daniel's legs and pushed back into it. His own cock was starting to press uncomfortably against his jeans. Pasha's breath hitched in his throat and he let out a little moan—but then Daniel stopped. He laid his chin on Pasha's shoulder and spoke quietly into his ear. "There's a lot of stuff we've gotta talk about before we get too carried away here, Sugar."

"Like what?"

"I said my viral load was next to nothing, not that it was completely undetectable."

And it felt like Daniel was holding his breath, waiting for what Pasha would say next. He turned so they were facing each other and looped his arms around Daniel's waist. "I'm not sure what that really means."

"It means you have to decide what you're comfortable with, how far you're gonna want to go with me. There's no rush," he added quickly. "I don't mean tonight. I just meant in general."

Pasha gave a slow, thoughtful nod. "That sounds a little one-sided," he said. "What about what you want?"

"The important thing to me is that we don't do anything you end up regretting later."

"I'm not going to regret this, Daniel."

"You don't know that yet."

His tone made Pasha wonder if somebody else had said something similar and then ditched and ran after things got intimate. He pressed a soft kiss to Daniel's lips. "The only way to find out for sure is to let it happen." But Daniel stiffened in his arms. "Or we could just watch some TV. I don't want to rush you, either." *God, what would Amy say if she could hear me now?*

Daniel studied his face for a long moment.

"What?" Pasha finally asked.

"I guess… I hope this doesn't screw up my chances here, but I keep waiting for the other shoe to drop. It's been a while since I've had somebody in my arms like this, and I'm realizing how much I missed it." Color tinted his cheeks. "I don't mean… it's not just that you're *anybody*, it's that you're *you*. I hope I'm making sense."

"You are." Movement on the other side of the room caught his attention. "Maybe we'd better eat before your cat decides our dinner is fair game." But before he pulled away, he pressed another kiss to Daniel's lips. When he felt Daniel's tongue brush against his mouth, Pasha opened to him. He deepened the kiss.

DRIFTING up from sleep, Pasha became aware of something heavy on his chest.

It was warm.

It was fluffy.

It was *snoring.*

He groaned and opened his eyes. Alex opened his eyes too. They stared at one another for several long moments in the dark before Alexander stretched out his front legs. One giant furry paw ended up on Pasha's chin. The other ended up on his shoulder.

"Do you mind?" he asked the cat.

Apparently, it didn't mind at all. Alex stretched a little more, just barely pricking Pasha's skin with his claws, then started kneading against his skin, purring at him.

"I suppose this means 'pet me'?" Pasha asked. It must have, because when he pulled one hand out from under the covers, Alex butted his head up against it.

Pasha sighed, but continued to scratch behind the cat's ears. He freed the other hand and reached over to the coffee table for his cell phone. It was four ten. The alarm was set to go off in fifteen minutes. He only vaguely remembered Daniel leaving at three thirty, kissing him good-bye. He smiled. As vague as the memory was, it was a pleasant one. Warmth spread from the pit of his stomach all the way up to his chest. It would have been nicer if they'd slept together, but at the same time, there was something strangely sweet about taking things slow. After dinner they'd made out a little, fully clothed, hands never roaming anywhere they shouldn't go, while the fireplace crackled. Pasha couldn't remember the last time he'd been with a guy and not gone any further than first base.

He checked the time on his phone again. Four fifteen. "Okay, cat, time for me to move—that means you have to move too." As he sat up, Alex maneuvered himself, managing to stay on Pasha's chest until he was almost completely upright. When he finally gave up and jumped onto the floor, he turned and gave Pasha a nasty scowl. "It's not like I *want* to be up. God. Now I'm talking to a cat."

Pasha shut off the alarm on his phone and, after attending to morning necessities, padded into the kitchen in search of coffee. He hoped Daniel had left some in the pot—but there was no pot. He turned around in a slow circle, scanning the countertop, blinking in disbelief.

Okay, he didn't actually remember seeing Daniel drinking coffee, but *everybody* owned a coffee pot. Didn't they? As soon as Pasha started rummaging through the cupboards looking for a coffeemaker—or even a jar of instant coffee—Alex jumped up onto the counter and started pawing at his arm.

"You tell me where he hides the coffee, and there's a whole can of tuna in it for you."

All Alex did was meow.

Right. Not only wasn't there a coffeemaker hiding somewhere, Daniel didn't even have a stash of emergency coffee singles. "Guess his friends don't drink coffee, either."

Fifteen minutes later, Pasha emerged from the shower and got dressed. His phone chirped. It was Daniel, texting him to say he'd be there in ten minutes. Pasha sent a quick text back to confirm he'd be waiting at the curb as planned, then packed his stuff, folded up the blankets, and hurried out the door. Within minutes, a familiar black and silver truck coasted to a stop in front of the house, much to the irritation of the car behind it.

Daniel pulled away from the curb as soon as Pasha had the door shut behind him. He probably hadn't been stopped for more than sixty seconds, but the guy behind them laid on his horn anyway. "Sorry," Pasha muttered. He was still fumbling with his seatbelt.

"Don't sweat it, Sugar. How'd you sleep?"

"Pretty good. But we have a major problem," Pasha told him, deadpan.

Daniel's smile faltered. "What's wrong?"

"I don't think I can see you anymore."

"Why? Did something happen?"

"I can live without sex, but not without coffee. I'm sorry."

Daniel blinked—but then the worry slowly drained from his face. "Do you think I could maybe talk you into giving me a second chance if I promise to get some before the next time you stay over?"

He hesitated, pretending to consider the matter. "Well. You are awful cute. I guess I can give you *one* more chance. But *just* one," he warned gravely.

"Remind me to thank my parents for the genes that gave me such awesome good looks."

"Don't push it, I said 'cute.'" Pasha scowled, but he was having a hard time not laughing.

"How about if I stop off at the nearest Starbucks?"

"That would help. A lot."

Daniel reached over and took hold of his hand. "Does this mean I get a third date?"

Pasha twined his fingers into Daniel's and gave a squeeze. "Yeah, I think so."

PASHA drained the last of his latte just as Daniel was turning onto Main Street. They would be at the diner in less than ten minutes and his stomach was in knots. "I ah… I was wondering about something," he began. "You said you had a doctor you really liked?"

"Yeah. Why?"

"I know I can go to a clinic to get tested, but it's been a while since I had a physical, and I thought maybe, if your doctor sees other people—I mean, does she only see HIV patients or will she see anyone?" Heat warmed his cheeks. He wasn't sure he would ever be comfortable talking about HIV.

"You don't have a regular doctor?" Daniel asked.

"Yeah, but he's Dad's doctor too, and I know all about confidentiality but it just… it would be really weird asking him for an STD test. The last time he saw me, I was fifteen and still a virgin."

"I'll text you with Doc Neumann's number later."

"Thanks."

And they'd reached their destination. In the front window, the Open sign was on, and Pasha could see his father moving around in the dining room. Daniel eased the big truck around the corner, into the lot, right to the spot where he'd been parked the first time they met.

"I guess this is where I get out," Pasha said when they came to a halt. He wasn't ready to leave. "I had a really good time last night."

"Me too. I ah—"

Before Daniel could finish what sounded like an awkward good-bye, Pasha leaned over and pressed a long, slow, sensual kiss to his lips.

"Damn," Daniel swore when they parted, both breathing hard. "I don't know what I did to deserve that, but if you tell me, I'll be sure to do it again."

Pasha smiled. "I told you coffee would help."

"Guess I'd better get that coffeemaker."

"Yes. You'd better."

He shook his head, chuckling softly. But then he sobered. "If anything happens and you need me, call, okay? I'll be on this side of town for the next couple of hours and I will drop whatever I'm doing—"

"Daniel, I'll be fine. Thank you for the offer, but I can handle this."

"Just promise you'll shoot me a text so I know for sure everything's okay."

"I'll text you as soon as I get settled in." He leaned over and pressed another soft kiss to Daniel's lips then grabbed his backpack and hopped out of the truck. "Drive safe."

"Always," Daniel promised.

Pasha watched as Daniel pulled out of the lot. Then he turned toward the restaurant. He wasn't surprised to see Dad waiting for him at the back door. Not just waiting. Watching. *Glaring.* There was no doubt he'd witnessed their kiss good-bye. *But if he didn't want to see it, he shouldn't have been watching.* Steeling himself as best as he could for whatever was going to happen next, Pasha headed toward the door.

"You're late," Ivan snapped.

Pasha bit his tongue on the fact that it was only a few minutes after six and there weren't any customers anyway. Dad was right. He should have been there before six. Not that Pasha thought it would have mattered. If he'd been there at five thirty, Dad would have just found something else to bitch about. He apologized anyway, then hung up his coat and dropped his backpack into the office before heading up front.

The only thing his father should have been doing in the dining room was starting a pot of coffee, and *only* because he wanted a cup himself. What Dad *had* done was nearly all of Pasha's opening sidework. *But none of his own.* There were over three dozen soufflé cups filled with ranch and Greek dressing—which was about three times as many as they needed—and the lemon wedges were overflowing out of the container. The ketchup and mustard bottles were set out, but Pasha doubted they'd been filled or wiped down.

Ivan trailed behind him. "I did your work. Now I'm behind in kitchen," he grumped.

Pasha just nodded. They both knew there was no reason for the old man to have done his sidework, and there was no point in stating the obvious. "You need a hand in there?" Pasha asked instead, his tone neutral.

"Just finish your damned own work."

Pasha got the pitchers of salt and pepper so he could fill up the shakers. Dad was still hovering. "Do you need something?" Pasha asked him.

"You gonna start coming and going whenever the hell you please now?"

"No." He continued working and the old man continued hovering.

"I got enough employees who are always late. I don't need another one."

So it's back to employee. Pasha wondered if he should ask his dad to be paid hourly. He'd figured it out once. If he made what most cooks did per hour, he'd earn a hundred bucks more a week than the salary his father paid him, and that *wasn't* counting the hours he put in waiting tables or all the overtime he worked. Amy was right; he'd make more money and have less grief if he worked somewhere else.

When Pasha didn't answer him, the old man huffed into the kitchen. Pasha headed toward the tables on the other side of the restaurant, out of his father's line of sight, so he could send Daniel a quick text.

Dad's pissy, but not much more than usual. TTYL.

Pasha set his phone on vibrate just in time; Daniel texted back almost immediately. *OK. Call if u need me.*

CHAPTER EIGHTEEN

"HEY, guys," Amy called out as she came in the restaurant's front door, bringing a blast of cold air in with her. She unwound a long scarf from around her neck, took off her coat, and sat down at the counter.

Ivan didn't look up—he'd kept his back turned to the dining room almost the entire morning—but Sean and Pasha both smiled.

"Hey, dude, how's it hangin'?" said Sean.

Amy rolled her eyes at him. It was a little after ten, and technically she should have been Sean's first customer, but he gave Pasha a quick nod and went back to checking messages on his phone.

Pasha poured Amy a glass of ice water and set it down in front her. "How's it going?"

"Not bad. You?" She cast a quizzical look at Ivan's back.

Pasha shrugged. Dad hadn't said more than half a dozen words to him since Daniel dropped him off, but that was fine. Pasha was used to his father being pissed and giving him the silent treatment. What bothered Pasha was that Dad hadn't come out to talk to Nate earlier, when he came in for coffee. The old man said he was too busy to sit around today—only they *weren't* busy. It was as dead as ever. Dad hadn't bitched at Sean over being on his phone either, even though he'd hardly put it down since he got in at nine forty-five. "It's going, I guess," Pasha answered Amy's question.

She looked from him to Ivan's slumped shoulders and back again, then slid from the stool and headed toward the ladies' room, motioning Pasha to follow.

Feeling more than a little dubious but not wanting to say anything where Sean—or worse, Samara—might overhear, he followed Amy into the bathroom and locked the door behind them. *Like this won't look even* more *conspicuous.* But the restaurant was too small to offer a whole lot of privacy, and this was one conversation he didn't want anyone to overhear. It wasn't really a conversation he wanted to have at all. Which was probably why the dirty grout looked so interesting just then....

"Okay, what's going on?" Amy asked.

"Daniel picked me up from the restaurant yesterday and...." He hesitated, but there wasn't any way to beat around the bush on something like this. He forced himself to meet Amy's gaze. "Dad caught us kissing in front of the house."

Her eyes grew wide. "Jesus Clooney Frog! What the fuck were you thinking?"

"That I'd met a guy I really liked and I wanted to kiss him," he offered up weakly.

"I get that, but why did you do it in front of your *own* house?"

"I don't know. I...." He bit his lip. "It's too complicated to talk about here." What would Amy say if he told her Daniel had HIV? *Should* he tell her? She was his friend. Didn't that mean she had the right to know? *Or does Daniel have the right to keep that kind of thing private?*

"Fine. But we're *having* this conversation. Coffee or booze?"

"Booze." There were some conversations that simply mandated alcohol. "My treat."

"Damn skippy it's your treat. Do you know the Emory in Ferndale?"

Pasha shrugged. "Just to drive past it."

"Well, tonight you're going in. Text me when you get out of here and I'll meet you there."

DAD waited until Amy left to tell Pasha that he wanted to see him in the office. With no little trepidation, Pasha trudged into the back. As it was, he knew Samara was going to give her mother an earful of gossip tonight. He didn't want to make it any worse by arguing with Dad in front of her.

Ivan stomped in after him and slammed the door shut. "What you do… mistakes you make… you keep it to *yourself*, you hear me?"

Pasha frowned. "What?"

"You keep your private life fucking *private*! You keep it to yourself!" Ivan yelled louder, as if that would somehow make the message more clear.

"Dad, what are you talking about?"

His face grew redder. "Don't you go spreading your goddamned business all over place like town whore! You keep your fucking mouth *shut*!"

And finally Pasha knew what he was talking about. "Amy's my friend, Dad. I'll talk to her if I want to."

"You're still *my* son," he seethed, slapping his palm to his chest as if to emphasize the point, "and I won't have you running your mouth off, disgracing me in my own goddamned restaurant!" He shook his head, pain and shame replacing anger on his face. "Pasha, you're *good* boy. I don't understand. Why are you doing this to me?"

"This has nothing to do with you. This is about me, *my* life, who *I* love."

"You don't love man, Pasha, *you're* man! You're supposed to find nice girl, get married, have children, not bring shame on me."

"Dad—"

"I raised you. People gonna look at me and wonder what I did to you to make you turn out like this. I don't got no answer for them. I don't know what I did wrong." He sounded completely heartbroken, but when Pasha reached for him, Ivan drew back, clearly not wanting to be touched.

Pasha tried not to let the rejection hurt. "You didn't do anything wrong," he promised softly.

"Then tell me why you're doing this. Don't you know difference between man and woman?"

"Can we please talk about this later?"

"*Nyet*. I want to know what happened to you. Who put these ideas in your head? Did… did somebody hurt you? Touch you?"

"Jesus. Dad. *No*."

"If somebody hurt you, it's not your fault. You can get help." Guilt and hope seemed to be waging a tug of war on Dad's face. "If I wasn't there, if I didn't keep you safe—"

"Dad, listen to me. Nothing like that *ever* happened. This is just… it's who I am, okay?"

"No, it's *not* okay. You're not *pidoras*, Pasha! You're *good boy*. You're my son."

"I love you too, Dad."

"If you love me, you'll stop this nonsense. You'll find nice girl, get married. Have kids. Who's gonna look after you in your old age if got no kids, huh?"

"I…." He wanted kids. He loved children. *But somehow I don't think that's going to happen.* Not with a man who had HIV. "I don't *want* to marry a woman. I don't… I'm gay. I don't look at women the same way you do."

"You don't have to be no fucking gay! Just find nice girl!"

"I can't change who I am."

"Then you don't really love me."

"*Dad*—" The accusation was like a knife to his gut.

Ivan waved him off. "I don't wanna talk to you no more."

Fighting back tears, Pasha nodded. "Yeah, okay. I'm going outside for some fresh air."

"Do whatever the hell you want."

Outside, the sky was crystal clear and the prettiest shade of pale blue Pasha ever seen. The air, however, was bitter cold and chilled him to the core. Pasha walked out to the dumpster, away from the building, out of the line of sight of anyone pulling into the lot. He wiped his cheeks dry and dialed Daniel's number.

Daniel picked up in two rings. "Hey, Sugar. Everything okay?"

"Right now nothing is okay." Which wasn't completely true, but it was close.

"Is there anything I can do?"

"You got a couple minutes?"

"For you I have all the time in the world. What do you need?"

"Just to talk to somebody who doesn't hate me."

"Baby, what happened?"

Pasha drew in a ragged breath and told Daniel about his morning and the fight he'd just had with his father. "I know we never really got along, but now it's like he can't even look at me. And I keep telling myself I'm glad he saw us, I'm glad it's finally out in the open because I was so sick of hiding who I am, but I just… I didn't realize how much this was going to hurt."

There was a moment's hesitation on the other end of the line. "Do you want to take a break, maybe give you and your dad some more time?"

"What do you mean?" He worked over eight hours a day with the old man, lived with him. How much more time did they need together?

"I'm saying maybe we shouldn't see each other again until after the holidays, so you and your dad can sort things out."

For half a second, Pasha's world bottomed out. "We *just* started seeing each other," he protested. "We've had two dates. I don't want to stop going out with you, Daniel. I…." Pasha swallowed back the words. *I think I'm falling in love with you.* "I just needed someone to talk to."

"I can do that. I'll talk—and listen—as much as you want, but if you need time or space—"

"That's the last thing I need."

"I just want you to know you can have whatever you need, okay?"

Pasha smiled. "Just like Mick says, huh?"

On the other end of the line, Daniel laughed. It was a soft, warm rumble in Pasha's ear, and it made him smile. "Yeah. Just like Mick says." He leaned back against the dumpster. "How about sending me your doctor's number so I can make that appointment?"

"I'll shoot you a text as soon as we hang up."

"Thanks. And thank you for talking to me."

"I'll be here, Sugar. Anytime you need me."

They said their good-byes and Pasha hung up. True to his word, Daniel sent a text just a few seconds later. And since there was no time like the present to make the call, Pasha dialed the number and asked about making an appointment for a physical.

"Doc's schedule is pretty full right now," the receptionist explained politely. "If you'd like, I can give you a referral to another physician nearby," he offered.

"No. I mean, yeah, if there's no way to get in I'll take a referral, it's just that my… my boyfriend is one of Dr. Neumann's patients. I was really hoping maybe there was some way she could squeeze me in. It doesn't have to be right away."

The receptionist's tone changed from politely friendly to genuinely cheerful. "All right, let's see what we can do. How long has it been since your last physical?" he asked.

"A few years. I… um…." Pasha licked his lips. "I haven't done anything that would make me think I *need* an HIV test or anything, but I probably should get one while I'm there. Um, and maybe…." He floundered. He'd never made an appointment for an STD test. After he and Michael split up, he just went to a clinic. "Maybe… you know, check for other stuff too?"

"No problem. How does Friday sound?"

Pasha blinked. "This Friday?"

"It's a little bit of a squeeze, but we can get you in at seven, if that works."

"Yeah, sure. Thanks."

"Great. Now, let's get some information."

Pasha swallowed. "Like what?"

The receptionist chuckled. "How about we start with your name?"

Heat rose in his cheeks. "Sorry."

"Don't be. A lot of people are a little anxious the first time they call. HIV is scary, but it's not a death sentence for your partner. It doesn't mean the two of you can't have a perfectly normal, healthy relationship, either."

"Thanks."

AT FIVE thirty, the restaurant was empty except for Art, Jimmy, and Rueben, who sat at their usual table near the back of the restaurant. Pasha sat down at the table closest to the door, which was as far away from them as he could get, and pulled out his phone. He typed *HIV* into the Internet search engine.

Sharon was on him before Google could bring up the first page of hits. "What are you doing?"

He turned his phone so she couldn't see what he was looking up. "Nothing that has anything to do with you."

"Don't you think you should be *working*? You know how your father feels about cell phones."

"Dad's not here right now, and as far as I know, he didn't promote *you* to manager. Why don't you worry about your work, and I'll worry about mine."

She looked so stunned, Pasha was sure that if she were a character in some old movie she would have said something like "I declare!" *Probably in a Southern accent, too.* But all she did was huff for a second before spitting out, "The apple fell an *awfully* long way from the tree, Pasha. You have absolutely no respect for *anyone*, and certainly not your superiors."

"What I have no respect for is a *coworker* who leaves half her sidework for me to do in the morning," he snapped right back. "When you come in, everything is all set, and all you have to do is start taking tables. When *I* come in, I have to stock everything, *make* everything. I'm sick of doing your work as well as my own. I'm even more sick of you acting like a manager when you're not. You're a *waitress* and I've worked here just as long as you have—longer if you count all the stuff I did around this place when I was a kid."

She balked. "You'd better believe I'm going to talk to your father about this when he comes back."

"Go for it. Now, if you'll excuse me?" He gave her an expectant look.

Sharon stomped off in a snit and Pasha returned his attention to his phone and the Internet. He wasn't interested in what Wikipedia had to say about HIV. He wasn't interested in WebMD or the CDC's websites, either. He knew the basics, just like everybody else. What he wanted to know more about was dating and HIV, but what he found wasn't encouraging. Safer sex meant that there would always be a latex barrier between them, maybe even for oral sex. Studies seemed divided on the issue, but if Daniel's viral load ever spiked, it would be safest to use a rubber for everything. And even though Daniel would in all likelihood live a long and healthy life, Pasha was right: someday he *would* get sick and it wouldn't be pretty. The best Pasha could hope for was that they'd keep improving HIV drugs or find a cure.

But the worst thing Pasha found online was what other people had to say about dating and HIV. It wasn't just the religious right, either. On a lark, he Googled the question "would you go out with a guy who had HIV?" It turned out that a lot of people on sites like Yahoo! Answers and LiveJournal had already asked the same question—and some of the answers made him heartsick. They ran the gamut from "Sure, why not?" to "Maybe, but I'd never have sex with him, I don't want to die," to "No, but I wouldn't play naked in traffic either. I'm not suicidal."

Then he read a post on some girl's blog. On it, she said she'd just met a guy who was everything she'd ever wanted in a partner: kind, funny, sexy, sweet, handsome. But most importantly, he was great with her six-year-old daughter, and the little girl really loved him. The only hitch: on their third date, her new boyfriend disclosed that he was HIV positive. Now she had to decide if she should keep seeing him or move on. She liked him, but she was afraid of pretty much all the same things Pasha was afraid of.

Like other questions, her query was met with answers ranging from "If you love him, stick it out and see what happens" to "Why would anyone put their child's life at risk?! Dump him and find someone healthy." One ass hat went so far as to call the woman an unfit mother for not having already dumped her HIV-positive boyfriend. The whole thing made Pasha's stomach turn sour.

But the next response he read stopped him cold. The respondent suggested that the only reason the boyfriend was so "perfect" was because he had HIV. If he were negative, he wouldn't have to be so great, he could—and very probably *would*—be an asshole.

And that made Pasha wonder.

If Daniel wasn't HIV positive, would he have come back to see me, or would he have just gotten directions to where he needed to go, said thank you, and driven off without a second thought? Daniel was gorgeous. Gorgeous men didn't have to settle for ordinary. *But maybe HIV-positive guys do.*

CHAPTER NINETEEN

PASHA picked at the label on his bottle of Bud Light. He shouldn't be drinking beer at all, but it felt strange walking into a bar and just ordering a glass of water. Then he thought about Daniel, who didn't drink, and that invariably made him start wondering about what Daniel *really* saw in him. *Does he like me for who I am or is he just happy to have someone who won't treat him like fucking Typhoid Mary?* Because if that was all it was, then Daniel was no better than the guys Pasha had been fucking all year. They didn't want *him.* They just wanted someplace to stick their dicks.

But God, Daniel didn't act like that was all he was after.

"Are you going to talk to me, or just make a mess?" Amy's sharp tone pulled Pasha up out of his thoughts. She was sitting across from him sipping a cosmo, nibbling on a plate of chili cheese fries.

Pasha knocked back a swig of his beer and looked out the big window at traffic passing by on Woodward. The sky had turned gray toward evening, making everything look gloomy and dark even before the sun set. "I guess I have a lot of stuff on my mind right now," he finally said.

"Gee, ya think?"

He took another big gulp of his beer and was given a few more minutes' reprieve when the waitress arrived with their entrées. Amy was having what he wanted, the chorizo burger. Pasha had opted to stick to his diet and go for the salmon burger. It was good, but Amy's looked better. *And I would just about kill for a side of fries or some onion rings right now.*

He sighed and knocked back the last of his beer. "Me and Dad got into it yesterday. I mean before the kiss," he said before she could crack another sarcastic comment. "And then there was all the stuff Daniel and me had to talk about."

"You mean like how you got so jealous over *nothing* that you went out and almost made the biggest mistake of your life over? *That* stuff?"

He supposed he deserved that. "Yeah." There was more, of course, but it wasn't his place to tell anyone about Daniel's HIV status. Was it? *If we get serious, don't I* have *to tell people?* Someday Daniel was going to get sick; it was inevitable. Shouldn't Pasha tell his friends now so it wasn't a shock later? *But if it was me, would I want my boyfriend of one whole week telling all his friends that I had HIV? Only wouldn't I feel left out of the loop and pretty hurt if my friend started dating a guy who had HIV and didn't tell me?* And what if Daniel cut himself or got hurt while they were out with other people? Wouldn't that be the *worst* time to tell someone they needed to wear gloves or whatever, before going near Daniel's blood? *Or maybe I'm being paranoid.* Pasha couldn't think of a single instance when he'd been out with friends and spontaneously started bleeding. He couldn't even think of any times when he'd gotten a cut, unless you counted the occasional paper cut, which was hardly the kind of wound people rushed to help someone with.

And all of that is assuming we're still dating next week. Because if Daniel wasn't what Pasha really thought he was, he didn't see any point in going out with him. *Except for the part where I'm starting to fall in love.* A dull throb worked its way from the base of Pasha's skull all the way to the back of his eyes.

"Earth to Pasha."

"Sorry, what was that?"

"I *said*, so what happened *after* your dad caught you and Daniel sucking face?"

"He basically called me a faggot, said he'd raised me better than that, and asked if Daniel had somehow put me up to being gay."

Amy rolled her eyes.

"Yeah. But it gets worse. After you left this afternoon, he called me into the office and he chewed me a new one for talking to you.

Apparently I'm shaming *him* by who I love… or, you know." He ducked his head as heat rose in his cheeks.

"You love him and you know it."

"I don't know how I feel," he lied. He wasn't ready to say it aloud, especially not with all the crap rolling around in his head. After all, Daniel had said himself that he used to be a different person. *Would the old Daniel have given me the time of day? Would I have wanted him to?* What if Daniel had been a conceited prick? Pasha took another bite of his salmon burger. "Anyway, after all *that*, Dad wanted to know if I'd been molested as a kid."

"Jesus Christ."

"Yeah. Oh and I almost forgot the part where he told me that all I needed was to find a nice girl and get married and I wouldn't be gay anymore."

"Look, if things get too intense over there, you can crash on my sofa, okay?"

He smiled. "You were the first person I thought of after I realized Dad saw us kissing."

"You know, as flattering as that is, I have to ask: Why don't you have any other friends?"

"Amy, I work, what? Sixty, seventy hours a week? I mean, there are a few guys I hang out at the bar with, but no one I'd want to crash with."

"What about friends from school?"

He shrugged. He'd stayed in touch with some of his friends from high school via Twitter and Facebook, but they'd all gone to college, gotten married and started families. "None of them even know I'm gay."

She reached over and took his hand. "Well, you've got a friend here."

"Thanks."

When Amy excused herself to the ladies' room, Pasha got out his phone. He thought about texting Daniel, but surfed back over to that blog post he'd read earlier, instead. The entry about the HIV-positive boyfriend was dated from two years ago, and it was the last post on the blog. Although there were twenty-four comments from visitors, the blogger herself hadn't responded to any of them or posted any kind of follow-up to let people know what happened. It was a long shot—who checked back to a blog they'd obviously abandoned two years ago?—but Pasha left a comment. He wanted—*needed*—to know if she'd dumped the guy because he had HIV, or if she'd stuck it out, and if so, were they living happily ever after somewhere? He explained that his situation was similar. He'd met a guy who was HIV positive, and while it was getting harder and harder to imagine his life without Daniel in it, there was just so much he was afraid of that he wasn't sure he wanted to pursue the relationship. He felt like an ass hat, but his biggest fear was of how other people would react when they found out his boyfriend had HIV. His second-biggest fear stemmed from what that one guy had said about the blogger's boyfriend: if Daniel had never gotten HIV, would he still have been interested in Pasha, or would he have given him the brush off? *Daniel is gorgeous*, he explained. *I'm just ordinary.*

He posted the comment and signaled the waitress to ask if he could get a shot of tequila. "No lime," he added.

"You can have anything you want if I can see your ID," she replied with a wink.

He smiled back at her—he hated guys who gave servers a hard time, especially when they were just doing their job—and pulled out his wallet.

"Thanks. Be right back."

Amy returned just as Pasha was downing his second shot. "Something you want to talk about?" she inquired.

"No. Maybe." He hung his head. He wanted to talk to Amy about what was bugging him, but there was no way to get into all the things he was afraid of without telling her Daniel had HIV. "Not right now. I… it's not something I'm even sure I *should* talk about. I just need some time to sort it all out."

She didn't look happy, but she didn't press the issue, either.

IT WAS almost eight thirty when Pasha slid behind the wheel of the El Dorado. If he went home now, he'd just have to turn around again to go pick his dad up in an hour. It made more sense to head back up to the restaurant instead, even though the last thing he wanted to do was hang out with Sharon. He started up the car and pulled out his phone. It was a stalling tactic—there was no way the blogger he'd contacted earlier had seen his comment yet—but he checked her blog site anyway.

As expected, his was the last comment on the feed.

She would probably never reply.

He didn't have any new e-mail either, so he surfed over to Facebook, just to see what was going on. Jeff Bellman, one of the guys he'd gone to high school with, was getting a divorce. Pasha typed *sorry man* on his wall. The guy had been married for less than two years. *Then again, better to get out now than end up like Nadia.* Not that he thought there was anything wrong with Jeff's soon-to-be ex-wife, it was just that Pasha's sister was miserable and he knew it.

A little farther down, he saw that Ty had a date with some guy he'd met yesterday at the gym. Sometimes Pasha thought the only reason his friend paid for a membership was to pick up muscle heads. Ty could keep them. Pasha loved Daniel's broad shoulders and strong arms, but he couldn't stand it when a guy got too bulked up. Who wanted to snuggle up against a rock?

He skimmed farther down his "home" page and found a whole lot of nothing: cat pictures, random posts from people he barely knew, silly memes, and e-card wisdom. He was about to close down his browser when he noticed he had a friend request pending. It was from Daniel, and there was an accompanying message:

*Hope u don't mind me "cyber stalking" u. If ur not comfortable accepting, don't sweat it, but I promise not to post pics of rainbows and unicorns. Or cats unless it's Alex. *g**

And I promise I'll never unfriend you. That counts for real life, too.

—D

Warmth surged through him—but it was quickly beaten down again by niggling doubt. How much *did* he know about Daniel?

Pasha clicked on Daniel's Facebook page and hit the About link. His basic information lined up exactly with what Daniel had already told him: he lived in Ypsilanti, he'd grown up in Hannahville, gone to U of M, and currently worked for Taps Microbrewery as a driver/salesman. He was interested in men and women, his political views were "independent," and his religion was "complicated." They hadn't talked religion or politics, but that seemed to fit. Nothing in Daniel's list of "Likes" was a surprise, either. He liked *Bones*, *Buffy*, *Angel*, and a handful of other TV shows, including *Medium*, *Law & Order*, *Criminal Minds*, and *Castle*. He also liked the Independent Players Community Theater, U of M Football, and a few HIV, LGBT, and environmental awareness groups. None of them looked scary or militant. He had a little over a hundred friends, including his parents, his sister, his brother, and a dozen or so other relatives, as well as his boss and some coworkers. A lot of the other people on list seemed to be friends in real life, at least if their comments on his wall were any indication.

And the only cat photos on Daniel's timeline were of Alexander. Pasha smiled. If nothing else, Daniel was honest. *Maybe he's been honest about other stuff, too.*

He accepted the friendship request and started up the El Dorado.

A SCOWL spread across the old man's face as Pasha walked in the backdoor. "What's wrong? Why are you so early?"

Pasha frowned. If he was late, Dad got pissed. If he was *early*, Dad got pissed. *There's just no way to win.* "Nothing's wrong."

"It's not even nine o'clock."

Pasha just shrugged and hung up his coat.

Ivan's scowl deepened as he looked Pasha over. He wasn't dressed up, but he'd stopped off at home to change clothes and shave before meeting Amy at the Emory.

"You go out?" the old man asked.

"I met Amy for dinner."

The statement didn't make Dad look any happier.

Pasha brushed past him and headed into the dining room for a cup of coffee. Sharon was standing talking to Nate and Sam, who were at a back table eating dinner. Pasha didn't say hello to her and she didn't speak to him either. The only other customer in the place was Jimmy, who sat on the other side of the restaurant, engrossed in a book. He was the only one to give Pasha a friendly smile. "Hey, Pasha. How's it going?"

"Pretty good," he lied. "You?"

"Can't complain."

Jimmy went back to his book, and Pasha poured his coffee.

Ivan stepped out of the kitchen. "Pasha? Can I see you for minute?" His tone was surprisingly civil. That didn't mean Pasha thought he was going to like what the old man had to say, but he followed him anyway.

Ivan walked around the corner into the prep area, taking them out of the line of sight of the dining room. He turned to Pasha and studied him for a long moment, as if he was trying to gather his thoughts. Finally, he spoke, his voice still calm. "Pasha, you gotta listen to me. Some things not other people's business. I know you think Amy's your friend—"

"She *is* my friend, Dad."

The old man's jaw tightened. "Fine. So she's your friend. But you don't gotta tell your friends everything. What if you change your mind? What if you find nice girl?"

"It's not *about* finding a nice girl." It was all he could do to keep his voice down. "It's about who I like, who I'm attracted to."

"You're not *pidaros*, Pasha. You're good boy." It sounded more like a plea than a statement.

"Dad… I wish I…." But even if he could, he wouldn't change who he was. There had been too many sleepless nights, too many long, hopeless hours spent wondering what was wrong with him, wondering if God was punishing him somehow, or testing him, maybe. He'd finally come to terms with his sexuality, and he was never going back to being that miserable. "I wish I wasn't such a disappointment to you. *Prastee.*" *I'm sorry.*

"You're not disappointment to me, Pasha," Ivan said, speaking in Russian. Pasha had never seen his father looking so heartbroken. "I love you. I only want you to be happy. I want you to have wife, children. I want you to be *normal.*"

"Dad—"

"Is this because we didn't let you play baseball?"

Pasha frowned. What did baseball have to do with anything?

Ivan continued in Russian. “Are you all mixed up because you were always here, always working? Never having time for sports or to spend with girls?”

Since Dad was speaking in Russian, Pasha did too. “You think I’m….” Except he couldn’t think of any Russian words for “gay” that weren’t insulting or demeaning. He settled for asking, “You think I’m this way because I didn’t get to try out for baseball?”

“I don’t know what to think. I don’t know why you turned into *pidaros*. What did I do wrong?”

“Dad, stop. Please. You didn’t do anything wrong. People don’t turn *gay*”—Dad’s face reddened when he said “gay” in English—“this is just the way I was born.”

“No!” Ivan slammed his palm against the counter. “You weren’t born this way. Nobody’s born this way!” More than angry, he sounded desperate—desperate for there to be a reason, desperate to understand it. “Somebody did something to you. Somebody touched you, hurt you. Somebody *forced* you. I read on website about what older men do to boys.”

“Dad, my first crush was on an actor. I was *twelve*. He was on TV—*and* he’s straight. I didn’t meet anyone else like me until I was… Jesus. I was seventeen the first time I went to a bar, okay? I swiped Peter’s ID,” he explained.

“You…?”

“I’m not saying it was smart. I’m just trying to tell you that I went there on my own. Nobody forced me and it had nothing to do with you.”

“How could you know you were… like this… when you were only a kid?”

“The same way you knew you liked girls, Dad.”

Ivan looked like someone had punched him in the gut.

“I’m not trying to upset you. I just want you to understand that I’ve always been like this. You don’t get to choose who you’re attracted to. It just happens.”

“It doesn’t just happen!” But it sounded like he was losing some internal argument. “I taught you right from wrong, Pasha.”

“Yes, you did.”

“This is *wrong*.”

Pasha picked up his coffee and started toward the dining room.

"Don't you turn your back on me!" Ivan snapped in English.

Pasha answered in Russian. "I'm not. I just can't argue with you about this anymore. Life is too short to fight all the time. You don't ever have to meet Daniel. You don't have to hear about him. And I wish to God you'd stop asking me questions you don't want the answers to because I'm sick of fighting, but I'm not going to lie to you about who I am anymore. Last year I was seeing someone I really cared about—"

"You had girlfriend?" he asked in dismay, slipping momentarily back into English.

Pasha answered in Russian so no one but his father would understand. "No. I had boyfriend."

"*Kto*?" *Who?*

"You remember my friend Michael? The one you said I spent too much time with?"

"He… was your…?" He couldn't seem to say the word in any language.

Pasha continued on in Russian. "He wanted me to move in with him. I told him I couldn't, not with everything we had going on here. I couldn't leave you, I couldn't leave this place. So he broke up with me and… you don't have to understand it, you just need to know that I'm not going to make the same mistake twice."

"You would *leave*? You would choose some *pidaros* over your own family? Is *that* how I raised you?"

"I'm not Peter," he snapped, still speaking Russian. "I won't leave unless you tell me to, and then it's on you, not me. But I won't give up the man I… someone who makes me happy just because you don't like what I'm doing."

"You… you *love* this… *moosheenah*?"

At least Dad had called him a man instead of a *pidaros*. Pasha supposed that was something. "We haven't been going out long enough to start talking about love. I just know I…" *want him.* He'd answered his own question. He didn't care who Daniel was six years ago. He loved who Daniel was now. Pasha wasn't the same person he'd been six years ago, either. He never would have stood up to his father back then. *And Daniel said he didn't want just anybody, he said he wanted me.* Pasha didn't have any reason not to believe that. "I really like this guy and I want it to work out," he told his father in Russian.

"It's *shameful.*"

"And that's why we can't talk about it."

"Because you're ashamed?" He sounded almost triumphant.

"No. Because you are."

"How else am I supposed to feel?"

"I don't know." He turned on his heel and headed toward the dish room, but he didn't get far.

"Pasha." Ivan's tone was sharp.

"What?" He was so tired, so worn out. *So sick of fighting.*

Ivan hesitated. He looked tired and worn out, too. "After you finish your coffee, tell Sharon she can go home. You wait tables."

He frowned—but then nodded. Maybe this was Dad's way of punishing him for how he'd spoken to Sharon earlier. *Or he's trying to punish me for being gay.* It didn't matter and there was no point in arguing. Pasha took his cup to the dish room and dumped the stone-cold coffee into the sink.

"Everything okay?" Kaja asked quietly, casting a wary glance toward the kitchen.

"Not really."

Kaja was the kind of guy Pasha had avoided in high school, tall and thin, with a scraggly goatee, long hair, and tattoos up and down both his arms. And maybe back in high school, Kaja was someone who should have been avoided; by his own admission, he'd been a troublemaker. But in the six months Pasha had known him, he'd felt nothing but respect for the other man. Kaja worked hard and never complained, even when he had every right to. "Anything I need to worry about?" he asked.

"It'll blow over. It always does."

Kaja wiped his hands off on his apron. "Since you're here, does that mean your dad wants me to pack it up and head home?"

"He told me to send Sharon home tonight." *Let's just hope she doesn't shoot the messenger.* Maybe that was his real punishment, telling Sharon Dad wanted her to go home at nine fifteen.

Kaja cast another quick glance toward the kitchen before telling Pasha, "Her and your dad have been sniping at each other all night."

"What do you mean?"

"Right after you left, Sharon laid into him. I tried to stay as far away as I could. But then you come back and all I hear is Russian coming from the kitchen." He shrugged. "I just wanna make sure I've still got a place to work."

"We're not in that kind of trouble yet." But he understood why Kaja was worried. He had a wife and a five-year-old son at home, and the diner was his only job. Instead of going to college after high school, he'd gone to prison for five years. Even when the economy was good, guys like Kaja had a hard time finding jobs. "Me and Dad weren't fighting about the business," Pasha assured him.

"You know I appreciate everything you and your dad have done for me," he said tentatively, like he wasn't real used to saying "thank you."

"We appreciate you too." Pasha answered. He gave Kaja's shoulder a quick squeeze and headed out to the dining room, where he found Sharon standing at the counter, wrapping silverware. She didn't look up until he was standing right next to her, and her smug expression gave Pasha the impression she'd misinterpreted his and Dad's tense conversation in the kitchen. Knowing she was wrong didn't make him feel any better. "Dad says you can go home. He wants me to take over on the floor."

"It's not even nine thirty."

Pasha shrugged; he could tell time just as well as she could.

She frowned—then threw down the silverware roll she'd been working on and marched into the office to get her coat and purse. A moment later, the back door slammed. When Pasha looked up, he saw Nate glaring. Sam seemed to be trying not to look at him at all.

It was going to be a long night.

CHAPTER TWENTY

"LET me ask you something."

"Dad, please, I'm sick of fighting." He'd taken a couple of ibuprofen, but his head was still throbbing.

"I don't wanna fight, I just wanna know something." It was eleven thirty and they were leaving the restaurant for the night. Sam and Nate had left shortly after Pasha came on the floor, and Jimmy stuck around until ten. No one else came in. Even though it was dead, the old man had kept Kaja on until closing, so for once all the night sidework actually got done.

Pasha sighed, set the alarm, and stepped out into the cold, biting wind. "What do you want to know?"

"How you gonna be happy with *moosheenah*, with *pidaros*?"

"*Stop it*!"

Ivan looked stunned by his outburst. "What?" He sounded genuinely startled, too.

"Stop asking questions you don't want the answers to!"

"What if I *do* want answers? What if I want to know how my son's gonna be happy with no family, no kids? What if I want to know who's gonna take care of you when you're old man like me?"

Before he found out Daniel had HIV, he would have told his father they could always adopt—and maybe they still could if things really worked out. *Can a guy with HIV adopt?* Hell, did Daniel even want to? *Do I?* Didn't he have enough to worry about without bringing children into the mix? *Or am I being unfair by deciding that all on my own, without even talking to Daniel?*

And maybe he was assuming too much anyway. There was no guarantee he and Daniel would stay together long enough to worry about whether or not to start a family. "I don't have the answers to any of those questions, Dad," he told his father as the headed toward the El Dorado.

"So why not find nice girl? You could get married, have children. You're gonna need somebody to take over restaurant when you want to retire."

They'd lose the business long before Pasha had to worry about that, but that wasn't the important part. "Do you really want me to lie to some girl?" he asked his father.

Ivan frowned. "Who said anything about lying?"

"I don't *like* women, at least not the same way you do. Getting into a relationship with one—marrying her—that would be the worst kind of lie there is." Judging by his father's expression, Dad had honestly never thought about in those terms before. Maybe now he would. "Now will you please stop needling me?" Pasha begged.

"Who's needling?"

"*You* are."

Ivan heaved a sigh and handed over the keys. "You drive. I'm tired."

Pasha didn't argue. He took the keys and unlocked the passenger side door, then went around to the other side to get in. In his pocket, his phone buzzed, but he let it go to voice mail. It was probably Daniel, and he felt guilty about ignoring the call—he hadn't texted or called Daniel all night—but he just wanted to get home. He was tired, too. He started up the car. "You're picking at this like you'd pick at a scab," he told his dad. "Every time you pick it, it hurts both of us. Please just give it a rest." He eased out of the lot and headed toward I-696.

"I got nobody else to talk to, Pasha." The old man sounded so despondent. It hadn't occurred to Pasha that he was the only person his father could talk to about it, but it made sense. "Nobody else gonna understand how you turned out like this. *I* don't understand it."

"Maybe if you did some reading—"

"*Ya cheetal*! I've *been* reading! For two days I've been reading Internet and *nothing* makes any sense. One person says it's natural, it's okay, but I know it's *not* natural. Men not meant to lie with other men, everybody knows that! Then on different website, that's exactly what they say, it's not natural, not normal. It's abomination." It seemed to hurt him to say the word almost as much as it hurt Pasha to hear it. "But it's not your fault if someone hurt you, only I don't want to think about anybody ever touching you like that." He sent Pasha a pleading look.

"For the last time, no one ever…." He bit his tongue on the word "rape." Dad didn't need to hear that. He was tearing himself up enough as it was. "No one hurt me, okay? No one touched me. No one forced me into anything."

"*Da*, okay. I just don't understand none of this. I read somewhere else where they say this kind of thing happens when boy doesn't learn how to be man, when he doesn't play sports or do things boys are supposed to do. But you never tried to dress up in women's clothes or play with dolls. You wanted to play sports, we just didn't let you."

"Dad, listen. My sexuality isn't your fault. You had nothing to do with it. Not all gay men are… just forget about the stereotypes." God, he was glad Dad had never met Ty. "Maybe I can't change my own oil, but I don't want to wear high heels and makeup and… look, I know I said that I wouldn't talk to you about him, but Daniel played football and hockey—and he was in theater and he sings and he's got a twin brother who's totally straight."

"He's got twin?"

"Yeah. An identical twin."

"And he's not *pidaros*?"

"If you don't stop using that word, this conversation is over."

Ivan opened his mouth then shut it again. "I don't understand none of this nohow." He turned to watch the scenery go by outside the passenger window.

Pasha didn't comment. Instead he nibbled at his lower lip as the miles ticked by. "What would you say if I asked Sean or Amy to pick up Sunday for me?" he finally asked as they neared their exit.

The old man frowned. "What? You need another day off?"

"I meant every Sunday."

"You… want… *what*?" he asked, sounding genuinely confused.

"I don't want to work seven days a week anymore, Dad. I never did."

"You think *I* want to work seven days a week! I was supposed to be retired already! You and Peter were gonna take over—"

"Peter was never going to take over the business. He never wanted it."

Ivan didn't respond. He just stared out at the road ahead.

"I'm sorry things didn't work out the way you'd planned," Pasha said quietly.

"You and your brother are exactly alike. Each of you doing whatever you want and to hell with who you hurt."

Pasha took a breath and let it out, counting silently to ten and back down again. He didn't speak until he was certain he could sound calm. "I'm not the one who left. That was Peter. Don't blame me for him hurting you."

"You didn't leave, you just…." He shook his head. "You're gonna be owner someday, Pasha. You gotta take responsibility for yourself."

"I wish you'd make up your mind."

"What the fuck is that supposed to mean?"

"It means that when you want me to feel guilty about something, you remind me that I'm going to be the owner someday. When you're pissed and want me to shut up, you tell me I'm an employee who's expected to do whatever you tell him to. Which is it? Do I work for you or am I your partner?"

The old man's jaw tightened. "You're my *son*. Place gonna be yours someday. I want you to fucking act like it."

"If you want me to act like an owner, how about treating me like one?"

"When you show *me* respect, maybe I'll show *you* respect," Ivan retorted.

"I do respect you, and for what it's worth, I don't think you should be working seven days a week, either. Your doctor—"

"Ah!" Ivan waved it aside. "What does he know? Doctors are all damn fools."

Pasha took another deep breath and let it out. "The bottom line is that I'm not going to work on Sunday anymore."

"Fine. You don't wanna work no goddamned Sundays, you don't gotta work no goddamned Sundays. But don't you expect me to *pay* you for Sunday, neither!"

"I suppose that's fair." Which wasn't really true. He wasn't paid fairly as it was, but he wasn't going to argue about it, especially when Dad was giving in and giving him his Sundays. "Maybe we could work something out so you don't have to work so many hours, either," Pasha suggested.

"How we gonna do that, huh? We can't afford to pay another cook."

"I know, but if we hired another server, I could cook full time and you and me could switch off in the kitchen. You could open some days and I could close, or vice versa." It would mean a cut in Pasha's income. On a good day he could make fifty or sixty bucks in tips—not that there were very many good days anymore. But they could afford to pay another server two fifty an hour a lot more easily than they could afford to pay a cook at twelve or fifteen bucks an hour. Maybe if Dad took some time off—got some rest—he'd feel better, be less unhappy. *Live longer.*

"You don't have car, remember? How we gonna 'switch off' if we gotta drive in together?"

"I'm working on that."

"You can't afford no car."

"I've got some money saved, and I was looking on Craigslist the other day. There were a lot of cars in my price range—"

"It's not just cost of *car*, Pasha, it's gas, it's insurance. What you gonna do when it breaks down, huh? You don't need car. And we don't need to make no changes at restaurant neither. Things fine the way they are."

Jesus Christ, De-Nile really isn't just a river in Egypt. "Dad, we *do* need to make changes. The place is going under."

"I told you. You let me worry about money. You just do your job."

"If my job is to be your partner—"

"Your job is to… to do your fucking job!" he snapped.

Pasha was never happier to pull into his driveway. His head was throbbing and all he wanted was to go to bed, but after Dad got out of the car and headed up to the house, Pasha got his phone out of his pocket. Instead of seeing Daniel's number on the caller ID, he saw Amy's. She'd left him a voice mail.

"I don't know if I should be calling you"—her voice trembled and it sounded like she was barely holding back the tears—"but I…. Brett… some kids attacked him. They beat the shit out of him, Pasha!" A sob broke free. "I made some calls but… I'm all alone right now in this stupid fucking hospital and I could really use a friend. We're at Beaumont. In Royal Oak. Gimme a call, okay? Maybe by the time you get this, I'll have some good news." She sniffled and disconnected the call.

Pasha sat there, trying to absorb what she'd said. Some kids had beat the shit out of Brett? *Why?* Pasha barely knew him, but he felt sick to his stomach. *Please let him be all right.* It was an earnest prayer. He started the car back up and called the house phone as he eased the El Dorado back down the driveway toward the street.

Dad picked up on the first ring. "Pasha?" His silhouette appeared in the kitchen window, and then the curtain pulled back and he peered out into the yard. "Where are you going?"

"That was Amy who called me earlier—"

"She okay?"

"*Nyet*," he answered without thinking. "I mean, yeah, she's fine, but a friend of hers is in the hospital. It sounds like…." *It sounds like a fucking gay bashing*, but he didn't know that for sure, so he shouldn't jump to conclusions. "He was attacked by some kids. I think it's pretty bad and Amy's all alone. I'm going to go sit with her for a while."

"*Da*, yes, of course. Go."

"Thanks, Dad."

“Pasha,” he said quickly, before Pasha hung up. “Call me when you know something, okay?”

“I will.”

He disconnected with his father and tried Amy again. When he got her voice mail, he left the message that he was on his way and then tried texting her. He prayed the only reason she wasn’t picking up was that she was somewhere in the hospital where she had to have her phone turned off, that it didn’t mean something awful. Feeling frustrated and helpless, Pasha dialed Daniel’s number. There was nothing Daniel could do, but hearing the sound of his voice would make Pasha feel better.

And just a little guilty too. He’d been putting off calling Daniel all day because he wasn’t sure what to say and now he was calling because he needed him.

“Hey, Sugar,” Daniel said when he picked up. His smile was audible. “I was about to hit the hay. What’s up?”

“Hi, sorry to call so late.”

There was a pause. “What’s the matter?”

“I ah… I just got off the phone with Amy.” He told Daniel about Brett being in the hospital; he just didn’t tell him how he knew Brett. “It sounds… he’s gay. It sounds like….” He swallowed hard.

“Do you want me to come sit with you?”

“It’s late.”

“So?”

“You barely know Amy. You’ve never met Brett.”

“They’re your friends, Pasha. They’re important to you and you’re important to me.”

“I….” For several seconds, words completely failed him. “You have to work in the morning,” he finally stated the obvious.

“I’ve already got my coat on. Just tell me what hospital.”

“Beaumont, Royal Oak. But I don’t know what room he’s in or anything.”

“Call me when you find out.”

"I… thank you. You don't have to do this."

"I want to, Sugar."

WILLIAM BEAUMONT Hospital's Royal Oak campus was a huge, sprawling affair. Five or six years ago, the restaurant had regularly gotten hospital staff coming in for breakfast and lunch, sometimes dinner. But little by little, those customers started going elsewhere. Whether it was for better food or faster service, Pasha didn't know. It wasn't like there weren't fifty other restaurants between them and the hospital.

He pulled into the parking deck nearest the ER and suddenly realized he had no way of tracking Amy or Brett down. He didn't even know Brett's last name. It was fucked up; they'd screwed and the only thing he could tell anyone about Brett beyond a vague physical description was that he liked rum and Coke, easy on the Coke. He was about to call Amy again when his phone rang. It was her. "Perfect timing, I just got here. Is there any news?" He stepped out of the car and headed for the building.

"Nothing. He's been in surgery for the last hour." She bit back a snuffle. "They said it might be a while before they knew anything, but…." The sniffle turned into a sob. "God, why would anyone do something like this? Brett's a good guy!"

"I don't know why stuff like this happens." He walked through the enormous glass rotating door and into the ER lobby, but Amy was nowhere in sight. "Where are you?"

She sucked in a ragged breath. "Standing in the main lobby waiting for Mark. I need a fucking cigarette, but I'm afraid to go outside." She took in another shaky breath. "You didn't have to come. I would have been fine with a phone call." But she sounded happy he'd shown up in person.

"What are friends for? I'll be there in a few minutes, okay?"

"Yeah. Thanks."

After disconnecting the call, Pasha stopped the first employee he spotted, a middle-aged woman wearing pink scrubs and an ID badge, and asked for the best way to get to the main lobby. Less than ten minutes later, Amy was wrapping her arms around his neck, hanging on as if for dear life, sobbing.

"Shhh," Pasha soothed as he guided her to a sofa so they could sit down together. "What happened?"

"I got a call from Brett's boss… Brett was… he was attacked by some kids and… Trish, that's his boss, she's upstairs in the waiting room, but Leon's in New York and Mark hasn't gotten here yet and Teddy's working and I can't even get ahold of Ben!" The words tumbled out in a rush.

Pasha feathered a soft kiss to her forehead. "What about Brett's family?"

"They don't care about him." She wiped the tears from her cheeks. "How's this for fucked up: Brett's sister Madison was my best friend for… for fucking ever. But when Brett came out his whole family just flipped right the fuck out. His parents forced him into 'therapy.' It was awful. Maddie said she hated him—they're the kinds of people that give Christians a bad name. And because I refused to stop being Brett's friend, Maddie stopped being mine. We went to the same stupid middle school, the same high school—we had classes together and she wouldn't even *look* at me. I haven't seen her in six or seven years. He hasn't either."

Christ. Pasha was suddenly grateful for his own fucked up family because even though the old man wasn't exactly embracing his sexuality, Pasha was still sure his dad would be there in a heartbeat if he ended up in a hospital. "Isn't there anybody in his family who would want to know what's happened?"

"His great-aunt Natalie took him in when his parents kicked him out. That was after the 'therapy' didn't work. But she died a couple years ago. Some kind of cancer."

Pasha used the cuff of his sleeve to wipe mascara-darkened tears from Amy's cheeks. "How bad was he hurt?" He finally asked what he wanted to know, even though he was afraid of the answer.

Her expression turned angry. "It took me almost half a fucking hour to convince the nurse that I was the only family he has, that none of his blood relatives were actually going to fucking show up! Trish backed me up. If she hadn't…. Goddamn, I hate these people! They didn't want to tell me anything because I'm not fucking family." She shook her head as if to clear it. "Trish told me that those kids—teenagers, like sixteen and eighteen years old—she said there were five or six of them in the store causing trouble and when Brett asked them to leave they started hassling him. Trish had to threaten to call the cops to get them to go. Then when it came time to close up, Brett took the trash out and he was gone for an awful long time." She was crying again. "So Trish went out back to check on him and… and… and they were holding him down and… and just beating the shit out of him! Hitting him. *Kicking* him. She screamed, but… but there was nothing she could do except call the cops and wait. By the time anybody got there, the kids were gone and Brett… they pounded his face in, Pasha." Amy dissolved into ragged sobs again and all he could make out was broken ribs, a fractured something, and internal bleeding. It didn't sound good.

Holding Amy, it occurred to him that he didn't even know where Brett worked. How could he know so little about the guy? "What do the doctors think? I mean, he's going to be okay, isn't he?" *Please God, don't let him die.*

"I don't know."

"What did the police say?"

She shrugged. "Who knows? There were detectives here talking to Trish earlier, but they didn't sound like they were going to put a whole lot of effort into finding the assholes who did this."

"Why not?"

"Because he works at Dorothy's Closet." Which was one of the largest LGBTQ bookstores in Metro Detroit, but it was located in one of the least savory neighborhoods. "You know what Detroit cops are like," Amy added. "Trish told them as much as she could, and I saw one of the detectives talking to the doctors, but I don't know what about. I'm not fucking family."

"Yes you are," he told her. "You're here. That's what counts."

Amy managed a weak smile. "Thank you."

Pasha pressed a kiss to her cheek. He didn't promise that it would be all right, but he prayed it would be. He didn't know what Brett wanted to do with his life, but he prayed that whatever it was, none of his injuries would keep him from doing it. When he opened his eyes, he spotted Mark walking in the revolving door on the far side of the main lobby and waved to get his attention. The worry etched on Mark's faced morphed into an angry grimace as he made his way over.

Mark took a seat on Amy's other side and pulled her over to him. "Amy, what's going on, what happened?"

Pasha sat and listened while Amy repeated the story. She was only marginally more composed the second time through and seemingly totally oblivious to the way Mark kept glaring at him. Pasha did his best to ignore it; he was there for Amy, not Mark.

"Why don't we go up to the waiting room?" Pasha suggested when she finished talking. "Maybe there's news." He only hoped that if anything had changed, it was for the better.

Amy nodded and all three stood up. Mark looked over at Pasha. "Thanks for being here, but you don't have to stick around. We're good." It sounded like he was doing his level best to keep a civil tongue. It wasn't working.

"I don't mind hanging out for a while," Pasha replied evenly.

Amy looked over at him. "Fuck, I just realized how early you have to be up tomorrow."

"It's okay," he said.

"You sure? I mean, I…." She swallowed hard, but it looked like she was all out of tears.

"I'll be here as long as you need me," he promised her.

Mark's expression darkened further, but Amy smiled. "Thanks, Pasha. We're up on the fifth floor." She started toward the elevators, but Pasha held back.

"I'll be up in a sec. I promised Dad I'd give him a call when I knew more."

Amy nodded and Pasha watched as she and Mark made their way toward the bank of elevators. He wasn't sure if Dad would still be up or not, but he'd promised, so he called.

The old man picked up at once. "*Da*, Pasha? Amy okay?"

"She's fine, Dad," Pasha assured him. "Her friend was jumped by a bunch of sixteen and seventeen-year-olds. He's in surgery now. I'm going to sit with her for a while more."

"*Da*, yes. I'll see you in morning?"

"I'll be home in time for work," he promised.

"You try and get some sleep. And you tell Amy I'll keep her friend in my prayers, okay?"

"Thanks. I love you, you know."

"*Ya tebya loobloo, tozhye*, Pasha," he answered back without hesitation.

Warmth surged through Pasha's chest—then he spotted Mark stepping back out of the elevators. "I've gotta go. See you in the morning." Pasha hung up and turned to face Mark.

"Why don't you just go the fuck home already? We don't need you here."

"Amy called me—"

"She called a lot of people."

"Look, Mark, I don't know what your deal is—"

"My deal? I don't have a 'deal.' You're not Brett's friend. You're not even Amy's friend. You're just some guy who… look, Brett's fucked a lot of guys. Being one of them doesn't make you special."

Pasha opened his mouth, then closed it again. The words stung, but this wasn't the time to say all the things he wanted to say in response to Mark's dig. "I have one more call to make and then I'll be up," he replied calmly.

"Why are you being such an asshole? Go the fuck home!" Mark pushed him hard enough that Pasha almost lost his balance.

Several nurses and a security guard looked their way, but before anyone could do anything, Pasha said, his tone still calm, "I get it that you don't want me here. Amy does. Maybe I haven't known her as long as you have, but she *is* my friend, so I'm staying. Excuse me." He turned away from Mark and dialed Daniel's number.

Mark stalked off.

BEN and Teddy arrived shortly after Pasha got up to the waiting room. When Pasha offered his hand, Teddy pulled him into a fierce hug. "Good to see you again," he said as he squeezed Pasha tight. "I just wish the circumstances were better."

"Definitely," Ben agreed, taking Pasha into his arms after his partner finally let him go. "Thanks for coming." He kissed the top of Pasha's head like they were old friends.

Mark glowered. Amy still didn't seem to notice his animosity toward Pasha, but Pasha saw the dark look Teddy shot at Mark.

Trish, Brett's boss, seemed too preoccupied with her own thoughts to pay either of them any attention. She was a petite woman, maybe in her midforties, and no matter how many times Pasha or Amy told her it wasn't her fault, she kept saying how she wished she'd done more to stop the attack. But if she'd tried to get in the middle of it, she'd be in surgery too—or worse. With no one to call the police, she and Brett might both still be lying behind her store, unconscious. It was a chilling thought, but when Pasha said it aloud, Trish just shrugged.

Daniel showed up at a little after one. Pasha got to his feet the second he saw him, and an instant later, Daniel's strong arms were wrapped around his shoulders. Pasha hadn't realized until that moment how raw and ragged he felt. "Thank you so much," he said softly.

"Anytime, Sugar."

As he sagged against Daniel's warmth, he closed his eyes, praying fervently—selfishly—that Mark didn't decide *this* was a good time to mention what Pasha's connection to Brett really was.

But it was Amy who made the introductions.

Mark shot Pasha another dirty look when she referred to Daniel as Pasha's boyfriend. Pasha could guess what Mark was thinking, but thankfully, Daniel didn't seem to notice.

"I'm glad you're here," Amy added when Daniel had finished shaking hands with everyone.

“I’m glad Pasha called me,” he replied. Daniel sat down in the chair Pasha had occupied, tugged Pasha into his lap, and wrapped his arms securely around Pasha’s waist.

Not having the will or even the desire to fight it, Pasha snuggled into the comfort of his embrace. Now wasn’t the time to worry about who might see him curled up in a man’s lap or what Mark thought of him. Pasha closed his eyes and let his whole world become the warm, woodsy scent of Daniel’s cologne and the soft steady beating of their hearts.

“Try and get a little sleep, Sugar,” Daniel whispered. “I’ll wake you up when they come in with some news.”

The offer was too good to refuse, but before he let himself give over to it, he opened his eyes again and reached for Amy’s hand. “You should get some sleep too,” he told her.

Amy nodded. Still holding on to Pasha’s hand, she leaned over and laid her head against Mark’s shoulder.

Chapter Twenty-One

"PASHA... babe." The soft rumble of Daniel's voice brought Pasha back to consciousness. It took him several long moments to figure out why Daniel was waking him up and not his alarm clock, why he was sitting Daniel's lap, why the room was so bright.

Then he remembered. Brett had been attacked. He was in a hospital waiting room.

"Brett just got out of surgery," Daniel told him in a quiet tone.

Pasha nodded. He noticed Amy and Teddy on the other side of the room talking to an older man in light-blue scrubs. The rest of the group was sitting, waiting, looking worried.

"What time—?" he asked Daniel.

"Almost 4:00 a.m."

Brett had been in surgery for five hours? Maybe closer to six. Crap. That didn't bode well.

"We don't know anything yet." Daniel stroked his cheek. "And just 'cause it took so long to fix whatever needed fixing doesn't mean it's bad."

"Thank you."

"For what?"

"Coming when I called. Staying with me. You didn't have to. I mean...." Daniel must have called off work to hang around so long.

He pressed a soft, sweet kiss to Pasha's lips. "Nothing to thank me for, Sugar. Like I said, Brett's important to you and you're important to me. That's all I needed to know."

"Yeah." His conscience nagged at him. He should tell Daniel the truth, but….

The doctor made his exit and Amy and Teddy came back over. Amy looked like she was going to start crying all over again.

Teddy put his arm around her shoulders. "He's in recovery," he said. Ben reached up and took his hand. "Overall, the surgery went well, but um, they're not sure when he's going to wake up."

Amy failed in stifling a sob.

Teddy pulled her closer. "The truth is, they don't know for sure that he will or… or what kind of, he ah…." He cleared his throat. "There was a lot of trauma to his head. They won't really know… well. There's a lot they don't know right now." He let go of Ben's hand so he could put both his arms around Amy's shoulders. "We're going to stick around, but the doctor said… there isn't anything anyone can do. There's no need for everybody to stay. It could be hours or days or… well." He shrugged and feathered a kiss into Amy's hair.

"I'm staying, too," Mark told him.

"Mark," Teddy began.

"*I'm staying.*"

Teddy nodded. Ben climbed to his feet, Pasha stood, and then Daniel got up too. Trish was already up. Pasha wondered if she'd sat down all night, or if she'd just paced the whole time. "We'll keep everybody posted," Ben promised.

Amy pulled away from Teddy and wrapped her arms around Pasha's shoulders. "Thank you for coming last night," she whispered. "I was sure I was going to fall apart."

"You're welcome, Amy. I just wish…." But what more could anyone do? "Let me know when he wakes up, okay?"

"I will. Promise." She looked up at Daniel. "Thank you."

"Anytime."

Amy stood back and Daniel helped Pasha with his coat. When Daniel hesitated, Pasha reached for his hand. Life was way too short to worry about anyone seeing him holding hands with another man. *The man I love.*

"When do you have to be in to work?" Daniel asked as they reached the elevators.

"We open at six."

"I guess that means you need to get going now, huh?"

Pasha nodded. "Yeah. Sorry."

"No worries, Sugar."

"I feel like I owe you something. You came all the way out here."

"You don't owe me anything, except maybe a phone call later, when you find out how your friend is doing."

"Daniel, I… will you walk out to my car with me?"

"Sure."

He waited until they were clear of the building to start talking, not that it took him very long to tell Daniel that he barely knew Brett, that they'd only met once, a couple of weeks ago, and within an hour of saying "hello," they were in Ben and Teddy's bathroom screwing. "I don't even know his last name," he confessed. They'd arrived at the El Dorado, and Pasha looked up at Daniel. It was impossible to tell what he was thinking. "I'm sorry."

"What for?"

"Not being a better person."

"Babe, I am the last person on God's green earth who should be judging anybody. All I care about is where we go from here. What you did before we started going out isn't my business. As long as you meant what you said about wanting it to be just you and me?" he questioned.

"*I meant it*. But I… there's one more thing." Pasha shoved his hands into his pockets. "I was kind of avoiding you yesterday."

"I thought you might've been."

Damn. A part of him had hoped Daniel wouldn't notice. "So why'd you come out last night?"

Daniel shrugged. "You called me. It sounded like you needed a friend."

"But—"

"Pasha, I laid something really huge at your feet yesterday. The day before yesterday," he amended with a smile. "Point is, I don't expect you to say 'everything's okay' and never worry about it or think about it or have doubts or fears ever again. And maybe my motivation wasn't entirely selfless." Color tinted his cheeks. "I wanted to see you. And I wanted you to know you could count on me to be there when you needed me. I hoped your calling meant that you weren't thinking about running for the hills—or that if you were, you'd at least talk to me first and give us a chance to work things out." Genuine fear shone in his eyes. "I don't know that talking will fix everything, but I have to hope you'll tell me when there's something on your mind, good or bad."

Raw emotion made Pasha's chest tighten. He didn't deserve a guy as good as Daniel. "There's nothing I could say about yesterday that won't make me sound like a total ass hat."

"I'd rather have you sound like an ass than lose you, babe."

"Not gonna happen. I… I just had some stuff going on in my head that I needed to work out. I did," he added quickly. Then he glanced at his watch. "I wish I could stick around, but I really have to get to work." He reached for Daniel's hand anyway and held it tight.

"Call me? When there's news. Or even if there isn't. Just to… to let me know you're not having second thoughts again?"

Pasha nodded and ran his thumb over the back of Daniel's hand. He didn't want to leave.

Several seconds ticked by and Daniel asked, "I ah, I don't suppose it'd be all right if I kissed you good-bye before you head out?"

"I'd like that."

"You sure? People might see."

"I don't care who sees. Life's too short to worry about shit like that anymore."

Daniel smiled. He cupped Pasha's cheek in his other hand and leaned in. His lips were soft, his kiss gentle. It made Pasha's knees feel like they were made of jelly.

EVEN though Pasha skipped a shower, only taking enough time in the bathroom to shave and brush his teeth before getting dressed, they still ended up leaving the house later than usual. For once, though, the old man didn't gripe; he just asked Pasha about Amy's friend.

Pasha filled him in on the basic details and cringed when Dad asked about Brett's family.

"They um… they're not… they had a falling out."

"What do you mean?" Ivan wanted to know.

"I mean they're not going to the hospital." He tried not to snap. "His parents kicked him out a long time ago. They don't want anything to do with him."

"It's wrong."

Pasha shrugged.

"Family is family, Pasha. You don't turn your back on family no matter what."

"Brett's gay."

Ivan didn't respond. He studied the highway ahead and didn't speak again until they were pulling into the parking lot behind the restaurant. "It's still wrong," he said. "Two wrongs don't make right." Then he turned to Pasha. "Is that why he got beat up, because he's… gay?" Instead of the anger or derision Pasha would have expected to accompany a question like that, the only thing Pasha heard in the old man's voice was concern.

"I don't know for sure," he answered truthfully. "The bookstore where Brett works is in a pretty rough neighborhood, and the kids who attacked him were causing problems earlier in the day." Maybe it was just because Brett was white. Maybe there wasn't a reason at all. He got out of the car and followed his father across the ice-slicked lot to the back door.

"What do police say?" Ivan asked.

"That they're doing the best they can."

The old man made a dismissive noise. "Police in this country no better than police in Russia." He unlocked the back door and flipped on the lights. It was almost as cold inside as it was outside.

Pasha's phone buzzed in his pocket. It was a text message.

"That Amy?" Dad asked.

"No."

Ivan stiffened. "Is it that boy?"

"*Da.*" He considered telling his father that Daniel was thirty and not exactly a boy but he doubted it would matter. He read Daniel's text.

Home safe and headed 2 bed. Just wanted 2 say good night before hitting the hay.

Pasha smiled and answered with *sweet dreams*.

"You talk to this boy an awful lot."

"I guess."

"Doesn't he have job?"

"Yes, Dad, he has a job."

"Well, so do you. Come on. Maybe we have busy day today."

IT WASN'T a busy day, but it wasn't the worst one they'd ever had either.

Amy stopped in at one, and Pasha's stomach knotted up the second he saw her. She looked like she hadn't stopped crying since he left her at the hospital.

"Brett woke up about an hour ago," she told him, but then she started crying again.

Pasha wrapped his arms around her and held her tight for several moments before guiding her over to the counter to sit down. There were a couple of customers in, but none of the regulars—not that Pasha cared just then.

Dad came out of the kitchen and Sean came over too. He laid a hand on Amy's shoulder. "You need anything, dude, just say so. I'm totally here for you."

Amy looked like she might almost laugh. "Thanks."

"How is he?" Pasha asked.

"In a lot of pain." She wiped the moisture from her cheeks. "They're already talking about more surgery. He was messed up really bad." She sniffled and tried to sit a little straighter. "But the important thing is that he's alive."

Pasha nodded and Ivan said he'd make Amy something to eat.

"I'm not hungry—"

"So you take it home for later," he told her and headed into the kitchen.

"Thank you," she said with a soft, resigned sigh. Then she leaned back against Pasha and smiled. "Thank you, too."

"Anytime. Do um, do you think it would be okay if I went by and visited him after work?" he asked hesitantly.

"I'm sure he'd love to see you. He's in room five twelve."

BEFORE going up to Brett's room, Pasha stopped off at the hospital gift shop. He didn't know what Brett liked, so he settled on a simple arrangement of red and white carnations stuck into a red coffee cup with a plush brown teddy bear tied to the handle. The bear was holding a heart with the message "get well soon" embroidered into it. Admittedly, it was probably the stupidest thing in the gift shop, but it was what he could afford. Pasha just hoped Brett would like the mug.

Only when he got to Brett's room, he almost bolted without even going in. It wasn't so much the cast on his arm or his swollen, splinted fingers, or the IV or the breathing tube in his nose—it wasn't even all the monitors Brett was hooked up to. It was his face, swollen and misshapen, covered in red and purple bruises. Half his face was bandaged and the other half… bile burned the back of Pasha's throat. Brett's eye was swollen shut, and there were cuts along his cheek and lip. Some of the bruising looked like a handprint, like someone had held his face so hard…. Pasha closed his eyes. He couldn't imagine the kind of force it must have taken to do something like this—the kind of hatred. Six guys. Six guys had held him down and—

"Hey." The raspy voice cut through the nightmare Pasha's imagination was creating for him.

He looked up and realized Brett could open up his un-bandaged eye after all, if only a little bit. "Hey," he responded, his throat so dry he could barely get the word out.

Brett seemed to smile, but it was hard to tell. "Flowers. You shouldn't have." His words were slow and slurred, but it sounded like a joke, so Pasha forced a laugh. He wished he hadn't come and then hated himself for wishing it. He set the flowers down on Brett's nightstand. "Pretty lame, huh?"

"Nah. Sit. Glad to see you." Brett gave him another what-looked-like-a smile. "I know what you're thinking: there goes his career as a beauty queen," he teased.

Pasha swallowed down the lump in his throat and sat in one of the chairs next to the bed. "I'm sure… I mean…." He didn't know what to say.

With his good hand, Brett waved it aside. "Docs keep telling me I'll be out of here breaking hearts in no time. But…." He shrugged. Winced. "Fuck. I keep forgetting I can't do that. Four broken ribs. Broken collarbone. My hand…. Jesus." He closed his eye.

"Hey, it'll heal." Pasha leaned forward, resting a hand on Brett's cast as gingerly as he could.

Brett opened his eye again. "I just don't know if it'll heal enough."

"What do you mean?"

He flashed another weak smile. "Right, I forgot. We never got past hello, did we?" He made it sound like a joke.

"I'm sorry," Pasha said anyway.

"Why? Wasn't I any good?" he teased some more.

"You were fantastic."

"Awww, I bet you say that to all the girls."

Finally, Pasha smiled for real. "Only the ones I wish I'd had the guts to call."

"Seriously? You would have called me?"

"Yeah."

Brett shrugged—winced. Swore. "Guess I won't have to worry about too many more hot dates, huh? Who wants to be seen with the Bride of Frankenstein?"

"It's not that bad."

"You're sweet, but yes it is. I guess it'll teach me for being so vain." It sounded like he was trying to make another joke.

Only Pasha didn't know what to say, so he just sat there for several long, awkward moments before finally asking, "Are you an art student?"

"Musician. Concert harp." He snorted. "Only you don't see too many one-handed harpists, do you? I was supposed to graduate this year, but no way that's going to happen now. And I had gigs lined up through New Year's. Christmas is almost as good as June—weddings," he explained. "In a good month, I could make almost a thousand dollars."

"Wow."

"Yeah."

"What do the doctors say?"

"To give it time. Like time's going to heal *this*." He nodded toward his damaged fingers.

"Maybe it's not as bad as you think."

"I had a guy *standing* on my hand, grinding the heel of his fucking boot into it as hard as he could."

"I'm sorry," Pasha said, feeling totally helpless. "I wish I knew what else to say. I suck at this. Hospitals. Cheering people up."

Brett's smile surprised him. "You're doing great." He reached over with his good hand, and Pasha took hold of it. Their fingers intertwined and Brett closed his eye again. Within seconds, he was asleep.

Pasha stayed until a nurse came by to say visiting hours were over.

As soon as he got down to the lobby, he called Daniel.

"Hey, Sugar, any news?" Daniel's voice was full of warmth. The sound of it made Pasha's stomach flutter, made him smile despite how unhappy he was.

"Hey yourself, and yeah, good news. Brett's awake. I just came from his room."

"How's he doing?"

"I don't know. I mean, he seems…. Christ, if it was me I'd be so *angry*. I'd probably want to kill whoever did that to me. Brett's a musician and he doesn't know… his right hand is pretty smashed up.

He's not sure he's going to be able to play again or even if he'll graduate." What would Brett do if he couldn't play? He'd just spent the last four or maybe even six years in college and now what?

"What do the docs say?"

"To give it time. I just… if it was me, I don't think I could be smiling about anything right now. But he was cracking jokes."

"There are only two choices at times like this, babe. You either get through it or you don't."

"Yeah, I know." He understood exactly what Daniel was saying. "How did you get through it? I mean… when you found out…," he faltered.

"You mean when they told me I had HIV? I considered some pretty stupid alternatives to getting my shit together and plugging forward," he admitted. "It's not easy finding out that your whole life is gonna be something other than what you had planned. But I'm sure if it comes to that, Brett'll be okay."

"How can you be so sure?"

"Because he has people around who care an awful lot about him."

"And a family who hates him," Pasha countered. "Amy told me his parents kicked him out because he was gay."

"Sugar, there's two kinds of family. The one you're born into, and the one you choose. I know what they say about blood being thicker than water, but sometimes it just doesn't work out that way."

"Yeah."

"Look, I know it won't actually help, but do you feel like meeting me for coffee or something? You've still got a little time before you have to get your dad, don't you?"

"No. I mean, I do and I'd love to see you, believe me, but I haven't been home yet and I need a shower."

"Okay."

"I'm not blowing you off this time," he promised.

"I know, Sugar. I'm just being selfish. I want to see you."

"I want to see you too. Um… if you're free Sunday, I'm off work. I sort of put my foot down and told my dad I was taking Sundays off whether he liked it or not. He's not liking it and I'm not sure it's going to work long term, but Sean's covering for me this week. So I thought maybe if you weren't doing anything…?"

"I don't suppose there's a chance you'd consider letting me pick you up Saturday night? I'm not trying to rush you into anything," he added quickly. He sounded nervous—hopeful. "I was just thinking we could catch a movie or go out for dinner or something. Or we could do takeout and a movie here again. Whatever you're comfortable with. I just want to spend as much time with you as I can."

"Will there be coffee?" Pasha inquired.

Daniel's chuckle was a warm rumble in his ear. "Yes. I already went out and bought everything I need to satisfy your addiction."

"Good." But then he hesitated a moment. "I'll make you a deal. If you tell me I don't have to sleep on the sofa again, you can pick me up Saturday and I'll bring an overnight bag."

"Pasha, that's not…. I'm not trying to rush you into something."

"You're not. I'm the one asking if I can sleep with you."

"Are you sure?" Daniel asked.

"Yes."

"Okay." But he still sounded nervous.

"I'm not going to regret this, Daniel."

"No offense, but the only way we're gonna know that for sure is to see how you feel Sunday morning, and by then it'll be too late."

"How about this: no matter what happens, we'll talk about it, okay?"

"I guess that's all I can ask you for."

Pasha agreed. They said their good-byes and he disconnected the call.

Before heading out to the car, Pasha dialed the number for the nursing home and talked to his mom for a few minutes. She didn't recognize his voice and didn't remember having a son called Pasha, but when he tried telling her he was *tvoy kotyonok*, your kitten, she responded and talked to him like she knew who he was.

CHAPTER TWENTY-TWO

AFTER work on Wednesday, Pasha stopped by the hospital to see Brett. He thought he'd find Amy there because Sean had covered for her at the restaurant, but instead, Mark was sitting next to Brett's bed.

"He's asleep," he said when Pasha stepped into the room.

Pasha nodded. "Amy said they were doing more surgery today. I just wanted to drop by and see how it went. I won't stay long." He expected Mark to shoo him out of the room, but instead, he started talking.

"There was still some swelling on his brain from where they… they fucking bashed his skull in." He shot Pasha a helpless, hopeless look.

He ventured closer. "How's he doing now?"

Mark shrugged. "Better, I guess. He said you came by yesterday."

"Yeah." His gaze flickered to the flower arrangement he'd brought. He wasn't sure why, but he hadn't expected it to still be there. But there it sat, front and center, with a bunch of other, bigger bouquets behind it.

"He was glad to see you. He didn't say it, but I could tell. I don't know what you said, but… it helped. Thanks."

"I didn't do anything special."

Mark didn't respond.

"I guess I should get going—" Pasha began.

"No. Wait. You don't have to go just because…. Stay?" Mark asked.

He hesitated, then sat down.

"Did he tell you that they had to put pins in his fingers? Nearly every bone in his hand was shattered."

"Damn." No wonder Brett wasn't sure if he'd be able to play again.

"Yeah," Mark agreed.

"I… is he going to be okay?"

"I hope so." Mark reached over and took Brett's hand.

Pasha studied them both for a long while, mostly watching the slow rise and fall of Brett's chest, but also watching the way Mark looked at Brett. *Like he's the most important guy in the world.* "I'm sorry," he told Mark at length. "About what happened that night at Ben and Teddy's."

"You didn't do anything wrong."

"Yes I did. I just didn't realize it. But that's no excuse. I was an ass."

Mark's smile surprised him. "You were, a little, but it doesn't matter. Me and Brett have been friends for too long for anything to ever happen. I'm the brother he never had." His smile turned rueful. "I guess it could be worse. He might not notice me at all. At least as his friend I get to be there when he needs someone to pick up the pieces. Damn it," he cursed, wiping the sudden drip of moisture from the corner of his eye. "I didn't mean it that way."

"Yeah, I know."

Mark nodded. "It's none of my business, but your boyfriend…?"

"We weren't together when… you know. But I told him about it anyway," he added, although he wasn't sure why.

"He seems like a decent guy," said Mark.

"He is." Pasha sat with him until visiting hours ended. Brett didn't wake up, but Mark said not to worry. He'd been sleeping most of the afternoon.

ON HIS way out, Pasha stopped by the hospital's chapel. As soon as he stepped inside the quiet room, he was struck by how much he missed going to church. He missed the candles and the incense, the beautiful mural walls and the gilt iconography. He missed the choir and the pomp and circumstance.

His chest tightened with anger, resentment. He was angry at God for Mom's sickness and furious at his father for not making her go to the doctor sooner. Everything he'd read said that if they'd caught it early, gotten her treatment, he might have had more time with her.

"I know being angry isn't right," he said softly. "I know everything happens for a reason, but what reason was there for Brett getting beat up so badly?" What good came from Mom being sick, from her blowing half of hers and Dad's retirement account? Why did *anyone* have to get AIDS?

Pasha was pretty sure Father Aaron would say that man, with his limited capacity for knowledge, could never hope to understand the mind of God. It was best to simply accept that God knew what he was doing and pray for the strength and the grace—Father was big on the concept of grace—to get through the hard times.

Pasha sat down and closed his eyes. He prayed for Brett, for Mark. For himself. *Because I think I could use an extra dose of grace right about now.*

"YEAH," Pasha answered his cell phone without checking the caller ID.

"I catch you at a bad time, Sugar?" Daniel asked.

"Yes. No. I don't know." He pinched the bridge of his nose. It didn't help. His head continued to throb in time to the music on the radio.

"You want me to call back later?" Daniel offered.

"No, it's okay." He shut the ledger he'd been staring at for the past half an hour and gulped down the last of his cold coffee. He was sitting at the counter with Sharon glaring at him every time she passed by. Pasha was sure Dad was going to get an earful when he got back. *Which hopefully is soon.* It was almost five thirty, and he needed to leave by six if he was going to make it to his doctor's appointment on time.

Behind him, Art, Jimmy, and Rueben were having dinner. Art's wife Gladys and Jimmy's wife Carol were with them. Rueben wasn't married.

Pasha tucked the ledger under his arm and headed into the kitchen so he could talk without being overheard. "I've been looking around this place all day, wondering what a guy like Gordon Ramsey would do with it." Gordon Ramsey was a British chef and host of several TV shows, including *Ramsey's Kitchen Nightmares*—but mostly he was famous for his hot temper.

"And?" Daniel asked.

"He'd probably recommend a wrecking crew and say the only thing that would help us is to tear it all down and start over."

"It's not that bad."

"Yes it is. It's not just that the menu sucks and the decor.... God, I don't know if it *ever* looked good. But I've been going through Dad's books and we're spending almost a thousand dollars more a month than we're bringing in. That doesn't count household expenses, it's just the restaurant. I have *no* idea where the money's coming from, and my brother doesn't seem to want to talk to me." He'd left two messages on Peter's voice mail already today.

"Are you sure your dad's writing everything down?"

"Even taking Dad's erratic bookkeeping practices into account, it looks like we've been operating in the red for over five years. I have *no* idea how we're still in business."

"Do you think he took out a second mortgage on the house?"

"That's what I'm afraid of. Either that or Dad emptied out the last of his retirement account."

"What are you going to do?"

"Hell if I know—I gotta go," he said, as the back door opened and his father came in. "I'll talk to you later," he promised, then disconnected the call. "Dad, you have a minute?"

Ivan shucked out of his coat. "I thought you had appointment."

"I do. But this is important."

The old man's gaze fell to the ledger in Pasha's hands, and his expression darkened. "What are you doing with that?"

"Trying to figure out how we're still open," Pasha told him, speaking in Russian so Sharon couldn't eavesdrop.

Ivan answered in kind. "I told you, you let me worry about money."

"Dad, this is my responsibility too."

"How is it your responsibility?"

Pasha blinked. Dad honestly didn't seem to get it. "When you put my name on the restaurant, you made it my responsibility. If something happens and we go under, I'm just as liable as you are."

"We're not going under. Now go on, get out of here." He waved Pasha toward the door. "Bad enough you're coming and going whenever the hell you want—"

"Don't try to change the subject. I'm not leaving until you tell me where all this money is coming from."

"You're making tempest in teacup, Pasha. It's not that much—"

"Bullshit!"

Ivan glared. "What gives you right to talk to me like that? I raised you," he snarled.

"And I love you for it," Pasha spat back him. "Now answer the question."

"I closed out me and your mother's retirement account. Happy?"

"Jesus. Of course I'm not happy! Why would you do something like that?"

"So we wouldn't lose business. Things are bad, Pasha. I wasn't going to let this place go. I wasn't ready to give up."

It didn't escape him that his father was speaking in the past tense. "We'll talk about his later, okay?"

"There's nothing to talk about. What's done is done." He put his apron on and headed into the kitchen.

Pasha followed him. "We'll find a way to turn the business around," he said with more conviction than he felt.

"Pasha, it's not just us. Economy is for shit right now." Ivan gestured broadly. "We're not special, everybody suffering."

"Take a drive through downtown Royal Oak sometime. It's *not* everybody. There are a lot of restaurants right down the street that are doing just fine."

Ivan scoffed. "We can't compete with places like that! We just have to keep going until economy gets better."

Pasha counted silently to ten and then back down again. "What are you planning to do when the money runs out?"

Ivan's shoulders sagged. "I don't know."

For the first time in his life, Pasha thought his father actually looked scared. "How much is left?" he asked.

The old man shrugged.

"Dad, *how much*?"

"Twelve, maybe fifteen thousand."

The throbbing in Pasha's head got worse. "Okay. We'll figure something out."

"It wasn't supposed to be like this, Pasha. We used to make good money. I thought… I thought you and Peter would run business after your mother and me retired. And then someday your sons would take over and run it after you. This place was supposed to be legacy."

"I know, Dad. I'll see you later." As he got his coat down from the peg by the back door, Pasha saw the worried look on Kaja's face and shot him a tight-lipped smile. He didn't just have to figure something out for Dad's sake; other people depended on them too.

PASHA was almost to Dr. Neumann's office when his phone rang. This time he checked the ID. "Finally," he muttered when he saw his brother's name. "*Preevyet*."

"You called me?" Peter sounded irritated.

"Yeah. I got one question answered already. What I want to know now is if you knew Dad had emptied out his retirement account to keep the restaurant from going under."

"It's his money. He can do whatever he wants to with it."

Guess that answers that question. "You should have talked him out of it."

"How the hell was I supposed to do that?"

"Dad listens to you, Peter. You could have told him it was a bad idea, maybe come up with some other plan to keep the place running."

"Since when do you care about the goddamned restaurant?"

"I don't know. Maybe I just care about Dad, which is more than I can say about you."

"Hey!"

"Don't even. You're the one who left us."

"Dad knew for years I wasn't planning on sticking around."

"You damned well know that's not true," Pasha retorted.

"Look, it's not my fault the old man is delusional. Now if there's nothing else—"

"Dad only has another twelve or fifteen thousand dollars left."

"That's not my problem. It's not yours either. Maybe when he's finally broke, he'll sell the place."

"Selling it will kill him."

"Bullshit. He'll be fine. Besides I thought you wanted him to sell."

So did I. "That isn't the point—"

"Look, I don't have time for this. I have a dinner reservation."

"Yeah. Have fun." He hung up before Peter could say another word. Pasha was so angry he almost missed his exit and ended up cutting off a guy in a big blue van. The driver blared his horn, and Pasha raised a hand in apology.

Dr. Neumann's office was on Plymouth Road in Livonia. Pasha had thought—*hoped*—it would be in Ypsilanti or Ann Arbor and he'd have an excuse to ask Daniel to meet him for coffee or something afterwards. *But I'll see him tomorrow.* He smiled. Tomorrow couldn't come soon enough.

He managed to navigate the rest of the way to Dr. Neumann's office without incident and parked as close to the door as he could. Pasha swiped his damp palms down his thighs and headed inside, where he found nearly a dozen people sitting in the cheerfully decked-for-the-holidays waiting room. Most were men, a few were women. Two looked like teenagers. The boys were huddled together in a corner by themselves, looking as terrified as Pasha felt. He wondered which of them had HIV. Maybe they both did.

In the corner opposite the boys sat a living scarecrow of a man. His cheeks were hollow, and his face, neck, and long, thin hands were dotted with rough, dark purple-brown spots. KS Lesions. Pasha recognized them because he'd been doing his homework, trying to prepare for what might happen someday. Only seeing it in person was a lot harder than looking at pictures online. The man in the corner didn't look any older than Daniel, but he looked… *like a walking gravestone.* Pasha swallowed back the lump in his throat and focused his attention on the receptionist.

She flashed a cheerful smile his way. "Come on in. Mr. Batalov?"

"I… yeah. Hi." His mouth felt dry and his voice crackled. He cleared his throat and stepped up to the window. "Pasha's fine. Pavel." He'd given his name as Pavel when he made the appointment. "Pasha's short for Pavel. It's Russian." Heat crept into his cheeks.

"Nice to meet you, Pasha." Her bright smile never faltered. "I'm Tess."

"Hi," he repeated. How could anyone be so cheerful working in a place like this?

"I just need you to get started on some paperwork." She handed over a clipboard. "Go ahead and have a seat, and we'll get you in just as quickly as we can."

"Thanks." He flashed a weak smile and turned back around, looking for a place to sit, and another lump rose in his throat. Probably everyone here had HIV. AIDS. His gaze fell on the boys again. Was this their first visit or were they coming back to get the results of an HIV test? Would it be good news or bad? *Please let it be good.*

He scoffed at himself. How much use could a prayer like that possibly be? The news would be what it would be. Once the damage was done it was too late to pray for the best. There was no "best," there was only dealing with it or doing something permanently stupid.

One of the boys looked up and flashed a tight-lipped smile. Embarrassment over being caught staring heated Pasha's cheeks—but he smiled back anyway, then found a seat and turned his attention to the clipboard. The first page started out with easy stuff: name, age, address, reason for visit.

Only how did he put his reason for being there into words? This was why he preferred to go to a clinic to get tested. Clinics were quick, convenient. Anonymous. He didn't have to tell anyone why he was there, they already knew. But this was about more than HIV. Besides, he was negative; he didn't have anything to worry about.

So why am I shaking?

He found himself looking at the man with the KS lesions again, imagining it was Daniel sitting there gaunt, covered with awful purple-brown spots. Daniel was so beautiful, so strong…. Tears burned the corners of Pasha's eyes and he bolted for the door.

Chapter Twenty-Three

PASHA stood shaking, frigid air burning his lungs as he leaned against the building, gulping in air, trying to get a hold of himself. He'd spent most of the week very successfully *not* thinking about HIV, AIDS, but now…. He closed his eyes. Someday, Daniel was going to look just like that guy in the waiting room. "I can't do it," he whispered. He wasn't strong enough. When Daniel looked like that—

"Pasha?"

He jumped at the sound of his name. He opened his eyes and brushed the tears away quickly. In the doorway stood a man about his age wearing dark-blue scrubs and a thick sweater. Pasha hoped the guy hadn't heard what he said.

He stepped out into the cold and smiled. "I'm Ronny." He was a little taller than Pasha, maybe a little heavier, with blond hair and dark eyes. "We talked the other day when you made your appointment."

"Yeah. Right. Hi. I ah…." He had no idea what to say.

"You mind if I smoke?" Ronny held up a cigarette.

"Sure, go ahead."

"You want one?" He reached for the pack in his breast pocket, but Pasha shook his head.

"I don't smoke."

"Good for you. The doc's been riding me to quit since she hired me."

"Yeah, I guess a… nurse… or…?"

"Nurse," Ronny confirmed. "Or at least I will be once I pass my board exam. Right now, I'm just an office assistant." He leaned against the wall and lit up his cigarette. "Either way, this is pretty dumb. And not just for the obvious reasons."

Pasha shot over a quizzical look.

"There's a reason I came to work for a doc who specializes in HIV."

Pasha blinked. "You…?" This guy had HIV? But he was going to be a nurse!

"Been living with it for five years now." He took a long drag off his cigarette, held it a second, and then blew the smoke away from Pasha's face. "I'm down to four a day. Cigs, not packs," he clarified with a laugh.

"*Moladyets*. Sorry. Good for you."

"Thanks." A moment of long, less than comfortable silence stretched between them. Pasha didn't want company, but he didn't want to go back inside either.

"You doing okay?" Ronny asked him.

Pasha opened his mouth to lie, to say he was fine, but instead, the truth came out. "No."

"You wanna talk about it?"

"I want it to not be happening." *God, could I get any more selfish?* He wasn't the one with HIV. Daniel was. Ronny was. That guy inside with the lesions was.

"I know the feeling."

"Yeah… I…." *I feel like an ass.* He cleared his throat. "I guess it's hard. Living with it."

"It's hard living with someone who has it too. My boyfriend got his first lesion a couple months ago."

"You… your boyfriend…?" He shook himself. "Sorry. It's none of my business."

"It's no big secret. Jeffery and me've been together almost three years. It just wasn't supposed to happen like this." He took another long, slow drag off his cigarette, making the end of it light up bright orange. "He wasn't supposed to get KS until his white cell count totally bottomed out. His count is better than mine. Guess the virus didn't get the latest handout telling it how to behave."

"Yeah, I guess not," Pasha replied weakly.

"No one can predict how it's going to go, Pasha. All you can do is take each day as it comes. I know, totally cliché, right?" He laughed.

"Yeah, I guess."

Ronny took another drag off his smoke. It was almost half gone. "Can I ask you a personal question? Something I'm really not supposed to ask?"

"Um. Sure, I guess."

"Don't worry, it's not that personal, especially not compared to the kind of questions the doc's going to ask. I just wondered who your boyfriend is."

Pasha blinked.

"On the phone, you said your boyfriend was one of the doc's patients," he explained.

Right. "His name's Daniel. Englewood," he clarified, because for all he knew Dr. Neumann had eight patients named Daniel.

"Damn. Good catch."

Warmth surged through Pasha's chest. "Yeah. He's… he makes me really happy."

"You know, this isn't easy on him either. I don't just mean the HIV. That sucks no matter how you cut it, but—and look, I can't speak for Daniel—but the guy I was with before Jeffery was negative, and it was really… challenging." He took one last pull from his smoke and snubbed out the butt. "It wasn't just him, either. I was terrified I would give him this thing somehow. And I know better. I *know* it usually takes more than one broken condom, and that even if there *is* a broken condom, there are drugs that practically guarantee the negative guy stays negative. I know it's nearly impossible to transmit HIV just by going down on somebody or letting him go down on you. But every time my ex tried to initiate anything, I reached for protection. He hated that. Eventually we called it quits. Jeff and me have to be just as careful, but he's not afraid to tell me I'm being a dumbass when I get all freaky on him. And if there is an accident—he's such a klutz." He rolled his eyes. "I swear, I should ban that man from the kitchen—but when something happens, neither of us panics. Carson—my ex—he didn't mean to be insensitive, but I cut myself once shaving and he wouldn't go anywhere near the bathroom until I'd bleached the sink twice." Only instead of sounding mad, he laughed. "Oh, it was funny, believe me," he said when Pasha gave him a mortified look. "He was trying so hard to stay calm, but he just couldn't keep it together."

"I've never… I mean, I'm sure I know guys who have HIV, I just don't know who they are."

"I'm not surprised. There's this huge stigma attached to being positive. It makes it hard to come out and say 'Hey, I've got this thing, but would you love me anyway?'"

"Yeah."

"Hey." He reached out tentatively, and when Pasha didn't flinch away, Ronny laid a hand on his shoulder. "There's a lot of support too."

He nodded. Daniel had mentioned belonging to a support group, but it sounded like it was only for people with HIV. "I just don't know what kind of support there is… I mean. You know. For guys like me, people who *don't* have it." Christ, could he sound any more selfish if he tried?

But Ronny smiled. "There are support groups for mixed-status couples too, Pasha. It might help to meet other men and women who are going through the same things you are."

"Did you and your ex belong to a support group?"

"We tried, but… look, just because something doesn't work for one person doesn't mean it won't work for you. There are some fliers at the desk inside. Why don't you at least check it out?"

He didn't feel particularly hopeful but agreed take a look.

"Ready to go back in?" Ronny asked.

No. "Yeah." He followed Ronny back in and Tess let him know they were ready for him in back. "I didn't get a chance to finish filling all the paperwork," Pasha told her, embarrassment heating his cheeks.

Tess smiled. "You can finish it in the exam room. It's no big deal," she promised. It didn't help. Pasha felt like everyone was staring at him as he picked up the clipboard and followed Ronny into the back—but maybe no one was staring at him, maybe he was just imagining it. What was it his dad used to say? *You're not center of whole world.*

"Come on, I'll take you back and get you started," Ronny offered.

Doing his best to get over feeling so self-conscious—so selfish—Pasha followed him down a long hall to an exam room. It didn't look any scarier than the rooms in Dr. Mullins's office, but Pasha's gut tightened as he stepped inside.

"I need you to take off your coat and shoes and come on out to the scale so we can get your weight," Ronny told him.

"Do you really need to know my weight?"

Ronny smiled at him. "It's painless, honest."

"It's been a while since I've been on a scale. I'm a little afraid of what it's going to say."

"It's just a number."

"Yeah." That's what Daniel had said too. Pasha set his coat and the clipboard down on one of the exam room chairs, pulled off his shoes, and trudged back out to the scale in the hallway. It was painless as promised. He didn't look at the number and Ronny didn't tell him what it was.

"Go on and take a seat on the table," Ronny said when they were done. "Doc Neumann'll be in, in just a few minutes."

"Thanks."

Ronny closed the door, leaving Pasha alone in the small, brightly lit room. It was decorated as cheerfully as the rest of the office, but that didn't help. He wanted… *Daniel.* Pasha fished his cell phone out of his pocket and dialed his number before he could talk himself out of it. After all, they were seeing each other tomorrow.

Daniel picked up on the third ring. "Hey, Sugar, done at the doc's already?" His cheerful tone made Pasha feel guiltier than ever. Daniel was always so happy to hear from him.

God, if he could see the way I acted in the waiting room…. "I'm still here." He swallowed hard, but the lump in his throat remained.

"What's wrong?"

"I'm being stupid. It's nothing."

"Pasha, come on, you promised to talk to me. What's the matter?"

He took a breath, let it out. “It’s honestly nothing. I’m okay.”

After a moment’s hesitation, Daniel asked, “Have you had dinner yet?”

“I never even got around to eating lunch. I was too tied up trying to sort out the books.”

“You ever solve the mystery of where the money’s coming from?”

“Yeah. Dad cashed out his retirement account.”

“Damn. What are you going to do?”

“I don’t know. Dad seems to be walking around in this bubble where everything will work out as long as we keep doing what we’re doing, and Peter… Peter’s a selfish fucking bastard.”

“I’m sorry, babe.”

He shrugged. “It’s not your fault.”

“So….” Daniel hesitated again. “You maybe feel like grabbing dinner with me after you finish up at the doc’s? If you like Mexican, there’s a place just up the road from her office called La Palapas. I go there almost every time I have an appointment.”

“But… you live in *Ypsilanti*.” That was almost forty minutes away.

Daniel chuckled. “There are these marvelous inventions called automobiles. I can get into mine and meet you in half an hour. If you want to see me, that is.”

“More than… I mean….” He took another deep breath and let it out. “There are all these people in the waiting room and some of them are really sick and I just… I started thinking about you. This one guy is so skinny and he’s….” Covered in lesions. “He’s really sick.” Shame made heat rush to his face. “I’m such an ass hat. Why do you even want me as a friend?”

“You are *not* an ass hat, Pasha. And for the record, I want you as a whole lot more than just a friend.”

Shame and embarrassment waged war inside his heart. “I ran out of the waiting room like a cat with its tail on fire.”

“Did you go back in?”

"Yeah. I'm sitting in an exam room now, waiting for Dr. Neumann."

"That's all that matters, babe. So how about dinner?"

God, he couldn't be serious. After what Pasha just admitted? "I came straight from work. I'm not really dressed to go out."

"La Palapas is a casual restaurant. No one's gonna care what you're wearing."

"What about my devastatingly gorgeous boyfriend?" he managed to tease.

"Your boyfriend—who isn't half as gorgeous as you seem to think he is—likes you just the way you are, Sugar."

"You are gorgeous, Daniel." But more than that, he was an amazing man. *He deserves better than me.* Or maybe what he deserved was for Pasha to *become* better.

"You're pretty good-looking yourself," Daniel told him, "and just in case you forgot, the first time I met you, you were wearing that uniform."

Pasha leaned back against the wall. "So you're saying you have a thing for waiter uniforms."

"Hey, everybody has a fetish."

He laughed. "Just try not to look too good, okay?"

"I will do my very best to look like a slob, just for you."

Pasha laughed harder. "So where's this place we're meeting?"

"Just take a right out of the lot and head west on Plymouth. It's just a couple miles down on the right side of the road."

"Got it. I'll see you soon." Pasha hung up and hopped up onto the table, causing the paper to crinkle loudly—or maybe it just sounded so loud because the room was so quiet. He took another deep breath and went back to filling out the forms. On the line after "reason for visit," he wrote *physical and STI tests* and wondered why that had been so difficult before.

The next section, however, genuinely *was* difficult. It covered his family's medical history, something Pasha knew almost nothing about. Dad had a bad heart and high cholesterol and Mom had Alzheimer's, but did she have anything else? Heart problems, blood sugar issues?

What about his grandparents? He had absolutely no idea. Dad didn't talk about stuff like that. He struggled through it as best as he could until the door opened again, and another young man stepped into the room carrying a small plastic tub.

"Hi, Pasha?" He had the brightest blue eyes Pasha had ever seen.

"I… yeah. Hi."

He smiled. "Hi. I'm Jamie, Doc Neumann's resident vampire."

Vampire?

The other guy laughed. "Sorry. Phlebotomist humor." He set the tub on a tall chrome table on wheels and rolled it over. "I need to get some blood."

"Oh." Right. Vampire. Blood. Christ he felt like an idiot. He set the clipboard aside and tried to relax.

"Don't worry, nobody around here is ever happy to see me. I don't take it personally." Jamie pulled on a pair of hideous blue gloves. "So I hear you're Daniel's boyfriend."

Pasha frowned. *How…*?

Jamie chuckled. "Word travels fast around this place. Can you roll up your sleeve and make a fist for me?" he asked. When Pasha did, Jamie examined his arm. "You have great veins—bet that's the first time you've heard that one," he teased. "You can relax a sec."

Jamie swabbed part of his arm with iodine and lined up a frightening number of empty vials on the chrome table. He winked when he noticed Pasha staring. "Hey, I said I was a vampire."

"Yeah."

"Don't worry, I haven't lost a patient yet, honest," he promised.

Pasha nodded. He closed his eyes and tried to relax, breathing through the hard pinch of the needle and making a fist again when Jamie asked him to.

"You're doing great. Just a couple more and we're done. So… restaurant work?"

"Guess the penguin suit gave it away."

"Pretty much. Whereabouts?"

"Royal Oak. It's just a little diner."

"Little diners are the best. Just one more. You're doing great… there." He pulled the needle out gently. "Hopefully that wasn't too traumatic."

"No. Thanks."

He smiled. "Anytime." Jamie placed a small sterile pad over the tiny wound. "Lift your arm. Good. Hold that there for just a second."

Pasha nodded again and watched Jamie dispose of the needle in the "sharps" box on the wall. Then he had Pasha relax his arm and taped the cotton pad into place with a bright blue bandage. "All done."

The door opened, and Jamie grinned. "Right on time, Doc," he said to the woman who stepped in. He gathered up his things and with a parting wave, left the room.

CHAPTER TWENTY-FOUR

"HELLO, Pasha." Dr. Neumann held out her hand. "I'm Edna Neumann." She didn't look like much, just a short older woman with thick bifocal glasses, but Pasha couldn't help feeling intimidated. After all, this woman had to face people like that guy in the waiting room every day. God, how was he ever going to cope when it was Daniel looking emaciated and covered in lesions?

Please just give me the strength to handle it. Forcing a smile, Pasha put his hand in hers. "Nice to meet you."

"Likewise. I understand you're here because you're seeing one of my patients?"

"Yes, ma'am."

"Why don't you call me Doc?" she invited him. "Pretty much everyone else around here does."

Pasha tried to smile, but it was hard when he felt so awkward and out of place. "I um, I started seeing Daniel a couple of weeks ago."

She gave a thoughtful nod, her expression remaining stoic, making it impossible to tell what she was really thinking. "You mind if I start out by asking you some tough questions?"

"No," he lied, swiping his hands down his thighs. Every time he moved, the paper under him crinkled.

"I'm here to help, Pasha. But I can only do that if we're completely honest with each other. There's nothing you can say that will shock me. I'm a card-carrying member of the dirty old ladies club."

Her wink caught him completely off guard, and after several embarrassing seconds of uncomfortable silence, Pasha managed to laugh. “Sorry. I guess I’m just nervous,” he admitted, as he tucked his hands up under his thighs.

“Can I ask what you’re nervous about?”

He hesitated, shifting his weight again and making it the paper under him crackle some more.

“This is a conversation between you and me,” Doc Neumann promised. “Daniel’s my patient, and someone I care about, but whatever you say to me stays right here in this room. Got it?”

“Yes, ma’am. Doc. It’s just… it’s so overwhelming. I’ve never really thought about it—HIV—before. I know I should have. I’m a gay man.”

“HIV and AIDS *aren’t* confined to the LGBTQ community.”

“I know. I just… I really care about Daniel, but I’m scared to death, and I feel like shit because of it,” he confessed.

Her smile was surprisingly kind. “It’s natural to be frightened, Pasha. You do know you can’t catch HIV through casual contact though, right? Hugging, holding hands, even drinking from the same glass—”

He nodded. “I know all that stuff. That’s not what scares me. Or… I guess it scares me a little.” It was stupid and selfish, but he couldn’t sit there and pretend he wasn’t afraid of contracting HIV himself. He knew he couldn’t get it from holding Daniel’s hand and the look on Daniel’s face when they touched, when they *kissed*—God, it made him wonder how many people had shunned Daniel because of his status. But how could he not be afraid? Accidents happened. Condoms broke. People cut themselves in the kitchen. Only that wasn’t what really scared him the most. “I’m afraid I won’t be able to be strong when he needs me to be. I’m afraid he’ll end up taking care of me when I should be taking care of him.”

“It’s likely to be a very long time before Daniel gets as sick as some of my other patients,” she pointed out. “I can’t ethically discuss his health with you, of course, but I’m sure I don’t have to tell you he’s in great shape.”

The tips of his ears burned. "I just… I want to be in this for the long haul. I *really* care about him, but I'm so afraid I'm going to freak out the first time he gets sick, even if it's not… related."

Her expression softened. "There are going to be days when it's overwhelming for both of you, Pasha. There's nothing wrong with feeling that way, nothing wrong with being afraid. You can call me anytime you need someone to talk to. There are some great support groups for sero-discordant couples, too."

He nodded. "Yeah, Ronny mentioned that. I'll grab a few fliers on my way out."

"Good. Now, let's get back to those tough questions."

AS SOON as he spotted Daniel coming in the door, Pasha got to his feet. Daniel looked his way and a warm smile spread across both their faces.

"Hope I didn't keep you waiting too long," Daniel said when he reached Pasha's table.

"I had good company," Pasha replied. He'd brought Daniel's paperback with him.

Daniel's grin broadened. "Looks like you're almost done."

"Just about." He was on the last chapter.

Daniel took off his coat. He wasn't dressed like a slob, but the jeans and Proclaimers T-shirt he had on made Pasha feel less out of place. Or maybe it was the way Daniel was looking at him, like nothing else in the world mattered, not even the fact that they were in a crowded restaurant. Besides, life was short. Pasha took half a step closer and leaned up, not sure how Daniel would respond—but when Daniel met his kiss halfway, Pasha let his eyes slide shut so he could savor the moment. Daniel tasted like peppermint and cranberry, and he smelled of burning wood and warm, spicy cologne. It was a brief, chaste kiss that seemed to go on forever—but it was over way too soon.

When they drew apart, Pasha cast an anxious glance around at their fellow diners. Only a few seemed to have even noticed. No one seemed to care.

He looked back up at Daniel. His expression was hard to read. "Sorry if I… I just… I've never done that before." Pasha shot another nervous look around the restaurant. No one was looking at them anymore. "I ah—"

Daniel pressed his finger lightly to Pasha's lips. "You can kiss me anytime you want, any*where* you want."

"You sure?"

"I am absolutely sure, Sugar." He waited for Pasha to retake his seat before sitting down across from him. "So how'd it go at the doc's?"

Pasha hesitated. He liked her, but talking to a woman his mother's age about sex wasn't easy. And she hadn't *just* asked about his sex life; she'd wanted to know how many partners he'd had in the past year—he'd had fifteen. Except at first he said fourteen but then he remembered Fred or Frank or whatever his name was. Forgetting him, not knowing his name, made him feel cheap. So did the fact that he'd been with fourteen other guys last year and honestly, he barely remembered *their* names, either. Doc Neumann assured him it wasn't the highest number she'd ever heard and added that she was a firm believer in a vigorous—safe—sex life. Then she'd wanted to know *exactly* what he'd done with those fifteen men and if he'd used condoms for oral sex as well as anal. He hadn't, although he hadn't engaged in a whole lot of oral sex. If some guy wanted to go down on him, Pasha wasn't going to say no, but when it came to hookups, he preferred to just get screwed. Doc Neumann gave him a long, embarrassing tutorial on condoms and cocksucking and sent him off with a handful of flavored condoms she'd pulled from the pocket of her lab coat.

Pasha could have gone his whole life without knowing that bubblegum was his doctor's personal favorite condom flavor.

Daniel snickered when he was done recounting his visit. "Maybe I should have warned you."

"Is she always like that?"

"It sounds like she took it easy on you."

He groaned and Daniel laughed again.

"I do have some good news," Pasha added.

"Oh?"

"I guess it isn't really news. I mean… I would have been…." *Shit.* His good news was that he was HIV negative, which wasn't news. It was what he'd expected to hear, he just hadn't been expecting to hear it tonight, but the doc used a rapid test. *Only how do I tell a guy who has HIV that my good news is that I* don't *have it?*

"Babe?"

"I'm negative."

A broad smile spread across Daniel's face. Pasha wasn't sure that would be his reaction, if their positions were reversed. "I never doubted you, Pasha," Daniel told him. "But I'm glad we both know for sure."

"Yeah… I—"

Only before he could say more, their waitress came by to ask if they were ready to order.

"You need another minute?" Daniel asked him.

"No, I'll figure it out. Go ahead." He scanned the menu quickly while Daniel ordered his dinner. It all looked good, but absolutely none of it was diet food. Promising himself an extra thirty minutes on the exercise bike tonight, Pasha ordered one of the combo plates.

The waitress smiled, collected their menus, and left to go put in their order.

Daniel shifted in his seat. "So…um… I was thinking about tomorrow night."

"Me too." Pasha smiled. He'd been thinking about it so much that there were several pairs of soiled sweatpants hidden under his bed. He wanted to touch Daniel, to kiss him, to go down on him and prove to them both that it was going to be okay, that they could have a perfectly normal relationship despite some stupid virus.

"I um, I was wondering if maybe I could just pick you up on Sunday morning instead."

"Why?" Saturday night had been Daniel's idea.

"I just… I don't want to jump the gun."

"Why not? I mean look, I know there's some more stuff we need to talk about, and I know I totally freaked out in the doc's office, but Daniel, I want this to work."

"Which is why I think we should wait."

"Fine, I'll sleep on the couch again." Even to his own ears, he sounded pissy.

"I… let's just do Sunday morning, okay? I can pick you up early and we can go out for breakfast and maybe… I know it's not the most romantic thing in the world, but I've gotta get some shopping done, so maybe we could go to the mall? Then maybe hit a movie and grab some dinner before I take you home."

All of which sounded perfectly fine, but it wasn't what Pasha wanted. "What happened to having dinner at your place and watching TV?" he asked, because being nervous about sleeping together was one thing, but it sounded like Daniel was going out of his way to keep Pasha out of his apartment.

"I thought something different might be more fun."

"Daniel, what's really going on here? On Tuesday, you asked me to spend the night at your place. I know I pushed you to sleep together, and if… look, I'll take the sofa if that's what you want, but I only get one day off a week. I don't want to spend it at the mall. If something's changed… if maybe you want to get back together with that guy from college…?" Maybe it was like Ronny had said: it would be easier for Daniel to be with someone who understood what it was like to live with HIV. *It would just totally break my heart.*

"Aiden and me are over. We've been over for years. Pasha, I swear, you are the *only* person I want to be with."

"Then talk to me. What's changed? Is this because I freaked out today? If it is, I'm sorry. I had a moment. I got over it."

Daniel heaved a heavy sigh and shook his head. He looked so completely defeated that Pasha reached across the table and took his hand. Daniel held it tight. "Remember I had that doctor's appointment last week?" he asked.

"You said it was just a routine checkup." A hard knot started to form in Pasha's gut; all he could think about was that guy in Doc Neumann's waiting room.

"Sugar, routine for me is getting my viral load and CD4 count checked."

"You're numbers are good—aren't they?"

He hung his head and the rock in Pasha's stomach suddenly felt like it was the size of Mt. Everest. "They were when we had that conversation. Or at least I thought they were. Doc called me today to tell me that my CD4 count has dropped to four-fifty. My viral load's spiked too. That's why I think we should slow down, at least until I get another test done."

"What will another test prove?" Pasha wanted to know. He'd been reading, and four-fifty wasn't a good number. It wasn't catastrophic, but it wasn't good.

"Numbers can fluctuate. It might not be as bad as it seems."

"What does Doc Neumann say?"

Daniel hesitated before admitting, "She wrote me a prescription for Stribild. It's an ARV. An antiretroviral drug. She wants me to start taking it."

"Okay." What was the big deal?

"No, Pasha, it's not okay. Once I start taking drugs, that's it. It's over. I'm on them for the rest of my life." He was trembling.

"It beats the alternative, doesn't it?"

"I don't know."

"Jesus… *Daniel*." He struggled to keep his voice down.

"I just want one more blood test. Numbers fluctuate," Daniel repeated. "My CD4 might go up on its own."

"What if it doesn't?"

"I don't know. We'll keep tabs on it, see how low it gets. Maybe I'll get lucky. If it stays stable, I can put off the drugs for a while longer."

What the…? "Why are we having this conversation?" Why was Daniel playing fucking games with his health? His *life*?

"I don't want you thinking the wrong thing about me not wanting to sleep with you."

"So how about you just take the damned drugs like your doctor says?"

"Because I met this really amazing guy, and I'd like us to have a little more time together before I have to start telling him we can't go out to dinner because I'm afraid that no matter what I eat, it'll make me sick, before I have to start cancelling dates because I'm too tired or sore to even get out of bed."

Pasha frowned, confused.

"The side effects of ARVs are a bitch. Nausea. Diarrhea. Fatigue."

"It still beats the alternative." *AIDS.*

"I just want a little more time to spend with you, Sugar. Doc Neumann's running another blood test. I should have the results in a week. In the meantime, four-fifty isn't that bad."

Pasha swallowed past the lump in his throat. "You're not going to kill yourself over me." His voice was so calm it scared him. He stood up and fished a twenty-dollar bill out of his wallet to cover his half of the dinner that hadn't arrived yet. "If you change your mind about taking care of yourself, call me. Otherwise… I… I'm sorry. I'm already watching one person I…." *Love.* "I'm watching my mother die of something we could have done more about if we'd caught it sooner. The drugs wouldn't have cured her, but we could have had more time—real time, not this fucking limbo I feel like I'm stuck in. I refuse to watch you die too. Not like this. Not when there's something you can do about it."

"Pasha—"

He turned and walked away as quickly as he could without causing a scene. There was moisture trickling down his cheeks before he even got to the door.

CHAPTER TWENTY-FIVE

IT WAS nine thirty when Pasha pulled back into the restaurant's lot and found himself parked in almost the exact same spot where he'd met Daniel for the first time. His phone hadn't rung once on the drive home. *But phone lines work both ways.* If he'd wanted to talk to Daniel that badly, he could have been the one to call. *I* won't *be the reason he fucking kills himself.* God, what the hell was Daniel thinking? He was half tempted to call Dr. Neumann—but he doubted it would do any good. She couldn't talk to him about Daniel's health.

He closed his eyes. *Please....* "I don't even know what to ask for," he whispered to God. "I just want Daniel to be okay. I want him… I know he's got this stupid thing and I know it's his fault, but everybody screws up. It was one mistake." Or maybe it was a bunch of mistakes. Pasha had gotten the impression that Daniel was pretty wild in college. "Please just let him be all right." He took a deep breath and headed into the restaurant.

Dad looked up from the grill and frowned. "You called Peter?" It sounded more like an accusation than a question.

Pasha bit back his initial response, that he couldn't believe his older brother was so fucking immature he'd called Dad and *tattled* on him. Getting mad wouldn't help. "I needed to ask him about something," he said instead, his tone carefully neutral.

"I thought I told you not to worry about goddamned money," the old man seethed.

Pasha took off his coat. Kaja was in the back peeling potatoes, his head down, bent over his work like he didn't want to be noticed. Sharon sat at the counter eating a bowl of soup. There weren't any customers.

Pasha turned his attention back to his father and said in Russian, "What do you plan to do when the money runs out, Dad?"

"It's *my* money—" He hit his palm against his own chest. He spoke in English.

Pasha continued in Russian. "I'm not arguing that. I'm asking what you plan to do when there's none left."

"Peter says you want me to sell restaurant."

Of course Peter would put it off on me. "If it's all the same with you and Peter, I can think—and speak—for myself." He surveyed the kitchen; even though it was early, it looked like Dad had gotten most of the cleanup done. All that was left was to put the food away and then sweep and mop. There was no reason not to get started, so he rolled up the heavy mat in front of the grill.

"Well?" Ivan demanded, settling his hands on his hips, finally switching into Russian—not that Pasha figured it would help at this point. "*Do* you want me to sell?"

"No." It wasn't a lie, he just didn't know when he'd changed his mind. "But we have to make changes if we're going to stay in business." He set the rolled up mat aside and went to get the broom from the dish room. Ivan followed.

"What kind of changes?" he asked.

"Do you really want me to answer that?"

"I asked, didn't I?"

Pasha regarded him a moment. He could think of several conversations they'd had where Dad asked questions he didn't actually want the answers to. "All right." He leaned against the counter. "The menu is too big. It's out of date. We need to start ordering from suppliers—"

"Suppliers are too expensive."

"It's cheaper in the long run than buying from the grocery store and Sam's Club. And we really need to think about opening later and closing earlier—"

"Regulars are used to our hours. If we start changing, we'll piss off most important customers."

"Dad, if there were enough of them, or if they spent enough money when they came in, I'd be happy to stay open all night if that's what they wanted." His father started to argue, but Pasha cut him off. "When did the last table come in today?"

"How should I know?"

"Do I have to go to the register and see when the last customer cashed out?"

"Fine," Ivan grumbled. "Eight o'clock. But it's still early yet. We don't close for another hour and half."

"How many customers did we get last night between nine and eleven?"

"I don't know. Three. Four."

"Three or four *people* or three or four *tables*?" Pasha pressed him.

"What difference does it make?"

"The difference is how much money it takes to keep the door open. It's not just what you pay Kaja. It's the gas, the electricity. It's the water. It's what working so hard is doing to your heart."

"You let me worry about my own goddamned heart."

He sighed. "I'm not in the mood to argue, okay? You asked about what I thought we needed to change and I told you. But just for the record, this is my place as much as it's yours—"

"I started this business with your *mother*—"

"And I've worked here my whole goddamned life! I gave up… I gave up a lot to be here, Dad. I've earned a say in what goes on around here."

Anger flashed across the old man's face. "If I'd known you were gonna act like this, I never would've put your name on business."

"Yes, you would have. It was the only way you could keep me from leaving the way Peter did."

"What's so wrong about not wanting to lose you, too?"

"Nothing. And I love you too," he added.

Dad waved it off.

"I know how important this place is to you, but you're important to me—"

"If I'm so important to you, how come you're with that… man?" Even though they were still speaking in Russian and no one else could understand the conversation, Ivan still looked uncomfortable.

Pasha swallowed hard. He wasn't even sure he *was* with Daniel anymore. But he wasn't ready to tell his father that. "This has nothing to do with me and Daniel," he replied evenly. "This is about you taking care of yourself and us getting this place back on track." *Somehow.*

The old man made a dismissive noise. "I'm gonna go sit down. If customer comes in, you cook."

"Sure." Before Pasha went back into the kitchen, he sent Daniel a text:

I'm sorry. Please call.

It didn't surprise him, however, when his phone remained silent.

IVAN shot Pasha an askance look when he came down the stairs for breakfast the next morning. "I thought you were spending night with… friend. How come you don't got nothing packed? I don't want you bringing that *pid*… that *man* back here after work," he warned. "What will neighbors say, huh? You already give them enough to talk about."

Pasha swallowed past the lump in his throat. "Don't worry. I'm not sure… I don't think me and Daniel are going to be spending any more time together." Saying it aloud hurt. He'd sent Daniel another text last night before going to bed, just to say good night. Daniel hadn't responded.

Dad frowned. "How come?"

"We had a fight, okay?" God, he didn't want to talk about it, least of all with his father. Regardless, he kept on babbling. "We went out to dinner last night, and I said something really stupid and… and I think I broke up with him."

"Pasha, I… I don't know what to say." The softness of the old man's tone surprised him.

He smiled. "Don't worry about it, Dad."

"I worry about *you*." He hesitated for a long moment before continuing. "I might not understand this gay business, but everybody has fights. Even me and your mother. We used to… well." He shrugged, a mask of sadness covering his features. "One fight doesn't mean end of world."

It felt like it. "Thanks," he said anyway, because he knew what an effort Dad was putting in.

"Why don't you tell me more about some of these ideas you have for restaurant," Ivan suggested.

"I…. Sure." Maybe the old man was just trying to cheer him up, but either way it was a step in the right direction.

AMY came in fifteen minutes late, took one look at Pasha, and asked him what was wrong. "Me and Daniel had a fight last night." Even though Dad knew, he kept his voice down.

Amy frowned. "What about?"

"I… I don't want to talk about it here."

She started to pull him out of the old man's line of sight, but Pasha shook his head. "No. I mean I don't want to talk about it at all."

"Oh, honey, was it that bad?"

"I think I broke up with him."

"You *think*?"

Ivan glanced up—then looked away just as quickly.

Amy lowered her voice. "Either you did or you didn't, Pasha. Now which is it?"

"I didn't mean to, I just… the words came out and I walked away, and I didn't even realize what I said until it was too late. I *really* don't want to talk about it." If they talked, he'd end up telling her Daniel had HIV, and even if he never saw Daniel again, he wasn't ready to have that discussion.

"Have you tried explaining to him that you fucked up?" Amy asked.

"I would if he'd call me."

"Give it time. He'll call."

Pasha nodded, but he wasn't so sure. He'd given Daniel an ultimatum. *Don't call until you're ready to take care of yourself.* If he wasn't ready.... Pasha closed his eyes. If Daniel wasn't ready, there was nothing he could do about it. As soon as Amy went to go do something in the back, Pasha pulled out his phone and sent one more text message, promising himself that it would be the last.

I just wanted to say that no matter what happens, I care about u, he typed. Then he pocketed his phone and tried very hard not to spend the rest of the day staring at the clock, wondering what Daniel was doing.

AT FOUR, Pasha's Aunt Anya came into the restaurant through the back door, just like always. Pasha's gut tightened; whenever she came in by herself, it meant there was going to be trouble.

"*Preevyet*, Pasha," Anya called as she headed into the office to hang up her scarf and coat.

"*Preevyet*," he replied as cheerfully as he could. Only employees were supposed to use the back door. *Which is funny, because Samara always comes in the front.* Of course, so did Amy half the time. Pasha turned his attention back to the thick, deep-orange soup he had cooking in the old stove back in the prep area. Before he left for the afternoon, Ivan had—begrudgingly—given Pasha the go-ahead to try a couple of new recipes for tomorrow.

When Anya came out of the office, she peered over his shoulder and frowned. "*Chto eta*?"

"Sweet potato soup," he answered.

"*Chto*?"

He contemplated saying it in Russian, but Anya's English was just as good as his. "Sweet potato soup," he repeated.

She still looked confused. "Who puts sweet potatoes in soup?"

Pasha didn't answer.

"What are you making it for?" Anya inquired after a moment.

"Tomorrow's lunch."

"At restaurant?"

"*Da*."

"Tomorrow Sunday. You serve vegetable beef on Sunday."

Before he could answer, Sean hollered from up front. "Hey, Pasha, I got an order for you!"

"Be right there!"

"Honestly," Anya hissed. "Do you have to yell?"

Pasha ignored that question too. He turned off the burner under his soup and headed into the kitchen. Anya trailed after him.

"Oh, hi, Anya," said Sean. "How's it going?"

She wrinkled her nose. "Hello, Sean." Under her breath, she muttered in Russian about the lack of good manners in today's youth.

Pasha didn't respond. He took the ticket from the window and hung it over the grill. It was an easy one: burger, gyro, fries, chicken strips. Anya stood next to him. "Does Ivan know about this sweet potato soup of yours?"

"Yes."

"Not everybody likes sweet potatoes, you know."

"I know." Not everybody liked beef vegetable either, but he didn't point that out to her. "I made up some tomato basil bisque for tomorrow too," he said instead.

"*Two* soups? And tomato is for Wednesday." Anya spoke to him as if she were talking to an errant child. "Customers not gonna like you mixing everything up like this."

"You let me worry about customers."

Pasha looked up at the sound of his father's voice; he hadn't heard the old man come in. Apparently, neither had Anya. Her scowl deepened. "You can't go changing things around, Ivan. You'll lose customers. Things are already bad."

"That's none of your business," he told her.

"My Nikita paid for you and your family to come over here, you owe—"

Ivan waved aside her argument. "I don't owe you nothing. Me and Vera paid you back ten years ago."

She balked. Pasha was startled too. He couldn't remember his father ever talking back to Anya like that. Ivan pulled off his coat and hung it up. "You come in for lunch?" he asked his sister.

Anya nodded, still looking stunned. "*Da.* I wasn't expecting to see you. It's not even four thirty. Why are you back so early?"

He shrugged. "I get back when I get back." Ivan looked at Pasha, hesitated, and finally said, "I think you got friend waiting for you in parking lot."

"What *friend*?" Anya wanted to know.

"Pasha has friends! Everybody got friends!" Ivan snapped. "Go sit down. I'll make you something to eat." He waved her toward the dining room.

Pasha frowned while his heart started to flutter with nervous excitement. The way Dad was acting, he could only mean it was Daniel in the parking lot, but… *there's no way it's him.* If Daniel wanted to talk, he'd call or text. He wouldn't just show up. He flipped the gyro meat for Sean's order.

Ivan took the spatula from him. "You go outside. I'll finish this."

"Is this how you run business?" Anya demanded. She was still standing in the kitchen, her hands on her hips. "Letting your son's friends show up and sit in lot—"

"How I run business is none of your goddamned business! Now go sit the hell down! Pasha, go outside and see your friend."

Heat rushed to Pasha's cheeks. "Thanks. I'm sorry. I wasn't expecting…." He didn't know what else to say, especially with Anya standing there glaring.

Ivan waved it aside. "*Da.* I know. Go on. *Boistra.*"

Dad didn't have to tell him a third time. Bracing himself for disappointment—after all, it couldn't *really* be Daniel—Pasha grabbed his coat and headed out the back.

Chapter Twenty-Six

PASHA'S heart skipped a beat when he saw the green Mustang sitting out by the dumpster. It couldn't be.

But it was.

As he approached the car, Daniel leaned over and opened the passenger side door. Pasha slid in. "Hey." He had to force the word out past the lump in his throat.

"Hey yourself," Daniel answered with a tight-lipped smile. "I hope your dad didn't see me."

"He did."

"I'm sorry. I wasn't trying… I was just sitting here trying to decide if I should text you or leave."

His heart sank. If Dad hadn't seen him… *if he hadn't told me….* "Why did you come?"

"I don't know. I started driving and this is where I ended up."

Despite everything, Pasha couldn't help the soft laugh that came out. "Looks like maybe you're lost."

Daniel's smile warmed. "Looks like." His expression turned sober again. "I'm sorry, Pasha." He offered his hand.

Pasha looked at it, then looked back up at Daniel's face, meeting his gaze. "I won't sit by and watch you kill yourself, Daniel."

"Open the glove compartment."

Pasha popped it open and saw the small white paper bag with a pharmacy label. Inside it he found a white pill bottle. The label read Stribild.

"I haven't taken one yet," Daniel admitted. "I'm too scared to."

Pasha laid his hand on top of Daniel's, twining their fingers together. He gave Daniel's hand a firm squeeze. "I'm scared too. But I'm more scared of what's going to happen if you don't do what the doc says."

Daniel gave a slow, shaky nod. "I have to take those with food."

"So why don't we go get some dinner?"

"You… um… do you want to go out or…?"

"I'd like to go home and throw some clothes into a bag so I can spend the night at your house—we can talk about sleeping arrangements when we get there," he added before Daniel could say anything. "If you don't mind stopping by the store so I can go shopping, I'll cook us dinner at your place and then you can take your pill."

"I'm not sure how this stuff is going to affect me."

"That's okay. The only thing that matters to me is that you're going to take care of yourself. Let me just run in and let my dad know what's going on."

"I'm sorry he saw me."

"I'm not." He leaned over and pressed a soft, warm kiss to Daniel's mouth. Daniel responded at once, and Pasha nipped at his lower lip. Daniel let him in, let him deepen the kiss. He let out a soft, happy sigh and cupped Pasha's face in both hands, drawing him in closer. By the time they separated, Pasha was out of breath, his whole body quivering, aching. He'd never believed it was possible to love someone so much it hurt. "I'll just be a few minutes," he promised as he reached for the door handle.

"I'll be here."

"YOU cooked, you shouldn't have to clean up too," Daniel argued when Pasha tried to send him out to the living room to relax after dinner.

He'd opted for a simple, light meal of sautéed chicken breasts with lemon, dill, a little garlic and olive oil, served with baby carrots over a bed of rice. *But to watch Daniel eat it, you'd think it a five-star dinner.* Or maybe Daniel hadn't eaten much that day either. Pasha's stomach had been in knots since last night.

He was about to insist on doing the washing up, but then he remembered what Ronny said about his ex always fussing over him. "Grab a towel. I'll wash, you dry," Pasha said. Daniel didn't have a dishwasher.

"Sounds like a plan, Sugar." He took up the spot next to Pasha at the sink and they fell into an easy rhythm of washing, rinsing, and drying.

It felt nice. Comfortable.

But it would have been better if Pasha could ignore the big, ugly elephant in the room. Or maybe there was more than one. "So… about those sleeping arrangements…?" He left it open-ended.

"It's up to you," Daniel told him.

"No, babe. It's up to *us*. We're in this together."

He watched Daniel's Adam's apple bob up and down. "I hope you realize what it does to me when you say stuff like that," Daniel said, softly, sounding very uncertain of himself.

Pasha rinsed off the last of the silverware and handed it over. "This is the happiest I've been in a long time. Walking out on you last night…. God, nothing has ever hurt so much. But when you said you weren't going to start taking the drugs Doc Neumann wanted you to, when you said it was because of *me*? I *won't* be the reason you kill yourself."

"I'm sorry. That was unfair." Daniel put the silverware away and turned to face Pasha. "All I could think about was you going out last week and almost hooking up with some other guy because you were mad at me."

"I was jealous and I'm sorry. If I'd known—"

"I know. Me too. I should've handled it better on my end. I should've handled yesterday better too. I just couldn't help wondering what it was gonna be like when I had to cancel a date because I was too sick to go out or when I spent half the night in the bathroom because something I ate hit me wrong. I figured if we had a few more good times—"

"We're going to have plenty of good times," Pasha promised, sounding far more confident than he felt. He picked up the white bag Daniel had laid on the counter when they came in and took out the pill bottle.

"Maybe I should wait 'til morning to start taking those things. I'm supposed to take 'em at the same time every day. It'll be easier to remember in the morning."

He was stalling and Pasha knew it. He glanced at the clock above the stove and said, "How about I call you every night at eight forty-five and remind you?"

"I can't expect you to do that."

Pasha unscrewed the cap and took out one of the ugly olive-green pills. "Of all the things anyone's ever expected from me, I think this will be the easiest."

Daniel gave in. He poured himself a glass of water and swallowed the pill. "Now what?" he asked.

Pasha smiled. "Now, we go to bed."

"It's still early—"

"I didn't say to sleep," Pasha informed him. In addition to packing clothes and a toothbrush, he'd also packed the condoms Doc Neumann gave him the other day.

"What if I get sick?"

"Then we stop until you feel better," he said sensibly.

Daniel hesitated. "We really don't have to rush into anything. We could watch a movie."

Pasha leaned up and pressed a long, slow kiss to Daniel's lips. It was like the first time they kissed: it took Daniel a few seconds to respond, but Pasha wasn't in any rush. When he felt Daniel relaxing, he let his eyes slide shut and teased at Daniel's lower lip with the tip of his tongue. When Daniel gave in and opened his mouth, Pasha captured his lip between his teeth. He gave a gentle tug and a nibble and Daniel let out a soft, sweet moan. Pasha stopped playing and kissed him in earnest as his cock continued to swell, pushing painfully against the tight confines of his jeans. He pushed into Daniel's crotch; they were both hard as hell, and there was way too much clothing between them.

But when he put his hand on Daniel's zipper, Daniel stopped him. "Sugar, there's really an awful lot of stuff we gotta talk about while I'm still capable of talking."

"I got the safer sex talk from Doc Neumann. If there's anything else I need to know, you can fill me in as we go."

"I just…."

"Shhh." Pasha leaned in and pressed another long, sensual kiss to Daniel's mouth. "I want this. I want *you*."

Daniel nodded. He pressed a soft kiss to Pasha's lips, but before Pasha could deepen it, Daniel pulled away. "Wait here a minute, okay?"

Pasha frowned. "What's wrong?"

"Nothing, there's just something I need to do."

"Yeah, okay." But he felt more than a little dubious.

"It won't take long, promise." Daniel gave him one more quick kiss and headed in the direction of the bedroom.

Pasha looked down at Alex, who hadn't strayed far from the kitchen the entire time Pasha had been there. He was pretty sure that had more to do with the chicken than with how much Daniel's cat liked him. Just the same, Pasha knelt down so he was at kitty level, and the giant beast came bounding over to be petted. When Pasha scratched behind its ears, the cat let out a loud rumble of a purr.

Pasha watched the seconds tick by on the clock. After five very long minutes had passed, he stood up and headed through the living room and into the short hallway that led to Daniel's bedroom. The door was shut, but a faint orange light flickered through the crack at the bottom. "Hey, I'm getting kinda lonely out here," he called.

"I'm sure Alex is keeping you company." Daniel's grin was audible. So was his nervousness.

Alex threaded eagerly between Pasha's legs, eventually coming to stand in front of him. He rose up on his hind feet, stretching, pawing at Pasha's stomach. "Yeah, he is, but he's not the guy I want to spend my time with tonight." He scratched behind the persistent cat's ears some more, anyway.

Finally, the bedroom door opened and Daniel stepped out into the hall.

Pasha's breath caught in his throat. Daniel was shirtless, and his hair hung over his broad, strong shoulders. Behind him, the bedroom was lit up by dozens of flickering candles. The light danced on Daniel's smooth, bronze skin, playing over his muscles, making him look almost ethereal.

"I wanted this to be special." Daniel sounded embarrassed. "I hope you don't think—"

"It's *beautiful*." No one had ever done anything like that for him before. Emotion surged in his chest, making him almost blurt out the words *I love you.* But he kept the words safely tucked inside in case Daniel wasn't ready to hear them yet. "You're beautiful," he said instead and reached out and brushed Daniel's hair away from his chest. Daniel shivered under his touch. "You have a tattoo."

"Yeah. I…." But Daniel didn't finish his statement.

It didn't matter. Pasha understood without being told that he had gotten it after he was diagnosed with HIV. Pasha traced the thick dark lines of the hourglass design with his fingertips. *Life is short.* He ran his hands lightly over the rest of Daniel's chest, causing goose bumps to rise on his skin and his nipples to harden into nubs. With a wicked smile, Pasha gave in to temptation and took one of them into his mouth.

Daniel gasped, then moaned. He wrapped his arms around Pasha's shoulders, and Pasha began to suck in earnest. He took Daniel's other nipple between his thumb and forefinger and gave a gentle squeeze.

"Oh God," Daniel rasped.

Smiling, Pasha swirled his tongue over the hard nub in his mouth and canted his hips so he was rubbing his groin into Daniel's crotch. The sensation was maddening, especially with so many layers of clothing keeping them from actually touching. He wanted Daniel's skin, he wanted his cock, he wanted his whole body.

"God, you're incredible," Daniel whispered, the words bringing a rush of warmth to Pasha's heart.

He looked up, but before he could respond, his mouth was devoured by a hungry kiss. Daniel's tongue darted between his lips. It wasn't slow and it wasn't sweet, but it was exactly what Pasha wanted in the moment. They could do slow and sweet later. Daniel's arms tightened around him and suddenly Pasha was hoisted up into the air. With a startled cry, he wrapped his legs around Daniel's waist and his arms around Daniel's neck. Daniel carried him with ease into the bedroom. He laid Pasha down onto the bed without breaking the kiss and straddled him, nudging Pasha's knees open. Pasha didn't resist. Daniel could have anything he wanted. *Everything* he wanted.

Except when Daniel started pulling Pasha's shirt up over his head, he felt suddenly self-conscious. Daniel's body was so beautiful. Lean. Golden. Nearly hairless. Exactly the opposite of Pasha.

But Daniel smiled down at him. "I meant what I said, babe. You are incredible. Beautiful. I…." He hesitated. "I want to see you. All of you." He leaned in and gave Pasha's mouth another kiss, and Pasha surrendered to it at once. This time Daniel's kiss was soft and slow. It was sweet. Gentle. It made Pasha's toes curl and his knees feel weak. Daniel nipped at his lips and nudged his cheek until Pasha turned his head so Daniel could kiss his neck. Daniel kept it up until Pasha was so desperate he stopped feeling self-conscious and lifted his arms so Daniel could pull off his shirt. He kept his eyes closed as Daniel's hands explored his body.

Pasha shivered and moaned, as moments later, fingertips were replaced by lips. Daniel feathered a trail of soft kisses from Pasha's neck all the way down to his belly button. His cock felt like it was going to burst out of his jeans, but he didn't care if Daniel wanted to take all night touching, exploring, getting to know each other's bodies.

He felt Daniel's lips curl into a smile against his skin and then Daniel shifted and kissed his way back up Pasha's stomach toward his chest. Very, very slowly, he ran the tip of his tongue around Pasha's right nipple. Pasha whimpered and squirmed as Daniel began to suck on it. His whole body felt like it was on fire—God, there was no way to have an orgasm just from this, was there? And if this was what Daniel did with his nipple, what was it going to feel like to have that mouth on his cock?

By the time Daniel shifted his attention over to the other nipple, Pasha was ready to promise anything just to find out.

When he felt Daniel's hands on his zipper, he didn't protest. He let Daniel finish undressing him even though he hated the way he looked. "What about you?" Pasha asked. Daniel hadn't made a move to take off his own jeans yet.

"I'm good for now."

"I want you inside me, Daniel. I want you to fuck me."

"We've got all night, Sugar. I promise, I will do whatever you want me to."

Pasha nodded—but the uncertainty that flickered over Daniel's features wasn't lost on him. "What is it?"

"There are things that get spread… HIV isn't the only STD out there. I'm willing to trust you if you say you're sure you don't have anything else." But he looked nervous.

It took Pasha a second to get it, to remember the part of Doc Neumann's lecture about how easily gonorrhea got spread orally. It made him glad he hadn't sucked off any of the anonymous hookups he'd been with last year, even though a few of them had gone down on him. "If you don't have anything, I brought the condoms I got from Doc Neumann with me just in case. They're in my backpack."

Daniel went from looking nervous to looking embarrassed. "I… went shopping. I wasn't assuming anything, I just figured better safe than sorry."

Pasha cupped Daniel's cheek and drew him into a soft, slow kiss. "Why don't we use whatever's closest?"

"I'm sorry this has to be so complicated."

He caressed Daniel's cheek with his thumb. "Weren't you the one who said it's not the complications that matter, it's what you do with them?"

Daniel smiled. "Guess I did, didn't I?" He leaned over to the nightstand and took three brand-new boxes of condoms and several bottles of lube out of the drawer.

Pasha snickered. "You planning an orgy or something?"

Color rose in Daniel's cheeks. "I didn't know what you liked."

"So you bought out the whole store?"

"Maybe I went a little overboard."

Pasha propped himself up on his elbows for a better look at what Daniel had got for them. One box of rubbers was just standard lubed condoms, while the other two were unlubricated condoms in different assortments of flavors. For lube, his choices were strawberry, cookies and cream, cinnamon, warming, and plain. Pasha flashed a wicked smile. "Please tell me there was some pimple-faced kid at the cash register."

Daniel laughed. "It was a little old man. He was mortified. I came this close to asking him if he'd like to stop by later, but I was afraid I'd give the poor guy a stroke."

"God I…." *love you.* He bit back the words at the last second.

"What is it?" Daniel asked.

"Nothing. I'm just really glad I met you."

For half a second, Daniel almost looked hurt—but then he smiled again. "Me too." He tore open one of the boxes of flavored condoms and made his selection. "Mint," he said, holding it up. "My favorite." He set the packet aside and reached for the plain lube. He squeezed a generous amount of it on his hands and rubbed them together. Then he took Pasha's shaft in one hand and stroked it slowly, coating it with lube from tip to base and back again.

Pasha's eyes rolled back in his head and his toes curled—and suddenly his cock was engulfed in warmth. He opened his eyes and peered down at the top of Daniel's head. Was Daniel putting the condom on him with his *mouth*?

When Daniel looked up, his triumphant smile told Pasha that that was *exactly* what he'd done.

"I sure hope you don't expect me to be able to do that," Pasha told him.

"I wasn't sure I still could," he admitted. Then he dipped his head and Pasha let out a soft, happy sigh as his cock was once more enveloped by the heat of Daniel's mouth.

There was a little loss of sensation with the latex between them, but Daniel seemed determined to make it up for him, laving his tongue around the head of Pasha's dick until Pasha was squirming. "Oh God," he moaned when Daniel took the entire shaft to the back of his throat. Daniel bobbed his head up and down several times very, *very* slowly, until Pasha thought he was going to go through the roof. “Please,” he begged. Then he gasped when he felt a lube-slicked finger pressing against his entrance. “Not too much.”

“I’ll go slow, promise.” Daniel’s voice was soft, reassuring. “You can tell I put a glove on, right?”

“No…. I mean… yeah.” He knew the difference between a naked finger and one covered in latex. “But I don’t….” Embarrassment heated his cheeks. “Not too much prep. I like it when it hurts a little.” Why was admitting that to Daniel so hard?

But Daniel didn’t seem bothered by it at all. “Whatever you want, Sugar, just as long as I don’t end up hurting you in a bad way.”

“You won’t.” He closed his eyes and let his head rest against the pillow as Daniel went back to work lavishing attention on his cock, one finger lazily circling his entrance, playing at it, making him shudder, teasing him until Pasha was ready to scream at Daniel to just fuck him already—and then he felt it. The tip of Daniel’s finger slipped past the tight ring of muscles. “Oh that feels so good.” Daniel’s finger was thick. Long. He pressed in slowly, carefully. Then he pulled out a little and Pasha mewled in protest—but a second later, Daniel pushed back into him. “More,” Pasha told him and he moaned when he felt Daniel’s knuckle breach his entrance. Daniel crooked his finger and went straight for the sweet spot, sending a sheet of fire and ice cascading through Pasha’s whole body.

When a second finger joined the first, it was too much. Pasha let out a strangled cry as the orgasm ripped through him. He’d wanted it to last all night, but it was hard to be disappointed when he opened his eyes and saw the happy look on Daniel’s face. He looked so satisfied, so pleased with himself. “Come here,” Pasha coaxed.

Before Daniel slid closer, he removed the spent condom, tied it off, and deposited it in the trash can under the nightstand along with the latex glove he’d been wearing. Then, moving very slowly like he still wasn’t feeling too sure of himself, Daniel straddled Pasha’s waist.

Pasha smiled. He reached for Daniel’s zipper. Daniel was trembling. Pasha undid his fly and, with Daniel’s help, he pulled the jeans and gray cotton briefs down past Daniel’s hips, freeing Daniel’s cock. The thick, uncut shaft rose in a graceful curve up from a patch of black curls. It was a good eight inches long and lined with dark veins.

A darkened head peaked out from behind the foreskin. When Pasha reached out and touched him, Daniel shuddered, but otherwise he remained motionless and silent as Pasha caressed his length.

Knowing the next move was his, Pasha reached for the box of lubed condoms on the nightstand and ripped it open. "I ah, I hope I don't sound totally stupid when I tell you I've never been with a guy who wasn't circumcised before. I'm not quite sure how to do this."

"You never sound stupid, Sugar." He took the foil packet from Pasha's hand and showed him how to put it on.

Watching Daniel pull back his foreskin and slide the latex into place was a definite turn-on. His cock had begun to come back to life while he was stroking Daniel, but now it stood at full attention. With both hands, Pasha reached up and twined his fingers into Daniel's hair so he could pull him down for another kiss. Daniel tasted vaguely of mint and latex, but it was hard to care about the strange flavors when he had Daniel's tongue exploring every inch of his mouth.

Daniel shifted and kissed Pasha's neck, nipped at his earlobe, then kissed his way slowly around Pasha's jaw to the other earlobe before making a trail of soft, sensual kisses down Pasha's chest and to his stomach. "And just for the record," Daniel whispered, when he got to Pasha's belly button.

Pasha looked down at him. "Hmm?" was the best he could do for words.

"I love your body."

Pasha smiled and lay back as Daniel shimmied the rest of the way out of his jeans and settled back between his thighs. He drizzled lube onto his shaft, coating it liberally before driving it home in one smooth stroke that had Pasha's eyes rolling back in his head.

CHAPTER TWENTY-SEVEN

PASHA woke encircled in strong arms, surrounded by Daniel's warmth and the musky sweet scent of sex. The room was cast half in shadow, as only one bright ray of sunlight streamed in through a cat-sized part in the drapes. Alex lounged on the sill looking at something outside. He didn't twitch a muscle when Pasha extracted himself from Daniel's embrace to reach for the flavored condoms and lube. He made a hasty selection and gently pulled back the covers.

As soon as Pasha began stroking him, Daniel stirred to wakefulness, a slow, lazy smile stretched across his face. "Morning, Sugar."

"Morning, yourself." Pasha slid Daniel's foreskin back carefully, doing his best to mimic the way Daniel had done it the night before, and slowly rolled the condom into place. A quick look at Daniel's face told him he'd done it right. Feeling pleased with himself, Pasha lowered his mouth over Daniel's hard cock. He'd chosen a strawberry-flavored condom, but as soon as he had it in his mouth, he realized it didn't taste like strawberry at all. The only thing he could taste was the latex. Worse, the texture was… *rubbery.* Pasha closed his eyes and tried to ignore the flavor and texture, but it was like trying to suck on a balloon and make it sensual.

Daniel must have noticed his discomfort. "Sometimes a little flavored lube outside helps."

"Yeah." Pasha doubted anything was going to help, but he reached for the strawberry lube anyway and squirted a little on his finger. It tasted more like strawberry gum or strawberry pop than actual strawberries, but he spread the lube on Daniel's cock and tried again. The combination of sugar and rubber made his stomach lurch.

A morning blowjob was supposed to be spontaneous and fun, not something he had to think about. He wanted to make Daniel feel as good as Daniel had made him feel last night. He wanted to prove to Daniel that he wasn't afraid of any part of him. He didn't want to be like Ronny's ex or some of the asswipes he'd seen online. But he couldn't do it, not with fucking latex between them. "I'm sorry," he said as he sat up.

The look on Daniel's face almost killed him. Daniel wasn't angry, he was just… sad. "Don't worry about it, Sugar." He took the condom off and dropped it in the trash can under his nightstand, then left the bedroom without another word.

Pasha sat there for several long moments, not sure what to do. Around the room, dozens of burned-down candles stood as a reminder of how beautiful last night had been—how beautiful Daniel had made it. *Because he wanted our first time to be special.*

That was all Pasha had wanted this morning to be. Special.

Only instead of making it special, I acted like an ass hat because I couldn't get past a little latex.

A high-pitched whir cut through his unhappy thoughts. He realized Daniel had been gone for longer than it should have taken to go to the bathroom and clean up—and there it was again, the whirring noise.

Pasha grabbed a T-shirt and sweatpants out of his backpack and padded toward the source of the sound. He found Daniel in the kitchen, wrapped in a dark-green bathrobe, standing over a coffee grinder. There was a French press sitting next to the electric tea kettle, where water was heating. Behind it sat three brown paper bags labeled "Italian Roast Espresso," "Kona," and "White Russian." The open bag at Daniel's elbow read "Jamaican Blue Mountain."

"I wasn't sure what you liked," Daniel said over his shoulder. "And the white Russian was kind of an impulse buy," he added with a wan smile.

Pasha made his way over to where Daniel stood. "You didn't have to go through all this trouble." He didn't know what else to say.

He'd expected Daniel to go out and get a cheap little coffeemaker and a tin of Folgers.

"The lady at the shop swore that if I wanted to impress my coffee-addicted boyfriend, this was the way to go."

"Coffee-addicted, huh?" Pasha challenged, doing his best to tease, to keep the mood light, despite the growing knot in his gut.

"You threatened to break up with me, remember?" Daniel teased back.

"Yeah, well. It was early and I was grumpy."

Daniel popped open the coffee grinder, filling the kitchen with the aroma of fresh ground coffee beans. *Because instead of getting a tin of Folgers, he went out and got a coffee press and some of the best coffee on the market.* It was more than Pasha deserved. "Daniel, about earlier—"

"It's okay."

"It's *not* okay."

"It's going to have to be," Daniel snapped. He took a breath and let it out, then turned back to the task of making Pasha's coffee. "I can't expect you—*no one* can expect you to do something that makes you uncomfortable."

"Going down on you doesn't make me uncomfortable. It was just… latex tastes like shit and strawberry-flavored shit is still shit."

"I get that, babe, honest. Come on, let's just have some breakfast and figure out what we're gonna do today, okay?"

"Yeah, okay." He didn't want to fight and he was pretty sure that was the only place the conversation would lead if he pursued it. "Just tell me you accept my apology?"

Daniel turned and gathered him into his arms. "Of course I accept your apology."

Pasha laid his head against Daniel's chest and snuggled in close. "I picked up some fliers at Doc Neumann's office for support groups. For sero-discordant couples. If, um, if you think that's something you might be interested in checking out."

"I'd like that."

Pasha let out the breath he barely realized he'd been holding. "There's a group that meets on Sundays at a church somewhere around here. I know it's not the most romantic thing in the world, but maybe—?"

Daniel feathered a kiss to his temple. "What time do they meet?"

"Three thirty."

"Sounds good."

Pasha looked up at him. "You sure?"

"I'm happier than I've been in a long time too, Sugar. I want this to work. I want… I want a lot of things." He pressed a kiss to Pasha's lips. "When we're together I start to think some of those things might really be possible."

"Me too." He shifted his weight away from Daniel. "It's still pretty early." It was barely 9:00 a.m. "If you want, after breakfast, we can go to the mall. I mean, if you've still got shopping to do."

"You sure you don't mind?" Daniel asked.

"I'm sure. I should probably try to finish up the last of my Christmas shopping, too."

"IT WAS the worst day of my life," said Stan, a tall, thin old man wearing khaki chinos and a pale-blue shirt. Like the guy at Doc Neumann's office, his cheeks were hollow and his hands looked like bone with skin stretched over them—but instead of acting like a man who was dying, he kept smiling, even as he was telling about the worst day of his life. His partner, an old, portly man named Terry, reached over and took his hand.

"It was the eighties," Stan went on, "we only barely had a name for all this back then. The only thing the guy at the health clinic told me was 'you have AIDS' and then he walked out of the room. I thought that was it, my life was over."

"I'm glad he was wrong," said Terry. "Otherwise I might never have met the love of my life."

Stan waved him off. "You're nothing but a sentimental old fool. God knows why I keep you around." But he was smiling and snickers ran through the circle, as if that was the kind of banter the rest of the group was used to out of the pair.

There were eight couples total in the basement meeting room at the Unitarian church—a room that was eerily similar to the ones in the church Pasha used to go to as a kid. Maybe it was a church thing. Maybe they were all the same. Sitting there reminded him of being in Sunday school and of sitting in old, too-big, metal folding chairs in a circle, listening to Matushka tell Bible stories. All things considered, it wasn't a comfortable memory. Matushka had never talked about homosexuality; Father didn't either. But Pasha knew the Russian Orthodox Church's stance on the subject, and he knew what was going on in Russia.

He shifted in his seat and the chair squeaked and scraped against the hard tile floor. Heat rose in Pasha's cheeks, and Daniel gave his hand a squeeze. When they'd arrived fifteen minutes ago, Stan and a guy named Steve had greeted Daniel by name, offering up warm hugs and friendly handshakes. Apparently, they were in Daniel's regular support group, the one for people living with HIV. It was stupid and selfish, but Pasha had expected they would both be new here. Knowing Daniel had friends in the group made him feel more out of place than ever.

Of the seven other couples, three were heterosexual. "Josh and I went into the clinic together," one of the women said. She was slim and dark skinned, with close-cropped, tight, curly hair, huge brown eyes, and a chunk of silver-wrapped quartz crystal on a braided cord around her neck. Her name was Cate, and she was HIV positive. "We weren't sure what to expect. I um… I'd had some problems with drugs," she admitted. "And when I got high, I did stupid things. But Josh stuck by me." She favored her boyfriend with a warm smile.

He smiled back. He was slender and tall with a long, curly red beard and a balding head, and he was wearing a plaid flannel shirt that made him look like a lumberjack. "When Cate came out into the waiting room and told me… man, I lost it," he said.

Even though Pasha and Daniel were the only new members of the group, everyone was recounting something about what it was like when they found out they or their partner had HIV. Pasha wasn't sure if it was a regular part of the meetings or if they were doing it because there were new people there today.

Josh went on. "All I could picture was me at her funeral."

She laughed. "At least he had the decency to put me in my favorite dress."

"You guys talked about it?" Pasha blurted out. Heat stained his cheeks and the chair squeaked again.

But Cate took it in stride. "I wanted to know what he was planning to make sure he got it right," she told him with a smile.

"There's no right or wrong way to cope with it," said a man named Keith. He was in his thirties and HIV negative; his partner was Steve, who had been living with HIV for eight years.

Like Daniel—and Cate for that matter—Steve was in great health. Looking at him, no one would guess that he had HIV. "All that matters is that you *do* cope with it," he said. "I went into a tailspin when I first found out. I totally drowned myself at the bottom of a vodka bottle. I just couldn't believe it had happened to me."

"I was the opposite," said Daniel, and Pasha's heart lodged in his throat. He was sure he could never be so calm talking about it, if it was him. "I um… I don't know for sure if I'm really an alcoholic or just a guy who doesn't know when to say when, but I did a lot of drinking when I was in college. That and some other stupid stuff is what landed me here. After I got HIV, I cleaned up my act, stopped drinking." He short Pasha a nervous glance. "I realized that if I didn't make some serious changes, I was gonna mess my life up even more."

Pasha pulled Daniel's hand up to his lips and kissed it. Nothing Daniel had said surprised him, and none of it made him love Daniel any less.

"Zack and me went in together," said a young man who had introduced himself as Jeremy. He was negative, his boyfriend was positive. They didn't look much older than eighteen or nineteen. When they introduced themselves, they said they'd been together for six months and that Zack had tested positive just four weeks ago. "When we got our results, I couldn't believe it. I mean, how did he have it and not me? We hadn't exactly been careful…. I felt so fucking guilty that he had it but I didn't. For a while all I could think was how we should keep on doing it without a condom, so I'd get it too, that way things would be level, you know? It wouldn't be so complicated. A bunch of people talked me out of it, including Zack." He glanced at his boyfriend. "I still don't know how you have it and I don't."

"I'm just lucky, I guess," Zack joked.

"If you look at the statistics," said Keith, "you start to wonder how anybody gets HIV at all. There's only something like a 1 percent chance that any given encounter will end with the virus being passed on. And yet, here we all are."

"And guilt is normal," Steve added, shooting his partner a look.

"Yeah," Keith agreed. "When we met, Steve had already been living with HIV for about four years. When he told me, I was gobsmacked. I couldn't believe this amazing, intelligent man had been dumb enough to get himself infected."

Steve rolled his eyes. "He overestimates how smart I am."

Around the room people chuckled, and couples held hands.

Keith went on, "And then I got to thinking about all of the less than smart things *I'd* done and suddenly I felt so guilty. How did he have it and not me? We broke up for a while because I was such an idiot about how I felt. We didn't talk to each other enough in the beginning."

"Talking's hard," Steve added. "I didn't want to tell him how scared I was of getting sick. I don't want anybody having to take care of me; I *don't* want my lover to see me as weak or frail. I can't help it. It's the way I was raised," he explained with a shrug. "Men are supposed to be the strong ones in the relationship, and being gay doesn't change that for me. But having HIV does. I know that someday he *is* going to have to take care of me and I'm going to have to let him."

Keith snorted. "And tomorrow, I might get run over by a bus and you'll be the one wiping the drool off my chin," he joked.

Everyone laughed and Pasha gave Daniel's hand another small kiss. He'd been so busy thinking about how scared *he* was that he hadn't stopped to think how Daniel must feel about getting sick someday and being dependent on someone else to take care of him. He leaned into Daniel's shoulder and Daniel kissed the top of his head. *Please give me the strength and grace I'm going to need*, Pasha prayed.

"When me and Dustin moved in together," said a woman named Anne, "and I started telling some of my friends that he had HIV, my ex tried to sue for custody of our daughter. I couldn't believe it. I couldn't believe the judge actually wanted to hear it. He finally ruled in our favor, said that Melody was perfectly safe, but that hasn't stopped my ex and his family from trying to poison her against us. It doesn't help that my mom is on *their* side. She's sure that both Melody and me are going to get infected. She's my mother. She's supposed to be on *my* side. We haven't spoken in over a year."

"Yeah, my brother flipped out too," said Josh. "He wanted me to leave Cate, get tested again, all kinds of stupid crap. I told him, no way."

"It's not stupid," Terry countered diplomatically. "People are scared of this thing because they don't understand it—and how can they? All they see is what's on the news or the Internet. What the hell did you kids do before Facebook, anyway, when you actually had to pick up a telephone and *dial* a number to talk to somebody?"

Everyone laughed.

Terry continued. "Too many people are afraid to come out and say 'I'm positive' or 'I'm partnered with someone who's positive.' We're afraid we'll lose our jobs, our homes, our families. We're not always wrong. But if we don't come out of the HIV closet, the only thing other people have to judge us by are numbers on a page. And it's easy to be afraid of numbers. Numbers aren't our neighbors and friends; they aren't our brothers and sisters. Numbers are just nameless, faceless black squiggles. But when we come out, like Anne with her ex, we risk losing everything. It's an awful, vicious cycle."

Stan chuckled—then coughed violently. "My husband, the philosopher, ladies and gentleman," he teased when the coughing finally subsided.

Terry shook his head and handed Stan his water bottle.

"YOU doing okay?" Daniel asked as they crossed the parking lot holding hands.

"I think so." Not everyone had families like Josh's or Anne's. Terry had been married before coming out and had grown children and grandchildren who visited him all the time. His daughter worried about Stan's health, but not about her kids getting HIV. Of course, looking at Stan and Terry made Pasha feel like he was looking into his future with Daniel.

When they reached Daniel's car, Pasha leaned against it and pulled Daniel in close for a warm, sensual kiss.

"Not that I'm complaining, but what was that for?"

"I figure I'd better get in as many kisses as I can before you take me home, because it's going to be almost three weeks before I get to see you again. You're headed home to your parents' place next weekend." He didn't expect to see Daniel again until he got back.

"I was thinking about that. How about I leave on Sunday afternoon next week instead of Saturday morning like I was originally planning? That is, if you want to stay over with me again," he added sheepishly.

"I'd love to, but are you sure?"

"Ma'll understand. They get me for two whole weeks. I only get one day a week with you." Daniel cupped Pasha's cheeks in both hands. "Call me selfish, but I don't want to give that up."

Pasha leaned in and Daniel met his kiss halfway. He nipped at Pasha's lower lip and sucked on it the way Pasha had done to his last night before finally kissing him fully. "Any chance we could go back to your place for a while?" Pasha asked when they drew apart.

"Not if we're going to get some dinner before I get you home."

"I don't need food."

Daniel rubbed his thumbs over Pasha's cheeks. "Yes you do. We'll have next weekend, Sugar."

"And then you're gone for two weeks."

"Yeah, but then I get to come home and show you how much I missed you."

God, I love you. But he still didn't say it aloud. He just got into the car so they could go find something for dinner.

"There's something I wanted to talk to you about," Daniel said as he slid in behind the wheel.

"Whatever it is, it doesn't sound good."

"No. I mean…." He took a quick breath and let it out, like he was trying to gather his thoughts. "I haven't said yes yet. My friend Erika is the stage director for a community theater troupe. She's trying to get me to audition for *Rent* next spring."

"And…?"

Daniel shot him a sidelong glance. "Do you have any idea what the play is about?"

"Sorry, I've never even heard of it."

"You're kidding."

He shrugged. When did he have time for plays? "I remember you said Erika dragged you on stage to sing some song from *Rent* the night you went out to karaoke for your birthday," Pasha told him.

"The CD's in the player if you want to listen to it. But ah… it's kind of another one of those bittersweet pills."

"How so?"

"It was written back in the early nineties and it's about a bunch of people living—and dying—with HIV. Erika's doing it to raise community awareness, so it's not going to be any big secret everyone in it is positive in real life. That's why she asked me to audition. I ah, I'm not real closeted about much of anything."

Pasha couldn't help but smile. Daniel was the guy who'd brought his boyfriend to a school dance. "Do you want to audition for it?"

"Only if it's something you're comfortable with me doing, Sugar."

Which was tantamount to saying yes. "Why wouldn't I be?"

Daniel was quiet for several long minutes. "I have to ask," he finally said. "Have you mentioned to any of your friends that I've got HIV?"

"I wasn't sure… I mean, I don't know what I should say," Pasha answered truthfully. Next to him, Daniel nodded and turned his attention to the road. It was starting to snow again, but Pasha was pretty sure that wasn't why Daniel was suddenly so interested in the traffic. "Talk to me?" Pasha said softly.

Daniel reached over for his hand and Pasha took it. "You heard what some of those guys said back at the meeting, and I told you what happened to me, how so many of the people I thought were my friends just… they abandoned me. I know I said I don't blame them, but that doesn't mean it didn't hurt, babe. It makes me scared of what's gonna happen when your friends start telling you not to go out with me."

"I'm not."

Daniel shot him a questioning look.

"I want this. I want *you*," he repeated what he'd said the night before. "Nothing is going to change that."

"Are you sure?"

Pasha ran his thumb over the back of Daniel's hand. "I'm completely sure." He leaned forward and turned on the CD player. "So. Which part are you trying out for?" he asked.

Daniel gave his hand a squeeze. "Click to track number thirteen. That's the duet between Collins, the role Erika wants me for, and Angel. I ah… maybe I should warn you that they're kind of a couple."

"Is Angel a guy or a girl?"

"Drag queen."

Pasha just grinned. "I think I'm looking forward to seeing this already."

CHAPTER TWENTY-EIGHT

"I S'POSE making out in front of your house again is probably a bad idea, huh?" Daniel asked when he pulled up to the curb.

Pasha smiled. A faint yellow-orange glow shone from behind the curtains in the front window, which meant Dad was in the living room watching TV. "Yeah, probably." He leaned over anyway and pressed a soft, chaste kiss to Daniel's lips. "Call me when you get home?"

"Will do."

Shouldering his backpack, Pasha gathered up his shopping bags from the backseat and headed across the street toward his house. When he got to the porch, he turned and waved. Daniel waved back and eased away from the curb. Pasha stood there with giant white snowflakes falling down around him until Daniel's taillights vanished around the corner. "Thank you," he whispered up quietly toward the sky before letting himself into the house.

"I was starting to think you were never coming home," the old man greeted him sourly.

Pasha forced a smile. "It's only eight o'clock." He left his shoes and bags by the front door and hung his coat up in the hall closet, then joined his father in the living room.

Instead of watching television, Dad was sitting on the sofa, flipping through an old photo album. "You eat supper?" the old man asked.

"*Da*." He and Daniel had stopped for a quick bite on the way—only figuring out where to go wasn't a quick or easy decision. Daniel still didn't know what would upset his stomach and what would be fine. *It won't always be this complicated.* They both kept saying it. Pasha just hoped it was true. "How was work?" he asked his father.

Ivan made a disgruntled noise.

"Was it busy?"

Dad just shrugged.

Pasha leaned against the doorjamb. "How'd the soup go over?" He finally asked what he really wanted to know.

Dad didn't answer.

"Customers hated it, didn't they?" he hazarded.

"We sold out of sweet potato soup." But Dad didn't sound happy about it.

"And the tomato?" Pasha asked.

"There's some left. Not a lot. Maybe we do lunch special or something tomorrow."

"Yeah, we could do that," Pasha agreed. Of course his mind was conjuring up images of grilled smoked-gouda sandwiches on artisan bread. More likely, it would be a slice of American on whatever bread they weren't out of. "I was thinking about Christmas Eve," he said slowly.

"What about it?"

"We close at four." That was nothing new; the old man had always closed for Christmas Eve. "I'm pretty sure Amy doesn't have class that day. Why don't I ask her if she'll come in for me—"

"Why, so you can go spend more time with that man?" Ivan snapped.

Pasha bit back an angry response. "No. So I can cook and you can have a day off."

Ivan balked. "I already have Christmas off."

"This would give you a day to actually rest. On Christmas you're going to be working your ass off around here."

"I told you, I'll rest when I'm dead."

Maybe Dad was just one of those people who wasn't happy unless he was miserable. "All right. I'm going upstairs."

"Pasha." Ivan called him back before he'd taken two steps. "Are you seeing that man again next Sunday?"

"Yes."

"Same as this week? He's gonna pick you up on Saturday?"

"That's the plan, why?"

"You gonna spend every weekend with him now?"

"He's going home for a couple of weeks over the holidays, but yeah, we're planning on spending our weekends together as much as possible."

Instead of some acerbic comment about how Pasha was going to be the boss someday, Ivan asked, "Where's he from?"

Pasha blinked in surprise. Why the hell did Dad care where Daniel was from? But he answered anyway. "Hannahville—it's up in the UP."

"He has big family up there?"

"Pretty big, yeah. Why?"

Ivan didn't answer him. "Come here. Sit down. I want to talk to you."

"We are talking."

"So come here and sit down," the old man grumbled. "You got plenty of time for this boyfriend, but no time for your own father?"

For a second Pasha was too stunned to move. Going from *pidoras* to "that man" was a huge step for his dad, but for the old man to actually call Daniel his boyfriend? Pasha made his way over to the sofa and sat down next to his father. "What're you looking at?" he asked.

"You kids, when you were little." Ivan tilted the book so he could see.

Pasha smiled. The first picture on the page was of him and Nadia, sitting on some mall Santa's lap. It was yellowed with age, faded around the edges, but he and his sister both wore huge, sappy grins. Only little kids who had no idea what life was really like could smile like that. He reached across his father's lap to turn the page, revealing more pictures of him and Nadia, a few of Peter, sitting in front of a colorfully decorated Christmas tree. Nearly all of the ornaments were made of construction paper, put together by children's clumsy hands.

They were gaudy, glittery, cheap. There were only a few brightly wrapped boxes under the tree, and none of them were big.

"That was your first Christmas in United States," Ivan told him.

"I don't remember it, but I remember that tree." He remembered sitting with Nadia making paper chains out of red and green construction paper and making folded paper bells and cutting out paper angels. It had been a long time since he and his sister were that close.

"We came here with so little. Travel was expensive. We couldn't afford to bring more than few suitcases on the plane. We had to mail trunk with your grandmother's dishes in it. Your mother was so worried they would break." His smile faltered. Neither of them brought up the fire in the microwave. "When we first got here, we lived with Anya and Nikita for three months before we bought this house. You remember that?"

"Only bits and pieces," he admitted.

"Ah. You were practically baby, how could you remember? Me and your mother came here because we wanted better life for you kids, better life for ourselves. Look what it got us."

"Can I ask you a question?"

The old man nodded. "*Da*. What is it?"

"If you'd known…. I mean, if there had been any way anyone could know Mom would get sick like that, would you still… would you have made the choices you made? Would you still have married her?"

"Pasha. How can you ask question like that?"

It didn't seem like the right time to mention that his boyfriend had HIV. "It's just that with everything that happened—"

"You listen to me. Your mother gave me best years of my life. No fucking disease gonna take that away. She gave me you and Nadia and Peter. Alzheimer's not gonna take that away, neither. I wouldn't change a goddamned *thing*. You got that?"

"I just… yeah, okay."

"Love is funny thing, Pasha. When I first saw your mother it was like I couldn't breathe. I couldn't think about anything but her. She was beautiful woman when she was younger." He flipped back to the beginning of the photo album to a faded picture of his mom in a swimsuit on some beach. She was standing, her hands shading her eyes, auburn hair flying in the wind, staring at the person taking the photo.

Pasha had seen it before, but he'd never really paid attention.

"That was first day we met," his father told him. "And that was me taking picture, before I even went up to say hello. My parents never liked her."

"You never told me that before."

"Why would I?"

Good point. Dad barely talked about his family at all. Anya didn't much either, but at least she had pictures of their parents hanging up in her house. "What did your parents have against Mom?"

"They said she was too old. You know she was almost thirty-one when we met—I was just your age, twenty-four. Your mother had never been married and she wasn't widow. My mother wanted to know what was wrong with her, how come she not have husband already."

"You know, thirty-one isn't that old, Dad."

"Russia is whole different world, Pasha. And it wasn't even Russia then, it was still Soviet Union. It's funny. Under Communist laws women equal to men—same pay for same work—but people… people are always people. My mother wanted me to marry woman like her. Someone to be wife to me and mother to my children. But your mother… oh she was smart lady, Pasha." A ghost of a smile flickered across his lips, then died again as quickly as it had appeared. "My mother and father wouldn't even come to church when me and your mother got married. They said I was making mistake marrying 'old maid,' that nothing good would come of it. If they could see me now…." He shook his head, the sadness seeming to weigh him down. "Tell me something, Pasha. Did I do right by you? Was I okay father? I know sometimes I was too hard on you, but you know I did best I knew how, don't you?"

"Of course I do. Being a parent isn't easy. I don't have to have kids of my own to see that."

"I *want* you to have kids." He hit his balled-up fist against his knee. "I *want* you to get married, be like Peter. Like Nadia. You're good man, Pasha. You'd make good husband. Good father."

"I want that too. I don't know if it's ever going to happen—"

"It *won't* happen, not as long as you're playing around with that man!" he snapped.

Pasha counted slowly to ten. "It's not playing around. This is my life. It's who I am. I wish you could understand it and I'm sorry that you don't, but I'm not sorry for being gay."

"I don't understand this homosexual business, Pasha. I don't understand how…." He hesitated. "I don't understand world no more. Things used to make sense. Now *nothing* makes sense. How could my own son… do you love this man? He asked the same question he'd asked the other day in the kitchen.

This time Pasha told him the truth. "Yes. I do."

Does he love you?"

Pasha swallowed past the lump in his throat. He wished he had some idea where the conversation was going. Just the same, he answered honestly. "I think so."

"You think?" Ivan questioned.

"We haven't said the words, but I'm pretty sure he loves me too." He was sure he'd never seen his father looking so defeated, so completely hopeless. It was like every time they talked about it, the old man lost something, maybe even a piece of himself. "Why do we have to keep discussing this?" he asked.

"Because…." Ivan faltered again. "I thought you weren't married yet because you were looking for good woman, someone better than that… that *gaduka* your brother married." The old man had never made a secret of how much he disliked Peter's wife, Cindy. Dad said she wasn't pretty enough, that if Peter and Cindy ever had children, they'd come out skinny and pale like her. The more Dad put Cindy down, the more Peter dug his heels in, until one day he came home and said he and Cindy were getting married and there was nothing Dad could do to stop them. Peter was right, too. Dad couldn't stop them.

"Dad, I'm sorry things didn't work out the way you wanted them to. I'm sorry Peter was the one who left and I'm the one who stayed. I can't change who I am—"

Ivan blinked at him. "Is that what you think I want? To have Peter but not you?"

"You've always liked Peter more than you liked me."

"*Nyet*, Pasha. I love you both. I'm sorry…." But he didn't finish his sentence. He pinched his forefinger and thumb over his eyes and was silent for a long time. Finally, he lowered both hands to his lap. Pasha watched his father staring at them and wondered what he was thinking. "I read this thing in newspaper today," he finally said, "about boy who killed himself. They say he did it because he was… *gay*."

Pasha had read the same article. "That kid didn't hang himself because he was gay. He hanged himself because other kids were picking on him. There's a difference."

"Is there?"

If the question hadn't sounded so sincere, Pasha might have lost his temper. As it was, he had a hard time holding in his anger. It wasn't just his father he was mad at. No one should ever feel so alone or be picked on until they killed themselves rather than face another day at school. *No one should ever get their nose broken by their older brother over a stupid swimsuit catalogue.* "You have no idea what it's like to be afraid that the people you love the most will turn their backs on you if they find out something like that. I wasn't…. Look, maybe there was a time when I was ashamed because I couldn't be more like Peter, because I didn't like girls the way other guys did. But more than anything, I was afraid of what would happen if you found out. I didn't want you to hate me."

"Didn't you ever… you never feel like that boy, did you?"

He knew the answer his father wanted to hear, but he told him the truth anyway. "Yes. I did." The old man looked like somebody had kicked him in the gut. "I didn't really want to hurt myself," he promised. "I mean, there were days when I thought about it. But I'm still here, right?" He forced a smile.

"Is that why you got into fight with that boy? That time you got your nose broke," he clarified. "Someone was picking on you, like on that boy who killed himself and you got into fight over it?"

He could lie. Maybe he *should* lie. "I didn't get into a fight with another kid," he said quietly instead. "I got into a fight with Peter."

"What do you mean, you got into fight with Peter? Peter was twenty—"

"Peter hit me, Dad. Then he told you I got into a fight with another kid because… I don't know. Maybe he didn't want to tell you that he found me looking at male swimsuit models."

"You were only fifteen!"

"And I'm sure you looked at pictures of girls in bikinis when you were fifteen."

"That's not same! Boys supposed to look at girls, not… never mind." He shook his head as if to clear it. "Just tell me this: is that what you really want for your life? This… this gay business?"

"It's not about what I want or don't want. It's about who I *am*."

"Okay."

Pasha blinked. "Okay, what?" Okay they would never talk about it again, okay Dad wanted him to move out…? *Okay he's going to run to Peter and demand some kind of explanation about why Peter didn't tell him he caught me looking at half-naked men when I was fifteen?*

"Okay," Ivan repeated. "I want to meet him."

Pasha's jaw went slack. "You want to meet…?" He had to be misunderstanding what his father meant. There was no way Dad wanted to meet Daniel.

"If this man is gonna be part of your life, I want to know if he's good man or if he's *paskudnyak* like Ryan or if he's snake like that woman your brother married. I want to know if he comes from good family, if he respects his mother and father, if he'll be good…. I don't even know if he's gonna be husband or wife!"

"Dad, we haven't been going out long enough to… it doesn't matter, we're both men. There is no husband and wife, just two men who love each other."

The old man's hands balled up. "Men don't—!" But he stopped midsentence and shook his head. Nodded. Relaxed his hands. "Okay. Two men," he repeated. "But he's good man? He's not *paskudnyak*?"

"He's a very good man, Dad. He's not a *paskudnyak*. He went to U of M, he has a good job, and he comes from a good family."

"So you fix it up so I can meet him."

He felt like Alice tumbling down the rabbit hole, like nothing was quite right or quite real. "Yeah, okay. We'll figure something out."

"Good."

"I, ah, I'm going to throw some laundry in. Anything you need me to wash while I'm at it?" Pasha asked him.

"*Nyet*. Thanks."

"Yeah." He leaned over and pressed a kiss to his dad's cheek. "I love you, Dad."

"*Da*. I love you too."

PASHA had just switched his laundry over from the washer to the dryer when his phone rang. He didn't have to look at the ID to see who it was. "Did you remember to take your pill?" he said by way of hello.

"Excuse me, doll face?"

Shit. "Ty. Hi. I was expecting someone else."

"And what kind of pill was this someone else supposed to take?" he asked.

"It's nothing. What's up?"

"The sky, the price of gas, my skirts. How about you?"

Pasha shrugged even though his friend couldn't see him. "Not much." Only the second the words left his mouth, he felt guilty. He had a boyfriend. His father wanted to *meet* his boyfriend. *My boyfriend has HIV.* But instead of saying any of that, he asked, "How'd your date go the other day with that guy from the gym?"

"Oh. My. God. What a waste of a perfectly good night!"

Pasha couldn't help but laugh. "That bad, huh?"

"The *worst*. But you can totally make it up to me by taking me out tonight and showing me a good time."

"Come on, you know I work in the morning."

"That's no excuse. You work every morning."

"I'm pretty wiped."

Ty let out a dramatic sigh. "Fine. How about next weekend?"

Pasha bit his lower lip. "Next weekend's kinda booked already."

"The *whole* weekend? Am I suddenly *not* your fairy godmother anymore?"

He rolled his eyes. "Fine. I'm free on Friday night. But I can't stay out too late this time."

"Don't you worry your pretty little head. I'll have you home by midnight, Cinderella."

Pasha's phone beeped to let him know he had another call coming in. "I have to go. I'll see you Friday," he promised. He barely let Ty say good-bye before he switched over. "Hello?"

"Hey, Sugar. I just wanted to let you know I'm home safe. And before you ask, yes, I took my pill."

Pasha smiled. "Good." He kicked the laundry room door shut and sank to the floor, his back resting against the dryer. "You are never going to *believe* the conversation me and the old man had tonight…."

They didn't say good night until well after Pasha's clothes were dried and in the basket. Nothing was set in stone, but Daniel suggested meeting up with Ivan next Sunday, after the restaurant closed and before he headed up north. It would put him on the road later than he'd planned, but he assured Pasha he didn't mind, and he was sure his mother would approve.

CHAPTER TWENTY-NINE

THE old man frowned when Pasha walked in the back door at seven o'clock on Monday night. "What are you doing back so early? And what's all that?" he asked of the grocery sacks Pasha set down on the counter in the prep area. "We didn't need nothing from store."

"I wanted some stuff for tomorrow." Not only was he planning new dinner specials, but he'd promised Amy he would make something for Brett's welcome-home party Tuesday night. Pasha hung up his coat. Before starting his errands, he'd gone home and changed into jeans and a heavy sweatshirt. "I came back early because I figured Mondays are usually slow, so it'd be a good night to go through the walk-in."

"What's wrong with walk-in?"

"Dad, when was the last time we cleaned it out?"

"It's fine, Pasha."

"I didn't say it wasn't, but the only way to keep it that way is to clean it out once in a while. You mind if I ask Kaja to give me a hand?"

Ivan waved him off. "Do whatever you want."

Before getting to work on the cooler, Pasha went up front and got himself a big to-go cup of coffee. Sharon regarded him coolly. He smiled. "How are the customers liking the new soups?" Today, he'd made broccoli cheddar and borscht—the hot version with beef broth and chunks of both lamb, because that's the way Mom used to make it. Technically, the lamb was a little extravagant—especially buying it from the grocery store across the street—but the soup had gone over so well at lunch, Pasha wanted to put it on as an everyday staple and make it their house specialty. No other restaurants in the area served anything like it.

As for his question, Sharon stiffened. “A lot of people wondered why we don’t have chicken lemon rice on today.”

Pasha looked around the restaurant. There were four tables sitting. Two of them were regulars who had been in at lunch and raved about the borscht. Pasha doubted Sharon had served “a lot of people” anything, but he didn’t comment. He took his coffee and headed into the dish room to enlist Kaja’s help with the walk-in.

They’d been at it for fifteen minutes when Sharon came back. “Kaja, your wife and son are here.”

“I hope everything’s okay,” Pasha told him.

But Kaja smiled. “Today’s Tommy’s birthday. Beth brought him in for dinner.” He picked up a milk crate full of vegetables to move it out of the cooler.

Pasha took it from him. “Go see your wife. I can finish this.”

“I—”

“Go. And if Dad doesn’t offer to pick up your dinner, it’s on me,” he added.

“Pasha I don’t…. I’ve only been here a few months. I don’t expect anything like that from you guys.”

“Get out there already. If it’s okay, I’ll come over and say hi as soon as I clean up a little.”

“Yeah, of course. Thanks.”

By the time Pasha got out to the table, Dad had already told Kaja’s family their meal was on him. Pasha wasn’t surprised. The old man could be a grouchy old jackass but he had softer moments, too. Ivan came out and sat with them for a few minutes, and before Beth and Tommy left, he boxed up one of the apple pies he’d pulled out of the oven earlier in the day to send home with them. As soon as they left, Kaja ran a load of dishes and came back to help Pasha finish up with the walk-in.

“You know what you guys really need, if you want to make this place special, is a gyro cooker,” Kaja said as they were carrying the last of the boxes back into the newly cleaned walk-in. Only as soon as he said it, he looked embarrassed. “I don’t mean to sound like I’m trying to tell you how to run the place. I was just thinking it'd be like the soup you made today, something nobody else around here does."

"I'm always open to new ideas," Pasha told him. "And I don't think I've ever even *heard* of a gyro cooker before." They'd always used the frozen premade gyro patties, just like every other Coney/Greek restaurant in the area.

Kaja swiped his hand across the back of his neck, looking like he was genuinely nervous about giving his boss advice. "Before… you know. Shit happened. I took Beth down to Atlanta. She wanted to see the new aquarium, something about these giant sharks." He shrugged. Clearly he wasn't interested in fish, but he loved his wife. "We ended up lost as all fuck downtown and stopped at this gyro place for lunch. It was a total freaking hole in the wall, but they had these big rotisserie things with slabs of gyro meat on 'em. When someone ordered a sandwich, the cook sliced off what he needed. It was a while ago, but it was way better… I mean, not that you guys don't make good food—"

"I don't mind you criticizing the food," Pasha assured him. "Some of it's total shit."

Kaja shrugged, keeping his eyes downcast. "I just never saw nothing like that around here."

"I'll look into it, thanks."

By ten o'clock, the restaurant was dead. There hadn't been anyone new in the door since eight forty-five and the last customers had left at nine twenty. For the past half an hour, Pasha had been sitting at the counter with a cup of coffee, menu, notepad, calculator, and his phone. His cup was empty and two notebook pages were full of numbers. He didn't like any of them. "Dad, who came up with the menu prices?" he called into the kitchen.

"Peter. Why?"

Pasha rubbed his forehead.

"What is it?" the old man asked.

"Do you realize that we actually *lose* money on some of these dishes?"

"How?"

Because Peter doesn't know the first thing about planning a menu.

Ivan came out and sat down next to him. "Where do we lose money?"

Pasha showed him his notebook and the old man frowned. "You have to be making mistakes."

He sighed but didn't argue. He'd checked his math twice. "The point is that we seriously need to redesign the menu. It's almost six pages long."

"People like variety."

"When was the last time anyone ordered half this stuff?"

"Customers don't like change, Pasha."

"They liked the soup well enough," he countered.

"That's just soup."

"We need to take a good look at what we want to do here, Dad. What kind of restaurant do we want to be—"

"The kind where people come in to eat!" He slammed his palm down on the countertop. "You think you're so smart, think you got answers. *Fine*. You make goddamned new menu, then maybe you'll see it's not so easy." He got up, grabbed a discarded newspaper from under the counter, and stalked over to one of the empty booths to sit down.

Sharon stepped next to Pasha. "It's disgraceful the way you talk to him. He's your *father*."

"At home, he's my father. Here, he's my business partner. Get used to it."

She opened her mouth to say more, but when Pasha's phone rang, he cut her off. "Excuse me," he said and picked it up to check the name on the caller ID. When he saw the name, he frowned and headed into the kitchen to answer the call. "Michael?" he said in lieu of hello.

"Hi."

"Yeah, hi. What's up?" Pasha asked.

"I ah… I got your message the other day. Last week, I guess."

More like two weeks ago by Pasha's reckoning, but he didn't feel like correcting Michael. "Yeah, I… I guess I was feeling pretty bummed out that night." In hindsight, he felt like an idiot. "If you're calling me to tell me to leave you alone or something—"

"No. No, that's not it. I'm glad you called. I um, I was wondering if that offer of a cup of coffee is still good?"

Something in Pasha's heart surged. He didn't want it to, but he couldn't help it. "Yeah, sure." What harm could it do?

"You want to meet at Java Hut?"

"When?"

"How's tomorrow?"

"Sorry, I can't. I have a thing to go to."

Michael laughed. "A thing?"

"Yeah, I ah… a friend of mine's getting out of the hospital and a few of us are getting together to welcome him home."

"Oh man. I'm sorry. I hope everything's okay. I mean—"

"Yeah." He cut Michael off to save him from any more uncomfortable babbling. It wasn't like Pasha would know what to say if someone told *him* something like that, either. "So how are things with you and… shit. I'm sorry, I don't remember his name."

"That's okay, we broke up last month."

"Damn, Michael, I'm sorry." As much as he'd hated seeing Michael with another man, he'd never wanted him to be unhappy. "What happened?"

"Nothing, really."

"People don't break up over nothing."

"He stopped calling. I stopped calling. There wasn't a big fight or anything, we just drifted apart. By the time we met to make it official, he was already seeing someone else."

"Ouch."

"It wasn't that big of a deal. But it got me thinking about all the dumb moves I've made this last year."

"Believe me, we all do dumb stuff."

"Look, there's something… back before, I mean way back when I said I didn't want to be friends, it was because I…. I never stopped loving you, Pasha. I've never loved anybody the way I love you. When you said you didn't want to move in with me, I…. It hurt. But the way I handled it didn't help any. I just wanted to say I was sorry for being such an ass about the whole thing."

"You weren't an ass. I'm the one… look, it's water under the bridge, okay?" If Michael wanted to be friends again, there was no point in rehashing the past. "I'm just glad you called."

"Me too." The smile in Michael's voice was audible, and it sent butterflies flapping around in Pasha's stomach. "I… um… do you think we could maybe make another go of it?" Michael sounded so sincere, so hopeful. "I can deal with you being in the closet, Pasha. I didn't think I could, but a year's a long time to get my head on straight. I had no right to try and dictate to you who you tell. And… this is going to sound awful, but… look, I liked Rob, but we didn't have half the connection me and you did."

God. If Michael had called him a month ago. Two weeks ago even. "I'm seeing someone."

There was a long pause on the other end. "I bumped into Ty over the weekend. He said you were, quote, 'footloose and fancy free.'"

If Michael hadn't sounded so dumbfounded—and so hurt—he might have laughed. That sounded exactly like something Ty would say. "The relationship is new, and it's a little complicated," Pasha told him.

"Complicated how?"

He leaned his aching head back against the wall. He was sore from hauling boxes and buckets, and tired from working all day and most of the night. "The kind of complicated I didn't feel like getting into it with Ty about."

"Is it serious?"

"Yeah."

There was another long pause on the other end of the line. "I guess… what was it you used to say? Mola-something?"

Pasha smiled. "*Moladyets*. Thanks."

"Yeah. Um… look, if you still want to meet for coffee… I mean, I won't lie, I was hoping for more, but… I miss hanging out with you. I know your work schedule is crazy, but… if you have time?"

"How about I give you a call after Christmas?" Pasha offered.

"Thanks. Take care of yourself."

"You too."

Pasha hung up with Michael and put on his coat before pulling the garbage from the kitchen and heading out to the dumpster. Kaja followed him outside with the dish room trash. His timing couldn't have been better.

"I need to talk to you a sec," Pasha began. "I'm trying to convince Dad to close up a couple of hours earlier during the week."

Kaja shifted his weight from one foot to the other. "Yeah, I ah, I guess that makes sense. The place is usually pretty dead after eight or nine."

"I know you can't afford to have your hours cut, so I wanted to ask you if you could come in earlier. I'm not sure I can cut Samara's hours too much"—not if he didn't want a war on his hands, anyway—"but if you came in at one, you could help with kitchen prep. If nothing else, it'll look good on your resume," he joked. No one stayed with them for long.

Only Kaja wasn't laughing. He leaned back against the dumpster and fished a crumpled pack of Pall Mall cigarettes and bright purple disposable lighter out of his jacket pocket.

"If you can't do it, I understand. I just want to help," Pasha told him. "I thought you wanted more hours, that's all."

"No, that's not it." His hands shook as he got his cigarette lit. It was the last cigarette in the pack. "We really need the money and I appreciate everything you and your dad…. Damn it," he swore.

"What's wrong?"

Kaja took a long drag off his cigarette. He held it, then let it out again, filling the air between them with cheap-smelling tobacco smoke. "I followed you out here 'cause I don't want to make trouble between you and your old man. I heard you on the phone."

A rock formed in Pasha's gut.

"I didn't mean to eavesdrop."

"It's okay. Dad knows I'm gay and he knows I have a boyfriend. He just doesn't want too many other people to find out."

Kaja closed his eyes and he raised his cigarette to his mouth again. "I don't know if I can work for you anymore."

"Why not?"

"Because when I was six… or I don't know, maybe seven, we had this neighbor and he used to watch me after school."

"Oh Christ. Please don't tell me…."

"Yeah."

"Kaja, I'm so sorry. But you have to know that what your neighbor did to you has nothing to do with being gay. It has nothing to do with *me*."

"Doesn't it?" he asked angrily. "What about all those priests you hear about? What about teachers who fuck around with little boys? What about all the fucking faggots who rape their neighbors' kids?" he snapped. "When my son was in here earlier, did you—"

"Did I *what*?" Pasha snapped right back.

Kaja shook his head and took another long drag off his smoke. "Nothing. I just don't think people like you should be allowed to run loose."

Pasha drew in a shaky breath. All he could think about were those six guys who had jumped Brett. But this wasn't some stranger. "Why don't you head home for the night?" he finally suggested.

"Yeah." He threw his cigarette to the snow and ground it out. "But you should probably know that if I had my way, every faggot in this country would be locked up and fucking castrated without anything to numb the pain. And I'd be the first in line with a knife."

Pasha swallowed hard and walked away as calmly as he could.

"YOU can't take that kind of threat lightly, Pasha," Daniel told him, when Pasha called later from his bedroom.

He'd been shaking so badly as he walked back into the kitchen he almost called Daniel then, but he was afraid if he did, he might break down completely, and then he'd have no choice but tell his dad what had happened. He didn't want to scare the old man too. Instead, he told Dad he'd sent Kaja home for the night because there wasn't much left to do and it was almost time to close, anyway. Dad bought the excuse without question.

"What do you suggest I do?" he said to Daniel, keeping his voice down in case Dad was still up. "Call the police and tell them our dishwasher threatened to castrate me because I'm gay?"

"That's *exactly* what I suggest you do."

"I can't. If they take it seriously.... Daniel, this guy already has a record. He was in prison for five years."

"All the more reason to file a police report!"

"He has a wife. A *kid.* Today's his son's sixth birthday, and now he has to go home and tell his family he... he said he was going to quit. There's no way he has any kind of savings to fall back on. Having the cops show up on his door would only make things worse for his family than they already are."

"I'm sorry this sucks for other people, babe, but you're the only one I care about here. I need to know you're going to be safe."

"He's *not* a bad guy. That's what's bugging me." Pasha rolled over onto his back and stared up at his ceiling. "I can hate those creeps who beat the shit out of Brett because they're nameless, faceless thugs. But Kaja's someone I've worked with for the last six months and tonight he told me that when he was a kid there was this guy who used to babysit him and... and why wouldn't he hate gay men?"

"Pasha—"

"I know. It has nothing to do with being gay. That's what I told him."

"Look, babe, what happened to this guy is... it's heinous. But bad stuff happens all the time. It's no excuse."

"I just thought...." He faltered. He didn't know what to think anymore.

"You thought he'd look at you and realize that not all gay men were to blame for him getting hurt," Daniel supplied in a gentle tone.

"Pretty naïve, huh?"

"No. Well, maybe. But it just proves what kind of person you are, that all you care about here is not making some other guy's life harder even after he threatened you."

"He didn't mean it. I mean... I'm sure he meant what he said, but I don't think he would have actually hurt me. He's a decent guy."

"He was in prison."

"It was for stupid shit. He was hanging with the wrong crowd, he made some mistakes. He's trying to get his life together. I just wish… I should have gone into the office to talk to Michael or been more careful about what I said."

"That wouldn't change the way Kaja feels about gay men."

"I know. My life was just easier before…." *Shit.* But it was true. His life was easier before he stumbled out of the closet and decided to stay out, only he hadn't meant to say that aloud. "I'm sorry, I didn't mean that," he lied. "I'm just really tired."

"I know. Look, why don't you get some sleep and call me tomorrow? Are we still on for Brett's welcome home shindig?"

"I don't know. If Kaja quits, I'll have to stick around and wash dishes."

"All right. Keep me updated. And be careful." He was back to sounding worried again.

"I will."

"And Pasha?"

"Yeah?"

"This guy's problems aren't your fault. If he does quit, it's on him, not you."

Daniel's words didn't make him feel any less guilty, but he said "thank you" anyway.

CHAPTER THIRTY

IVAN hung up the phone. "That was Kaja," he told Pasha.

Knives twisted in his gut. "Yeah?"

"He quit. I don't know what we're gonna do. I can't ask Samara to stay all day." The old man looked as if he was genuinely at a loss.

"I'll call Randy later and see if he can come in," said Pasha.

"What if he can't?"

"Then either I'll stay, or… who knows, how much do you want to bet Randy knows someone who's looking for a job?" He was a high school kid and probably had plenty of friends who needed money.

Ivan was still shaking his head. "I don't understand. Kaja never said anything was wrong. His wife was here last night."

"Did he tell you why he was quitting?"

"He didn't give no reason. He just said he couldn't work here no more. Did he say something to you?"

"I… yeah." He wanted to lie, but he couldn't.

The old man frowned. "He told you he was quitting?"

"He gave me the idea that he might."

"Why didn't you tell me?"

"I hoped he'd change his mind."

Ivan's scowl deepened. "What did he say to you?" It sounded more like an accusation than a question, like somehow Ivan knew it was Pasha's fault.

But that wasn't why Pasha hesitated in answering him. Samara was only as far away as the dish room and she spoke fluent Russian just like him and the old man. "Kaja overheard me talking on the phone last night. I ah…. Michael called me." He shoved his hands into his pockets. "We talked for a little while."

"Michael?" he questioned—but then his expression soured. "That boy you were…?" He stopped midsentence and glanced toward the dish room. "Pasha, what did you say? Why were you talking where other people could hear?"

"I don't know. I called Michael a couple of weeks ago, and…. Look, it's complicated, okay? I was so surprised he actually called me back that I wasn't thinking."

"It's *not* okay. And it's not fucking complicated. You just gotta learn to keep your big fat mouth *shut*. Or maybe you wanna go put ad on billboard and tell the whole world your business, huh?"

"I didn't tell Kaja anything. He overheard me talking."

"And because you can't keep your goddamned mouth shut, now I gotta hire new dishwasher!"

"I'm sorry—"

Ivan waved him off. "Go put sign in fucking window. I have work to do."

"What about my idea to hire another server?"

"How am I supposed pay another server? We don't got no extra money."

"You can cut my salary."

Ivan stared at him, dumbfounded.

"Dad, I would have suggested it sooner if I'd realized how bad things were—this is why you have to talk to me."

"Money *my* problem, Pasha!" He thumped his chest with his palm. "Not yours."

Pasha understood what he was really saying. It was embarrassing for his father to admit how far they'd gotten into the red. "I can manage on two fifty a week." That was only a little more than Kaja earned, and *he* had a wife and kid to support. What did Pasha have? He didn't even pay rent.

"I thought you wanted to buy car?" said Dad.

"I do. And I will. It just won't be an expensive car."

"You gotta have good car, Pasha."

Pasha decided not to remind his father that he'd been against him getting a car since Pasha first brought it up. "It'll be fine. And it's just until we turn things around," he added when his father continued to scowl.

Finally, Ivan gave in. "*Da*. Okay." His expression softened. "You're good boy, Pasha. This Daniel better not be no *paskudnyak*."

Pasha seriously didn't understand how his dad's mind worked sometimes. But that wasn't what mattered. "He's not," he promised.

"Good." Then Ivan paused a moment. "Kaja didn't give you no kind of trouble last night, did he? About what he heard? That isn't why you told him to go home, is it?"

"No," he lied. "We just talked. I really hoped he wouldn't quit."

"His loss. Go on. Put sign in window. Lots of people looking for work. We'll have new dishwasher by end of week."

Pasha only wished it was that simple. It wasn't just Kaja's loss. His wife, his kid.... *But Daniel's right. It was his choice to quit.*

AT THREE o'clock, with fingers crossed, he called Randy to see if he could come in to cover Kaja's shift. He breathed a sigh of relief and sent a prayer of thanks as soon as Randy said yes—it sounded like Randy was pretty happy about getting in a few extra hours too. As soon as he got off the phone with Randy, Pasha called Daniel to let him know they were still on for going over to Brett's.

"What time do you want me to pick you up?" Daniel asked.

"Dad said he'd be back around five. Maybe six to be safe?"

"Sounds good, Sugar. I'll see you soon."

They said their good-byes and Pasha pocketed his phone so he could check on the contents of the oven. The whole restaurant smelled like roasting garlic and simmering lamb; opening up the oven door only made the smell stronger. His stomach growled. Inside the oven were two pans each of homemade spanakopita and moussaka for tonight's dinner specials. Dad used to make moussaka all the time, but that was years ago, back before Mom got sick. Pasha had had to look the recipe up online, then tweak it a bit because most people made moussaka with beef, but lamb had such a richer flavor. *Maybe it'll be one more thing set us apart from every other Greek restaurant in the neighborhood.* He'd been looking at gyro cookers online today too.

Christ, how could someone who's worked with me for the last six months lump me in with the kind of monster who molested him when he was a kid? How could Kaja think Pasha would look at Tommy like that? *Because he was hurt*, he answered his own question. *And because he loves his son.*

As soon as Pasha cleared the oven, he put in a couple of smaller pans of moussaka and spanakopita for the party tonight. There was nothing he loved more than cooking for other people, and after yesterday, he needed something to make him feel good.

He set the timer on the oven and started to work on the rest of tonight's specials. Instead of the usual side dish of rice slathered in red sauce, there would be lemon rice with roasted garlic on the side of both the moussaka and spanakopita. In addition to those two dishes, tonight's menu would also feature almond-encrusted center-cut pork chops with Fiji apple slices and roasted garlic mashed potatoes.

"YOU'RE making too much work for me," the old man grumbled when Pasha showed him the night's specials—the *only* specials Pasha had put up on the board. Normally, there were eight or nine of the same tired old "specials" crammed onto the whiteboard every day. It looked a lot neater with just three. *And they're specials that are actually* special *for a change.*

"The chops are already breaded, so all you have to is sauté the meat, slice up the apples, and put a scoop of mashed potatoes on the plate." He emphasized the fact that it was *a* scoop of mashed potatoes by plating up a pork chop dinner right in front of his dad and Sharon. Pasha had made up a sample plate of the spanakopita and moussaka as well, so they could taste all three dishes. He called Randy in from the dish room to try it too. It wasn't like there wasn't enough food to go around.

"It's too much goddamned fuss," Dad complained.

"Dad, it's Tuesday. It's not going to be that busy. You'll have time to fuss."

Ivan still wasn't happy. "What's wrong with specials we usually serve on Tuesday?"

"I keep telling you. Nobody eats like that anymore."

"What about all of our regulars?" Sharon wanted to know. "What if *they* want what we always have?"

"Then I'm sure Dad will make them whatever they want." *He always does.* His cell phone chirped, letting him know he had a new text message. A quick look at the phone confirmed that it was Daniel and that was almost there to pick Pasha up.

Sharon frowned. "Don't you ever turn that thing off?" She shot Ivan an expectant look, but the old man didn't say anything. He just took another bite of moussaka.

"Tastes a lot like your mother's," he said.

Pasha beamed. "I was hoping you'd like it."

Ivan frowned—but a hint of good humor twinkled in his eyes. "Who said I ever liked your mother's moussaka?"

Pasha rolled his eyes and dashed into the office to change into jeans and a long-sleeved shirt. He only wished he had time to shave. Most days he had what other guys considered five o'clock shadow by three in the afternoon.

"You need a hand with that?" Randy offered when Pasha came back out and started loading the pans of food for Brett's party into tote bags. The insulated food-service quality bags were one of the few things Mom had bought that were useful. Pasha just wished she hadn't felt the need to buy four dozen of them.

Before Pasha could tell Randy no thanks, it was just the two pans of food, Dad stepped in. "I got it," Ivan said. Pasha shot him an inquisitive look. Dad had to know he didn't actually need help. But the old man was reaching for his coat. "I'll carry one of these out to car for you," he said.

Pasha continued to frown. His father had already agreed to have dinner with him and Daniel on Sunday. Why was he pushing to meet him now?

"What?" Ivan challenged. "I can't go out and say hi to your friend?"

"I… sure." He just hoped Dad hadn't sunk into some kind of weird denial where Daniel was just a friend. *Or that he doesn't totally lose it when we get outside.* Either was a possibility, but unless he wanted to get into it with his father in front of everyone, the only thing he could do was give in and let his dad take one of the totes.

Daniel was parked in his usual spot out by the dumpster, but even at that distance, Pasha could see the look of surprise on his face when Dad stepped out the back door after him. He flashed an apologetic smile in Daniel's direction, and Daniel smiled back. *Dear God, please don't let this turn into a disaster.*

At Pasha's elbow, his father hissed, "He's not white."

"Oh, God, Dad. Please don't—"

"Well, he's not!"

"He's Native American."

"*Indian*?"

"*Da*. Now please, this was your idea." They were getting close enough that Daniel would be able to hear, so in Russian Pasha said, "Act polite."

"I'm always polite!" Ivan snapped back in Russian.

Pasha refrained from commenting.

"Hey." Daniel greeted them with an uncertain smile. He took the tote from Ivan first. "Thanks."

"You hair's long."

"*Dad*!"

But Daniel took it in stride. "Yes, sir." He set the first tote into the backseat and took the second from Pasha's hands.

"Pasha says you're Indian," Ivan went on.

"Oh God." Was there a rock around there anywhere Pasha could crawl under?

"Potawatomi," Daniel answered smoothly. "And a little Cherokee and maybe some Portuguese, if Great-great-grandma Seka's stories are to be believed," he added with a half smile.

"Are you Christian?" Ivan wanted to know.

"Dad! You don't go around asking people questions like that!"

"He's not people," Ivan argued.

Pasha didn't know what was more infuriating, Dad's stupid questions or how hard Daniel was trying not to laugh. Pasha was pretty sure *he* was the cause of Daniel's barely suppressed snicker. "If he's not 'people,' what is he?" Pasha asked his father.

"He's your *drook*. That means boyfriend," he added, for Daniel's benefit. "And if you're gonna be part of my son's life, I want to know if you're Christian or some kind of Indian heathen."

"Dad, please stop."

"It's all right," Daniel assured him. He turned back to Ivan. "I'm sure if I say 'both' it'll just be confusing, so let me explain. My family goes to a nondenominational church pretty much every Sunday, and sometimes I go to the Unitarian church near my place. But we still observe a lot of cultural traditions too. My folks' philosophy is that as long as you lead a good life and believe in a higher power, it'll all work out in the end. And for the record," he said, turning to Pasha, "you can expect exactly this kind of grilling from Ma and Joyce. That's my sister," he added for Ivan's benefit.

"And your family is okay with this gay business?" the old man asked.

"I came out when I was sixteen. But ah… you should probably know that I'm not gay—"

Ivan's brows knit together. "*Chto*? What do you mean, 'not gay'?" He shot an angry look at Pasha. "What's going on here?"

"Mr. Batalov, I'm bisexual."

"That means—" Pasha began.

"I know what it means!" Ivan snapped. "I read. I read *a lot*." He shifted his angry gaze from Pasha to Daniel and back again. "Bisexual means he has girlfriends." It sounded more like an accusation than a statement.

"Sir, it means I've *had* girlfriends," Daniel corrected him gently. "And boyfriends too, just like Pasha dated other guys before me."

"But you could be with woman." Ivan looked more confused than ever. "Don't you want wife? Don't you want *family*?"

Pasha swallowed hard, wondering what Daniel would say. Wondering just how uncomfortable the topic was for him.

But Daniel smiled. "Two men can have a family—and so can two women, for that matter. Not that we've actually started planning that far ahead or anything." He sounded a little embarrassed. "But there are options. Surrogacy, adoption. Anything's possible."

Pasha let out the breath he hadn't even realized he was holding and smiled up at him, hoping that a family—children—was something Daniel would consider.

Ivan, however, looked less than pleased. "I know you boys got to be someplace, but I need to talk to my son for few minutes. *Alone*." The old man's tone left no room for argument.

Daniel nodded and walked around to the driver's side of his car. "Take your time," he said, mostly looking at Pasha.

He licked his lips and nodded. "Yeah, sure. I… we won't be long." He shot his dad an expectant look, and the old man motioned for him to move around to the other side of the dumpster. Pasha followed, but for several long, nerve-racking moments, Ivan just stood there, silently staring at the cold ground beneath their feet. "Dad?" Pasha finally asked him.

"He seems like nice boy. Man. And you say he has good job that he's no *paskudnyak*?"

"He drives a delivery truck for a microbrewery."

"That's good job?" Ivan questioned.

"He makes good money and he likes what he does," Pasha offered up, hoping it would be good enough for his father.

"And you're not worried he's gonna leave you for woman? What if he decides he doesn't want no more of this gay business? What if he decides he wants normal life? Where you gonna be, huh? After you invested time into this… this boyfriend."

Pasha blinked. Of all the things his father could say, all the things he could be worried about, *that* wasn't one Pasha had expected. "Dad, being with a man who's bisexual is no different from being with a man who's gay—"

"It's *not* same thing!" He glanced around and lowered his voice. "He likes girls. He could meet nice woman someday. He could get married."

"*We* could get married. Dad, DOMA was overturned, remember? One of these days, same-sex marriage is going to be legal in every state."

"It's still not same thing, Pasha."

He sighed and shoved his hands into his pockets. "If I didn't trust him there wouldn't be much point in being together."

"He's good-looking boy."

Pasha smiled. "He's a very good-looking boy."

"And you're sure he don't want nobody else? Not woman? Not wife?"

"I'm sure."

"*Da.* Okay. We talk more on Sunday. Now you go and… and tell Amy something nice from me."

"In other words, you want me to lie," he teased.

Ivan gave a sour look and waved him off. "Get out of here before customers see you with *drook* in my parking lot." But underneath the scowl, Pasha saw a hint of a smile.

"See you in a few hours," Pasha promised. The plan was for Daniel to bring him back to the restaurant around ten so he could help his dad clean up, since technically Randy wasn't supposed to work past ten because he was still in high school.

Daniel looked up when Pasha got into the car. "Well? What's the verdict?"

Pasha couldn't help but smile; Daniel sounded so nervous. "You realize that no matter what he says, it won't change how I feel about you, right?"

"I'm glad, Sugar. But you weren't expecting him to come around at all, so if there's anything I can do to help…?" He left it open-ended.

"Besides wanting to make sure you're not a *paskudnyak* like my sister's husband Ryan, Dad's biggest fear is that you're going to leave me for a woman."

Daniel reached over and took his hand. "You know that's not gonna happen, right?"

"I know. I trust you."

"I'm glad."

IT WASN'T until they got into the brightly lit hallway of Brett's apartment building that Pasha noticed the dark circles under Daniel's eyes. "Are you okay?" he asked.

"Today was just a little rough. I'll be all right," Daniel assured him with a wan smile.

Guilt needled at Pasha's conscience. He'd been so worried about Dad's reactions to everything that he hadn't even thought to ask Daniel how he was feeling today, even though he knew the side effects of the ARVs—the antiretroviral drug—were starting to take a toll. The last couple of times they'd talked on the phone, Daniel had mentioned being worn out and not having much of an appetite. He kept downplaying it, saying it was nothing. Now Pasha wasn't so sure. "I wish you would have said something. You didn't have to come tonight if you weren't feeling up to it."

But Daniel smiled. "If I'd told you I was feeling like something the cat dragged in, I might not've gotten to meet your dad tonight. That makes it all worthwhile, Sugar. And I'm okay, honest."

"Just promise me that if we need to leave early, you'll say so."

"You got it, Sugar." Daniel assured him.

By then, they were at Brett's door. Pasha knocked, and a couple of seconds later, Mark let them in and took their coats. A flicker of concern crossed Mark's face when he looked up at Daniel and no doubt saw how haggard he looked, but all he said was "Glad you guys could make it."

"Thanks," Pasha replied. There was no need to ask where the kitchen was. Brett's place was an efficiency apartment, probably not more than six-hundred-square-feet, and built long and narrow. The dozen or so guests milling around seemed to fill the place completely. Colorful Chinese lanterns hung from the ceiling, providing subdued lighting—Pasha wasn't sure if they were a regular part of the décor or only up because of the party—and Abba played on the stereo. He was pretty sure Abba *was* a regular fixture in Brett's apartment.

"Hey, you made it!" Brett hollered with a grin over the loud music and conversation. He hauled himself to his feet with help from Amy and hobbled over toward the door. He looked like he was in a lot of pain but trying to ignore it. The first time Pasha met Brett, Brett had been wearing snug-fitting jeans with a crisp cotton shirt tucked into them; today, he had on a T-shirt that was at least two sizes too big and loose-fitting gray sweatpants. His hair was clean and combed, but not styled like it had been that night at Ben and Teddy's. Besides the cast still on his arm, there was a flesh-colored cloth bandage peeking out from underneath the loose neck of Brett's shirt, and while most of the bruises had faded to a dull, ugly yellow-brown, there were several long gashes on his face that still had stitches in them. But he never stopped smiling. "So *you're* the reason Pasha never called me," he teased Daniel.

Daniel grinned back at him. "Nice to meet you."

"Likewise," Brett agreed. Then he turned to Pasha. "Maybe after some of this hardware comes off, you guys'll consider a threesome? Assuming you can get past the Quasimodo looks."

Mark looked hurt and Amy rolled her eyes. "You're incorrigible," she said.

Pasha's stomach churned with acid. He wanted to tell Brett that he looked fine, but there was no way he wasn't going to have scars. He'd be able to hide some of them, Pasha was sure, but he couldn't hide his face. *And there's no way he can afford plastic surgery.* He just hoped Brett would be able to play again someday.

"You should be sitting down," Mark told Brett.

"I've done nothing but sit on my ass for the last week," Brett argued—but it looked as if just walking across the room had worn him out.

"You mind if I use your oven to heat some stuff up?" Pasha asked.

"Help yourself. And thanks for cooking."

"You can thank me after you've tried it." Pasha managed to smile. He leaned up to give Daniel a quick kiss before heading for the kitchenette. And he wasn't surprised when he found Amy at his elbow.

"Is everything okay?" she asked quietly.

"Not exactly. Kaja quit." He set the oven to broil and pulled the pans out of the tote bags. While he worked, Pasha gave Amy the *Reader's Digest* version of last night's events in hushed tones. By the time he finished the story, the food was in the oven and Amy was perched on the countertop like a little kid.

"Fucking… what a jackass," she muttered, glancing out into the other room at Brett. "You realize that I don't care what his fucking excuse is. If I ever see him again, I'm going to kick his nuts right into his throat."

If she hadn't sounded so deadly serious—and if Brett weren't sitting right in Pasha's line of sight—he might have laughed. "Yeah, I know. It just sucks for Kaja's family."

"No comment." Amy hopped down from the counter and opened the fridge. "I need a beer. And so do you."

"Just a pop or tea or something, thanks."

She frowned, then glanced over to the living room where Daniel was chatting with Ben and Teddy. "Is there something going on that I don't know about?"

"Yeah. But I ah… I'd rather go somewhere a little more private to tell you about it."

"Well, I seem to remember someone I know being very well acquainted with other people's bathrooms," she reminded him.

Heat rose in Pasha's cheeks. "I'm never going to live that down, am I?"

"Eventually. Maybe." She grabbed a beer out of the fridge for herself, poured some Coke into a red plastic Solo cup for Pasha, and led the way to the bathroom.

AMY stared up at him from her seat on the edge of the tub. "HIV?"

Pasha nodded and held his breath, praying she wouldn't react the way Anne's ex had or go off on him the way some of those guys online went off on that blogger—she still hadn't contacted Pasha. Maybe he would never know if she stayed with her boyfriend or not.

And it seemed to take Amy several seconds to formulate her next words, but finally she asked, "Is he all right?"

Pasha sagged back against the counter. "I think so. I hope so."

"Oh honey." She stood up and wrapped her arms around his shoulders. "Are *you* all right?"

"I think so," he repeated, but he was trembling. "He just started taking ARVs—antiretroviral drugs. They're hitting him pretty hard." He was *not* going to start crying. It was like Keith said the other day at the support group meeting: Pasha could get hit by a bus tomorrow and Daniel would be the one taking care of him. Just because Daniel looked like death warmed over didn't mean he was dying.

Amy tightened her grip on him. "When did he tell you he had it?"

"On our second date."

"Does anyone else know?"

Pasha knew that what she was really asking was whether or not he'd told his dad yet. "No."

"If you need anything—and I mean *anything*—I'm here, okay?"

"Thanks, Amy."

"SHOULD I even ask what you two were doing in the bathroom?" Brett teased when Pasha and Amy joined him and Daniel on the sofa.

Heat flushed Pasha's cheeks, and the bemused expression on Daniel's face wasn't helping.

"Oh like you have any room to talk," Teddy interjected. "Or maybe we *shouldn't* tell that story in front of Pasha's boyfriend." He shot a wink at Pasha.

"Why do I have the feeling you and me are gonna be having a long talk later?" Daniel asked, grinning.

Teddy laughed. "Just remember, make-up sex is the best."

Daniel slung his arm over Pasha's shoulder and pulled him in close. "A *real* long talk," he teased.

"What you need to do is get him feeling so guilty he starts baking for you," Amy advised, settling in on Daniel's other side.

"I'll keep that in mind," said Daniel.

Pasha let out a sigh and shook his head, but he couldn't help smiling.

THEY left at eight fifteen with Daniel feeling queasy and didn't get more than three blocks before he had to pull over so he could throw up.

Pasha dashed around to his side of the car and crouched down next to him in the snow, holding Daniel's hair back as he heaved again. The only saving grace was that the side street Daniel had pulled onto was dark and no one seemed to have noticed them.

"I haven't done this since I was in college," Daniel muttered—then heaved for a third time, swearing violently as everything he'd eaten that night came up. Helpless to do anything else, Pasha rubbed his back and promised it would be all right.

At last, Daniel slumped back, leaning heavily against the side of his car. "I'm so sorry, Pasha. I *hate* this." He sounded so tired, so defeated.

Pasha sat down next to him. "It's okay, babe. We'll get through it."

Harsh anger played across Daniel's face. "No, *we* won't. I'm sick because I ate more than I should have, and I only ate as much as I did because… *crap*. I'm sorry," he repeated as the anger drained away, leaving almost as quickly as it had appeared. Only what replaced it was worse, because Daniel looked so hopeless, so helpless, it broke Pasha's heart. Moisture ran down his cheeks. "It's not your fault. It's mine. This whole fucking *thing* is my fault. If I hadn't been so *stupid*—"

"Don't," said Pasha. "Don't go there, don't beat yourself up."

"Why not?"

Pasha didn't answer him. Instead, he moved so he was straddling Daniel's lap. He pulled off his gloves and brushed his tears away with his fingertips. Under his touch, Daniel shuddered. He wrapped his arms around Pasha's waist and Pasha held on as tight as he could.

"Thank you," Daniel whispered.

Pasha understood. People were afraid of tears, of drinking out of the same glass. *Of being in the same room.* And he understood why Daniel had eaten too much, too. *He knew I was worried about him. He wanted to prove he was all right.* "Why don't you let me drive?" he suggested softly.

Daniel nodded against his shoulder. "I didn't mean to ruin your night. I know you wanted to stay longer—"

"Shhh. It's okay," Pasha told him. "Come on." He stood up and offered Daniel his hand.

Pasha stopped at the first gas station they passed and got Daniel a bottle of Vernors ginger ale and some crackers to help settle his stomach. "It's going to be all right," he promised when he got back into the car. Daniel hesitated, so Pasha opened the pop bottle and handed it to him. "Drink."

Daniel took a very small sip. "It doesn't feel like it's going to be okay," he said. "I'm afraid… I'm afraid it's going to be like this for the rest of my life."

"It won't be. The side effects are supposed to subside after a couple of weeks. If they don't, we'll talk to Doc Neumann."

"We?"

"We're in this together."

Daniel licked his lips and studied Pasha for a long moment. "Every time you say stuff like that, it gets me thinkin' about the long haul," he said softly. "Only I ah… I have a hard time convincing myself that's what you really mean. You know I'm… never mind." He shook his head quickly.

Pasha opened his mouth, but before he could say anything, the alarm on his phone went off.

"Let me guess," said Daniel, "it's time for me to take my pill?"

"Yeah. You should eat some crackers first."

Daniel let out a heavy, bitter-sounding sigh.

Pasha took his hand. "It really will get better."

"I know. Thanks."

CHAPTER THIRTY-ONE

WHEN Pasha turned from Twelve Mile Road onto Main Street, he saw red lights flashing up ahead. His mouth went dry and a hard knot started forming in his gut as he realized they were coming from the behind the restaurant. It was all he could do not to speed the rest of the way there. Just as he was rounding the corner into the lot, his cell phone started to ring, but all he could focus on were the flashing red lights, the fire truck—God, it was enormous!—the red EMT truck, and the wide-open back door. He only barely felt Daniel's hand squeezing his.

Pasha pulled the Mustang to a halt and sprinted toward the restaurant. He stopped dead in his tracks when the paramedics emerged from the building, bringing someone out on a stretcher. Even if he hadn't already spotted Sharon and Randy hovering in the doorway looking worried, he would have known it was Dad.

Pasha didn't hear Daniel's footsteps; he just felt strong, warm arms wrapping around his shoulders, and he leaned into Daniel's embrace. "Everything was supposed to be fine," he said. Dad was going to take more time off. Okay, he hadn't agreed to it yet, but Pasha was going to find a way to make it happen. They were going to turn the restaurant around. Dad had accepted that Pasha was gay. He'd met Daniel.

Oh God... what if*...?*

The paramedics closed up the back of the truck and pulled out of the lot, sirens wailing. And that was it. Dad was gone, and Pasha didn't even know what had happened. He looked blankly up at Daniel and then toward Sharon and Randy, and he realized that Sam and Nate were standing behind them. "Sharon—"

"I tried calling you." She cut him off. The gap between them grew shorter, but Pasha couldn't honestly have said who moved, him and Daniel or Sharon and the others. Maybe they all started walking at the same time, closing the distance so they were standing face to face. "I tried but you didn't pick up and…." Sharon stopped short, her gaze drifting from Pasha to Daniel—who was next to him, one arm slung around Pasha's shoulders—and then back again. Sharon's expression turned sour, but Pasha was past caring who saw or what they thought.

"What happened?" Daniel asked.

Sharon hesitated and Randy answered for her. "Ivan was acting funny all night. I don't know, it was like he couldn't breathe right or something, but he kept saying it was nothing."

"The stubborn old bastard was having chest pains!" Nate interjected angrily. "I tried to tell him, let us take him to the hospital, but he wouldn't listen. He said he'd go *after* the place was closed for the night. He's a damned fool!"

"He just fell over," Randy said. He looked as lost and confused as Pasha felt.

Daniel tightened his grip on Pasha's shoulders and feathered a soft kiss to his temple. It helped, but only a little.

One of the firemen joined them. "Is anybody here family?" he asked.

"*Da.* Yes, me," Pasha stammered. "He's my dad. I'm his son." He was shaking.

"Take it easy. I know we put on quite a show out here, but it was a mild heart attack. Your dad was giving the boys a hell of a hard time before they got him out of here," he added with a good-natured smile. "They're taking him to Beaumont. You know where that is?"

Pasha nodded and heard Daniel saying "yes."

"Thank you," Pasha added; he wasn't sure who he was thanking, Daniel or the fireman. Maybe it was both.

The fireman took his leave, and Sam stepped up next to Sharon. He gave Pasha a hard, cold look, but all he said was, "We'll meet you up there." He motioned Nate and Sharon toward his car.

"Wait—Sharon," Pasha called after her, "did you call Nadia?"

She turned and cast another dark look in his direction. "And Peter, and your aunt and uncle. Nadia and Anya are on their way. Peter will be here in the morning."

"Thanks," he told her, even though he would have preferred it if no one else was coming out. Selfishly, he wondered if there was any way to avoid the rest of his family tonight.

"We'll be right behind you," Daniel said as Sharon and Nate got into Sam's Buick. No one answered him.

Randy shuffled his feat. "I um, I wish I could, you know, go with you guys and stuff," he said awkwardly. "But my brother's on his way to get me. I was supposed to leave at nine thirty and, I mean—"

"You've got school tomorrow," said Pasha. "Go ahead and wait for your brother inside. Just make sure both doors are locked when you leave, okay?"

"You want me to clean up and stuff?" Randy offered.

Pasha gave him a grateful smile. "Go ahead and turn everything off and put away what you can. And don't worry about it if you miss anything. Thanks, Randy."

"I just hope your Dad's okay."

"Yeah, me too."

ON THE way to the hospital, Pasha called Amy to let her know what had happened. She offered to drive out, but he told her to stay with Brett. Dad was probably fine, and Daniel was still with him. Amy made him promise to call the second he had more news.

"I will," he agreed. He hung up with Amy, and he held Daniel's hand tight as they walked into the ER waiting area, where a dozen or so anxious-looking people sat in little clusters of two and three—a few all by themselves. It was like déjà vu. *Except walking into the ER when Brett was here, I only had to deal with one person who hated me.*

Daniel gave his hand a tight squeeze and reminded him, "We're in this together, Sugar."

"Thanks."

They made their way over to the far corner, where Sharon and Sam sat next to each other. Nate was on his feet, even though there were plenty of empty chairs nearby.

Dark anger etched its way across Nate's face as Pasha and Daniel approached. "This isn't a place for… *that*." He glared at Pasha and Daniel's clasped hands. "I'm sure your *friend* will understand if you want him to leave."

Pasha held Daniel's hand tighter. "Daniel is my *boyfriend* and he's here because I asked him to be." He didn't make any effort to hide how pissed he was by Nate's words.

Sam stood up. "Maybe this isn't the time for that kind of discussion—"

"There's no such thing as not the right time for it," Nate snapped, his voice growing louder. "It's all that political correctness crap that's turned this country upside-down! I swear, if my boy brought home a… one of you people, I'd toss him out on his goddamned faggot ass so fast he wouldn't even see it coming!"

People were starting to stare. Pasha swallowed back the lump of burning rage and replied in the calmest voice he could muster, "Then I guess it's a good thing for both of us that I'm not your son."

Before Nate could say more, Sam stepped in between them. He looked up at Daniel with a clearly feigned smile. "Daniel, is it? Hi, I'm Sam McMiller." He held out his hand. Daniel accepted and Sam went on. "I'm sure you're a perfectly nice man and your personal choices are entirely your own business." His tone was patronizing, bordering on smarmy. "I'm just as sure that you can see for yourself that it would be in everybody's best interest if you left before someone causes a scene."

For half a second, Pasha thought Daniel was going to cave. He looked so tired, and he'd gotten so sick on the way back from Brett's place. Maybe he *should* go home and get some rest.

But instead of backing down, Daniel pulled himself up to his full height. "With all due respect, Mr. McMiller, you're not the one who invited me. It's really not your place to tell me to leave."

Sam turned to Pasha. "Son, I think right now you need to think about your father. What would he say if he saw… this?" He spread his hands wide.

"Dad knows about Daniel. He likes him."

"Horseshit!" Nate yelled. "There is no way in hell Ivan would cotton to this nonsense!"

Before Pasha could form an answer, a woman wearing light-blue scrubs and a hospital badge approached them. "Is there a problem here?" she inquired.

"No, ma'am," Pasha lied.

"What's the name of the patient you're here for?" she asked.

"Ivan Batalov."

The woman pursed her lips, but it was hard to tell who she was pissed at. "Then you're who I'm looking for. Mr. Batalov wanted to know if his son was here." She gave Pasha a speculative look.

"Yes, ma'am, that's me. Is he all right?"

"He's stable and he'd like to see you."

"What about the rest of us?" Sharon wanted to know.

The woman in blue shot Pasha another look—but she didn't wait for him to respond. "Just family for right now. Mr. Batalov?" She nodded at Pasha to follow her.

"Just a second," he said and turned to Daniel. He really did look like something the cat had dragged in. It was completely selfish to ask him to stay, especially if it meant dealing with Nate.

But Daniel smiled and feathered a soft kiss to Pasha's forehead. "I'll be here when you get back, Sugar. Promise."

"Thank you. I…." He didn't even know what he wanted to say.

As usual, Daniel understood. "No worries. Go be with your dad."

God, I…. "I love you," he whispered, praying it wasn't the worst time ever.

Daniel's smile made warmth bubble up in Pasha's chest. "I love you too, babe," he said.

Pasha leaned up and pressed a quick, chaste kiss to Daniel's lips, then turned and followed the nurse out of the room. "Is Dad really okay?" he asked her once they'd reached the hallway.

"Dr. Sanjay will be able to tell you more, but I know we're going to want to keep him overnight for observation and to run a few more tests." She was quiet for a minute, then asked, "Are they going to be all right back there, or should I have security swing by?"

"They'll be all right. Nate's just… he is who he is." He shrugged.

IT WAS hard not to react when Pasha saw his father lying in a hospital bed hooked up to almost as many monitors as Brett had been hooked up to.

"It's not as bad as it looks," Ivan told him. "These damned doctors gotta squeeze every penny they can outta you, so they hook you up to every goddamned machine in hospital."

Much to Pasha's surprise, his escort chuckled. "What did I tell you earlier about not getting yourself worked up?" she asked him with a good-natured wink. "One heart attack per night is your quota. If you have another one we'll have to charge you extra."

He waved her off, but he was smiling too, and Pasha could finally breathe. If Dad was well enough to give his nurse a hard time, well enough joke with her, he really was okay.

The nurse turned to him. "Just let me know if you need anything," she said before making her exit. She drew the curtain shut behind her, giving them at least the illusion of privacy. There wasn't much privacy to be had when the only thing separating Dad's bed from the rest of the ER was a thin piece of cloth that didn't even reach the floor.

Pasha moved to stand by his father's side. "How are you feeling?"

"Like my damned heart stopped working right," Ivan grumbled. "How am I supposed to feel? Like getting up and dancing?"

Pasha heaved a sigh. "I told you that you needed to take better care of yourself. Maybe now you'll listen to your doctor."

"Doctors are full of shit!" But then he shook his head. "Look at me. What a mess, huh?" he said, his tone more subdued.

"It'll be all right. You gave everyone at the restaurant a good scare, though."

"How's Sharon?"

"Pretty shaken up. Sam and Nate came with her to the ER."

Ivan scowled. "They came here?"

"Yeah. Randy would have come too, but his brother was already on his way to the restaurant to pick him up."

"Too much goddamned fuss for one old man," he said. Then he asked, "What about that… Daniel? He come with you?"

"Yeah. He ah… everyone saw us together. I'm sorry. It all just happened so fast—"

Ivan waved off his apology. "Let them think what they're gonna think." He shifted like he was trying sit up, but the IV and oxygen monitor clipped to his finger made it difficult.

"Here." Pasha tried to help.

"I'm not invalid!" Ivan snapped. Then he wheezed and started coughing.

The knots in Pasha's stomach felt so tight he wasn't sure he could breathe either, because he didn't know what to do except step outside the curtain and flag down a nurse to see if Dad could have some water. By the time she got back with a little plastic pitcher and cup and straw, the old man's coughing fit had subsided enough that he could drink, but Pasha had to hold the cup.

"Maybe I am invalid." Ivan sagged back against the pillows.

"You're not an invalid, Dad, but you did have a heart attack."

"*Da*." For once the old man didn't fight him. "Okay. Sit down. We gotta talk about restaurant."

CHAPTER THIRTY-TWO

IT WAS a short, mostly unpleasant conversation that Pasha won only because Dr. Sanjay came in to check on Ivan and told the old man that if he didn't take time off, the next time he had a heart attack, they wouldn't be calling an ambulance, they'd be calling an undertaker. Then he told Pasha that his father needed to get some sleep.

"I'll sleep when I'm dead!" Ivan grumbled.

"And that will come sooner than you like if you don't start taking better care of yourself, Mr. Batalov," Sanjay warned.

Pasha leaned in and gave his father a kiss on the cheek. "I'll come by in the morning."

Ivan shot him an askance look. "Who's going to run restaurant if you're here, huh?"

"I'm not opening tomorrow. No more arguing." He cut his father off before he even started. "I'll see you in the morning. Now try to get some sleep."

Ivan waved off the suggestion. "Who can sleep with all this goddamned noise?"

"I don't know," Pasha said. "Just close your eyes and rest."

"We'll get you moved up to a room soon," Dr. Sanjay promised. "Mr. Batalov—Pasha," he clarified when they both looked up. "Could I see you a moment?"

He nodded and followed Dr. Sanjay out of the ER ward. "How bad is it?" he asked once they were in the hallway.

"Not as bad as I told your father," the doctor promised. "But he *must* start looking after his health. When I asked him about diet and exercise, he asked me what was the point of living if he couldn't enjoy himself."

Yeah, that sounded like Dad all right. "His own doctor's been after him for years to change the way he eats. I get on him, too, but he's stubborn."

"Some of the things your father says makes me think it might be more than just a case of him being stubborn. I'd like to ask a psychiatrist to come down and talk to him. I know sometimes people become upset at the word 'psychiatrist,'" he said quickly. "They think mental health issues can't happen to them, to their family. But they can happen to anyone. I think your father might be suffering from depression. Perhaps it's just seasonal. A lot of people are afflicted this time of year."

"It might be more than just seasonal. About a year ago, Dad had to find a nursing home for my mother. Alzheimer's," he explained. "It was pretty bad. He probably should have found her a place before he did. It's been a really rough… I don't know, maybe ten years."

"Has he gone to see a counselor through any of this?" asked the doctor. "There are support groups—"

Pasha shook his head. "I never even brought it up to him." Truthfully, it hadn't even occurred to him that either of them might need help.

"Perhaps you should."

"I'll see what I can do. Thanks."

PASHA found Daniel leaning up against the wall a few dozen feet from the waiting room, holding a cup of Starbucks coffee in his hand. "They didn't have cheesecake flavor. I hope white chocolate will do."

"God, I love you," he said. It came out flippantly, but Daniel smiled. "I'm sorry," Pasha told him anyway.

Daniel's expression faltered. "And that means…?"

"It means I didn't intend to put you on the spot like that. Before, in the waiting room," he clarified. "I just… I don't want you to think you have to say it back if you don't want to."

"Just answer me this: did you mean it?"

Heat burned in Pasha's cheeks, but he didn't hesitate to answer "Yes."

"Good. Because I meant it too." He leaned in and pressed a soft kiss to Pasha's lips.

Pasha closed his eyes and savored the moment—

"*Bozhe moi*!"

Pasha cringed at the sound of his aunt's shrill voice.

"Sorry," Daniel whispered. "I should have warned you it had gotten a little crowded in there."

"It's okay. I should've remembered Sharon called her. Is my sister here too?"

"Nobody introduced themselves—"

"Pasha!" Anya stomped up to him. "What the hell is going on here? Who the hell is this?"

"This is Daniel. *Moi drook*," he said in Russian, just to make sure there wouldn't be any miscommunication. "Daniel, Anya, my dad's sister."

Daniel offered his hand, but she slapped it away. "Pasha… we'll talk about this *drook* business later. Why the hell won't those idiots let me to see Ivan? They're saying 'family only.' I'm his goddamned sister! I drove from *Bloomfield Hills* just to see him!"

"I don't know why they wouldn't let you see Dad. Why don't we go back into the waiting room?" Pasha suggested, speaking as calmly as he could. Bloomfield Hills was just a few miles up Woodward Avenue. Anya hadn't had to drive far to get there. The point, however, was that she was *from* Bloomfield Hills; she had money and was used to getting what she wanted because of it.

In the waiting room, Pasha's uncle, cousin, and sister were sitting with Sam, Nate, and Sharon. *Because of course Anya couldn't come by herself. She had to drag Nikita and Samara out with her.* Nikita looked exhausted. Samara looked the way she always did: pissed. Nadia seemed paler and thinner than ever. She was the one to notice Pasha and Daniel first, and she nodded to Sharon to turn around. Even before Sharon turned, the hushed conversation the group had been having stopped dead.

Pasha cleared his throat. They were all staring. Glaring. “I’m sorry you guys all drove out here,” he said. “But it’s late and it doesn’t sound like they’re going to let Dad have any more visitors tonight.”

“You’re not gonna go fix it?” Anya demanded. She’d trailed in behind him but was quick to rejoin the others, leaving him and Daniel standing by themselves.

“There’s nothing to fix,” said Pasha. “The doctor asked me to leave too.”

She stared at him in stunned silence for several long moments before finding her voice again. “Well. I guess you’d better go home and get some sleep. You’re gonna have to run restaurant all by yourself tomorrow. Maybe you’ll appreciate your father more after few days of filling his shoes. We’ll talk about this”—she waved a hand at Daniel—“later.”

“We’re closed tomorrow, Anya. And as far as my private life goes, there’s nothing to talk about.”

She gaped at him as if he’d sprouted a second head. “What you mean ‘closed’? You can’t close. Me and Nikita helped your father open that restaurant—” She looked to her husband as if she expected his help.

Before Nikita could say a word, Pasha jumped back in. “Dad paid you guys back. Your name isn’t on the business. You don’t get a vote in how it’s run.”

“You can’t just close up whenever you *want*,” Anya snapped.

“Yes, I can. My name *is* on the business.”

Nadia shifted in her seat. “How’s Dad?” she asked.

“He’ll be okay. He just needs to get some rest and start taking care of himself.”

“He’s not gonna be okay when he finds out what you’re doing,” said Anya.

“How long are you planning on keeping the restaurant closed?” Nadia asked.

"Honestly, I don't know. Probably until after the New Year."

Nadia balked. "What will Dad do for money?"

He bit his tongue; what Nadia really meant was what would *she* do if she couldn't come to Dad for her mortgage payment this month. But he stuck with answering the question she'd asked aloud. "We'll get by. We always do. Things will just be a little tighter for a while."

"Pasha, you can't do that."

Anya put her hand on Nadia's shoulder. "Your father will never stand for this *zaoika*. You just wait until tomorrow when you can talk to him yourself. Ivan will fix it."

"You need to get it through your head, both of you—*all* of you," Pasha snapped. "Dad doesn't have a choice anymore. The doctor told him that if he had another heart attack, we wouldn't be calling an ambulance, we'd be calling the goddamned undertaker!" He paused for a second to let that sink in. "We're *all* going to have to make some changes. Don't come back here tomorrow if all you're going to do is get him riled up." He directed the last at his aunt.

It was an awful thing to wonder whether the stricken look on his sister's face was over the fact that their father really could die, or if it was because she realized she might not have any choice but to tell her husband to get up off his ass and find a job.

And maybe in the morning when he was less tired, he'd be able to care more. Right then all he wanted was to go to bed. Swallowing back the last of his fears—and with his heart pounding like mad—Pasha reached out for Daniel's hand. "Would you mind giving me a lift back to the restaurant?" he asked softly—but loud enough for everyone to hear.

"You got it, Sugar."

Pasha was shaking as they walked down the hall, but he refused to look back.

"It's okay," Daniel told him.

"I'm just sorry you got dragged into it."

Daniel shrugged. "You know what they say. When you get involved with somebody, you're not just getting involved with one person, you're getting involved with his whole family."

"GUESS this is good night," Daniel said when he pulled in behind the darkened restaurant.

Every light was off, even the ones Dad usually left on at night.

"You think maybe I can talk you into coming in for a minute?" Pasha asked. "I know you're probably tired, but…." It was almost midnight, but he wasn't ready to say good night yet.

Daniel cut the engine. "I think I can manage that."

Pasha unlocked the back door and let them in out of the cold. "Why don't you go up front and nudge up the heat a little," he said as he hit the lights. "I just need a few minutes to make sure everything's put away, but there's no reason for us to freeze while I'm doing it." It was a bald-faced lie. Well, mostly a lie. Pasha did need a few minutes to make sure Randy hadn't forgotten anything, but what he really wanted was to get Daniel out of the kitchen so he could start cooking without having to answer too many questions. By the time Daniel rejoined him, Pasha had the two chicken breasts on the grill and a small pot of chicken broth heating on the stove.

Daniel shot him a quizzical look.

"You lost your dinner, remember?" Pasha stated the obvious.

"Which is why I don't think eating now's a real good idea."

"You have to eat."

"Pasha—"

"You don't have to eat a lot, but you have to eat something." The chicken broth had started to boil, so he poured in a cup of rice and added a little dill and parsley. "Do you have Gatorade or something at home?" he asked. "What about bananas? If you want, you can take some from here. No one's going to eat them anyway."

"You *don't* need to mother me," Daniel snapped.

"I'm not," Pasha snapped right back. "There's a difference between taking care of someone and mothering them." He gave the rice a stir and flipped the chicken breasts.

Daniel huffed out an exasperated sigh. "I should get going. I have a long drive home." He started toward the door, but Pasha stepped in front of him.

"Don't you dare!" said Pasha.

"Look, I don't need you to cook for me, okay? I just want to go home."

"You have to eat something."

"Haven't you been paying attention? When I eat, I throw up!"

Pasha stood his ground.

"Please don't," Daniel begged.

"Don't what? Cook you dinner after you sat with me in the hospital for over two hours?"

The pained look in Daniel's eyes was enough to break Pasha's heart. "Don't start treating me like I can't take care of myself."

Pasha stepped closer and laid his hands on Daniel's hips. "Babe, I'm not. All I'm trying to do is feed you."

"I just don't want you to start looking at me like I'm somebody who can't fend for himself. I'll be *fine*."

"I know you will." Pasha tightened his grip. He understood what Daniel was trying to say: he didn't want to be a burden; he didn't want Pasha to wind up resenting him. "Daniel, would you be upset with me if you had a cold and I showed up at your place with a pot of chicken soup?"

"That's different."

"How? I love to cook. I love making people happy. Most of all, I love you."

"I don't want—"

Pasha placed his fingers on Daniel's lips, silencing him. "I know. Now how about making a pot of hot water and seeing what kind of tea we have? All you have to do is turn the coffeemaker on and flip the lever next to the on/off switch. Just make sure there isn't a filter full of coffee grounds still in it," he added quickly. It was the kind of thing that was easy enough for him to forget at the end of the night. He wouldn't be upset at Randy if he hadn't thought about it.

"I don't mean to be difficult," Daniel said softly when Pasha took his hand away from his lips.

"I know that too." He leaned up and pressed a kiss to Daniel's mouth.

While Pasha was waiting for the rice to finish cooking, he sent Amy a text to let her know Dad was okay, but they weren't going to be open tomorrow. He promised to call her in the morning. Then he went into the office and found a piece of cardboard and a marker so he could make a sign for the front door.

CLOSED FOR THE HOLIDAYS, SEE YOU ON JANUARY 1ST!

NEW HOURS:

MON-FRI: 7 a.m.—9 p.m.

SATURDAY: 9 a.m.—9 p.m.

SUNDAY: 9 a.m.—3 p.m.

HE WASN'T about to advertise Dad's heart attack, but tomorrow he'd start making calls to let their regulars know what was going on. As far as the rest of the world was concerned, they were just a small business taking some time off for Christmas.

And of course, Dad hadn't actually agreed to changing their hours—he hadn't agreed to anything—but Pasha was doing it anyway. *Next on the list is hiring a new cook.* Because whether Dad liked it or not, he was going to have to take some time off. That, at least, could wait until tomorrow. *Or maybe the next day.*

By the time he had the sign up in the door, the rice was almost done. Pasha grabbed a handful of spinach from the cooler and gave it a rough chop before dropping it into the pot. He covered it, turned off the burner, and let it sit for a few minutes.

"Smells good," Daniel said when Pasha emerged from the kitchen carrying two plates on one arm. He used his free hand to grab a couple of silverware rolls from the tub under the counter. He'd plated up small portions on salad plates, so it wouldn't look like he was catering to Daniel's easily unsettled stomach.

"Looks good too," Daniel added when Pasha set his plate down in front of him. His tone was subdued. "I really am sorry I was such an ass before. I'm trying not to be so oversensitive. I'm just not used to feeling like this."

"I know and that's why you're welcome and forgiven. But I need you to understand that this is hard for me too."

"I do know that."

"Good." Pasha nodded. "Then you can let me cook for you. Let me pester you and take care of you and maybe even mother you a little sometimes, because it makes feel like I'm doing something useful. And if I end up having to hold your hair back while you throw up once in a while, I'm okay with that too."

Daniel flashed an embarrassed smile. "I'd be just as happy if we never had to do that again."

"Me too. But if we do, we will."

"Thank you." Daniel finally picked up his fork and took a bite of rice and chicken. "It's good."

"Glad you like it." But he wasn't looking for compliments. It was a simple, bland, and fairly balanced meal, which was all that mattered.

Daniel took another bite, and Pasha watched as he chewed slowly and deliberately before swallowing it down. "So far so good," he reported.

Pasha stopped staring at him and ate some of his own meal. They ate in companionable silence, and when Daniel pushed his plate back, Pasha stopped eating too.

"You don't have to stop on my account."

"I'm good," Pasha told him.

Daniel nodded. "Look, I ah, I'm not one to invite myself or anything, but if you happened to want company tonight…. I'm not up for more than sleeping or anything, but I'm not real sure I can make it back to Ypsi."

"I'd love the company, but don't you have to work in the morning?"

"I called off work while you were in talking to your dad."

"Shit, I'm sorry."

"It wasn't because of this," he promised. "I would have called off to be there for you if you'd asked, but truth is I didn't sleep more than a couple hours last night. I didn't eat anything today—yesterday," he amended, "except what I ate at the party and… well…." He shrugged. They both knew what had happened there. "I wasn't gonna be able to make it in to work today, I just kept putting off making the call."

"Why didn't you tell me how sick you were?"

"I didn't want you to worry."

"Daniel, please promise me you'll talk to me from now on. I will worry, but I'll worry more if you start hiding stuff from me."

He nodded, but he didn't look happy. "I know it'll get better, and if it doesn't, we'll go in and talk to the doc." He shot Pasha a tight-lipped smile. "But right now I can't eat. I can't sleep. I didn't want to call in to work because doing that meant admitting I needed time off."

"Was your boss pissed when you called?" Pasha asked, worried. The last thing Daniel needed was to lose his job.

But Daniel shook his head. "Nah. He told me to go ahead and start my vacation early. The new guy'll just have to get his act together without me there to keep holding his hand. If I'm still feeling rough around the edges when I come back, we'll talk about shifting me over to a sales position."

"I'm sorry. I know you hate office work."

He shrugged. "I'll still get to hit the road to meet with customers. I'll be okay as long as I'm not cooped up all day, every day. So… back to me spending the night?" he prompted.

"I should warn you all I have is a twin bed."

Daniel grinned. "Damn. We might have to get close."

Pasha smiled too, and reached across the table to take Daniel's hands. "Guess I can deal with that."

Chapter Thirty-Three

WAKEFULNESS crept up on Pasha slowly, but thankfully without the piercing whine of the alarm clock. His room was dark and there was a warm, firm body pressed tightly up against his back. The faint scent of Daniel's cologne lingered in the air. Pasha snuggled back against Daniel. They were both naked, but that had more to do with convenience than anything else. Besides, with someone to sleep next to, the house didn't feel so cold.

When Daniel slid his hands slowly over Pasha's stomach, he shivered. With one hand, Daniel caressed his stomach, tickling him. With the other, he circled Pasha's nipples, first one and then the other, his light touch turning them into hard nubs.

"I'm not sure," Pasha murmured, "but I think there's a law about molesting people in their sleep."

"Guess it's a good thing you're awake," Daniel replied. He feathered soft kisses to Pasha's neck and shoulder, causing his already stiff cock to strain harder. "You happen to have any lube hiding anywhere?" he whispered.

"There's lube and condoms in the drawer next to you."

"Just need the lube. Don't move." The last statement was the kind of rough command that made Pasha quiver. He stayed completely still while Daniel rolled over. Pasha heard the drawer open and stuff sliding around as Daniel rummaged in the dark for what he was after. Finally, he felt Daniel's arms around him again. A moment later, lube-slicked fingers grasped Pasha's cock and he gasped.

"That feels so good." He moaned as Daniel began working him slowly.

"That's the idea." Daniel slid his other hand up Pasha's chest and rolled one nipple between his thumb and forefinger.

"Harder," Pasha begged.

"I'd rather take my time."

"No…. I mean yeah, slow is good. I just meant you could pinch harder." Why was it so embarrassing to admit that he liked it a little rough? But when he felt Daniel's mouth on his neck again, he whispered words of encouragement and Daniel's soft, tender kisses gave way to nipping—sucking. "God yes, like that." Pasha's toes curled and his eyes rolled back in his head. "I'm not going anywhere today, you can leave a mark," he rasped into the darkness. Weren't hickeys for teenagers? But damn, the harder Daniel sucked, the more Pasha wriggled and moaned, and when he finally came, an explosion of stars danced behind his eyes. "Love you. Daniel. God, I love you." His whole body shook.

Daniel wrapped both arms around him and held him through the aftershocks. "I love you too, babe," he whispered right in Pasha's ear. He pressed a series of soft kisses to Pasha's shoulder and waited for him to stop trembling before he spoke again. "I didn't realize you liked it like that. Rough," Daniel clarified.

Heat flooded Pasha's cheeks. "Only sometimes."

Daniel squeezed him a little tighter and pressed another kiss to his skin, right on top of the aching bruise he'd just left on Pasha's neck. "Sugar, I can do rough. I can do soft. I can do whatever you want, just tell me."

"You don't think there's something wrong with me?"

"What, because you like it a little rough? Pasha, I am totally flexible."

He smiled, and not just because Daniel was flexible. "How about rolling over onto your back?"

Daniel obliged, but he put his hands on Pasha's shoulders when Pasha started to go down on him.

"Trust me. I won't do anything I know makes you uncomfortable," he promised.

With a reluctant look on his face, Daniel let go and Pasha settled himself between his thighs. It wasn't the cock that presented any kind of risk—although Pasha wasn't convinced that sucking Daniel off would really be that risky—it was the semen. All he had to do was avoid Daniel's cockhead and he could go down on him all he wanted. He sucked and nibbled his way happily up and down Daniel's shaft, savoring the feel of his velvety skin and light salty flavor until Daniel was begging him to stop so he could jack off.

But Pasha had no intention of stopping yet. He maneuvered lower, kissing and caressing Daniel's balls with his lips and tongue, gently sucking one and then the other into his mouth, causing Daniel to moan louder. When he was sure he'd taken Daniel almost to the edge, he slid his hand up underneath Daniel and caressed the sensitive spot between his testicles and entrance.

"Oh God," Daniel groaned in response. "So close."

"Hand me the lube."

Daniel didn't question him. He just handed it over. Pasha slicked up one hand and wrapped it around Daniel's cock.

"Oh God.... Pasha," he moaned and his hips began to buck. "*Pasha*," he repeated as creamy white cum splashed over Pasha's hand and onto Daniel's chest. He sagged back against the mattress, breathing hard, looking utterly sated and completely happy.

PASHA stepped out of the shower first so he could shave while Daniel enjoyed a few more minutes under the hot spray. "I have to get up to the hospital and then the restaurant," he said as he lathered up his face. "But I was wondering if you'd mind being a guinea pig for something I'm thinking about putting on the new breakfast menu."

"Sure. What am I trying?"

"Whole grain carrot pancakes."

"Sounds… healthy."

Pasha laughed at the dubiousness in his tone. "That's the whole idea. There's cinnamon in them," he added, mostly hoping it wouldn't be too spicy for Daniel.

"I'll give it a try, just don't take it too personally if they don't stay down."

"I won't."

When Daniel stepped out of the tub, Pasha handed him a clean towel from the cabinet next to the sink. The dark circles under Daniel's eyes were almost completely gone. Pasha turned back around to finish shaving, but he couldn't help watching Daniel in the mirror. "Would it be okay if I said I could get used to this?" he asked after rinsing his face.

Daniel smiled. "I was thinking the same thing. Maybe someday."

"Can I ask you something?"

"As long as it doesn't involve more health food," Daniel teased him.

Pasha laughed, but his stomach was turning nervous flip-flops. "What you said yesterday to my dad, about how anything's possible…. Did you really mean that?"

"What sort of 'anything' did you have in mind?" Daniel asked.

"I'm not sure. I mean, there's a lot to consider, I just wondered if…." God, it was way too soon to be thinking the kinds of things he was thinking about. "Forget I said anything."

Daniel wrapped both arms around his shoulders and pulled him into a warm embrace. "Anything *is* possible, Pasha. I'm just not sure what I want."

Pasha nibbled his lower lip. "I guess that's fair."

"I didn't mean that the way it sounded. I just meant… there are some things I do know I want, okay?"

"Like?"

Daniel feathered a soft kiss to Pasha's neck. "Mornings like this. You next to me at night." He shifted, holding him closer. "I want to take you up north to meet my folks and I'd like—eventually—to figure out some way to make things work so every morning is really like this. I don't necessarily know how to do all that, but I know I want to try. I'm just not sure about the rest of it."

Pasha knew what he really meant: Daniel didn't know whether or not he wanted kids. "I can live with that."

"You sure? Because if that's some kind of deal breaker, this would be a good time to figure it out. I'm not saying no, I'm just saying I don't know because there's an awful lot to think about."

"Then why don't we put it in the category of things to figure out later down the road?"

Daniel nodded. "Sounds good."

THE sound of heated whispers coming from the other side of the curtain around Dad's bed didn't bode well, especially not when Pasha recognized that one of the voices belonged to his brother. He heard Cindy, too, urging them—or at least Peter—to keep it down. He and Dad were arguing in Russian about Pasha. Daniel. The restaurant. Money.

Pasha pulled the curtain aside and the conversation stopped dead. Dad scowled, Peter glowered, and Cindy looked uncomfortable. It was Thanksgiving all over again—except that instead of scowling at Pasha, Dad was scowling at Peter.

As soon as Pasha came in, however, Dad's attention shifted to him. "Tell goddamned doctors I'm ready to go home! There's nothing wrong with me."

"Dad, you had a heart attack," Pasha reminded him. "But I'll see if I can find out when they're going to let you out of here."

Peter stood up, causing his chair to scoot noisily against the hard tile floor. "We need to talk," he told Pasha in Russian. When he turned to his wife, he spoke in English. "Cindy, stay here."

She didn't answer, but she didn't look happy either.

"There's nothing for you to talk about," Ivan said in English. "What's done is done. Leave it be, Pyotr."

"Like hell it's done!" Peter snapped. He stalked toward the hallway. "Pasha, get out here!"

"Pasha—" Dad began as he started to follow his brother.

"It's okay," he said. "I'm not fifteen anymore." He leaned in and kissed his father's cheek, then flashed a tight-lipped smile at his sister-in-law and followed Peter out into the hall. Dad had been moved out of the ER and onto a regular floor where hospital staff, patients, and visitors were coming and going up and down the long, wide hall.

Peter stood next to Dad's doorway, glowering. "What in the hell is going on?" he demanded in a hushed tone as soon as Pasha emerged.

"Sounds to me like you already know."

"Don't play games—"

"Where do you want me to start, Peter? Back in high school, with you cutting back your hours and leaving me to pick up the slack? With me dropping out of college so *you* could take more classes? With you moving halfway across the state and leaving me to take care of Dad and the restaurant all by myself? With the fact that Dad is literally working himself into an early grave? Because as far as I'm concerned, *that's* what's going on."

Peter's hands balled into fists and blood rose in his face. "I went by the restaurant. And I talked to Nadia and Anya. I know all about that… person."

"If you mean Daniel, then no, you don't know the first thing about him—but do *not* pretend you don't know I'm gay."

"Do you have any idea what you're doing to the people around you?"

"Jesus fucking Christ. I'm done." He turned to go back into Dad's room, but Peter grabbed his arm.

"Don't you *dare* walk away from me!" Peter seethed.

Pasha wrenched himself free. "Touch me again and you'll be the one with the broken nose."

Several hospital employees were gawking at them, including the security guard walking quickly down the hall.

Pasha unballed his fist. "Take your wife and go home, Peter." He walked over to the nurses' station to see if they could tell him when the old man would be released to go home.

"HEY!" Amy hollered as she came in the back door of the restaurant on Thursday morning. She and Sean had both been in yesterday to take down the Christmas decorations and start going through the walk-in and pantry. There was a lot of food that had to be given away before it went bad. "I brought some more help," Amy said.

"Cool! We're up front," Pasha called out. He and Daniel had just gotten there and were making a list of what needed to be done before he could paint. Not that he'd picked out a color, but anything he chose would be better than beige.

When Pasha looked up and saw who Amy had brought with her, he blinked in surprise. The last person he expected to see was Mark.

Amy stopped halfway through the kitchen to look at the two new vertical rotisseries sitting on the counter next to the grill. "So this is a gyro cooker?"

"Yep." Pasha joined her in the kitchen. Daniel was right behind him. "I have to find a better spot for them, but for now, this'll do." Each rotisserie stood three feet tall, was over two and a half feet wide, and would hold a thirty-five-pound slab of meat—and each one had set him back a thousand bucks. One had been charged to his credit card, and he'd paid for the other out of his savings account. Now he just had to tell Dad what he'd done. *But one battle at a time.* "So ah…." He looked from Mark to Amy and back again.

"She wants me to fill out an application," Mark explained. He didn't sound especially enthusiastic or even hopeful that Pasha would hire him.

"What are you looking for?" he asked anyway.

Amy answered for him. "You're going to need another cook and Mark just graduated from Henry Ford Community College's Culinary Arts Program. He's good," she added with a wink.

Mark heaved a sigh. "I told her you wouldn't hire me."

"And I told him," Amy countered, "that you wouldn't let the rough start you two got off to stop you from considering him."

"I haven't even begun to figure out what kind of hours I've got to offer someone," Pasha said. "And I'll level with you, money is super tight right now. We've been operating in the red for the last five years, I just lost my night dishwasher, and I'm pretty sure I'm on the verge of losing my day dishwasher and my night waitress."

"Good riddance," Amy muttered.

"Maybe, but unless you and Sean want to start working doubles…." He shrugged. But he didn't want to work double shifts either, so he turned to Mark. "Are you working now?"

"No, I ah, I graduated last spring and got a job at this four-star restaurant, and long story short, it didn't work out."

"And you think you'd like this better?" Pasha had to ask.

Mark blinked, as if he finally realized he was being interviewed and didn't believe it. Amy snickered and elbowed him before heading up front for a cup of hot cocoa.

"I worked in a place like this when I was in school," Mark said. "I liked the work, but the restaurant isn't one I'd want to go back to."

"You might be saying that about this place in a month."

"Amy told me it can get a little interesting around here."

"That's an understatement," Pasha told him. "Look, I'd love to hire you, but I have to be honest. The pay sucks and I can only offer part-time."

Mark's grin surprised him. "So in other words, this is your way of getting back at me for being such a dick."

"Maybe a little," Pasha teased. "What do you say?"

"When do I start?"

"Depends. You any good with a paintbrush? I've got Sean, one of the servers, coming in tomorrow to help us paint," he explained. "We could use an extra pair of hands."

"What time do you want me to show up?"

EPILOGUE

WHAT the condo lacked in space, it made up for in personality—which meant that Daniel loved the woodsy ravine a stone's throw from the back door and the great big wooded park just across the street. The fact that there was a pool and exercise room in the complex didn't hurt as a selling point either, and not just on Pasha's end. Daniel had shifted over to sales full time in June and, as a consequence, wasn't getting in any real exercise at work. Since keeping fit was important to his long-term health, they worked out together three times a week—although Pasha was only down a couple of inches around his waist.

They painted the living room teal and used Daniel's furniture and throw pillows; Daniel got some of his friends from the community theater's prop department to come out and help him build bookshelves. Lots of bookshelves. Pasha cooked but otherwise endeavored to stay out of the way—after the *Rent* cast and crew party that Daniel talked Pasha into catering, all Daniel ever had to do was offer Pasha's cooking as bribery and he could get anybody from the theater to come out and help with anything they needed.

They painted the kitchen yellow and the dining room dusky rose. The table and chairs came from Pasha's basement. The set was antique and had belonged to Pasha's mother; he got her good china and teacup collection too.

After intense debate, Pasha finally caved and let Daniel talk him into painting the bedroom dark forest green, but *he* got to pick the new bedroom set. It included a king-sized four-post bed that barely fit the room. Instead of saying "I told you so" on the day it was delivered, Daniel went out and bought several dozen new candles and candleholders.

PASHA checked the goose for the fourth time. It was only at a hundred and fifty-eight degrees; it needed to get to one sixty-five before he could pull it out. He'd been on Skype all morning long with Daniel's mom because he'd never cooked a goose before, and he wanted it to be perfect. Or more accurately, he wanted to get it as close to the way she made it as possible.

Crammed onto the rack under the goose were pans of whipped potatoes, corn, and apple-walnut stuffing. Pasha would have liked to use the big oven at the restaurant, but that would have meant transporting twelve pounds of roasted goose and all the trimmings twenty minutes each way. Possible, but not practical.

He just hoped his sister and the kids showed up; as of last night she'd still been unsure. Pasha wasn't honestly sure if it had to do with his being gay and living with a man, something she was decidedly uncomfortable with, or if she was still pissed at him for cutting the purse strings. When Ryan had failed to be able to hold a job, they'd lost the house and she and the kids moved back in with Dad, while Ryan moved back in with his parents. The divorce was pending.

The doorbell rang just as Pasha was checking the goose for the fifth time.

"I've got it!" Daniel hollered from the living room.

"Okay, be there in a sec!" he called back. The goose was a beautiful golden brown, just like Daniel's mom said it should be. Just the same, he stuck a digital meat thermometer into the bird's breast one more time.

One sixty-seven. *Perfect.*

Out in the living room he heard Clara's excited cry of "You have a Christmas tree!" and smiled. The tree was another compromise. Daniel wanted to go out and chop down his own tree from some tree farm, but a live tree would never survive from Thanksgiving to

Christmas. He'd promised Daniel that next year they could have a live tree, but this year—if the kids came—he wanted them to have a Christmas tree up, just like they'd always had at his house, when Mom was around. He hoped the kids could talk to her later, when they called the nursing home. She'd been getting worse, but she still had good days as well as bad ones.

Pasha wiped his hands off on a dishtowel and put the cover back on the pan to keep the bird safe from prowling cats—in addition to Alex, they now had Tatiana—and headed into the living room.

"Uncle Pasha!" Clara and RJ cried almost as one. "*S dnyom blagodaryeneeya*, *s dnyom blagodaryeneeya*!"

He pulled them both into a fierce hug. "*S dnyom blagodaryeneeya*," he said and gave each a big kiss on the cheek. At Nadia's request, they hadn't explained to the kids the nature of his and Daniel's relationship. Daniel had been introduced a few months ago as Uncle Pasha's friend. With any luck, the kids wouldn't pick today to notice that the condo only had one bedroom.

Pasha straightened and held his hand out to his father—Dad pulled him into a hug.

"*S dnyom blagodaryeneeya*, Pasha."

"Happy Thanksgiving, Dad," he replied.

The old man turned to Daniel. "That's what *s dnyom blagodaryeneeya* means. Well. Sort of," he amended. "It translates more like 'with day of giving thanks.' But it's same thing. Go ahead, you try saying it."

"I've been trying to teach him all morning," Pasha cut in before Daniel could slaughter the words again.

Daniel explained, "I never was any good at foreign language."

"You just need good teacher," said Ivan. "Pasha can't teach for shit."

Pasha shook his head and turned to his sister while Daniel collected coats from Dad, RJ, and Clara. "I'm glad you guys could make it."

"Thank you for inviting us," she answered stiffly. She was still standing in the doorway looking pensive with Abbey in her arms and Bailey standing next to her.

Pasha knelt down and held his arms out to the three-year-old. When she came over to him, he scooped her up into a hug. "*S dnyom blagodaryeneeya*," he said. "Can you say that?" Bailey nodded but didn't repeat the words.

"Can I get anyone anything to drink?" Daniel offered.

While he was getting drinks sorted, Pasha set Bailey back down and turned to his father. "Would you give me a hand in the kitchen?"

"What you need my help for?" the old man teased. "I thought you knew all about cooking." His harsh tone was mitigated by the smile on his face.

"I could still use an extra pair of hands," Pasha answered. But when they got into the little kitchen, he closed the door behind them.

"Something wrong?" Ivan asked.

"No. I mean… nothing's wrong, but there's something I need to tell you and I just…. I need you to not flip out." Which probably made this the worst time imaginable to bring it up. Or maybe the best. Pasha was betting on—and praying for—the latter.

Dad's brows knit together. "What is it?"

"It's about Daniel. He ah… there's this thing, and—"

"He told me."

Pasha blinked. "What? No, I'm not… this is something else." He had no idea what Daniel had told the old man, but it *wasn't* what Pasha needed to say to him. It took all of Pasha's resolve to meet his father's gaze, but before he could start to say the words, Dad cut him off.

"He told me on opening night of that play that he has same disease. Virus." He corrected himself.

"But…." *Rent* had opened at the community theater back in April. "How…. I mean…. Daniel never told me he talked to you." In fact, Daniel had let him stew all week, worrying about how he was going to tell his father, afraid the old man would lose it—afraid he would lose his father. Afraid he would lose everything.

Ivan laid his hand on Pasha's arm. "He said you were having hard time knowing how to tell me, that you were afraid of what I would say. He asked me not to tell you. Don't be mad, Pasha," he said, correctly reading the frown that tugged at the corners of Pasha's lips. "Daniel figured you'd tell me when you were ready. He didn't want to take that away from you. What we talked about was between us, me and him. It was something he needed to do."

"He told you he has HIV?" he asked, just to be sure they were *really* talking about the same thing.

"*Da.*"

"And… you're okay…. I mean…." He couldn't get any of the questions whirling around in his head to come out as coherent sentences.

"Of course I worry about you. I worry about him, too. I worry somebody's gonna do to you what those boys did to that friend of yours, Brett. I worry you're gonna get sick. I worry Daniel's gonna get sick."

"You know we would never do anything… we always use… I mean…." He didn't know how to talk to his father about sex.

"Only thing I need to know is that you're both good boys. Good men. I trust you to make right decisions."

"Thanks, Dad. I love you."

"*Ya tebya loobloo*, *tozhye*, Pasha. Now come on, let's get the food on the table, huh?"

HELEN BARBARA PATTSKYN lives with her husband and children (both human and four footed) in a quiet suburb of Detroit, MI. She is working on becoming a full-time writer as well as doing volunteer work and still trying to find time to putter in her garden, watch the stars, and paint.

Helen describes herself as a storyteller, a science fiction geek, and a bookworm; as introverted, but not shy. Her favorite jobs (besides being a writer) have been hawking left-handed mugs at the Georgia and Michigan Renaissance Festivals and painting polyurethane corpses for Gag Studio. She's also waited tables, cut fabric, and worked as a library assistant. If anyone ever asks, she describes her life as "quiet"—but even she'll admit that when you condense it into two paragraphs, it suddenly looks a little more interesting.

Visit Helen's website: http://helenpattskyn.com. You can also e-mail her atthylacine.yawn@gmail.com.

Also from H.B. PATTSKYN

http://www.dreamspinnerpress.com

Also from H.B. PATTSKYN

http://www.dreamspinnerpress.com

Dreamspinner Press
For more of the best M/M romance, visit
Dreamspinner Press
www.dreamspinnerpress.com

www.ingramcontent.com/pod-product-compliance
Lightning Source LLC
Chambersburg PA
CBHW050032030726
47506CB00001B/240

* 9 7 8 1 6 2 7 9 8 1 2 7 9 *